Richard Clarke Cabot

A Guide to the Clinical Examination of the Blood

for Diagnostic purposes

Richard Clarke Cabot

A Guide to the Clinical Examination of the Blood
for Diagnostic purposes

ISBN/EAN: 9783337387402

Printed in Europe, USA, Canada, Australia, Japan

Cover: Foto ©Andreas Hilbeck / pixelio.de

More available books at **www.hansebooks.com**

A GUIDE

TO THE

CLINICAL EXAMINATION

OF

THE BLOOD

FOR DIAGNOSTIC PURPOSES

BY

RICHARD C. CABOT, M.D.

WITH COLORED PLATES AND ENGRAVINGS

Third Revised Edition

NEW YORK
WILLIAM WOOD AND COMPANY
1898

PREFACE TO THE THIRD EDITION.

About forty pages of new matter have been added, but the book is no larger than before, as a corresponding number of pages have been omitted from the bibliography. A complete bibliography of the subject would now need a separate volume, and it has therefore seemed best to omit all but the most important references.

The principal additions to the book include an account of Professor Óliver's tintometer and hæmoglobinometer (which are the only new instruments of importance), new matter in the chapter on the primary anæmias, and on leukæmia, and a description of Müller's "blood-dust" (the newly discovered constituent of normal and abnormal blood). Bremer's and Williamson's tests for diabetic blood and the iodine reaction in the blood during acute suppurative processes are described, and blood exminations are recorded in Malta fever, yellow fever, epidemic dropsy, beri-beri, relapsing fever, tetanus, chicken-pox, whooping-cough, and epidemic cerebro-spinal meningitis, diseases not included in previous editions. New observations on poisoning by alcohol, opium, corrosives, and ptomains, on aneurisms, on paroxysmal hæmoglobinæmia, and on cretinism are recorded.

I have wished to draw especial attention to the tendency to an *oval* or sausage shape among the red corpuscles in cases of grave anæmia and to the occurrence of adventitious forms of leucocytes in leucocytosis.

Some of my critics have regretted that there was so little theoretical discussion in the book. In this edition I have for the most part eliminated what little there was before. It had already become out of date. But though I cannot see my way to change the general plan of my book, there has been hardly any other suggestion of my critics which has failed to help me. I am especially indebted to those who have been good enough to send me detailed criticisms, and in almost every instance I have been glad to make the changes suggested. For such help I owe thanks above all to Dr. J. B. Herrick of Chicago, Dr. J. Ewing of New York, and Dr. Greene of the Marine Hospital Service.

It is impossible to keep such a book as this up to date. While the sheets of this edition have been passing through the press, three important works upon the blood have appeared, viz.: Ehrlich and Lazarus' "Die Anaemie," Türk's "The Blood in Acute Infectious Diseases," and Coles' "The Blood." I have greatly profited by reading these books, but unfortunately have been unable to incorporate their observations in the present edition.

190 MARLBOROUGH STREET, BOSTON.
July, 1898.

PREFACE.

In order to keep the size of this book within reasonable limits I have omitted all historical account of the steps by which our present knowledge of the different branches of the subject has been built up.

Wherever it has seemed to me that a point was definitely established, I have stated the conclusions generally accepted without special reference to the names of those who worked them out. On the other hand, where our knowledge has seemed to be insufficient I have given some of the names and findings of those who are responsible for the opinions generally current.

Theoretical discussions have been omitted on account of the strictly clinical plan of the book.

The absence of any account of the origin of the blood cells, the chemistry of the blood, coagulation, and many other subjects of great scientific interest is due to the lack of any considerable clinical value in them so far as at present understood.

The body of data referred to from time to time as the "Massachusetts Hospital Blood Counts" consists of nearly four thousand blood examinations, about three thousand of which were made by Drs. Moffitt, Hewes, Joslin, Denny, Franklin White, Capps, and Barney—medical internes of the hospital since 1893. Permission to avail myself of these data was very kindly granted me by the visiting physicians of the hospital. To these I have added about one thousand examinations which I have made both within the hospital and outside. The technique used in all the four thousand examinations was essentially that described in the following pages.

The accumulation of this body of facts and the great mass of foreign hæmatological literature (untranslated) have seemed to me sufficient reasons for the existence of this book—the first of its kind in English, so far as I am aware. Further, it has seemed to me a great pity that there should be no book available con-

taining colored illustrations of stained blood preparations which
bear some resemblance to their original, and are not wholly or
partly works of the imagination ("diagrammatic").

Funke, of Leipsic, has, I think, been as successful in dealing
with the stained blood in the present work as he was with the
fresh blood in the beautiful illustrations for W. S. Thayer's
monograph on "The Malarial Fevers of Baltimore."

Any one who writes on the blood must be constantly indebted
to the following standard text-books: Hayem: "Du Sang,"
Paris, 1889. v. Limbeck: "Grundriss einer klinischen Patho-
logie des Blutes," Jena, 1896 (second edition). Grawitz:
"Klinische Pathologie des Blutes," Berlin, 1896. Schmaltz:
"Pathologie des Blutes," Leipsic, 1896. Rieder: "Beiträge z.
Kentniss der Leucocytosis," Leipsic, 1892.

I have usually referred to them in the text as "Hayem,"
"Rieder," etc., always meaning one of the above works.

The quotations from Schreiber in the text refer to manuscript
notes of his lectures in 1896, kindly loaned to me by Dr. Mark
W. Richardson.

I am indebted to Dr. F. P. Henry for permission to use the
cuts from his recent article on the filaria sanguinis hominis.

December, 1896.

PREFACE TO THE SECOND EDITION.

A NEW chapter on the serum reaction in typhoid fever has
been added, and the more obvious mistakes in the text have
been corrected. I wish to express my thanks to those who have
called my attention to mistakes in the text, especially to Dr.
Joseph A. Capps, who has furnished many valuable suggestions.

TABLE OF CONTENTS.

BOOK I.

Introduction.

PART I.

METHODS OF CLINICAL EXAMINATION OF THE BLOOD.

CHAPTER 1.

CHAPTER II.

CHAPTER III.

OLIVER'S TINTOMETER—CENTRIFUGALIZING THE BLOOD—HÆMOGLOBIN ESTIMATION—SPECIFIC GRAVITY—STAINED SPECIMENS—BACTERIOLOGICAL EXAMINATION.

PART II.

PHYSIOLOGY OF THE BLOOD.

CHAPTER IV.

CHAPTER V.

PART III

GENERAL PATHOLOGY OF THE BLOOD.

CHAPTER VI.

CHAPTER VII.

CHAPTER VIII.

CHAPTER IX.

BOOK II.

Special Pathology of the Blood.

PART I.

DISEASES OF THE BLOOD.

CHAPTER I.

CHAPTER II.

PART II.

ACUTE INFECTIOUS DISEASES.

INTRODUCTION.

CHAPTER III.

CHAPTER IV.

ACUTE INFECTIOUS DISEASES (Continued).

PART III.

CHRONIC INFECTIOUS DISEASES.

CHAPTER VI.

PART IV.

DISEASES OF SPECIAL ORGANS.

CHAPTER VII.

PART V.

DISEASES OF THE NERVOUS SYSTEM, CONSTITUTIONAL DISEASES AND HEMORRHAGIC DISEASES.

CHAPTER VIII.

CHAPTER IX.

PART VI.

MALIGNANT DISEASE, BLOOD PARASITES, AND INTESTINAL PARASITES.

CHAPTER X.

PART VII.

EXAMINATION OF THE SERUM.

CHAPTER XIII.

BOOK I.

INTRODUCTION.

SCOPE AND VALUE OF BLOOD EXAMINATION.

HÆMATOLOGY is still so new a study that no confident statement can be made as to the exact limits of its usefulness in the practice of medicine. It has solved some problems where least was hoped from it, and given us disappointingly little help where great expectations had been aroused. We might have expected from it some light on the nature of rheumatism, furunculosis, uræmia, diabetes, but none has come.

On the other hand, who could have hoped that it would help us in the diagnosis of central pneumonia, of deep-seated suppurations and of trichinosis, or in the prognosis of relapsing fever or of pneumonia?

There are probably not more than five or six diseases in which the blood examination gives us the diagnosis ready-made, but there is a very considerable number of conditions in which the blood examination will help us to make it. Not pathognomonic signs, but links in a chain of evidence are what we are to expect from blood examination. Very often the simple discovery that the blood is normal may be a fact of the greatest value in diagnosis.

On the whole it seems to me that the examination of the blood gives evidence similar in kind and not much inferior in value to that obtained by examination of the urine. Both methods of examination give us (a) a ready-made diagnosis in a few diseases; (b) side lights on a good many obscure conditions; and (c) the frequently great assistance of a negative report. In certain wards of the Massachusetts General Hospital it has been for some years the rule to examine the blood of every patient as a matter of routine at the time of entrance. In a small proportion of cases this gave negative evidence only; in a much larger proportion it materially assisted in the making of a diagnosis.

Improvements in technique have lessened the labor and increased the accuracy of blood examination. The most important facts about the blood of nearly every case can be obtained by a practised observer in fifteen minutes. The experiments of Reinert and others have shown that with due care no error sufficient to mislead judgment need occur.

The blood is the only tissue that we can study easily during the life of the patient. Its relations to all other tissues are such that it is typical of them all in a way that no other tissue is, acting on all and being acted on by all. As yet we have studied chiefly its morphology, and from that single aspect obtained most of the clinically valuable information which we possess about it. But the field of the blood chemistry is in many respects even more promising at the present time, and there seems reason to believe that the study of the blood is still in its infancy and will take a higher place in the future as an aid to diagnosis, prognosis, and treatment.

Like all methods of physical examination it has especial usefulness when we cannot communicate with a patient, either by reason of his unconsciousness, stupidity, or insanity, or because he speaks no widely used language. In such cases the detection of marked anæmia, leucocytosis, a typhoid serum-reaction, or a malarial organism may be of great assistance. Malingering is made more difficult by it, and in the differentiation of organic from functional disease it is often very helpful. There is no febrile disease on which it may not throw light.

The evidence for these and many other aids furnished by the blood examination in clinical work is given in the later chapters of this work.

PART I.

METHODS OF CLINICAL EXAMINATION OF THE BLOOD.

CHAPTER I.

CONFINING ourselves to the clinically available processes by which we can gain information of diagnostic or prognostic value, blood examination at the present time embraces eight processes.

1. Examination of the fresh blood (with or without a warm stage).
2. Counting the red and the white corpuscles.
3. Estimation of the relative *volumes* of corpuscles and plasma by centrifugalizing the blood.
4. Estimation of the amount of coloring matter.
5. Estimation of the specific gravity of the blood.
6. Examination of dried and stained specimens.
7. Bacteriological examination of the blood.
8. Examination of the serum.[1]

To describe these processes in detail is the purpose of the next chapters.

I. EXAMINATION OF THE FRESH BLOOD.

(a) *Obtaining the blood by puncture.* In all the processes about to be described, except the bacteriological examination, the first step is as follows:

Wipe the lobe of the patient's ear with a damp cloth and then rub it with a dry one. This serves to remove gross dirt and also to make the tissues hyperæmic, so that a slight puncture will draw blood. Attempts to sterilize the skin, or washing it with alcohol and ether, are unnecessary.

Use a three-sided (bayonet-pointed) surgical needle or a small lancet—a sewing needle, even a sharp one, gives more pain and

[1] See Chapter xiii. of Book 1l.

draws less blood from a given depth of puncture. The needle need not be sterile. In several thousand blood counts made at the Massachusetts General Hospital since 1893 the needles have never been sterilized and no signs of sepsis have been seen in any case.

Possibly this is due in part to the fact that the next step in the process after the puncture has been made is always to wipe away four or five successive drops as they emerge, which serves not only to get the blood flowing freely, but also to wash the ear in its own blood.

The puncture is best made into the lower surface or edge of the lobe, which is steadied with the fingers of the left hand. A very quick stroke gives least pain, the hand rebounding like a piano hammer. If the skin of the lobe is stretched tight with the fingers of the left hand so that no "give" is possible, the quick puncture gives hardly any pain. I have repeatedly taken blood from a sleeping child without waking it. What hurts the patient is the mistaken tenderness that slowly *presses* the needle through the skin. The puncture must be deep enough to make the blood flow freely and without pressure, after it is once started by pressing out a few drops. Blood squeezed out with pressure should never be used for counting, as it is likely to be considerably diluted with fluid pressed out of the neighboring tissues. If the skin is moderately thin and the ear easily made hyperæmic, a puncture one-eighth of an inch deep is sufficient. With thick, bloodless skin it may be necessary to go in one-quarter or one-third of an inch—never more. *Beware of bleeders.* I have seen bleeding from a puncture made for a blood count which could not be checked for three-quarters of an hour. It is always safer to ask after a history of hæmophilia as a matter of routine before taking blood, just as one asks after false teeth before etherizing. If there is a history of hæmophilia, a mere touch of the needle point will give us all the blood we need without embarrassing us with a troublesome hemorrhage.

There is no question as to the superiority of the ear over the finger for drawing the drop. The ear is less sensitive than the finger, and a slighter puncture gives us all the blood we need. Moreover, it is a distinct advantage, especially in children, that the patient cannot watch the puncture of the ear, or the preparations for making it, and cannot easily withdraw the part. A sleeping patient often needs to be roused to get at his finger, while his ear is usually easily accessible above the bed clothes. Again, the absence of any bony prominence against which to press makes us less likely to use too much pressure than if we puncture the finger.

When one is making frequent examinations of the blood of a sensitive person, as in pneumonia, these details are of real importance, and in cases of pernicious anæmia in which the previous attempts to get blood from the finger had been absolute failures, I have found no difficulty in getting it from the ear. In this disease the advantages of the ear over the finger are peculiarly great.

Spreading the Blood.

(b) When, after wiping away the first four or five drops, a good-sized drop exudes spontaneously, touch the centre of a perfectly clean cover-glass against the summit of the drop *without touching the skin itself at all,* and drop the cover-glass face downward upon a slide so that the force of the impact will help to spread the drop of blood thinly and evenly between slide and cover. It is recommended by Ehrlich and others to hold the cover-glass with forceps, but there is no harm in holding it with the fingers, provided we avoid touching either of its surfaces, *i.e.,* hold it always as in Fig. 1.[1]

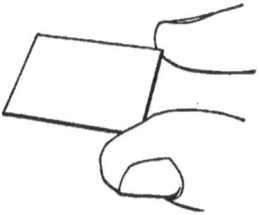

Fig. 1.—Proper Method of Holding a Cover Glass.

Slide and cover must be perfectly clean, else the blood will not spread out in a layer thin enough to avoid the corpuscles overlying each other so that not one of them is clearly seen. Further, as dirt simulates fairly closely some of the pathological appearances for which we are on the lookout, its presence on the slide leads to loss of time or to mistaken conclusions. Cover-glasses, as they come from the shops, may be coated with a substance not easily to be removed. To get them really clean

[1] I am not unmindful of Ehrlich's warning that the moisture of the fingers spoils the specimen ; but in practice I do not find it to be true except as regards the margin of the film, the good preservation of which is not essential.

nothing is so simple as or more effective than soap and water. After several years' use of the method of cleaning usually advised (viz., strong mineral acid, followed by alcohol and then by ether), I have become converted to the use of plain soap and water as the best and simplest way of cleaning slides or cover-glasses. Rub soap over every part of the glass, wash it off thoroughly with water, and polish it with a clean handkerchief (most towels are apt to leave a scrap of lint on the glass).[1] If slide and cover are perfectly clean, are held as in Fig. 1, and allowed to touch only the summit of the blood drop and not the skin, the blood will spread out properly between them, and no pressure on the cover-glass will be needed to make the layer of corpuscles thin enough. Pressure is undesirable, as it often makes all sorts of artefacts in the preparation and hastens crenation of the red corpuscles. Better results are obtained if slide and cover are *warmed* just before using.

Prevention of Cell-Death.

Slides so prepared are usually best examined with a one-twelfth oil-immersion lens. As a rule they keep long enough for purposes of examination without any further precautions, but if we desire to keep the blood fresh and uncoagulated for a longer period, it is best to exclude air in this way: Paint upon the slide with vaseline, cedar oil, or any gummy substance a hollow square or ring of about the size of the cover-glass, so that when the latter with its drop of blood is put down upon the slide the drop will spread out inside the ring of oil, which seals the margins of the cover-glass to the slide. Specimens so prepared will keep for many hours unchanged, and without crenation or coagulation, if the weather is warm or if the slide be kept in a warm place.

In examining blood suspected of containing malarial parasites it is sometimes useful to put the whole microscope into one of the warming apparatuses devised for the purpose. This is better than any of the various kinds of warm stage in use, but in clinical work there is rarely if ever any need for artificial heating

---

[1] Further experience has convinced me that water alone is generally sufficient, provided the polishing is thorough. Tissue paper is very useful for polishing cover-glasses. After polishing, it is well to pass them through a Bunsen or alcohol flame once or twice.

apparatus of any kind, provided the room and the slide are warm.

What Can be Learned from Fresh Blood.

Examination of the fresh blood by the method just described is the best way known for ascertaining the presence or absence of—

1. The Plasmodium malariæ.
2. The Spirochæte of relapsing fever.
3. The Filaria sanguinis hominis.
4. Rouleaux formation among the red cells.

It is also a quick and convenient method of finding out with approximate accuracy :

(a) Whether the blood contains an increased amount of fibrin ;

(b) Whether any considerable anæmia or leucocytosis[1] is present;

(c) Whether or not the amount of hæmoglobin in the red cells is much decreased;

(d) Whether the red corpuscles are deformed;

(e) Whether the "blood plates" are increased or not.

A practised observer can also make a diagnosis of leukæmia by this method in most cases, but here mistakes may easily occur.

So much can sometimes be learned from a specimen prepared in this very quick and easy way that it should be as much a matter of routine as a urine examination. But in order to get any information from such a preparation we must previously have familiarized ourselves with the appearance of normal blood under such conditions—with the size, shape, color, and refractions of the red cells, white cells, and blood plates and their ratio to one another, and with the great variety of curious phenomena to be seen as a drop of blood gradually dries up between slide and cover. No book can teach this: it must be learned by actual experiment.

Some of the commoner sources of error will be referred to later. Here I will mention only the Brownian movement in the protoplasm of the corpuscles, to be distinguished clearly both from the amœboid movements of the leucocytes or of the malarial parasite and also from the irregular contractions of the dying

[1] More accurately it is only the ratio of red to white corpuscles that we can determine, and when the red are very much diminished in number we may be deceived into supposing that the white are increased.

protoplasm, which give rise to pseudo-amœboid motions in the crenated points of normal red cells or in the irregular projections of corpuscles deformed by disease (vide infra).

For a more detailed description of normal red corpuscles, white corpuscles, and blood plates the reader is referred to Part II.

An account of the pathological changes to be observed in the fresh blood will be given in later chapters.

CHAPTER II.

COUNTING THE CORPUSCLES.

I. The Thoma-Zeiss counter.

II. Durham's modified counter.

I. Out of the many instruments devised for this purpose that of *Thoma-Zeiss* is much the most commonly used. In the use of this instrument there are five steps or stages:

1. Puncturing the ear.
2. Diluting and mixing the blood thus obtained.
3. Adjusting a drop of diluted blood in the counting chamber.
4. Counting the corpuscles.
5. Cleaning the pipette.

To count the white corpuscles, a different instrument is often used from that employed for the red.

The technique is nearly the same for both instruments, but for clearness' sake I shall describe them separately. To save time I shall call the small-bore pipette used for red corpuscles (Fig. 2, *A*) the "red counter," and the large-bore pipette (Fig. 2, *B*) the "white counter."

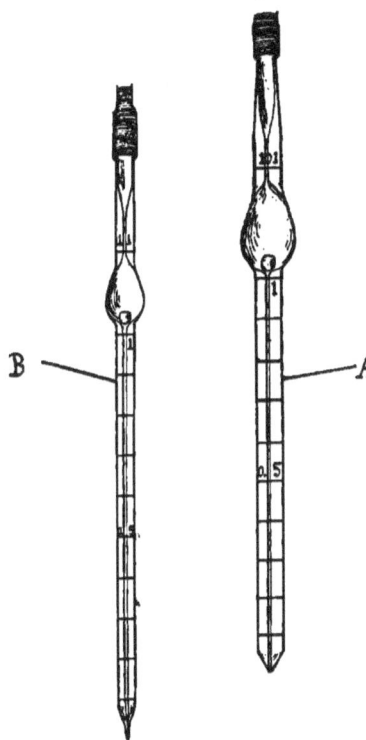

Fig. 2.—Thoma-Zeiss Pipettes. *A*, For red corpuscles; *B*, for white corpuscles.

Counting the Red Corpuscles.

(*a*) After puncturing the ear as above described, and as soon as the blood is flowing freely, put the point of the "red counter" into the drop as it emerges from the ear, and by sucking gently on the rubber tube attached to the other end, draw up blood to the mark 0.5 on the pipette. It is convenient to rest the end of the pipette on the thumb as shown in Fig. 3. It needs some

practice to stop exactly at the mark, but if we happen to draw the blood up *a little* past the mark 0.5 no considerable error results, provided we draw the column down again to the mark by tapping the point of the pipette on a towel, and provided also that the instrument is perfectly clean and dry. The aim and intention, however, should always be to stop exactly at the mark 0.5, and with a little practice we can do it, except with nervous or delirious patients,

FIG. 3.—Method of Resting Point of Pipette on the Thumb while Sucking in Blood.

and those who carelessly move the head just at the critical moment. With such patients we usually have to content ourselves with drawing the blood a little beyond the mark 0.5 and then drawing it down again to the mark as above described.

Diluting the Blood.

(*b*) The bottle of solution to be used for diluting the blood should be ready uncorked at the bedside. Of the many solutions suggested by various authors none is better than *Gowers'*, the formula for which is as follows:

Sodii sulphat., . .	. . gr. 112
Acid. acetic., . .	. . 3 v.
Aquæ, . . .	. . ℥ iv.

Toisson's solution is also very useful and stains the white corpuscles so that they can be easily distinguished from the red. Its composition is as follows:

Methyl violet, 5 B., ...	.025 gm.
Sod. chlor., ...	1.000 "
Sod. sulph., ...	8.000 "
Neutral glycerin, ...	30.000 cm.
Aquæ destill., ...	160.000 cm.

We must wait about ten minutes after mixing before the leucocytes are fully stained. Except for this delay, the only difficulty of this solution is that it is rather difficult to clean the pipette after using it. If the white cells are counted with another pipette the staining fluid can be as well dispensed with.

Into a bottle of one of these solutions, ready at the bedside, the point of the pipette is to be plunged as soon as the blood has been drawn up to the point 0.5 and the outside of the pipette wiped clean of blood. Suction is then exerted through the rubber tube *the instant* the point of the pipette is below the surface of the diluting solution. This suction is continued until the diluted blood has filled the bulb of the pipette and gone past it up to the point marked 101. It is not difficult to stop at this point, provided the pipette is perfectly clean and dry inside. Otherwise it is impossible. Should any mishap occur at this point, the whole process must be begun over again after carefully cleaning and drying the pipette. If no accident happens and the mixture is sucked up to and not past the mark 101, we have diluted the blood with two hundred times its bulk of neutral solution. If, instead of drawing the blood up to the mark 0.5 we draw it as far as the point marked 1, and then dilute as above described, the mixture will be 1 to 100. Some observers habitually use this dilution. The objections to it are: (1) That if the blood is accidentally drawn up too far (*i.e.*, past the mark 1) we cannot draw it down again but must painfully clean and dry out the pipette (see below, p. 16) and repeat the process. (2) If the blood contain approximately the normal number of corpuscles, they will be so crowded when adjusted on the ruled surface of the disc A that it is more difficult to count them. If we use another pipette for the white corpuscles the dilution of 1:100 has no advantage to counterbalance these drawbacks.

While sucking in the diluting solution, it is well to roll the pipette on the long axis with the fingers of the hand which holds it in the diluting fluid. This mixes the blood instantly and prevents any of it from floating on the top of the solution and thereby coming up undiluted into the narrow portion above the bulb of the pipette, where it might possibly escape thorough mixing. [1]

[1] Care must be taken that no saliva finds its way through the rubber tube and into the pipette. Never blow through the rubber tube.

Next we thoroughly mix the blood and diluting fluid by shaking and rolling the pipette, its ends being closed by the fingers. The little glass ball within the bulb helps this process materially. A minute's brisk rolling and shaking is as good as five minutes', as I have convinced myself by many experiments, and the distribution of the corpuscles throughout the mixture is very even, provided there is no delay in proceeding to the next step, 'viz. :

(c) *Adjusting a Drop of Diluted Blood in the Counting Chamber.* —Remove the rubber tube from the pipette and blow out the portion of diluting solution which *last entered* the pipette, and which consequently has not been thoroughly mixed with the blood in the bulb. Five or six drops should be blown out before any is used for examination. Next put upon the surface of the counter (A, Fig. 4) a drop of such size that when the cover-glass (B)

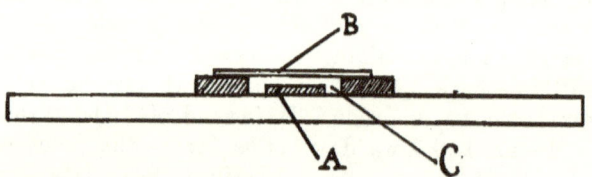

Fɪɢ. 4.—Thoma-Zeiss Counting Slide. *A*, Ruled disc ; *B*, cover-glass ; *C*, moat.

is let down over it the whole of the disc A is covered with the drop without any being spilled into the "moat" (*C*) around it. Just how large such a drop should be can only be learned by practice. It is not literally necessary that exactly the whole disc A should be covered, provided nine-tenths of it is covered, but any spilling over into the "moat" (*C*) entails serious error.

After the cover-glass has been let down upon the drop, we should be able (provided the whole instrument is *clean*) to see concentric rainbow rings between the cover-glass and the body of the instrument. These are known as Newton's rings. A little pressure with a needle on the cover-glass will often bring them out if they do not at once appear, *but they must remain visible* after the pressure is taken off. Otherwise we know that there must be some dirt or dust under the cover-glass preventing its settling exactly into position, and this will cause error in

[1] If we have to pause before going on to the next step, we must take care to roll and shake the pipette again when ready to proceed.

the count, though not a very considerable error in most cases. (To see Newton's rings we should get our eyes near to the level of the counting chamber so that the light from window or lamp is reflected from the surface of the cover-glass.)

If the above conditions are not all fulfilled the instrument should be washed and another drop tried, after shaking the pipette and blowing out a few drops as before.

The cover-glass must be let down as soon as possible after the drop has been put on the disc A, and before the corpuscles have time to settle. It is best to let it down with a needle as in mounting microscopic specimens.

Counting.

(d) After waiting two or three minutes so that the corpuscles may settle thoroughly upon the space ruled off on the disc A,

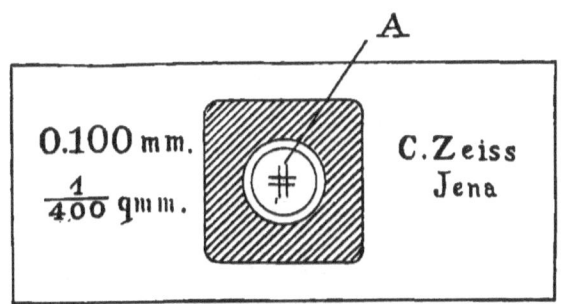

Fig. 5.—Thoma-Zeiss Counting Slide. A, Ruled disc.

the counting is begun, using preferably an objective 5 of Leitz or D of Zeiss and a No. 1 or 2 eyepiece.

The ruled space on the surface of the counter (A, Fig. 5). is divided into four hundred squares, every group of sixteen squares being enclosed in double lines to make it easier to know how many squares we have counted (see Fig. 6). Including the squares with double lines we have a group containing thirty-six small squares, a group convenient to count at one time as it just about fills the field of the objective Leitz No. 5, or Zeiss D with a No. 2 eyepiece.

To avoid considerable error we should count the corpuscles

in five fields of thirty-six squares each, such as is shown in Fig.
6, taking the fields in various parts of the whole ruled space.
The instrument should then be washed[1] and the whole process
repeated with a second drop. If the count of the second drop
differs widely from that of the first, a third drop should be
counted and the average taken of those two which are most
nearly alike. Thus at least three hundred and sixty small
squares should be counted; with such a number the error is not
over three per cent for practised observers.[2] In normal blood
this means counting about 2,160 corpuscles, as six or seven to a
small square is about the normal average when we are using a
dilution of 1 : 200 such as has been described (twelve to fourteen
cells per square in a dilution of 1 : 100).

Among the difficulties encountered in counting is the presence of a few corpuscles on or touching one or more of the lines
bounding the space to
be counted. Shall we
count these out or in?

In counting, for in-
stance, a field like that
in Fig. 6, what are we
to do with the cells
which sit astride the
lines AA, BB, etc.?

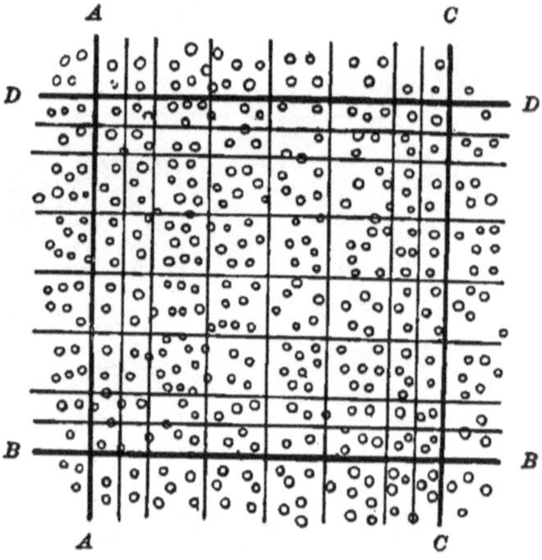

To get round this
difficulty, it is best to
make it a rule to count
in all the corpuscles on
or touching some two of
the boundary lines (e.g.,
AA and BB) and to
take no notice of any
cell on or touching the

Fig. 6.—Field of Thirty-six Squares on Ruled Disc of
Thoma-Zeiss Counter Covered with Normal Blood
Diluted Two Hundred Times.

lines CC and DD. In this way the exclusions just balance the
inclusions. Of course all cells within these outer boundary
lines are to be counted whatever their position.

[1] Use only water—alcohol dissolves the cement which holds the ruled
disc in place.

[2] See Reinert's "Zählung der Blutkörperchen," Leipzig, 1891, p. 48 et
seq.

Beyond this the details must be settled by each man for himself. My own habit is to count through the squares in the order indicated by the track of the serpentine arrow in the accompanying Fig. 7, and to count by twos or threes.

A movable stage makes the counting easier, especially for beginners. Either natural or artificial light may be used, with a small aperture diaphragm, and if the instruments are clean and the diluting solution fresh and free from sediment,[1] there is no difficulty in deciding how many cells each square contains, and no extraneous fragments to be excluded. We must distinguish the white corpuscles from the red, not by their size but by their stain if Toisson's solution is used, otherwise by their peculiar shining look when the lens is drawn up so as to put the red cells slightly out of focus. The blood plates are not noticeable and lead to no errors.

When the number of corpuscles in 360 squares has been counted the number is divided by 360 and multiplied by 800,000 (*i.e.*, by 200 to make up for dilution and then by 4,000 because each square is equivalent to $\frac{1}{4000}$ of a cubic millimetre), which gives us the number of corpuscles per cubic millimetre.

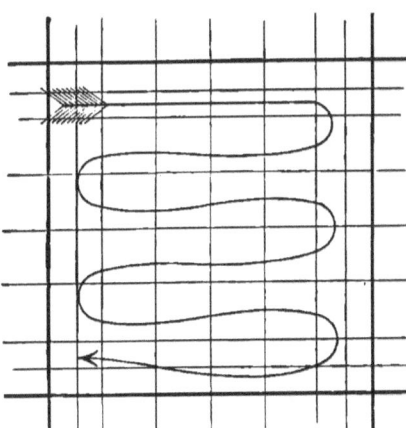

These figures need not be committed to memory, for we have marked on the instruments used all the data necessary for the calculation, *i.e.*, the dilution figures on the pipette and the area and depth of a single square on the counting slide.

Fig. 7.—The Arrow Indicates the Order in which the Squares are Counted.

(*e*) The importance of *cleaning the pipette* as soon as the counting is done is so great that it should be reckoned as one of the regular steps on every count. First water, then alcohol, and

[1] Most diluting solutions precipitate or accumulate spores, and need to be frequently renewed or filtered.

2

lastly ether must be sucked into the pipette and brought into contact with every part of the bulb and tube. After this air must be sucked or pumped through the tube until it is perfectly dry and the glass ball will roll about freely in the bulb without sticking anywhere.

These precautions take but two or three minutes, and if they are omitted and the blood dries in the pipette, it may take several hours' work to get it clean. Further, if it is not thoroughly *dried* after cleaning, the mixing of the blood when it is used next cannot be done accurately.

The first three steps of the above process (*i.e.*, the obtaining, diluting, and mixing of the blood) must be done as swiftly as is compatible with accuracy, but when once the blood is mixed in the pipette it can be kept there indefinitely and counted at leisure. None of the corpuscles are destroyed or lost, and if the bulb is thoroughly rolled and shaken up whenever we are ready to count the blood, no error results from keeping it twenty-four hours or more in the pipette.

It is not necessary, therefore, to carry a microscope to the patient's house or bedside; the pipette and the diluting solution' are all that we need to take with us, and when the blood is mixed in the pipette, the latter's ends can be closed with a rubber band and the blood carried home and counted at leisure. The pipette should be kept approximately horizontal during the transit.

Counting the White Corpuscles.

To make a reasonably accurate count of white corpuscles, using the "red counter" and the dilution of 1:100 or 1:200, we need to count an immense number of squares, far more than was necessary in estimating the red cells—in fact, at least ten times the whole ruled space. It is therefore far quicker and more accurate to use the "white counter" or large-bore pipette with a diluting solution which renders the red cells invisible and leaves only the white to be counted. Such a solution is the one-third of one-per-cent. solution of glacial acetic acid in water. With this the white corpuscles stand out very clearly and the red can barely be seen at all. The technique is the same as that already described, with the following exceptions:

1. The drop of blood needed is nearly three times as large

as that used in the "red counter;" it is about as big as can be made to stay on the ear without rolling off.

2. The bore of the tube being large, it fills and empties more readily. Hence our suction must be gentler, and it is rather harder to stop exactly at the mark 11. For the same reason the diluted blood will run out of the pipette if the latter is not kept nearly horizontal, and the bottle of diluting solution should accordingly be tipped up as we plunge in the point of the pipette, so that the latter is depressed as little and for as short a time as possible before suction begins.

3. Instead of counting separate fields of thirty-six squares each, we should count the whole ruled space and then repeat the process with a second drop. This takes never over fifteen minutes, often not over five, and is very accurate.

The advantages of this pipette are obvious. The only drawbacks are its expense and the need of a somewhat deeper and more painful puncture to get blood enough for it. The technique is not at all difficult.

Counting Both Red and White Cells With the Same Pipette.

We may avoid buying both large-bore and small-bore pipettes in one of the following ways:

1. We can count both red and white corpuscles with the "red counter."

2. We can count both red and white corpuscles with the "white counter."

The reason why we cannot use the "red counter" for counting white cells, unless modified in some way, is that in the whole ruled surface of the counting chamber not more than three or four white corpuscles are to be found in normal blood when diluted two hundred times. If we dilute less, we cannot see the cells distinctly because they are so crowded. If we find, say, three white corpuscles as the number to be used as a basis in calculating the number of white cells in a cubic millimetre, the chance of error is very great, the multiplier being so large (2,000) and the multiplicand so small (3).

To get over this difficulty we may utilize the cells spread over the disc of the counting chamber *outside the ruled space* in one of the following ways:

(a) *By measuring the field of the objective used.* The writer's objective, No. 5 of Leitz, has a field of very nearly one-quarter of a square millimetre or one-quarter of the whole ruled space. Four fields of this lens, taken anywhere outside the ruled space, therefore, contain the same number of cells as will cover the whole four hundred small ruled squares, and when we have counted the white cells in a series of four fields of this lens, we have accomplished as much as if we have put a fresh drop upon the counting chamber and counted all the ruled squares over again; the latter process is tedious, the former very quick. Thus it is my practice in some cases to proceed as follows (see Fig. 8): Supposing the large circle CCCC to represent the surface of the small disc (A, Fig. 4.) in the centre of the counting chamber, and AAAA the ruled squares in the mid-

dle of this disc, four microscopic fields are taken in the direction away from the centre indicated by circles and arrows in the figure. Starting, say, to the right of the ruled squares with the left edge of the microscopic field just touching the outer boundary line of the squares, count all the white cells to be seen in the field.

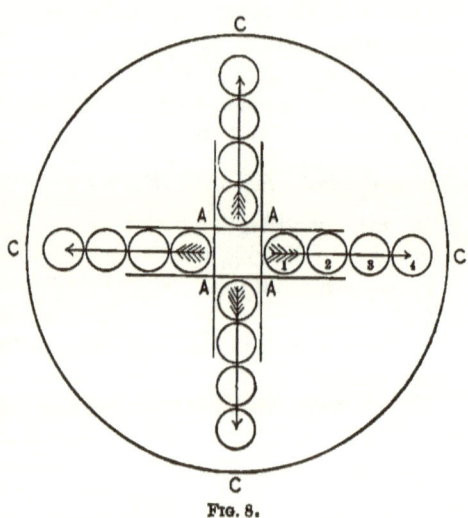

FIG. 8.

Then move along to the right till the corpuscles which were on the extreme right of the first field have gone out of sight to the left. Your field is then in the position of the circle marked 2 (Fig. 8). Count all the white cells in this field and so on for four fields. With my objective, four such fields are almost exactly equal to the whole ruled space AAAA. With other objectives of course the number of fields is different.

When we have counted four fields in each of the four directions indicated by the arrows we have covered as much ground as if we have put four successive drops on the slide after the first one and counted all the ruled squares in each, and we have saved much time and labor.

(*b*) Another and better method of attaining this same end is as follows: Cut out of black cardboard a piece of the shape shown in Fig. 9 and of such a size that it will fit into the tube of the eyepiece—the square aperture allowing a space of just one-quarter of a millimetre (one hundred of the ruled squares) to be seen through it with a given objective (say Leitz No. 5). Four fields as seen through such an aperture can then be counted in various parts of the slide outside the ruled space as explained above.

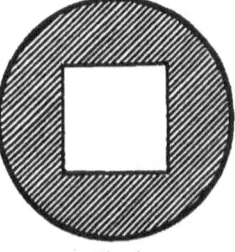

FIG. 9.

(*c*) For any one living where microscopic ruling on glass can be done at a moderate cost, by far the best way is to have the rest of the disc A (Fig. 5) ruled off as shown in Fig. 10. Leitz & Zeiss

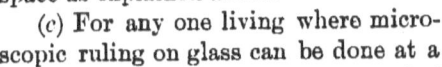

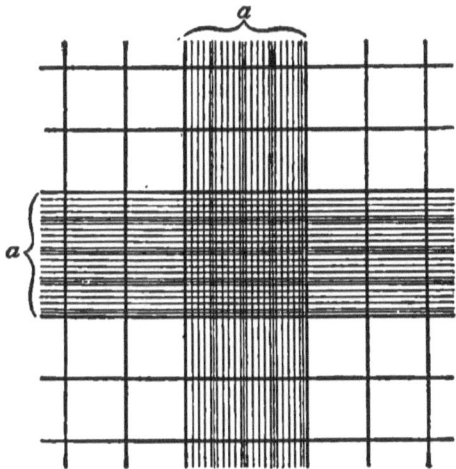

FIG. 10.—Modified Ruling of Thoma-Zeiss Counting-chamber.

now make to order instruments so ruled. I have not been able to hear of any one in America who could do such work at a moderate expense.

(d) We may work out mathematically what number of squares would be contained on the whole disc *were* it all ruled like the central portion. This can 'be done with the aid of a micrometer eye-piece and a mechanical stage. There is some variation in individual instruments, but as a rule the disc *outside* the central ruled space has an area of about two thousand of the small squares.

2. We may use the "white counter" for red corpuscles in the following way: Suck up blood only to the first mark up from the point (*i.e.*, one-fifth of the usual distance) and then Gowers' or Toisson's solution up to the mark 11. This gives a dilution of 1:100, and in anæmic cases, in which the cells are not very numerous, answers well. The same pipette can then be carefully cleaned and used for counting white cells with the acetic acid one-third per cent, and a dilution of 1:10 or 1:20.

Whatever method of counting white corpuscles is adopted, we ought to have at least one hundred corpuscles actually counted to use as the multiplicand of our computation. A single drop from the white counter with a dilution of 1:10 gives us normally about seventy white corpuscles in the four hundred ruled spaces, and by repeating the process with a second drop the result may be made reasonably accurate. This was the method adopted by Rieder[1] in the immense number of counts made by him.

II. Durham's Modified Hæmocytometer.

In the Edinburgh *Medical Journal* for October, 1897, Herbert E. Durham, of Cambridge, England, describes a self-filling capillary pipette which has considerable advantages over the ordinary Thoma-Zeiss instrument. The account of the device is here given in his own words.

"The apparatus entails no new principle; it is rather to be considered as an adaptation of a number of details, which together seem to present some advantages. As in the Gowers' instrument, there is a separate capillary pipette for measuring the blood, one for measuring the diluting fluid, a mixing vessel, and. the counting chamber. A few words may be said about each of these.

"*Capillary Pipette.*—There is an obvious advantage in the

[1] "Beiträge zur Kenntniss der Leucocytosis," Leipzig, 1892 (Vogel).

use of a self-measuring pipette. It cannot go wrong by acci-dent. Durham has availed himself of the pipettes introduced by Dr. Oliver, namely, small pieces of thick-walled capillary tube—5 and 10 c.mm. in capacity. These are carefully recali-brated by the makers of Dr. Oliver's instrument—The Tinto-meter Company.

"There is, moreover, another important advantage attaching to Dr. Oliver's pipette; this consists in the readiness with which it may be cleansed. As he has described, all that is necessary is to pass a piece of darning cotton by means of a needle through the bore of the pipette. All the adherent serum, etc., is completely removed thereby. Durham generally wets the end of the cotton with ether, but this is not absolutely necessary. In passing the needle, it is better to pass it into the pointed end, in case it is not withdrawn perfectly axially, when there is a liability to chip the thinner unsupported glass.

"Any one who has worked much with the Thoma-Zeiss pipette will know how troublesome it is to clean, especially when a number of observations have to be made in a limited time. Unless it is frequently cleaned out with strong acid, there is a tendency for the deposition of sticky serum remains which interfere with true readings.

"For use, Dr. Oliver's pipettes are mounted by means of a

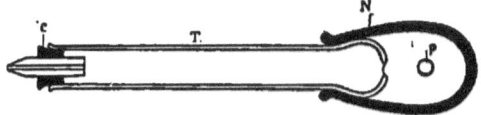

FIG 11.—Cross-section of Durham's Automatic Blood-Pipette. *T*, Glass tube (like that of medicine-dropper); *N*, rubber nipple (like that of medicine-dropper); *p*, perforation in the nipple; *c*, Cork holder, perforated by capillary pipette.

small cork (*c*) in a large glass tube (*T*), which is provided with a rubber nipple (*N*), having a lateral perforation (*p*) (Fig. 11).

"The *mixing vessel* consists of a small test tube ($2\frac{3}{8} \times \frac{7}{16}$ in. for 1 c.c., or $2\frac{3}{8} \times \frac{3}{8}$ in. for $\frac{1}{2}$ c.c.). Several such tubes may be kept, so that a number of observations can be made if necessary. For thoroughly mixing the blood and diluting fluid, one or more small glass globules are placed in the tube. By using different colored glass globules, different specimens can be readily differentiated.

"For *measuring* the diluting fluid, *pipettes* containing 1 and ½ c.c. are used; these are marked at 995 and 990 c.mm. and 495 and 490 c.mm. respectively. With these graduations the following dilutions may be obtained: 1:200, 1:100, and 1:50, with the appropriate capillary pipette.

"Having measured the diluting fluid, according to the eventual dilution desired, the blood capillary is filled by touching the exuding drop of blood and allowing it to completely fill itself. The blood may be obtained in the usual manner from the lobule of the ear, the first drops being wiped away.

"The hole in the nipple allows free air-way so that there is no hindrance to the action of capillarity. When filled, any blood on the outside of the pipette is rapidly wiped off and the tube is inserted into the mixer until the point is one-half to three-fourths of an inch above the level of the contained liquid.

"The nipple is then held in such a way that the hole lies under the thumb of the operator. When this is the case it is slightly squeezed, and then, while the pressure is continued, the bulb is rotated so that the hole is free again. In this way the blood is squirted out, but not sucked back again. The procedure is extremely simple and really requires no practice, given an operator who is not possessed of 'five thumbs.' In order to wash out the remains of the blood the point of the capillary is dropped into the diluting fluid; the bore instantly fills itself. It is then withdrawn and the pressure and rotation of the nipple are repeated. This has to be repeated several times, and occupies a few seconds of time. It has been suggested that a certain amount of error is introduced by measuring the diluting fluid in a pipette, the inner surface of which retains some moisture; this is extremely small in amount if the pipette is emptied slowly, and comparative readings with the Thoma-Zeiss apparatus show that the error is negligible.

"To mix the blood and diluting fluid thoroughly, the mixer is placed between the opposed hands, which are rubbed backward and forward; the mixer is rotated thereby, and the glass globules cause a thorough dispersion of the corpuscles in the fluid.

"A drop of sufficient size is then placed upon the counting chamber, and the cover-slip is slipped on sideways in the usual way I prefer the Thoma-Zeiss counting chamber.

"The advantages of this method are:

"1. The ease and thoroughness with which the pipette can be cleaned.

"2. The manifest advantage of the self-measurement of the blood.

"3. The avoidance of the objectionable necessity of using the mouth to suck fluids into the pipette.

"4. The measurement of the diluent can be done carefully and calmly beforehand, and any error corrected without taking any more blood.

"5. The greatly smaller cost of the pipette.

"6. The same pipette is useful for making various dilutions in serum diagnosis, by using several mixing vessels filled beforehand with dilute fluid."

CHAPTER III.

OLIVER'S TINTOMETER—CENTRIFUGALIZING THE BLOOD—
HÆMOGLOBIN ESTIMATION—SPECIFIC GRAVITY—
STAINED SPECIMENS—BACTERIOLOGICAL
EXAMINATION.

OLIVER'S TINTOMETER.

RECENTLY a method of estimating corpuscles by means of their optical effect, and without directly counting them, has been introduced by Dr. Oliver. For practical purposes an actual counting of the corpuscles must be considered a necessity; not only since the number of leucocytes is not without importance (*e.g.*, in the diagnosis of enteric fever), but also since these cells may be so abundant that they may interfere with the use of optical methods, as in the case of leukæmia. Nevertheless the instrument is very accurate and useful in many cases. Its principle is based on the fact that if a small quantity of blood is gradually diluted with Hayem's solution[1] in a test tube whose sides are flattened so that its mouth forms a rectangle about 15 mm. by 5 mm., and a candle flame is looked at through the mixture, there is to be seen, *when a certain degree of dilution is reached*, a bright *horizontal* line on the glass (see Fig. 15). This line is made up of a large number of minute images of the flame, produced by the longitudinal striation of the glass. If the quantity and quality of blood used is in every instance the same, the degree of opacity depends wholly on the amount of Hayem's solution added. It is found that with normal blood the amount of diluting solution necessary to allow the image of the candle flame to be seen through the mixture is always the

[1] Hydrargyri perchloridi, ...   0.5 gm.
Sodii chloridi, ...   1.0 "
"   sulphatis, ...   5.0
Aquæ destillatæ, ...   200.0 c.c.

same, and can be very accurately fixed, so that a variation of one per cent in the number of corpuscles can be distinguished by noting the amount of diluting solution which must be added before the image of the flame appears. To collect the blood, Oliver uses a capillary pipette containing about 10 c.mm. (one large drop), and used exactly in the same way as the v. Fleischl capillary pipette (see Fig. 12).

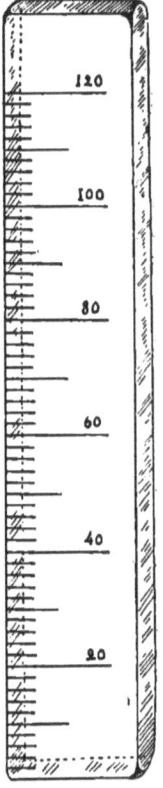

F ι g. 12. — Capillary Pipette for Oliver's Tintometer.

One pipette full of normal blood is gradually diluted in the flattened tube with Hayem's solution until a bright horizontal line caused by the image of candle flame becomes visible through the mixture. The point to which the column of the mixture *then* reaches is marked 100, and then space between that point and the bottom of the tube is divided into 100 equal parts. The point marked 100 is then equivalent to 5,000,000 red corpuscles; 90 = 4,500,000, 80 = 4,000,000, and so on, each degree on the scale corresponding to a difference of 50,000 corpuscles (Fig. 13).

Use of Oliver's Tintometer.

The capillary pipette is filled in the usual way, and the outside carefully and quickly wiped if necessary. The medicine dropper (previously filled with Hayem solution) is then connected with the polished blunt end of the pipette by means of the rubber tube (Fig. 14), and blood washed into the test tube as shown in Fig. 14. If the previous hæmoglobin estimation has shown ninety to one hundred per cent of coloring matter we can safely add the

Fig. 13.—Measuring Tube for Oliver's Tintometer.

diluting solution rapidly until the point marked 80 is reached. If the coloring matter is lower we must cease our rapid dilution correspondingly sooner. When we get near the point at which the flame-image is likely to appear, the diluting fluid must be added a few drops at a time. After each addition put the thumb over the mouth of the tube and turn it upside down once or twice to mix the blood thoroughly, wiping

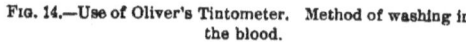

FIG. 14.—Use of Oliver's Tintometer. Method of washing in the blood.

FIG. 15.—Method of Holding the Tintometer while Diluting. Note the bright horizontal line in the fluid, indicating that enough diluting fluid has been added.

the thumb each time on the edge of the tube so as to put back what fluid has adhered to it. At a certain point the image will suddenly become visible. It is seen soonest if we rotate the tube on its long axis, as the image becomes visible earliest at the sides of the tube. The whole process should be carried on in a perfectly dark room, and the diffused light of the candle must be shut off from the eye. This is best done by fitting the tube into the hand as shown in Fig. 15 with the long axis in line with candle, holding the tube *close to the eye*, and standing about ten feet from the candle. In the use of both of his instruments Oliver uses only the small wax candle known as Christmas candles, whose flame is of the most convenient size.

THE HÆMATOCRIT.

THE hæmatocrit of Hedin, though a comparatively new instrument, has undergone considerable modification and improvement in the last few years and as remodelled and improved by Judson Daland is now coming into use in this country. Its direct and obvious object is simply to ascertain the relative volume or mass of the corpuscles and of the plasma in a drop of blood; but the hope of its advocates has usually been that it would supplant entirely or mostly the long, tedious, and eye-destroying process of counting with the Thoma-Zeiss instrument. Whereas the latter needs sometimes an hour's hard work and eye strain to make an accurate count of red cells, with Daland's centrifugal machine one can get the result in five minutes without any strain on the eyes.

Daland maintains the superior *accuracy* of his instrument in most cases as a further advantage of its use. The estimation of corpuscles depends on the length of the column of corpuscles packed down by centrifugal force at the end of a capillary tube filled with blood and whirled with great rapidity in a horizontal plane. The more corpuscles the longer the column.

Wherever there is much variation in the shape or size of the cells, as in many forms of anæmia, leukæmia, etc., the hæmatocrit is evidently inaccurate, inasmuch as the misshapen, under- or oversized corpuscle will pack down differently from the normal cells, three million undersized cells making a shorter column in the tube than three million healthy ones. This is recognized by the advocates of the instrument, which is accordingly recommended only in those cases in which we know that there are no considerable variations in the size or shape of the red cells. These are usually cases in which no very great anæmia is present and in which consequently the labor of counting the large number of corpuscles is greatest. It seems, therefore, as if the hæmatocrit might relieve us of the most irksome part of blood-counting without loss of accuracy.

Against this there is to be said that we do not as yet know how far the elasticity and compressibility of otherwise

healthy corpuscles may vary and how far such a variation may
invalidate the standard of tight packing established from other
cases.   Further, there is known to be a certain amount of variation in the size and volume of a healthy person's corpuscles, both
between nations and between members of one nation, and it is
yet to be shown whether this variation is sufficient to make the
result of the hæmatocrit liable to a greater error than those of

FIG. 16.—Capillary Tube of Hæmatocrit with Rubber Attached.

the Thoma-Zeiss instrument.   There is no doubt that the latter is a slower, more tedious instrument; the question is still
open whether or not it is the more accurate.   Daland reports
wide variations between his counts and those of his colleague
and between different counts by one observer at different times,
using the Thoma-Zeiss instrument, while with the hæmatocrit
the variations are but slight.

In testing these results I have made parallel counts of a patient's blood with several of the house physicians at the Massachusetts General Hospital during the last two years and our
differences have never exceeded the limit of error laid down by
Reinert—namely, two per cent.   I think Daland must have
been unfortunate in his results.

If, then, the error of the Thoma-Zeiss instrument is, as I
believe, not over two per cent under ordinary circumstances and
with correct technique, it does not seem likely that the hæmatocrit is a more accurate as well as a simpler and quicker instrument.

To use the Daland hæmatocrit we prick the ear as usual and
with the help of a bit of rubber tube attached to one end of the
capillary tube (Fig.16) suck in enough blood to fill it entirely.
Usually we draw in more than enough and it enters the rubber
tube as well, but this is no harm.   It is nearly impossible to fill
the glass tube exactly and no more, inasmuch as the proximal
end of it is hidden inside the rubber tube.   The commonest

mistake at this point is incomplete filling of the capillary tube, as a very large drop is needed to do it.

As soon as it is full, put the finger (greased with vaseline)

Fig. 17.—Daland's Hæmatocrit. Two capillary tubes in place on the horizontal whirling beam. The instrument is to be fastened to the edge of some solid and bulky piece of furniture by means of the thumb-screw seen at the bottom of the cut. If not very tightly secured, it will work loose when the handle is revolved rapidly.

tightly over the free end of the glass tube and then, *but not till then*, draw off the rubber tube and adjust the glass as quickly as possible in the place prepared for it on one of the horizontal arms of the whirling machine (Fig. 17). A similar tube (empty) should be put on the other arm of the crosspiece to make the balance true. We must be quick about this, else the blood will coagulate. The handle of the instrument is then revolved at least seventy times a minute for two minutes, at the end of which time (sometimes less) the column of blood cells is packed so tight that no further whirling has any effect on its length. Great care should be taken that the horizontal beam is securely attached to the main part of the instrument, as it is capable of doing serious damage should it come off while whirling nine thousand revolutions a minute, which is the rate usually attained.

It is well to put a little vaseline on the point where the blunt end of the tube rests (a, Fig. 17) to prevent any of the blood sticking there when we come to take the tube out and read it.

The capillary tube is marked off into one hundred equal divisions and provided with a magnifier like that on clinical thermometers. Laid on a piece of white paper it is easy to read off the number of divisions occupied by the blood column, although the end of it is often frayed or bevelled in a way that precludes great accuracy. In normal blood the white corpuscles hardly show at all in the tube. They accumulate at the free end of the column of red cells, but unless a leucocytosis is present their presence is indicated, if at all, only by a slight grayish blur at the end of the red column and cannot be accurately measured. This blur is another difficulty in the way of deciding precisely where the end of the red-cell column is.

To estimate the number of red corpuscles from the length of the column, we call each degree of the scale on the tube 100,000 cells, or a little more. Thus if the blood column in the tube ends at about the mark 50 we consider that the blood has rather more than 5,000,000 red corpuscles per cubic millimetre. So far all observers agree on the figures, but as to just how much more or less than 100,000 each degree on the scale is worth there is some variation between different observers. Daland,[1] in a long series of comparative observations of making blood counts and hæmatocrit estimations on the same case, conclude that each degree of the scale on the capillary tube corresponds to 99,390 corpuscles.

[1] University Med. Mag., November, 1891.

The writer in a series of forty observations on healthy persons, in each of which a count of corpuscles with the Thoma-Zeiss instrument and a volumetric estimation with Daland's hæmatocrit was made, found the value of one degree on the glass scale to vary between 105,000 and 123,000 red corpuscles, the average being 112,000.

It certainly seems *a priori* as if variations in the specific gravity of the corpuscles or in the properties of the plasma might make a considerable difference in the number of revolutions needed to reduce the column of corpuscles to its smallest size.

So far as I can learn, the use of this instrument in Europe has been chiefly for the direct information it affords as to the *volume* of the red cells and the amount of respiratory surface in the blood, rather than for the indirect information it may give us as to the *number* of the red cells. It does not seem as yet to be supplanting the Thoma-Zeiss counter.

Its bulk and the noise it makes must for the present, I think, prevent its extensive use outside of hospitals. The noise it makes is a very loud and disagreeable one, and will deter many from using it in private practice.

HÆMOGLOBIN ESTIMATION.

I. *Von Fleischl's Hæmoglobinometer.*

Until recently the instrument most used both here and in Europe is that of v. Fleischl. In France Hayem rules supreme in the matter of instruments, as in everything else concerning the blood, and in England Oliver's apparatus is used to a certain extent. The v. Fleischl instrument will be described first. The principle of its use is that of directly comparing the tint of the blood with various parts of a strip of colored glass ("*goldpurpur*") whose color shades gradually from a deep red at one end to clear glass at the other. The glass and the blood are brought before the eye side by side and a direct color judgment is attempted.

3

Use of v. Fleischl's Hœmometer.

(*a*) To use the instrument fill one side of the metallic cell (*a*, Fig. 19) about one-quarter full of distilled water and carry it to the bedside, together with the little capillary pipette (B, Fig. 18) and the needle for puncturing. The capillary pipette

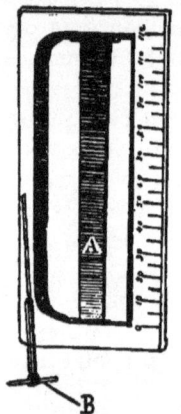

must be scrupulously cleaned and dried before use. This is best done by drawing a needle and thread (the latter wet with alcohol and ether) through the eye of the capillary tube. When the drop of blood is flowing freely from the ear, put the end of the little pipette horizontally into the side of the drop, which will at once fill the tube by capillary attraction if the latter is clean and dry. Carefully but quickly wipe away any blood that may be on the outside of the pipette, and make sure that the blood in it is just flush with the surface at each end and does not present a concave or convex surface. Then put it into the water contained in one of the partitions of the metallic cell and rattle it quickly back and forth, so that the water may be forced in first at one end and then at the other. So far in the process we must work very quick to prevent coagulation which in some cases takes place very rapidly.

Fig. 18.—*A,* Colored glass; *B,* capillary pipette.

(*b*) After this the cell with the capillary tube still immersed in it may be put in place on the body of the instrument (see Fig. 19) and carried to a room or closet where daylight can be excluded and artificial light used to read the instrument by. Then the expulsion of the blood from the capillary tube may be completed by forcing a few drops of water from a medicine dropper through the capillary pipette and into the compartment where the mixing has been begun. Using the metal handle of the pipette as a stirrer, mix very thoroughly the blood and water in every part of the compartment, looking after the corners especially. Then using a medicine dropper, fill both compartments of the cell to the brim with distilled water, taking care that neither overflows into the other, and adjust the compartment containing the clear water so that it comes over the slip of colored glass, while through the compartment containing the blood light thrown upward by the reflector below passes directly to the eye. Turn the thumb screw (see Fig. 19, T) back and forth until the color of the glass is the same as that of the blood, and read off the number on the scale which corresponds

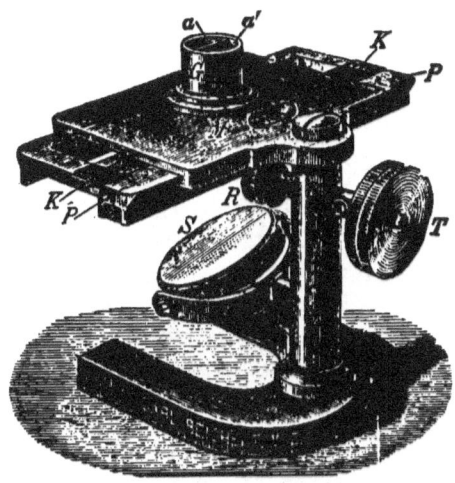

FIG. 19.—v. Fleischl's Hæmometer. *a*, Partition into which blood is put ; *a'*, partition into which water is put ; *G*, mixing cell ; *K*, *K*, colored glass slip (see Fig. 11, *A*) ; *P*, *P*, metal frame on which scale is marked ; *R*, *S*, reflector ; *T*, screw which moves the frame, *P*, *P*.

to that color. This gives the percentage of hæmoglobin, 100 being the color of normal blood for men and 80–90 for women.

(c) *Matching the colors* is not at all easy at best, but may be somewhat aided by observing the following precautions :

1. *Do not stand (or sit) facing the light, but sideways (i.e.,* at A or B, never at C, Fig. 20). For we wish to avoid that the image of one compartment should come on the upper half of the retina and of the other compartment on the lower half, inasmuch as the upper half of the retina is less sensitive to light than the lower and so a less accurate judge of color. By sitting as in Fig. 13, A or B, we get the compartments whose colors we are to match, on the right and left halves of the retina, which are equally sensitive in most persons.

2. *Use as little light as possible,* and always less light for a blood having a low hæmoglobin percentage than for one nearer the normal. Slight color distinctions are abolished if there is any more light than is necessary for simple illumination; too much light dazzles us slightly and so makes us less sensitive in color discrimination.

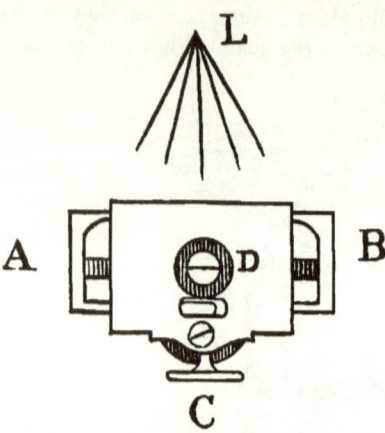

3. *Roll up a piece of paper (preferably black) into a tube* of such size that it will fit over the metallic cell (D, Fig. 20) and rest on the platform of the instrument. *Looking through this* with one eye we can judge more accurately than without it. Keep the other eye closed.

FIG. 20.—*L*, Light; *A* and *B*, right positions for observer; *C*, wrong position for observer; *D*, cell in place.

4. *Use first one eye and then the other, and never look more than a few seconds at a time,* as the eye very quickly gets sufficiently fatigued to lose its finer sensibility. Hence the impression of a first glance is better than a long look.

5. *Move the thumb screw with short, quick turns rather than slowly and gradually,* for sudden color changes affect the retina more than gradual ones. Suppose, for example, we have got as far as to decide that the tint of the diluted blood corresponds to that of glass *somewhere* between the numbers 40 and 60 on the scale. Move the screw suddenly from 40 to 55; the shock of the change will probably convince you that the blood color is lighter than 55. Therefore start this time at 55 and move it suddenly to, say, 45, which may show that 45 is too light. Thus by a series of quick movements of the screw getting shorter and shorter each time (with frequent rests for the eyes) we can probably get it down to a matter of doubt between, say, 42 and 45. Beyond that few persons can go and many can never learn to read without an error of five to ten per cent.

6. If the preliminary reading shows a reading of thirty per cent or less, two or three pipettes full of blood should be used and the reading divided by 2 or 3. A considerable error can thus be avoided.

Necessary Errors.

So far as I can see, a certain amount of error is absolutely necessary, inasmuch as the bit of colored glass to be seen at any one time through the aperture of the instrument is not (like the blood) all of one tint, but includes a *variation of twenty per cent in color*, *i.e.*, if the glass appearing at one end of the aperture is opposite 50 on the scale, that seen at the other end of the aperture will either be at 30 or at 70. We have, therefore, to pick out as well as we can the color of the *centre* of the bit of glass showing through the cell and compare the color *at that point* with the color which is evenly distributed throughout the whole of the blood-and-water compartment. This is of course, strictly speaking, impossible. We can no more get hold of and separate out the color of that central point than we can seize and hold fast the present moment. It eludes our grasp. This difficulty is somewhat lessened by shutting off from view all but a small section of both compartments with a bit of black cardboard or metal in which a slit is cut as in Fig. 21. The slit is put at right angles to the partition which divides the cell so that the blood tint is seen at *b* and the glass tint at *w*.

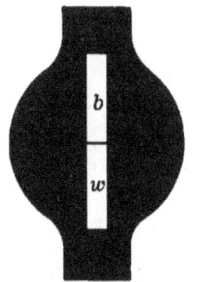

Fig. 21.—Shield for Use with v. Fleischl's Hæmometer.

Many persons are not sensitive enough to colors to attain any reasonable degree of accuracy with the instrument, and there is moreover a very considerable difference between different instruments in respect to the color of the glass slip.[1] Finally the instrument has been shown to be entirely unreliable for percentages of hæmoglobin under 20. This error, however, can be mostly eliminated by using several pipettes-full of blood and making corresponding reduction in the reading.

All these difficulties render the instrument an unsatisfactory

---

[1] Old instruments read lower than those recently manufactured.

one in many ways. Its bulk and expense are also considerable drawbacks.

II. *Oliver's Hæmoglobinometer.*

Oliver's instrument corrects two errors which are inherent in v. Fleischl's.

1. It has no sliding scale of color, but compares the blood tint successively with definite tints of glass, each of which is even. The tints are worked out to correspond to the specific dilution curve of blood, for:

2. Since every colored liquid changes color at a different rate when diluted, the dilution curve of blood does not correspond to that of glass (which behaves in this respect like a liquid). The glass wedge of v. Fleischl's instrument represents a single color regularly diluted and does not correspond in its degrees to the colors of blood diluted at a similar rate. The scale of Dr. Oliver's instrument is measured to correspond to the actual colors of the blood's dilution curve, by means of the tintometer.

In other respects the principle of the instrument is like v. Fleischl's, and the method of using the two is practically the same except that in Oliver's reflected light is used instead of transmitted light. Oliver's instrument consists of a series of twelve tinted glass discs corresponding to the hæmoglobin percentages from 10 to 120 and arranged in two rows (see Fig. 22a). The intermediate degrees are measured by means of "riders" of colored glass, which can be laid on top of the primary color discs so as to deepen the tint seen.

The capillary pipette (Fig. 22 *b*) is somewhat stouter than v. Fleischl's, but is used in the same way to collect the blood, which is then forced out of it with water from a medicine dropper (which is fitted with a rubber tube to slip over the blunt end of the pipette) (Fig. 22 *c*) and washed into a mixing cell (Fig. 22 *d*) similar to v. Fleischl's, except for the absence of a central partition. Here the blood is mixed in the usual way with water and the cell filled to the brim and covered with a small glass plate. The blood thus prepared is brought close to the scale and there compared with the tint of the different standard color discs. If it matches one of them the observation is complete;

if not we use one of the glass riders which enables us to read within two and a half degrees. A fuller set of riders can be obtained so as to make it possible to read down to 1 per cent.

The standard is usually arranged for candle-light, but another set of discs can be obtained adjusted to daylight read-

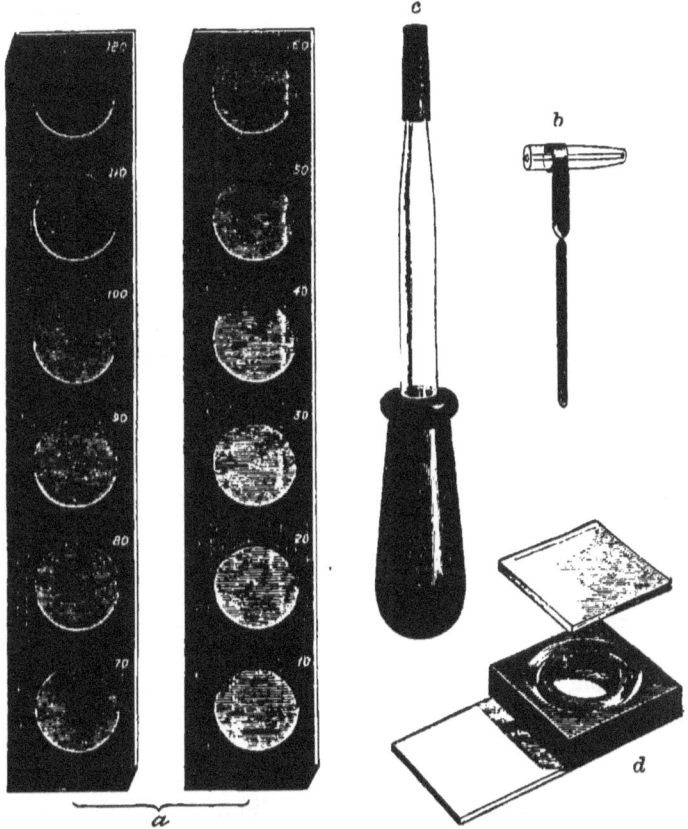

Fig. 22.—Oliver's Hæmoglohinometer. *a*, Standard color disks; *b*, capillary pipette; *c*, washing tube; *d*, mixing cell.

ings. The latter are less accurate. The same precautions as to the exclusion of outer light by means of a "hydroscope" tube, resting the eye frequently, etc., must be observed with this instrument as with v. Fleischl's. [It can be obtained of J. H.

Smith & Cie., Zurich (Wollishofen), for 115 francs plus duties
and expressage, or of the Tintometer Company, 6 Farringdon
Avenue, London, E. C.] The candle should be placed three or
four inches from the instrument and arranged to light both the
blood and the color discs alike.

A word as to the use of the riders. The instrument as used
for clinical work usually has two riders: the one having the
deeper tint is used on the upper half of the scale, the other on
the lower. Suppose we have decided that the blood color is
between 60 and 70. Put the rider on the 60 disc and compare
again. If the blood is darker than the 60 disc plus the rider
the percentage is approximately 67½ (since it is higher than
60+5 [the rider] and lower than 70). If it just matches the
60 plus its rider, the reading is 65. If the blood is paler than
this, yet darker than 60, it is about 62½. An error of about 2 degrees is obviously inevitable.

ESTIMATING THE SPECIFIC GRAVITY OF THE BLOOD.

The simplest and most available method for clinical use is
that of Hammerschlag,[1] a modification of Roy's[2] method.
Chloroform is heavier than blood; benzol is lighter. Mix in a
urinometer glass such quantities of the two that the specific
gravity taken by an ordinary urinometer is about 1059, *i.e.*, that
of normal blood. Puncture the ear, draw a drop of blood into
the tube of a Thoma-Zeiss pipette, a small medicine dropper, or
any other capillary tube, and blow it out again into the chloroform-benzol mixture. The blood *does not mix at all* with these
liquids but floats like a red bead. If it sinks to the bottom add
chloroform, if it rises to the top add benzol, until finally the
drop remains stationary in the body of the liquid, showing that
its specific gravity is just that of the surrounding mixture.
Then take the specific gravity of the liquid, as we do of urine,
and you have the specific gravity of the drop that floated in it.
The following precautions are needed:

1. Have the inside of the urinometer glass perfectly dry and
clean; otherwise the drop of blood may cling to it and flatten
out against it.

[1] Wien. klin. Wochenschrift, iii., 1,018, 1890.
[2] Proceedings of Physiological Society, 1884.

2. It is usually well to have more than one drop of blood in the glass in case any mishap occurs with the first one.

3. Add the chloroform and benzol a few drops at a time, and after each addition stir the whole mixture thoroughly with a glass rod.

4. If we have reason to suppose the blood will be lighter than normal (*i.e.*, if the hæmoglobin is probably low, *vide supra*), it saves time to start with a lighter mixture of chloroform and benzol.

5. Avoid having any *air* within the blood drop. This can generally be seen either in the capillary tube or after the drop is in the mixture. It is safer to take the *middle portion* of the blood drawn into the capillary tube, as both the first and the last portions of the column are more apt to have air in them.

6. The whole process should be done as quickly as possible, else the chloroform or benzol may work into the blood drop and affect its weight.

It is better to have a urinometer with a scale running as high as 1070, but this is not essential, for the clinically important specific gravities are *low*, not high.

The importance of the specific gravity of the blood, as hinted above, is not so much for itself, but because it runs parallel to the percentage of hæmoglobin and gives a figure from which the latter can be computed.

The specific gravity of the blood plasma varies very little (except in *dropsy* from any cause), and in the corpuscles themselves the variable element is the hæmoglobin.[1] Consequently in most non-dropsical patients the specific gravity of the whole blood varies directly as the hæmoglobin. The following exceptions to this rule must be borne in mind.

1. In leukæmia the specific gravity is relatively higher than the hæmoglobin on account of the weight of the leucocytes.

2. In pernicious anæmia with high color index (see below) the hæmoglobin is about two per cent higher than we should gauge it to be judging by the specific gravity.

Now, as it is far easier to take the specific gravity accurately than to use the v. Fleischl hæmometer, and as the instruments needed are already in the possession of most physicians and

[1] Except in dropsy in which the corpuscles themselves may get water-soaked.

the solutions not expensive, there are evidently great advantages in taking the hæmoglobin in this indirect way. The chloroform-benzol mixture can be filtered and then used over again indefinitely, and the bulk and weight of the urinometer with its glass and the chloroform and benzol bottles, are far less than that of the hæmoglobinometer.

In dropsical cases we must still use the hæmoglobinometer. In other conditions I do not see why it should not be supplanted by the cheaper, easier, more accurate, and equally quick method of calculating by specific gravity. To do this one of the following tables may be used. (I. is from Hammerschlag, using the method above described; II. is modified from Schmaltz, "Pathologie des Blutes," etc., Leipsic, 1896, using a direct weighing method.) Apparently a degree of specific gravity means much more at the top of the scale (*i.e.*, 6.6 per cent) than at the bottom (1⅔ per cent). These tables are of course not accurate, and further research will be needed to make them so.

I.		II.	
Spec. Grav.	Hæmoglobin.	Spec. Grav.	Hæmoglobin.
1033–1035 = 25–30 per cent.		1080 = 20 per cent. ±	
1035–1038 = 30–35 "		1035 = 30 " "	
1038–1040 = 35–40 "		1038 = 35 " "	
1040–1045 = 40–45 "		1041 = 40 " "	
1045–1048 = 45–55 "		1042.5 = 45 " "	
1048–1050 = 55–65 "		1045.5 = 50 " "	
1050–1053 = 65–70 "		1048 = 55 " "	
1053–1055 = 70–75 "		1049 = 60 " "	
1055–1057 = 75–85 "		1051 = 65 " "	
1057–1060 = 85–95 "		1052 = 70 " "	
		1053.5 = 75 " "	
		1056 = 80 " "	
		1057.5 = 90 " "	
		1059 = 100 " "	

STUDY OF THE FINER STRUCTURES OF THE BLOOD.

The study of dried and stained specimens with the help of the aniline dyes gives us much of interest and importance in regard to the blood. More can be told about a given case by the study of a dried and stained cover-glass specimen than by any other single method.

Preparation of Cover-Glass Specimens.

(*a*) Covers carefully cleaned with soap and water are arranged at the bedside in such position that we can quickly pick them up without touching their surfaces (see Fig. 1).[1] The ear is punctured in the usual way, and one of the cover-glasses touched to the summit of the drop as soon as it emerges. This cover-glass is then let fall upon another in such a way that their corners do not coincide (Fig. 23). If the covers are clean the drop spreads *at once* over their whole surface; as soon as it stops spreading, slide off the top one *without lifting them apart*, but exactly in the plane of their surfaces. Have a gas or alcohol flame at hand and dry instantly if you want to get the very best specimens; but this is not at all necessary for most clinical purposes. The *under* cover-glass is always better spread than the *upper*.

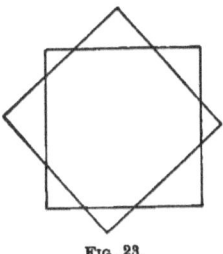

Fig. 23.

(*b*) These covers have now to be *fixed* either by heat or by half an hour's immersion in absolute alcohol and ether (equal parts), or by the same mixture (30 c.c. each) plus five drops of a saturated alcoholic solution of corrosive sublimate (five minutes' immersion), or by exposure to the vapor of forty-five per cent formaldehyde. I have used all these methods, but found none of them to compare favorably with the method of heat fixation when we wish to study the leucocytes or the nuclei of any cell.

When we wish to see chiefly the changes in the red cells (as in studying the malarial organism, nucleated red corpuscles, degenerative changes, etc.), the alcohol and ether method is good. But when, as in the majority of cases, it is the white cells in which our interest centres, the use of heat is very greatly to be preferred. Heat serves not simply to fix the cells on the glass and to prevent degenerative changes, but also to modify and greatly improve the staining power of the cell when Ehrlich's triacid stain is used.

The method of fixation by alcohol and ether needs little comment, the cover-glasses being simply left in the mixture half an hour or as much longer as is convenient. Half an hour

---

[1] I often poise them on corks so that their corners are readily accessible to the fingers. The process of making blood films is far easier if another person prepares the drop for us so that we can stand ready with a cover-glass in each hand to catch the drop as soon as it emerges.

is enough. In most cases we use dry heat. The best way to do this is in a dry-heat sterilizer at a temperature of 140°–155° C., according to the stain used. The temperature must be watched very closely, and as soon as it reaches the desired point the heat should be removed. Gradual heating and gradual cooling are best. If we cannot easily get access to such an instrument, we can manage very well with any small iron or copper box having a door or lid and a hole for a cork which is perforated for the thermometer bulb. This supported over a gas or alcohol flame does very well. It needs about ten minutes to get the temperature to 150° C., and as soon as it gets there the specimens should be taken out. The same end can be accomplished somewhat less accurately with a strip of copper supported over a Bunsen burner or a small gas or oil stove. The copper plate should be about a foot long and two or three inches wide. Such a plate supported on an iron tripod over a flame gets, after a few minutes, to have a fixed temperature at any given distance from the flame, the heat passing off at the end of the plate as fast as it comes, and so not accumulating. On this plate find the boiling point of water by dropping small drops of water on it, and put the cover-glasses at this point *face downward*. They may be left there for from fifteen minutes to as long as you please; but with the stain which I have used, fifteen minutes' heating gives as good results as a longer period, and excellent specimens can often be made with five minutes' heating.[1] After allowing the specimens to cool they are ready for staining.

Staining.

For all details of structure the Ehrlich tricolor mixture or one of the numerous modifications of it is most convenient.

---

[1] With a little practice one can learn to make excellent specimens by simply passing the cover-glass through a Bunsen or alcohol flame about twenty times very rapidly. The rate of speed must be learned by experiment, *i.e.*, *such* a speed and *such* a number of exposures to the flame as turns out to give on staining a bright *yellow* color to the red corpuscles (*never* red or brown or gray), a good definition to the blue-stained nuclei and to the violet or pink granules of the polynuclear leucocytes. These are the essentials of a well-stained specimen, and they depend (*a*) on the heating, (*b*) on the make of stain, but only slightly on the length of staining (*vide infra*).

The most useful and easily obtained of these is made by mixing:

Saturated watery solution of orange G,	.	. . .	6 c.c.
" " " " acid fuchsin,		. . .	4 c.c.

To these add a few drops at a time, shaking between each addition:

Saturated watery solution of methyl green, . . . 6.6 c.c.

Then add:

Glycerin, ...	5 c.c.
Absolute alcohol, ...	10 "
Water, ...	15 "

Shake well for one to two minutes. Let stand twenty-four hours. Do not filter.[1] G. Grubler's colors are best.

I have used only this stain for the past two years, and have never seen any other which compares with it in brilliancy and general usefulness.

The staining process is remarkably simple. A drop of the stain is simply spread over the surface of the cover-glass specimen with a glass rod and washed off again with water after two or three minutes or as much longer as is convenient. *With this mixture it is impossible to overstain.* If the specimen look too dark (brown or red instead of orange-yellow) it is not because of overstaining, but because of *underheating.* It needs a good deal of heat to bring out the full brilliancy of the three colors, and the 100°–120° C. usually recommended for heating is entirely insufficient with this stain unless continued for a long time.

If overheated the specimen looks pale lemon yellow to the naked eye, and under the microscope everything is blurred and dim.

I am convinced that any one who has once seen how much is brought out by a *good* make of triple stain will never use any other for clinical purposes. Eosin (one-per-cent alcoholic solution) followed after a few minutes by Delafield's hæmatoxylon for one minute, or methyl blue one-half minute, gives a very

---

[1] An absolutely reliable triple stain from Ehrlich's latest formula can be had of Walter Dodd, apothecary to the Massachusetts General Hospital. A 65-cent bottle will stain several thousand specimens.

striking contrast stain, but does not bring out the points most essential in clinical blood work. To "control" Ehrlich's triple stain with eosin-hæmatoxylon or eosin-methyl blue is like controlling a chronometer with a fifty-cent clock. The latter stains are very valuable for the study of the finer structure of nuclei, for karyokinetic figures and basophilic granules, but *not* for diagnosis.

After staining and washing in water, the covers are dried between layers of filter paper and mounted in Canada balsam, ready for examination with the one-twelfth oil-immersion lens, with wide-open diaphragm.[1]

Differential Counting.

The only procedure in the microscopic examination of such specimens which needs any description is that of making the so-called "differential count" of the leucocytes (*i.e.*, determining what percentage of the leucocytes present belongs to each of the sub-varieties as described on pp. 62–67). To do this accurately we should examine at least five hundred leucocytes—the examination being simply the classification of them under their different sub-varieties. A movable stage is very convenient though not essential for this purpose. With such a stage the technique is simply to start with the lens in, say, the *upper left-hand* corner of the blood film and, by turning the screw of the mechanical stage, move the preparation slowly past the eye until the *upper right-hand* corner is reached. During this process as the cells appear in the field they are checked off and put down under one or another heading. Then move the stage so that the lens is just one field's diameter nearer the *right-hand lower* corner of the preparation, and go back again from right to left, following the serpentine track indicated above in Fig. 7. To move the lens just one field's diameter we have only to fix the eye on a cell at the extreme edge of the field, and then move the stage till that cell disappears out of sight on the *oppo-*

[1] Of late I have used dry lenses a great deal—the 7 or even the 5 of Leitz —on account of their larger field. Most cells can be easily recognized with this power *after* we have well learned their looks by earlier study of specimens with the immersion lens. If in doubt about any cell, it is easy to pull out the tube of the microscope or put on the immersion lens.

site side of the field. Thus we avoid any chance of counting the same cells twice, and yet are sure not to miss seeing any.

As we go back and forth in this way, we notice chiefly the white cells of course, but yet keep our eyes open for any unusual appearances in the red cells. Usually these move by in a monotonous stream, one looking much like another, but in pathological blood we must always be on the lookout for nucleated red cells, degenerative changes, and variations in size and shape. In malarial cases of course our scrutiny is directed chiefly upon the *red* cells.

If we have not the help of a movable stage we try to do the same thing moving the slide with the fingers. With moderate care there is no danger of counting the same cells twice, but we cannot help missing a good many altogether, so that although accurate the process takes longer.

When leucocytosis is present, at least one thousand leucocytes can be found in a single well-spread seven-eighth-inch coverglass specimen. In normal blood we may need to go through two to three covers.

BACTERIOLOGICAL EXAMINATION.

Blood obtained by the ordinary method of puncture is not fit for bacteriological examination.[1] The following is the better way:

Sterilize the skin over the flexor surface of the bend of the elbow, and wash off thoroughly the agents used for sterilization with boiled water or boiled normal salt solution. Have an assistant grasp the upper arm so as to prevent the venous return and distend the large veins at the elbow. Into the most prominent of these plunge a sterilized hollow needle connected with the bulb of a sterilized syringe. All traces of antiseptics must be carefully washed out of the needle and the syringe bulb before using.

When the needle penetrates the wall of the vein the blood usually begins to flow into the bulb of the syringe, and this is hastened by gently withdrawing the piston until 1–2 c.c. of blood are in the bulb. Then withdraw the needle, press a pad of sterilized gauze over the wound, and expel the blood before it

[1] See Kühnau's comparative experiments in Deut. med. Woch., 1897, No. 25.

coagulates into a blood-serum culture tube so that it shall run down over the whole surface of the "slant" and collect a little at the bottom.   The tubes are then put at once into the thermostat.

In examining for the gonococcus the blood is to be mixed with equal parts of agar-agar (previously melted down so as to be mixable but not hot enough to kill the organisms), and then plated.

The further examination of cultures falls outside the scope of this book.

In the above procedure the only difficulties are: 1. Sometimes it is hard to find a vein and to get the needle into it. 2. Occasionally we get the needle entirely through the vessel into the tisuses on the other side.

If the blood does not flow readily into the bulb one of these two mistakes is usually the cause, but occasionally in those whose vessels are very small or whose circulation is very feeble (as in the moribund) it is very hard to get the requisite amount of blood.   Only practice helps us to avoid these difficulties.

The procedure causes hardly more pain than the use of an ordinary subcutaneous injection; the process of sterilization is usually more irksome to the patient than the puncture.

Bleeding is trifling, and within twenty-four hours there is usually no trace of the puncture left.   A sterilized dressing with moderate pressure should be applied.

OTHER METHODS OF BLOOD EXAMINATION.

It is perhaps worth while briefly to mention some other methods of blood examination of which no account will be given.

1. Determination of the *alkalinity* of the blood.   No accurate and clinically available method has yet been devised.   Despite the interesting work of Kraus, Caro, Löwy, Biernacki, v. Limbeck, and others, I am still unable to get hold of any clinically valuable information given by the determination of alkalinity.

2. *Resistance of the red corpuscles to the influence of distilled water.*   As is well known, water breaks up red cells, but if we add a certain amount of alkali, say NaCl, the cells remain uninjured.   The amount of NaCl which has to be added

to prevent the destruction of red cells is from 0.44 to 0.48 per cent. Under certain pathological conditions it needs either more or less of the salt to keep the cells intact, *i.e.*, they possess an increased or diminished power of resistance against the destroying influences of distilled water. The degree of concentration necessary to maintain red corpuscles intact is known as the *isotonic coëfficient* of the blood as stated in terms of a given salt; 0.44–0.48 is thus the coefficient of normal blood corpuscles in NaCl.

Possibly this method of examining blood may in the future give us knowledge of clinical value. At present it is not clinically applicable.

The resistance of the blood cells to the influence of electricity, heat, and mechanical pressure has also been investigated in various conditions of health and disease.

3. The rapidity of coagulation varies markedly in different diseases, but no reliable way of measuring it has yet been found.

4. The amount of solids in a given quantity of blood can be determined by weighing a given amount of blood before and after six hours' drying at 65° C. Inasmuch as the hæmoglobin percentage and the specific gravity run practically parallel with the amount of solids this method has no considerable clinical value.

4

PART II.

PHYSIOLOGY OF THE BLOOD.

CHAPTER IV.

ONLY such portions of our knowledge of blood physiology will be entered upon here as are necessary for an understanding of the small group of pathological changes which can be profitably investigated by clinicians. This limits us for the present to the *morphology* of the blood, its *coloring matter*, and its *density* under physiological conditions.

APPEARANCE OF FRESH NORMAL BLOOD.

A drop of normal blood spread between slide and cover-glass as directed on page 7 and examined immediately with a one-twelfth immersion lens, amazes us first of all by the entire absence of any red color. All we see is a colorless liquid in which masses of very pale greenish-yellow discs are floating or lying.

I. Red Corpuscles.

(a) If the blood is spread thickly the blood discs are often arranged in the *form of rouleaux* (Fig. 24). The entire absence of this tendency to rouleaux formation is pathological. It is to be avoided, of course, as far as possible, as it gives us only the thin edges of the corpuscles to look at and covers up much that we need to study. Thin spreading of the blood is therefore important.

(b) There is not much variation from the *accurately round shape* of each corpuscle in normal blood, except where one is indented by another. As they are moved about by the currents set in motion by the gradual drying up of the plasma and strike against each other, they bend, double up, or indent each other,

like bags of jelly, but yet always have a strong tendency to
return elastically to their round outline when free from pressure. Thus a corpuscle passing through a narrow passage between two leucocytes will be flattened out like a worm; but as
soon as it emerges on the other side, it will be as round as
before.

(c) The central *biconcavity* of the cell, being thinner than the
rim, is lighter colored. Just how much lighter should be learned
by practice so that we may detect any abnormal *pallor of the
corpuscles* due to lack of hæmoglobin. Pallor is to be seen
mostly in the centre of the cell, which in extreme cases seems
almost transparent. This is not to be confounded with the
highly refractile, glistening-white centres seen as a mark of
necrosis as soon as the blood begins to dry up. A fuller description of these appearances is given in the chapter on the
malarial organisms, with some forms of which they may be
confounded.

(d) Slight *variations in size* are present among normal red
discs, and here again only practice can teach us where the normal
limits end and the pathological begin. Cells may be (patho-
logically) *all* undersized or *all* oversized, so that a standard of
comparison is not always to be looked for in the preparation
itself.

(e) If we focus carefully on a single red cell we can usually
make out a fine, wavy, so-called *molecular motion* in it. This is
quite different from the active amœboid movements observed
in dying cells, and from the rapid dancing of malarial pigment.

(f) The familiar appearance of spines all over the cells
usually called " *crenation*" need not be described here (see Fig.
27, p. 86).

But it is the very earliest beginnings of crenation that lead
to mistakes, as when only one projection has been developed
and that points toward the eye, so that a bright spot in the corpuscles is all we see.

(g) Unless we disinfect the skin before puncturing we must
be prepared to find in fresh preparations (a) oil drops[1] (b) epi-
thelium; (c) particles of "dirt;" (d) small colorless motile

[1] In some conditions the blood really contains fat. (*Vide infra*, "Lipæmia.")

organisms about 1 μ in diameter, which are not at all rare but whose nature is unknown to me.[1]

(*h*) We may make a rough estimate of the *number of red cells* present if we take care to spread the drop of the same thickness each time. The eye gets used to the ordinary look of a well-filled field of corpuscles and notices a look of thinness if any considerable anæmia is present.

(*i*) The *degenerative changes* to be seen in normal blood after long exposure to the air, which can get in between slide and cover, are described in detail later on. In pathological blood we may find these as soon as the blood is drawn.

II. White Cells.

(*a*) *The white or colorless corpuscles* are but little different from the red in color, the latter being so nearly colorless. We first notice them either by their amœboid movements, or because they are not moved by the plasma currents, but stand like a rock round the sides of which the current of red cells is broken. They are slightly larger in most instances than the red cells; but this difference shows less in the fresh specimens where the leucocyte keeps its spherical shape than in the dried and stained preparations, where it is usually somewhat flattened. Their shape is very irregular and their edges often look tattered.

In some leucocytes the amœboid motions are entirely absent. These are the smallest cells, and in them a single nucleus filling most of the cell can often be seen. They are much more nearly spherical and less irregular than the amœboid cells.

The large amœboid leucocytes are more or less granular, and in certain lights these granules look quite dark and are sometimes mistaken for bits of malarial pigment. This is especially true of the *coarse granular* cells seen occasionally; staining shows these large granules much more distinctly (= eosinophile—see below, p. 65); cells of this type are the most actively amœboid of all.

(*b*) The most important point in connection with the leucocytes is their ratio to the red cells. This is estimated in fresh specimens not by any actual counting but by reference to a standard fixed in the mind by study of normal specimens, and

[1] Since this was written the same appearances have been carefully studied by Müller and Stokes (see page 50).

any considerable increase of the white cells would be noticed at once. Naturally we must not judge from any one part of the slide, as the distribution of the leucocytes may be unequal in different parts of it.

III. Blood Plates.[1]

Unless the number of these elements is increased by some pathological influence, we seldom notice them at all in normal blood. This may be because we do not work quickly enough in preparing our specimen. Hayem recommends that the cover-glass be laid upon the slide before the puncture is made; as soon as the drop emerges it is allowed to run in between slide and cover by capillary attraction, thus avoiding contact with the air.[2] The blood plates are irregularly shaped, very cohesive elements, about one-half the diameter of a blood disc, usually seen cling-ing together in masses like zoögloea. They are colorless and not amoeboid and look like débris.

IV. Fibrin Network.

After a specimen of fresh blood has stood for some time ex-posed to as much air as can creep in between slide and cover-glass, we begin to notice a network of fine straight lines in the spaces between the corpuscles. Here and there these filaments seem to radiate from a centre where irregular, colorless masses, apparently blood plates, are to be seen (Fig. 24).

No stain is needed to demonstrate these fibrin threads, but a small-aperture diaphragm and very little light makes them plainer. Their only importance is that under certain pathologi-

[1] It is probable that the elements included under this heading comprise several different things. It is beyond the plan of this book to discuss their origin and significance, since they possess at present no clinical value.

[2] This is a very satisfactory way if we wish to see the corpuscles as fresh and unspoiled as we can. Put a cover-glass on a slide so that the edge of one corresponds with the edge of the other, and, holding them in this position with finger and thumb, put their superimposed edges into the side of the drop as it emerges. It will run in between them by capillary at-traction. The blood plates can be stained with eosin, and in the eosin-hæmatoxylon stain are easily seen and their number approximately estimated.

cal conditions the fibrin network is very much increased and helps us in the diagnosis (Fig. 25). Hence it is of importance

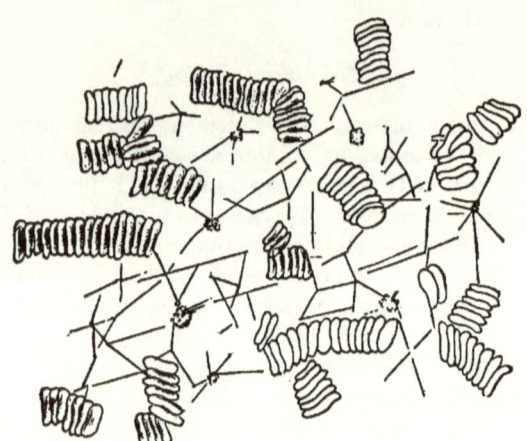

Fig. 24.—Rouleau Formation and Fibrin Network of Normal Blood.

to be familiar with the ordinary closeness of the network in normal blood as a standard of comparison.

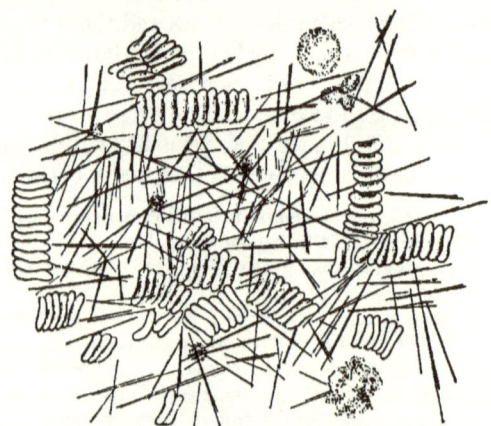

Fig. 25.—Increased Thickness of Fibrin Network.

For an account of the conditions of its increase see Chapter IX., page 124.

AVERAGE DIAMETER OF RED CELLS.

The blood under normal conditions shows considerable variations in the size of its corpuscles in the fresh state as well as in stained specimens.[1]

The following table (v. Limbeck) shows the results of various observers.

	Normal Limits.	Average Diameter.
Welcker	diameter = 4.5–9.5 μ.	7 μ
Valentin		7 μ
Malinin		7.7 μ
Hayem	diameter = 6–8.8 μ..	7.5 μ
Mallassez		7.6 μ
Laache	diameter = 6–9 μ....	8.5 μ
Bizzozero		7.075 μ
Gram	diameter = 6.7–9.3 μ	7.850 μ

Average = 7.5 μ

These differences depend partly on differences in the method of measuring (wet or dry), and partly on the fact that the age

[1] A method of measuring, approximately accurate, and easily applicable in clinical work is the following:

Using a camera lucida, trace on paper the divisions of a fine stage micrometer as seen under a one-twelfth oil immersion lens; such micrometres are usually ruled to one one-hundreth of a millimetre. Approximate accuracy in our tracing can be obtained if the process is repeated till the divisions marked in successive drawings correspond accurately one with another. Care must be taken that the paper is flat upon the table beside the microscope, and not raised on a block or otherwise; also that the part of the paper on which we draw should be perpendicularly under the centre of the mirror and not off to one side. When a drawing has been made with these precautions, we have only to divide the space between each of the lines in our drawing into ten equal parts, and we have a scale, each division of which represents 1 μ as seen under a one-twelfth oil-immersion lens, with the length of tube of the particular microscope used. To use our μ-scale we have only to draw with the camera lucida any cell whose size we want to know, using always the same microscope, the same length of tube, and the same lenses, and having the drawing paper (as before) flat on the table and perpendicularly under the mirror. The drawing thus made is measured with the μ-scale like any other object.

With this method a cell can be measured in a few seconds and with sufficient accuracy (i.e., within 0.5 μ).

and conditions of nutrition in the persons selected make a difference. In the new-born, and to some extent throughout childhood, the normal limits of variation are wider than in adults (3.3–10.5 μ, Hayem). Sex appears to have no constant influence.

Gram [1] noted that the measurements published by observers living in southern Europe are smaller than those of northern Europe (Italians 7–7.5, Germans 7.8, Norwegians 8.5).

The majority of any individual's red cells are certainly about 7.5 μ *in diameter, and this may accordingly be taken as our standard* (Hayem counts twelve per cent under 6.6 μ, twelve per cent over 8 μ, the rest 7.5 μ).

NORMAL NUMBER OF THE RED CELLS.

1. At the level of the sea and in adult life the normal number of red cells per cubic millimetre is about 5,000,000 for men and 4,500,000 for women. This is not infrequently increased in very vigorous, healthy persons; 6,000,000 is by no means rare among healthy young men, and higher figures are seen occasionally. Thus Hewes [2] in fifty young medical students found an average of 5,809,000 per cubic millimetre; of these fifteen exceeded 6,000,000, the highest being 6,400,000, while the lowest of the whole series was 5,120,000. *Altitude above the sea level* raises the count invariably (see page 79).

2. The influence of *menstruation, childbirth, and lactation* is to diminish the red cells temporarily, the amount of the diminution depending not only on the amount of blood lost but on the capacity of the individual organism for blood regeneration. At puberty, when sexual functions are being established, we expect lower counts than after the establishment of the function. Normal pregnancy does not affect the count of red cells.

3. The count of red cells per cubic millimetre is raised by any cause inducing *concentration of the blood,* such as profuse sweating, and is lowered by the temporary dilution of the blood after large draughts of liquid. In these changes, which are always very transient, the hæmoglobin and specific gravity in a given drop are of course increased with the corpuscles.

---

[1] Fortschritte der Medicin, 1884.
[2] Transactions of the Boston Society of Medical Science, May 18, 1897.

Vasomotor influences affecting the calibre of the peripheral vessels (hot or cold baths, exercise, etc.) may temporarily concentrate or dilute the blood by affecting the interchange of fluid between the vessels and the surrounding lymph spaces. By these processes the blood in the peripheral vessels may show an increase or diminution in the cellular elements, the hæmoglobin and specific gravity corresponding to the greater or less concentration of the blood at that point (on these points see below page 76).

Hayem noted that in young people especially the number of red cells varied considerably without any notable change in conditions.

4. Influence of Nutrition on the Number of Red Cells.

A. *After a meal*, especially when considerable liquid is taken, the blood is temporarily diluted and hence the count of red cells per cubic millimetre is diminished (v. Limbeck; Reinert). This is illustrated by the following case from v. Limbeck.

ADULT, MALE, HEALTHY.

	Red Cells.	White Cells.	Hb
11:15 A.M.	5,530,000	7,660	98 per cent.
12 M. dinner.			
12:15 P.M............	5,320,000	6,166	
1:15 "	5,480,000	8,500	
2:15 "	4,733,000	12,000	
3:15 "	4,872,000	14,000	89 per cent.
4:15 "	4,720,000	10,830	89 "

As the white cells rise (digestive leucocytosis, see below, page 83) the red fall.

Fasting, by concentrating the blood, temporarily increases the number of red cells (400,000–500,000 increase after twenty-four hours' fast).

B. *General Nutrition.*—Lean, muscular people have on the average more red cells per cubic millimetre than fat people (Leichtenstern, quoted by v. Limbeck), other things being equal.[1]

As above said, fasting (by concentrating the blood) raises the number of red blood cells, so that it is not simply hunger that

[1] The influence of stasis in the obese, whose fat loads the surface of the heart, is to cause an apparent increase of red cells (see below, p. 75).

gives us the *diminution* in red cells commonly found in *poorly nourished people*, but rather the influence of bad hygiene in the slums, etc.

5. *Seasons* and the *time of day* seem to have no influence in themselves. The same is true of *race* and *climate*. The only exception to this is reported in the work of E. Below,[1] who found in yellow fever districts an average count of only 4,700,000 red cells per cubic millimetre and the diameter of the individual cell reduced to 5.9 μ on the average (7.5 μ = normal).

6. *Fatigue.*—Hayem noted a loss of from 500,000 to 1,000,-000 red cells per cubic millimetre in the blood of a number of farmers after a hard summer's work, the counts made in September having been compared with those of April and always found to be lower. Whether fatigue is the only cause of this diminution may be doubted.

7. *Age.*—In the new-born the number of red cells is very high for a few days (7,000,000 to 8,800,000), but falls at the end of seven to ten days (see page 86).

In the very old a certain degree of anæmia is, so to speak, physiological; but this, which like the plethora of the new-born is to be referred *not* to the fact of age, but to concomitant influences, is by no means invariable. Schmaltz reports 6,766,000 red cells in a man of eighty-one and 4,816,000 in a woman of seventy-four.

NORMAL NUMBER OF WHITE CELLS.

The figure usually given for adults is 7,500 per cubic millimetre. This varies a good deal, according to the nutrition of the individual (see page 81) and also at different times of the day, owing to influences not explained. The influence of digestion will be mentioned later. In animals a slight shock[2] is sufficient materially to affect the count of leucocytes; 5,000 to 10,000 may be called the normal limits. Romberg finds 9,058 as the average count in fifty-five healthy young women. There is, I believe, no evidence to show whether or not mental disturbances (fear, rage, emotion of various kinds) affect their

[1] "Deut. Tropenhygiene," Berlin, 1895. O. Coblanz.
[2] Löwitt: "Studien z. Physiol. und Pathol. d. Blutes," etc., Jena, 1892. Fischer.

number, but my impression is that they do. Other causes of variation will be discussed under Leucocytosis.

BLOOD PLATES.

The number of blood plates is from 400,000 to 700,000 under normal conditions. They are the chief constituents of white thrombi, and wherever they are diminished (*e.g.*, in hæmophilia, purpura) clotting is apt to be slow. They are increased in leukæmia and in many cases of grave anæmia. In the severer types of many infectious diseases (typhus, erysipelas, malaria) they are diminished, and in malaria they are sometimes wholly absent during the fever. In pneumonia and tuberculosis they are normal or increased. In purpura and hæmophilia they are sometimes much diminished or absent.

The physiological limits of the amount of *hæmoglobin* and of the *specific gravity* have already been mentioned. Under physiological conditions their variations follow those of the count of red cells.

MÜLLER'S "BLOOD DUST."

Müller[1] has recently described under the title of "Hæmoconien," or blood dust, a constituent of normal and pathological blood not hitherto noticed. This consists of small round colorless granules about the size of the finest fat drops—or about $\frac{1}{4}$–1μ in diameter, their size being very variable. They are highly refractile and have rapid dancing (molecular) motion, but no power of locomotion. They are insoluble in alcohol and ether, not stained by osmic acid, and take no part in the formation of fibrin. Stokes and Wegefarth,[2] who have confirmed Müller's observations, note that the "blood dust" can be seen much more clearly by the light of a Welsbach gas burner than by daylight. The latter observers present a body of evidence tending strongly to show that these bodies are the extruded granules of neutrophilic and eosinophilic leucocytes. Granules apparently identical with them can be stained in fresh specimens with eosin or Ehrlich's triacid stain in a way apparently

[1] Centralbl. für allg. Path., etc., viii., 1896.
[2] Johns Hopkins Hospital Bulletin, December, 1897.

like that of the intracellular granules.[1] They are also to be seen in pus and in hydrocele fluid.

I have frequently noticed these granules in studying fresh blood, but hitherto supposed them to come from the patient's skin (see page 52, footnote). No special diagnostic or prognostic significance has yet been attached to them, though the work of Kanthack and Stokes renders them of great interest with reference to the problem of immunity. They remind one somewhat of the description given by Kahane of the supposed organism of cancer.

[1] Nicholls: Phil. Med. Jour., Feb. 26, 1898.

Examination of the Blood.

PLATE I.

Fig. 1. Varieties of Leucocytes.

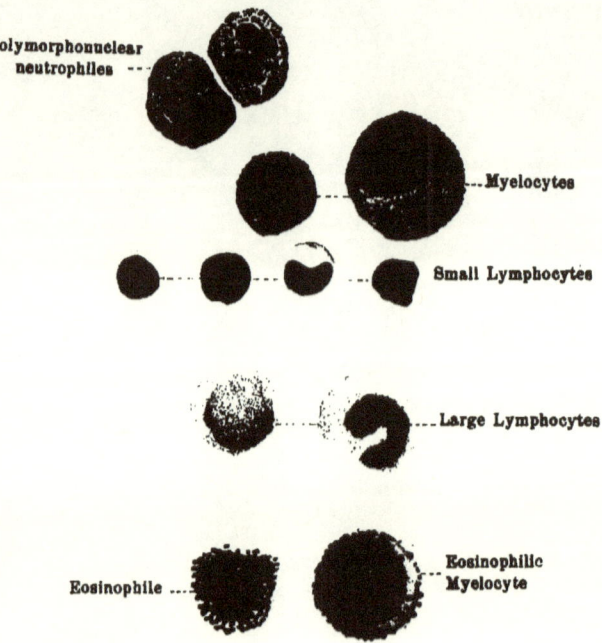

Polymorphonuclear neutrophiles ---

---Myelocytes

Small Lymphocytes

---Large Lymphocytes

Eosinophile ---

Eosinophilic Myelocyte

The Malarial Organism.

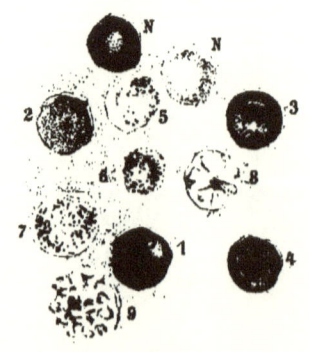

Fig. 2.

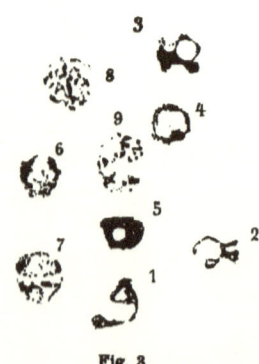

Fig. 3.

R. C. Cabot fec.

Lith. Anst. v. E. A. Funke, Leipzig.

PLATE I.

FIG. 1.—(a) *Polymorphonuclear Neutrophiles.* Note the varieties in size and shape of granules, the irregular staining of the nuclei, the light space around them, their relatively central position in the cell.

(b) *Myelocytes.* Note identity of granules with those just described; the even, pale stain of nuclei; their position near the surface (edge) of the cell. The two cells figured indicate the usual variations in the size of the whole cell.

(c) *Small Lymphocytes.* In the cell at the left note transparent protoplasm; in the cell next to it note *very* pale pink ring of protoplasm around nucleus which is deeply stained, especially at the periphery. The next cell has an indented nucleus; its protoplasm relatively distinct. The cell on the extreme right shows no protoplasm and is probably necrotic. In all note *absence of granules* with *this* stain. With basic stains blue granules appear in the protoplasm.

(d) *Large Lymphocytes.* Note pale-stained nuclei and protoplasm, irregularity of outline; indented nucleus in one. Every intermediate stage between these and the "*small*" lymphocytes occurs, and the distinction between them is arbitrary.

(e) *Eosinophile.* Note irregular shape, loose connection of granules, their copper color, their uniform and relatively large size, and spherical shape.

(f) *Eosinophilic Myelocyte.* Note similarity to (b) ordinary myelocytes except as regards granules. Color of granules may be as in (e) ordinary eosinophile.

All the above were stained with the Ehrlich triacid stain, and drawn with camera lucida. Oil-immersion objective one-twelfth and ocular No. iii. (Leitz).

FIG. 2.—*Malarial Parasites in Fresh (Unstained) Blood* (Tertian Forms). *N, N,* normal red corpuscles; 1, red cell containing *hyaline body;* 2, 3, 4, 5, successive stages in the development of the parasite, showing acquisition of pigment; 6, 7, full-grown parasites, the corpuscle no longer visible; 8, beginning of segmentation; 9, segmentation. In 6 and 7 note brownish blur behind the pigment dots. Drawn as in Fig. 1.

FIG. 3.—*Tertian Parasite Stained with Eosin and Methyl Blue.* The remains of the corpuscle containing the parasite stain pink, the parasite blue, and its pigment black. The stages of growth correspond with the numbers attached. Note in Figs. 1, 2, 3, and 4 the shape of the parasite, shown better than in fresh specimen.

[Owing to a mistake the cells in Fig. 3 are not drawn according to a single scale and their relative sizes must be disregarded.]

CHAPTER V.

FINER STRUCTURE OF THE BLOOD.

I. Appearances of Dried and Stained Specimens.

COVER-GLASS specimens prepared and stained as above directed give us more information of interest and importance than can be obtained from any other one method of blood examination. Approximate ideas of the quantity of red cells, of white cells, and of hæmoglobin can be formed, parasites and bacteria can be seen, and the whole mass of evidence based on the finer structure of the leucocytes can only be obtained in this way. The appearances of a specimen of normal blood prepared in this way are as follows:

RED CELLS.

1. The hæmoglobin stains with the orange G of the tricolor mixture, and in a properly heated specimen the red cells are of a brilliant yellow or pale orange tint. If overheated they have a feebly stained, washed-out look, while if *underheated they are more or less brown or gray.*[1]

The degree of pallor of the centres corresponding to the amount of hæmoglobin in the corpuscle can be gauged much more accurately with this stain than in the fresh preparations. The color of the edges is not much affected by pathological changes, the centres being the test. But in cases with extreme poverty of hæmoglobin the colored rim may be reduced to a mere shell and the rest may be almost completely colorless. The power to estimate the amount of coloring matter in this way can be easily acquired.

An approximate idea of the number of red cells may be formed by any observer who has learned to use a uniform technique in each case and to spread the blood of a standard thickness.

[1] This is a fruitful source of error. Many suppose that because their specimens come out too dark they must be "burnt," and so heat less. In fact the dark tint means that the specimen is not heated enough.

2. Nothing is seen of the fibrin or blood plates as a rule. In normal cases the plasma does not stain at all. A certain amount of débris is often present, usually pink stained.

WHITE CORPUSCLES.

3. The chief purpose and use of the "triple stain" is for distinguishing the varieties of white corpuscles, and the pathological states of the red. About the normal red cells it gives us no information that cannot be obtained as well by various other stains, but our knowledge of normal leucocytes has been immensely enlarged by its use.

In normal blood stained as above directed, we recognize the following varieties of white cells:

(1) *Small lymphocytes* or "small hyaline forms" (Kanthack) (see Plate I.). These consist mostly of a round blue nucleus about the size of a red cell, and surrounded by a thin coating of protoplasm, faintly stained or invisible (with Ehrlich's triple stain).

The nucleus may be considerably smaller than a red cell, and may or may not be deeply stained. In my experience it is usually pale-stained, but slight differences in technique will greatly affect its staining power. The larger it is the more apt it is to be pale (see Plate I.).

(2) There is no line to be drawn between this form and that now to be described, namely, the "large lymphocyte" or "large mononuclear cell," which is simply larger and paler.

The small lymphocyte is the form most frequently seen in the lymph channels and in chyle and at the periphery of the follicles of adenoid tissue. Whether it grows in the circulating blood into any other form of leucocyte is uncertain. In the so-called "large lymphocyte" the nucleus occupies relatively less of the cell than in the small lymphocyte.

In many cases we do not see in the blood any intermediate forms. Lymphocytes are either "small" (5–10 μ in diameter) or "large" (13–15 μ in diameter) (see Plate I.).

In other cases we find every intermediate size, both of nucleus and of the cells as a whole, and in such cases it is absurd to attempt a division into "large" or "small," though we may be able to say in a general way which size predominates.

The theory that the "*large*" *mononuclear* cells or "large hyaline forms" (Kanthack) come from the spleen and the small mononuclear from the lymph glands has been abandoned on all sides of late years.

The protoplasm of all lymphocytes, as has been said, is always hard to stain with Ehrlich's triple stain. Sometimes it has a faint pinkish tinge, more frequently it is grayish or very light blue, and in some cases it stands out brilliantly transparent and colorless against the faint purplish tinge of the surrounding plasma (see Plate I.). Although non-granular with the triple stain many of the lymphocytes show basophilic granules at the periphery of their protoplasm when stained with eosin and methylene blue. When thus stained a ring of unstained protoplasm appears around the nucleus. Sometimes the protoplasm stains diffusely blue with basic stains and no granules can be made out.

I have described the lymphocytes so far as "mononuclear," but it is not rare to find even very small ones (6 μ in diameter) whose nucleus has a deep cut in one side or has divided into two parts. I believe it is commoner to find a divided nucleus in the small forms than in the "large lymphocytes." The inapplicability of the term "small mononuclear cells" or "large mononuclear cells" to this variety of corpuscle is evident. The distinguishing mark is not the single nucleus but the absence of granules, with Ehrlich's stain. (See also below under "Mast cells.")

In the smaller forms of lymphocytes the nucleus, even when dividing, is compact and fills most of the cell. But in the large forms, instead of simply being larger and paler, the nucleus may begin to bend and branch in the cell, and then we get the so-called

(3) "*Transitional forms*" (Ehrlich), which are no bigger than the larger size of lymphocytes, from which they differ only in that they have an indentation in their nucleus—either a narrow cut or a bay so wide that a "horseshoe" nucleus results. This is *the* transitional form according to this nomenclature. There is no reason for calling it so, as all the forms of leucocytes are transitional, but there is some convenience in the name. Like most large lymphocytes it is pale all through—pale in both nucleus and protoplasm—and often escapes notice in hasty ex-

aminations.   Sometimes its protoplasm is sparsely covered with faint neutrophilic granules.

(4) The cells usually known as "polynuclear" are more properly called *polymorphonuclear neutrophiles.*   These cells constitute the vast majority of those found in ordinary pus. The main difference between them and those last described is in the possession of granules, best seen when stained by Ehrlich's methods.   The nucleus stains usually quite deep blue or greenish-blue, and irregularly, *i.e.*, more intensely in some parts than in others.   It is very irregular in shape, being twisted about in the body of the cell.   Here and there it may dive down so deeply beneath the surface of the cell that it is hidden under a thick layer of granules, reappearing in another part of the cell so that it *seems* to be broken in two.   Occasionally, no doubt, this is actually the case, but generally there are "underground connections" between the apparently separate pieces of nucleus. Now and then we see a cell (degenerating) where the granules have fallen away, leaving the nucleus like a short, thick snake, very rarely two, or like several sausages joined by strings.

One never sees any two of these cells whose nuclei are of the same shape.   Hence the term "polymorphonuclear."   The windings and twistings of the nucleus have suggested comparisons to the letters Z, S, E, etc.

The granules which fill the body of the cell and in which the nucleus is embedded stain well only with triple stains like Ehrlich's.   Acid stains like eosin, and basic stains like methylene blue, do not bring them out clearly.   Hence the term "neutrophilic," which is not strictly accurate; more properly they are faintly oxyphilic [1] and can be faintly stained with eosin. [Hence Kanthack and other English observers have called them "fine granular oxyphiles," while the term "coarse granular oxyphiles" is applied to the cells generally known as eosinophiles. These terms are in some respects more accurate than Ehrlich's, but are even more cumbrous than his.]   With Ehrlich's triacid mixture the granules stain violet or purple, sometimes pink. They are very small and irregular in shape and size, contrasting with the large, round, "eosinophile" granules (see below). The cells being spherical the granules lie *over* and around the nucleus, not simply *at the side* of it.   In their interstices we

[1] Ehrlich's stain is really a differential acid stain and not neutral.

sometimes seem to see a pinkish background of cell substance, but this is probably composed of granules somewhat out of focus. In normal blood these "neutrophilic" granules, which are so small that except with very high powers they look like a diffuse stain,  rarely if ever occur except in cells whose nucleus has reached the polymorphous stage. Occasionally we seem to see *mono-nuclear neutrophiles*, having a round nucleus with neutrophilic granules, but careful focussing usually shows that the appearance of a round or rod-shaped nucleus is given by the tight coiling of the ribbon-like nucleus round one of its ends, or else 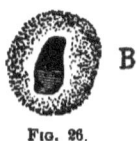 that a horseshoe nucleus is seen from the point of view indicated in Fig. 26. Thus if the eye be at the point A the nucleus will appear of the shape indicated in B (Fig. 26).

FIG. 26.

(5) The *eosinophile* or "coarse granular oxyphile" cell has, like its predecessor, a polymorphous nucleus and granules; but the nucleus is paler and more loosely connected to the granules, and the latter are spherical or oval, of uniform size, and much larger than any seen in the neutrophilic cell. They have strong affinity for acid coloring matters (eosin, acid-fuchsin, etc.), hence their name. In specimens stained with eosin or eosin and methyl blue they are very brightly colored pink. With the Ehrlich triacid mixture they are more of a copper or burnt-sienna color. Some individual granules stain much darker than others in the same cell, and may be of a different nature.

The eosinophiles are the most actively amœboid of all the corpuscles, and it may be for this reason that the different parts of the cell seem so loosely strung together. Or, if the hypothesis of Kanthack and Hardy, recently supported by Stokes, be true their loose arrangement may serve to make them easily detached for bactericidal purposes (see above, page 59). The granules may be all at one side of the cell and the nucleus on the other, and in cover-glass specimens we very frequently find actual separation of the two. Whether or not the actual separation is brought about by the technique of spreading the blood is unimportant, as we find such broken cells much more often

5

among the eosinophiles than among any other variety—which argues a looser structure.

Sometimes there seem to be two or more distinct and separate nuclei in the cell, no "underground connection" being traceable. The granules are seldom *over* the nucleus as we see it in cover-glass preparations, but cluster round it loosely.

The cell as a whole is usually a little smaller than the "neutrophile" and more irregular in shape. In stained specimens the neutrophile is seldom seen with a pseudopod extended, whereas the eosinophile often shows it.

The staining of the nucleus is more even as well as paler than that of the neutrophile, and with the Ehrlich stain often has a robin's-egg tint. To sum up:

The four varieties which we usually find among leucocytes in the blood are these:

1. Small lymphocytes, or "hyaline cells."

2. Large lymphocytes and transitional forms.

3. Polymorphonuclear neutrophiles, or fine granular oxyphiles.

4. Eosinophiles, or coarse granular oxyphiles.

5. A fifth variety of leucocyte—the basophilic "mast cell"—has lately been described as a constituent of normal blood, though in very small numbers. In leukæmia it is very common, but no special significance is attached to it.

With Ehrlich's stain the basophilic granules of this cell are not seen or appear only as clear white spots. Stained with the following solution they are easily seen:

Dahlia (saturated alcoholic solution filtered),   .   .   .   50
Glacial acetic acid, ...   10–15
Distilled water, ...   100

Covers should be left twenty-four hours in this mixture, then washed and mounted in the ordinary way. The nucleus is usually trilobed. Though very common in all connective tissue as well as in the wall of the intestine and the serous cavities, these cells rarely stray into the circulating blood.

TERMS.

No one can feel more unsatisfied with the terminology used in this book than the writer. It rests partly on a theory of the origin of the cells ("lymphocytes"), partly on the properties of the nucleus ("polymorphonuclear"), and partly on affinities for aniline dyes ("neutrophile"—"eosinophile").

All that can be said for it is that it discards certain very misleading names like "splenocyte" (a term applied by some to the large lymphocytes according to the now exploded theory that they come from the spleen), or like "small mononuclear" to designate cells not rarely polynuclear.

The cumbrous word "polymorphonuclear" is a shade better than "polynuclear," and that is all to be said in its favor.

It is greatly to be hoped that we may ere long have a new and improved terminology by some competent student. The English terms above referred to are so cumbrous that I have not as yet felt compelled by their slightly greater accuracy to adopt them unconditionally, but they certainly show a tendency in the right direction.

For some unknown reason we do usually find the leucocytes of the blood only in these four forms (the frequent presence of transitional stages between "small" and "large" lymphocytes has been mentioned as an exception). There are far too few transitional forms between the four varieties to be seen in the circulating blood for us to suppose that they grow from one type to another there. It may be that they all have a common leucocyte ancestor and are "specialized" in various extra-vascular tissues into the forms which we meet with in the blood. There seem to be well-marked sets of leucocyte forms adapted respectively to the blood, the serous spaces, the intestinal wall, the marrow, the connective tissues, and the adenoid tissues, as has been well shown by recent English observations.

NORMAL PERCENTAGE OF EACH VARIETY.

In the blood of healthy adults the proportions of the different varieties above described are the following:

(a) {	Small lymphocytes, ...	20–30 per cent.	
	Large "	4–8 "	
(b)	Polymorphonuclear neutrophiles, . .	62–70 "	
(c)	Eosinophiles, ...	$\frac{1}{2}$–4 "	
(d)	"Mast cells,"	$\frac{1}{10}$–$\frac{1}{2}$ "	

(a) In infancy the percentage of lymphocytes is much larger

(forty to sixty·per cent) and the polymorphonuclear neutrophiles are only eighteen or forty per cent.

In a variety of debilitated conditions not usually thought of as definite diseases, the number of lymphocytes is comparatively large and that of the polymorphonuclear cells small. The general vigor and health of the individual can sometimes be estimated simply from the leucocytes. Persons calling themselves well, but never vigorous or active, may show no more than fifty per cent of polymorphonuclear cells, the lymphocytes running up to forty or even fifty per cent.

Not all cases of debility show this change, and we are not yet in a position to say under just what conditions it occurs. It certainly is not peculiar to tuberculosis as Holmes has supposed. Presumably the conditions are such as decrease the nutritive value of the plasma.

(b) Changes in the percentage of neutrophiles will be discussed later.

(c) The percentage of eosinophiles often changes in a way hard to explain. We know that eosinophiles are present in large numbers in various parts of the body outside the blood-vessels (bone marrow, gastro-intestinal tract, cœlomic spaces, thymus gland), and in many ways they seem to live their life in comparative independence of the' other members of the leucocyte group.

In the free interchange of fluid and cells that is constantly going on between blood-vessels and lymphatic tissues and spaces, it is evident that a part of the life history of the leucocytes goes on outside the vessels, and there is reason to suppose that it is chiefly outside the vessels that cells divide and produce others like themselves. At any rate, we·rarely find evidence of mitosis or amitosis in the circulating leucocytes, while in the lymph glands and the marrow, and elsewhere, such dividing forms are common.

The bone marrow seems to be such a dividing-place for eosinophiles. They are always numerous there and mitoses are often seen in them. Indeed their number is so small in normal circulating blood that they might almost be said to be there "by mistake," belonging normally elsewhere. Whether or not this has any connection with their active amœboid properties, I do not know. The "mast cells" are even more "an accident" in the blood, and Ehrlich denies that they are a constituent of normal blood.

The increase or decrease of eosinophiles in the circulating blood does not follow that of the polymorphonuclear neutrophiles, in fact is often inversely proportional to it, and the eosinophiles are often markedly increased in a blood otherwise normal, for reasons wholly unknown to us.

An increase in the lymphocytes or neutrophiles does not occur without other blood changes, and points, not to disease of one place or function, but to general conditions like inflammation or malnutrition. The diagnostic indications of an increase of the eosinophiles are more specific (*vide infra*, articles "Trichinosis," "Asthma," "Dermatitis Herpetiformis," etc.).

I have spoken of the eosinophiles and "mast cells" as comparative strangers, though not intruders in the circulating bood. They are thus intermediate between the regular inhabitants (lymphocytes and neutrophiles) and the variety next to be mentioned, which are real intruders—*i.e.*, never found in normal blood. These are the

MYELOCYTES (EHRLICH).

The normal[1] abiding-place of these cells appears to be the bone marrow, hence their name of myelocytes or marrow cells. They are perhaps the most numerous leucocytes to be found in the marrow, although lymphocytes and polymorphonuclear cells are also to be found there, and eosinophiles and basophiles are numerous.

I describe them here because they are peculiar to no one disease and are occasional visitors of the blood in various diseased conditions and in conditions on the borderland between the pathological and the physiological (starvation—various intoxications).

The myelocyte (see Plate I.), like the polymorphonuclear

[1] Frankel (15th Congresse für innere Med., 1897) has reported the finding of myelocytes in the swollen lymph glands of a case of scarlet fever. In leukæmia they are found in the metastases and infiltrations in various organs as well as in the blood. Otherwise they are confined to the marrow so far as I know, except that very small numbers may enter the blood in conditions involving leucocytosis or grave anæmia.

neutrophile, is recognizable only by Ehrlich's staining methods. With Ehrlich's triple stain it appears as a spherical cell nearly filled by a large, pale-stained nucleus immersed in neutrophilic granules. One sees at once how little it differs from the large lymphocytes (simply in having granules) and from the poly-morphonuclear neutrophile (only in the shape of its nucleus). Were it present in normal blood we should undoubtedly con-sider it an intermediate stage between the large lymphocyte and the polymorphonuclear neutrophile. I see no sufficient reason for thinking otherwise merely because it does not appear in normal blood. The leucocytes are so cosmopolitan in their habits that we can hardly call them *blood* cells at all. It is better to think of "blood leucocytes," "gland leucocytes," and "marrow leucocytes" (perhaps "skin and mucous membrane leucocytes" too, see page 117) and to consider that "missing links" among blood leucocytes are to be looked for among those that live and grow up elsewhere. Perhaps the condi-tions in the marrow (rest, nutrition?) are such as bring out sides of the leucocyte nature suppressed in the blood. Staining with eosin and methylene blue shows that myelocytes also con-tain fine basophilic (blue) granules. The suggestion of their transitional nature is thereby increased, since they have baso-phile granules in common with the lymphocytes, and neutrophile granules in common with the polymorphonuclear cells. I am indebted to Dr. H. F. Hewes for calling my attention to this point. With Ehrlich's stain the granules of the myelocyte are precisely those of the polymorphonuclear leucocyte and need no second description (see Plate I.). The nucleus, by which alone we distinguish the myelocyte, shows none of the twists and turns characteristic of the polymorphonuclear neutrophile, but is usually spherical or egg-shaped, and is in close contact with the cell wall for a comparatively large portion of its extent—*i.e.*, if egg-shaped it is placed eccentrically.

Not infrequently the nucleus shows signs of old age (vacuoles) or of mitosis, for not infrequently we find two nuclei at the poles of the cell. It is then to be distinguished from the polymorphonuclear neutrophile by the fact of its having the nuclei in close contact with the surface of the whole cell for a comparatively large portion of their extent, while in the poly-morphonuclear leucocyte the nucleus abruptly leaves the surfaces again if it chances to approach it. The dividing myelocyte is also to be distinguished from the polymorphonuclear neutrophile by the *even* staining of the nucleus in the former.

Size of Myelocytes.

Almost every account of the myelocyte which has come to my notice speaks of it as a very large cell, the largest variety of leucocyte ever seen in the blood.

This is true of many of them; diameters of 18–21 μ are not uncommon, but we also find them of *every* other size down to 10–11 μ diameter, that is, down to the size of a lymphocyte. This is true both of the myelocytes in the circulating (leukæmic) blood and of those in the marrow. No distinction from other varieties of leucocyte can be based on size alone, unless we say their *average* size is greater than the average size of the leucocyte. Perhaps the following table may be of interest:

Average diameter of 100 myelocytes = 15.75 μ.
"   "   " 100 polymorphonuclear neutrophiles = 13.50 μ.
"   "   " 100 "large" lymphocytes = 13 μ.
"   "   " 100 eosinophiles = 12 μ.
"   "   " 100 "small" lymphocytes = 10 μ.
"   "   " 100 red corpuscles (normal) = 7.5 μ.

EOSINOPHILIC MYELOCYTES.

Under the same conditions where we expect to find the ordinary (neutrophilic) myelocyte, we often find a small number of cells identical with them in all respects, except in possessing eosinophilic in place of neutrophilic granules. Such cells are found in abundance in the marrow, and this fact together with the resemblance to the ordinary myelocyte both in morphology and in the conditions of their occurrence, seems to me to justify the term *eosinophilic* myelocyte.

CORNIL'S "MARK CELLS."

By most observers these are supposed to be the same as Ehrlich's "mark cells" or myelocytes. Cornil worked before the days of Ehrlich's staining methods and therefore before the presence of neutrophilic granules could be used to distinguish a myelocyte from a large lymphocyte. Cornil's description of them would answer for either. Schreiber considers Cornil to have discovered a different variety of non-granular cell, but the description of it given by Schreiber seems to me to leave it indistinguishable from a large lymphocyte.

Mononuclear Neutrophiles.—Capps[1] observed in general paralysis of the insane a variety of leucocyte possessing a deep-staining centrally placed nucleus like that of a lymphocyte, but containing also neutrophilic granules. He considers it either a variation from the ordinary type of marrow-bred cell visiting the blood temporarily, or more likely an ordinary lymphocyte in which the granules have developed before the nucleus has become polymorphous. Thayer has observed similar cells, but has given no explanation of them. Klein[2] mentions them under the name above given and figures them in his plates, but does not comment on them. I am inclined to think them ordinary myelocytes.

So far I have described the *type cell* of each variety. As we should expect, atypical forms are numerous. Some of the commoner ones are as follows:

1. Small lymphocytes whose nucleus is pale blue instead of dark blue.

2. Large lymphocytes, whose protoplasm has evidently forsaken them (degeneration forms, often more or less deformed or tattered).

3. Cells on the borderland between the "marrow cell" and the "polymorphonuclear leucocyte," the nucleus having some of the characters of each variety.

4. Cells the nature of whose granules we cannot settle (eosinophilic or neutrophilic).

Other rare varieties will be mentioned under leukæmia.

[1] American Journal of Medical Sciences, June, 1896.
[2] Volkmann's Sammlung klin. Vorträge, December, 1893.

PART III.

GENERAL PATHOLOGY OF THE BLOOD.

CHAPTER VI.

UNEQUAL DISTRIBUTION OF BLOOD—PLETHORA—DILUTION
AND CONCENTRATION OF THE BLOOD.

I. *Unequal Distribution.*

How far is the single drop used for blood examination typical of the whole?

It has been experimentally proved that specimens of the blood of the smaller venous and arterial twigs do not differ from each other materially in corpuscular richness. Capillary blood is slightly richer in corpuscles than that either of veins or of arteries. But as capillary blood is everywhere of the same corpuscular richness, we may consider one capillary network or set of venules as typical as another, provided our technique is good, that is, provided lymph is not squeezed into the drop by strong pressure. It is indifferent, therefore, so far as accuracy is concerned, whether the drop of blood be obtained from one or another part of the body. All standard estimates of the number of corpuscles per cubic millimetre of normal blood refer to capillary blood.

2. *Apparent Polycythæmia.*

So far we are speaking of normal conditions. It is a familiar fact, however, that the vessels of a given part of the body can be overcrowded with blood, e.g., by the use of an Esmarch bandage. A drop taken from such a part would certainly not be typical. Now as the same effect can be produced by a variety of diseases, under these conditions we must modify considerably any inferences made from examination of a single drop.

Such conditions, entailing a false polycythæmia or apparent increase in the number of corpuscles are:

I. Any disease involving either (a) general cyanosis or (b) cyanosis of the part from which the drop of blood is drawn.

(a) *General cyanosis* results either from cardiac insufficiency (valvular or parietal disease of the heart itself, blocking of the lung circulation by emphysema or thrombosis), from insufficient aëration of the blood (pneumonia, congenital malformation of the heart), interference with the heart's action by pressure of tumors, effusions (pericardial, pleural, peritoneal), or enlarged organs (liver, spleen), or from vasomotor disturbances. It is evident that some of these conditions (*e.g.*, congenital heart disease) may not involve any peripheral *stasis* at all, and in the absence of this it is not easy to account for the increased number of corpuscles in the drop. Some observers have supposed that there is a real overproduction of blood cells under these conditions; others suppose that the life of the individual corpuscle being lengthened, reproduction of cells at the normal rate soon leads to the "glut." There seems to be no reason to suppose that there is in these cases any unequal distribution of cells in favor of the periphery, such as is obviously the condition in ordinary cyanosis with stasis. Whatever the explanation may be, there is no doubt of the fact that general cyanosis from any cause whatever produces an increase of cells in a drop such as we usually examine.

The cases of cyanosis which I have classed under "vasomotor" (for want of a better explanation), cases in which, in the absence of disease in any organ, the skin and mucous membranes are persistently and markedly bluish, are not very uncommon. I have seen three such, all in stout, elderly women. In one the cells in a drop of blood from the ear, finger, or toe were more than *double* the normal number (see below, page 81).

(b) *Local Cyanosis.*—The pressure of a tumor, or any other hindrance to the circulation of any part, may give a similar increase in the number of corpuscles in a measured amount of blood from that part. Here again vasomotor conditions may cause cyanosis and apparent polycythæmia.

In markedly cyanotic patients the count of red cells is notably above normal, we should naturally guess the reason, and make allowances. Error is more likely to arise where we have cyanosis in a person whose blood is poor in red corpuscles. The combination of these two factors may give us a normal blood count and lead us to overlook the anæmia. Thus a person might have really a severe anæmia and yet the count of red cells be actually above the normal. This element of stasis should never be lost sight of. Many high counts reported in pneumonia or hysteria are to be explained by abnormalities not of *production* or *destruction* but of *distribution* of the blood cells.

II. Certain patients, whose circulations are feeble without being feeble enough to produce actual cyanosis, first give us evidence of the fact by an increase in the count of blood corpuscles in a given amount of peripheral blood. Following up the hint thus given, one may sometimes be brought to note and investigate an element in the case which might otherwise have been lost sight of.

With these exceptions the drop of blood taken at the periphery is typical. We have next to consider some *general* conditions under which a person's whole blood may be inferred to be abnormal from the findings in a drop taken from the periphery. Consideration of *special* diseases will follow later.

FULL-BLOODEDNESS (PLETHORA) AND ITS OPPOSITE.

There is no direct evidence for the existence of any long-standing over-filling or under-filling of the blood-vessels; there is a good deal of experimental evidence to show that if by artificial means we succeed in forcing into the vessels an abnormal amount of fluid (transfusion of blood or normal salt solution— large draughts of water), it does not stay there many hours, but comes out by the kidneys.

The red-faced persons popularly known as "full-blooded" show no abnormalities in their blood discoverable by any means of investigation known to us. The condition is probably dependent on the presence of a rich capillary network near the surface of the skin, or a dilatation of individual venules and arterioles at the periphery. Such a person may be markedly anæmic without any considerable changes in the color of the face. The fact that people of such complexion often end their lives with a ruptured cerebral artery is due presumably to the circumstance that "high living" produces in the same individual dilated peripheral capillaries and weakened arterial walls.

Temporary increase or diminution in the amount of fluid within the vessels can be brought about not only by a change in the mechanical conditions of pressure and osmosis, but by any influence affecting the tone of the peripheral vessels. We have then:

(a) *Temporary serous plethora or dilution of the blood* from transfusion of fluid in large amounts or its ingestion by mouth or rectum.

(b) From decreased blood pressure, as in acute failures of compensation in cardiac disease.

(c) From vasomotor dilatation.

As an example of this last Grawitz reduced the specific gravity of the blood from 1041 to 1038.7 within eight minutes by the inhalation of nitrite of amyl. This decrease of specific gravity can only mean an increased amount of watery constituents in the blood, as there was no evidence of any destruction of the heavier elements of the blood, and only water (and chlorides) pass through the vessel walls easily. In the above case the specific gravity was again at 1041 within a few minutes.

(d) In cases of severe anæmia which recover, the blood regeneration may attain such vigor that the number of red cells shoots up *above* normal, even as high as 7,700,000. This is *temporary cellular plethora* or polycythæmia.

(e) The same condition can be temporarily produced by transfusion of actual blood from one individual to another. It lasts but a few days as a rule.

The polycythæmia of the new-born will be discussed later.

Concentration of the Blood.

It is obvious that influences opposite to those producing temporary full-bloodedness will produce temporary lack of fluid within the vessels. So acute diarrhœa, purgation, deprivation of liquids (as in starvation), rapidly accumulated serous effusions, profuse vomiting or sweating (by skin and lungs) produce a temporary *concentration of the blood* by draining out its diffusible elements (water chiefly). All these influences are transitory. More permanent drains on the system, like chronic diarrhœa, diabetes insipidus or mellitus, or long-standing suppurations, show no evidence of lessening the volume of blood in the vessels.

They drain albumin out of the serum and corpuscles and so decrease the weight of the blood (see below, page 85), but the blood volume is not changed. Indeed, any influence has to work very quickly in order to concentrate the blood, for in an astonishingly short time the other tissues repay the vessels their loss of fluid and the normal blood volume is restored.

The same temporary effects can be produced by influences constricting the vessels (cold, pain, suprarenal extract), and a concentration of the blood results which lasts a few minutes or hours.[1]

In all these interchanges of contents between the bloodvessels and the other tissues it is, as above said, the watery elements chiefly that change. The red cells are not affected by the give-and-take of the vessels and tissues, and although cold produces in the peripheral circulation an increase in the number of white cells greater than can be accounted for by simple concentration, the weight of evidence seems to be against any new production of cells and in favor of a change only in distribution, the white cells accumulating at the periphery.

Now as the number of cells is not affected by these temporary variations in the volume of liquid within the vessels, it follows that the number to be counted in a cubic millimetre, though typical of the whole blood *at that time*, is not to be reckoned from in the ordinary way. For example, after a severe diarrhœa or in phthisis after a night-sweat the blood may be temporarily so concentrated that we find 6,000,000 or more red corpuscles per cubic millimetre. Under normal conditions of the blood mass we should infer from such a count that the body contained onesixth more red corpuscles than usual. Here obviously it only means (if anœmia is absent) that the blood mass is reduced by one-sixth by concentration. It is only in such sudden reductions of blood volume that we can measure the amount lost by

[1] Oliver has shown recently (Lancet, June 27th, 1896) that any influence causing rise of blood pressure will slightly concentrate the blood. Thus raising the arm over the head and holding it there by muscular effort slightly concentrates the blood in that arm. Electrical stimulation or massage of the arm has the same effect. *Lowering* blood pressure, as when the arm is supported *passively* over the head, dilutes the blood. This confirms the results of Mitchell (Med. News, May, 1893) and of Chéron (Comptes Rend. de l'Acad. d. Sciences, 1896, No. vi.). Oliver uses a new method for estimating the number of red cells, the accuracy of which has not yet been tested by others (see above, page 27).

this method. Long-standing causes of drain on the plasma might at any time act as destroyers of red corpuscles as well, through the changes in the nutritive fluids in which they live.

Further, it is only where we know the number of corpuscles just before the sudden drain on the plasma comes, that we can measure the amount of plasma lost by the amount of *apparent* increase in the red cells.   Stasis and any other cause that heaps up corpuscles at the periphery must also be excluded before we can judge of the loss of plasma in this way.

The conditions of an abnormal concentration of the blood are those already alluded to as temporarily sucking away its watery constituents, namely:

(*a*) Watery diarrhœa, especially in cholera and other acute diseases accompanied by diarrhœa;

(*b*) Large and rapidly accumulating serous effusions (slow accumulations would give time for the blood to take up water from the tissues and make up for its loss);

(*c*) Profuse sweats;

(*d*) Persistent vomiting or starvation of liquids;

(*e*) Increased blood pressure (exercise, massage, electricity).

Blood already lacking in red cells, if suddenly concentrated by such a loss of fluid, might deceive us into supposing it normal, because the number of cells in a cubic millimetre might be normal. *In the presence, therefore, of any such reason for concentration of the blood, we should always modify our ordinary methods of inference from the blood count.* For example, v. Limbeck records a case of hepatic cirrhosis with ascites, where before tapping the ascites the count of red cells was 3,280,000 per cubic millimetre.   Within twenty-four hours after tapping there were 5,160,000 cells per cubic millimetre, the reaccumulation of the ascitic fluid going on so fast that the blood was unable to adjust itself and became overconcentrated. A careless observation might have inferred a great gain in the corpuscular richness of the whole blood, when in fact not a corpuscle has been gained and those present have probably grown poorer in albumin.

Dilution of the Blood.

Causes of temporary *dilution of the blood* are less common than those of temporary concentration.

Immediately after the inhalation of nitrite of amyl or the in-gestion of a large amount of fluid by mouth or rectum, the blood would be diluted so that a blood count would show a diminu-tion in the number of cells per cubic millimetre, which yet would be due to no changes in the number of red cells in the body, and might be wrongly taken for an anæmia. The dilu-tion in cases of heart disease will be discussed later (see p. 296). Any condition involving *lowered blood pressure* has the effect of diluting the blood by allowing the entrance of perivascular lymph.

Summing up the discussion so far: There is no evidence for a *chronic* plethora nor for a chronic diminution in the volume of the blood. Where such takes place temporarily, it is by the ad-dition or subtraction of water and salts only, and not of the cor-puscles or organic materials, so that we must guard against false inferences from the resulting apparent increase or decrease of corpuscles per cubic millimetre.

But although there is no positive evidence of a true increase in the whole amount of blood in the vessels (except temporarily), there are some conditions which lead to an increased richness of the *peripheral* blood in red corpuscles even after excluding the influence of stasis or loss of fluid. Such a condition of what *appears to be* true polycythæmia is found:

1. In persons living at high altitudes;
2. In persons suffering from phosphorus or CO poisoning.

1. The Blood in High Altitudes.

The polycythæmia of those living at high altitudes increases the higher one goes. Köppe[1] gives the following tables:

Place.	Height above sea level.		Red cells.	Author.
Christiania................	O		4,974,000	Laache.
Göttingen	148	metres	5,225,000	Schafer.
Tübingen	314	"	5,322,000	Reinert.
Zürich	414	"	5,752,000	Stierlin.
Auerbach	425	"	5,748,000	Köppe.
Reiboldsgrün........	700	"	5,900,000	"
Arosa	1,800	"	7,000,000	Egger.
The Cordilleras.............	4,392	"	8,000,000	Viault.

[1] Münch. med. Woch., 1890, No. 41.

This extraordinary change takes place within two weeks of the time of taking up residence in a high place, and independent of any change in diet or manner of living. The sick and the well are equally affected and animals show similar changes. The hæmoglobin is also considerably increased, although it lags somewhat behind the corpuscles.

Köppe states that the individual corpuscles under these conditions are so much smaller that their volume in a given amount of blood (as determined by the hæmatocrit) is not increased at all.

On returning to low land, the blood returns within a short time to its normal condition.

Many explanations have been offered for this interesting phenomenon. If it were a true new production of corpuscles we should expect some signs of blood destruction (icterus, hæmoglobinuria) on returning to the sea level. But there are no such signs. On the other hand, if the polycythæmia were a simple result of concentration due to the dryness of the high air, one would expect that the blood would quickly adapt itself, as in other (temporary) concentrations, by taking up water from the tissues. But in fact it does not do so. The cause of the increase is still a mystery.

2. Phosphorus and CO Poisoning.

The polycythæmia of acute phosphorus poisoning may reach as high as 8,650,000. This may be partly explained by concentration due to the occurrence of vomiting, but in some cases the increase seems out of proportion to the amount of vomiting.

With illuminating-gas poisoning there is usually no vomiting to speak of, and the cause of the marked increase in the red cells is unknown. Von Limbeck in two cases of CO poisoning showed respectively 6,630,000 and 5,700,000 red cells. Münzer and Palma[1] record 5,700,000. The white cells are also increased (see page 330).

Possibility of a True Plethora.

Although there is no *direct* evidence that the whole blood mass in its relation to the weight of the body ever varies more

[1] Zeit. f. Heilk., vol. 15, p. 1.

than temporarily from the traditional 1 to 13, one cannot help getting the *impression* in some cases that the blood mass *is* increased or diminished, though we cannot prove it. Thus in certain cases of phthisis in which in spite of all the signs and symptoms of anæmia the blood count is normal, and simple concentration of a really anæmic blood seems to be excluded by the absence of a cause for such concentration, we cannot help thinking that the whole amount of blood is too small. Again, it is possible that in individuals who eat and drink much and exercise little the blood-vessels may gradually accommodate themselves so as to hold a *large* bulk of liquid, and thus a true plethora or "full-blooded" condition might be brought about. Experiments show, however, that fat, "sedentary" animals (pigs) have *less* blood in proportion to their weight than lean, active animals (horses, dogs). Pigs' blood is only one twenty-second of their total weight, while horses' is one-tenth.

I have repeatedly examined the blood in two patients with chronic cyanosis without known cause and found from 8,000,000 to 9,000,000 corpuscles in each case. One of these patients died of cerebral hemorrhage, and the autopsy revealed no lesions whatever except a stuffing of all the internal organs with blood and the results of chronic passive congestion *everywhere*. This certainly *seems* like a true plethora.

Young, fast-growing animals have relatively more blood than adults, and males more than females. Our impression that old people are more or less "dried up" gets some support from the analogy of these animal experiments.

Until some method is devised for estimating the total amount of blood during life, we shall never be sure upon this point.

6

CHAPTER VII.

ANÆMIA AND HYDRÆMIA.

1. ANÆMIA.

In the absence of any proof that the total volume of blood can be more than temporarily diminished, our definition of anæmia must be this: *A deficiency in corpuscle substance, i.e.,* a deficiency in red corpuscles, in hæmoglobin, or in both.[1]

It is important to bear in mind that the color of the skin is not a safe guide in judging whether a person is anæmic. Thus out of 100 cases shown to be anæmic by actual blood examination, Townsend[2] found a good color in the cheeks of 4 and a fair color in 7 others. Eighty-nine were pale. The color of the lips is but little better as a guide, as the following table from Townsend's article shows:

Table of Color in One Hundred Cases of Anæmia.

	Pale.	Fair.	Good.
Nails	95	5	0
Cheeks	89	7	4
Tongue	84	15	1.2
Lips............................	76	21	2.4
Conjunctivæ....................	64	25.5	10.5

My own impression would be that the lips and conjunctivæ were better guides than they are shown to be in this table.

In examining the color of the nails, the fingers should be flexed, as full extension may partly cut off the circulation under the nails.

[1] This is a clinical definition and makes no attempt to go to the root of the matter. I have little doubt that chemical or other changes in the serum are the cause of the corpuscular changes, which only mirror the deeper disease. But these chemical changes are as yet so little understood that we have to judge of their presence chiefly by their effect on the corpuscles.

[2] Townsend: Boston Medical and Surgical Journal, May 28th, 1896.

A. K. Stone [1] and his assistants estimated the hæmoglobin of 189 female patients who looked anæmic, and found over 75 per cent of hæmoglobin in 89, or nearly one-half of them. For a woman a hæmoglobin percentage of 75 per cent or more means practically normal blood.[2]

The most striking example of the fallacy of judging of anæmia by the color of the skin and mucous membranes is in the so-called "tropical anæmia." Practically all persons belonging to white races who take up their residence in the tropics acquire after a time an extreme pallor of the skin and mucous membranes, and this appearance has usually received the title of "tropical anæmia." It turns out, however, from the careful studies of several different investigators, that the blood of such persons shows absolutely no anæmia or other variation from the normal.[3] The appearance of the skin is probably due to the action of the extreme climate on the peripheral nerves and vessels. Tropical anæmia is a condition not of the blood, but of the skin and subcutaneous tissues.

Every one's experience includes a few persons who are perfectly well despite an almost bloodless condition of the skin.

On the other hand, anæmia may exist where there is a good color in the face.

We are to judge of anæmia, then, solely by the blood examination, and this judgment can be accurately made on the basis of the small fraction of a drop used for examination, *provided* always that our technique is good, and provided we make allowances for a considerable error wherever there is reason to suppose that any venous and capillary stasis is present, or that the blood is temporarily concentrated or diluted.

Distinction between Primary and Secondary Anæmia.

In one sense all anæmia is secondary. It is due to some cause, a symptom in a chain of events. But in some cases we know the cause and in some we do not.

(a) *Primary anæmia is that in which the causal factors are*

[1] Boston Medical and Surgical Journal, August 23d, 1894.
[2] Where the hæmoglobin is high the number of corpuscles is never considerably diminished.
[3] So far as present methods of examination go.

either entirely unknown or are apparently insufficient to cause so severe a disease. This division, like most of our statements about the blood, is a rough-and-ready one, held to provisionally until a better classification is discovered. It has a certain utility if not used with any less simple meaning than that given above.

In view of our ignorance of the blood-making functions, there is little difference between saying that a primary anæmia is a disease of the blood-making organs and saying that it is one whose cause is unknown, especially as the pathological appearances in the bone marrow recorded in cases of so-called primary anæmia do not differ from those which can be brought about experimentally by bleeding. There is no good evidence that there are any primary diseases of the blood-making functions. A case of secondary anæmia is one in which we have an obvious cause such as hemorrhage or malaria for the loss of corpuscle substance. Remove the cause and the anæmia ceases. Sometimes, however, after removal of the cause, *e.g.*, after cure of a case of syphilis, the anæmia set agoing by the syphilis persists. On the other hand, there are few patients with "primary" anæmia who cannot recall some event in their past lives sufficient to account for *a certain grade of anæmia* (*e.g.*, a nervous shock, a hemorrhage, an attack of tertian malaria). Yet if the anæmia that occurs after so slight a cause is of the pernicious or fatal type, we may fairly call it *"primary."* By this we mean that though the "cause" assigned might produce *some* anæmia, it was not sufficient to produce *this* fatal anæmia and has presumably little or no connection with it. "Primary" means not the absence of *any* cause of anæmia in the history, but the absence of any *sufficient* cause so far as is known.

An attack of tertian malaria or a history of bleeding piles does not cause fatal anæmia in 999 out of 1,000 people who have such a history. In the 1000th it is a case of *post hoc* and not *propter hoc*. Given the unknown cause that *does* lead to "primary" anæmia, and it might be that a pregnancy, a nervous shock, or the presence of intestinal parasites would act as the straw that breaks the camel's back; but *the important causal factor is the unknown factor.* It is, then, by their etiology and not by their symptoms or by the blood examination alone that we distinguish primary from secondary anæmia.

It is true that in the majority of cases we can tell from the blood examination alone whether a case is without known cause

(= "primary") or symptomatic (= "secondary"). But there appear to be enough exceptions to this rule to make us cautious about stating it as a law.

$$
\text{ANÆMIA} = \left\{ \begin{array}{l} \text{Primary} = \left\{ \begin{array}{l} \text{Chlorosis,} \\ \text{Pernicious anæmia,} \end{array} \right\} \left\{ \begin{array}{l} \text{To be discussed under} \\ \text{Special Pathology of} \\ \text{the Blood, Chapter} \\ \text{VII.} \end{array} \right. \\ \text{Secondary.} \end{array} \right.
$$

Secondary Anæmia.

I. *First Stage.*—I defined anæmia above as *a diminution in corpuscle substance.* In the milder types of this condition the number of red corpuscles is not diminished at all, but the individual cell is small, pale, and of light weight, through loss of nitrogenous matter. This is appreciated:

(*a*) As a lack of coloring matter;

(*b*) As a lowering of the specific gravity.

In the mildest grades of secondary anæmia there are no further changes. Such cases are those due to errors in hygiene —bad air, poor food, lack of light or exercise—to small hemorrhages, and to the earlier stages of the diseases next to be mentioned.

The lack of coloring matter is usually not present in every cell, as is seen in the stained specimens. Some are very pale at the centre, while others are well stained.

II. *Second Stage.*—Usually the next changes to appear are, like those already mentioned, *qualitative,* the number of red cells still remaining normal or approximately so.

The individual cell as seen in fresh preparations is more or less deformed and varies from its normal diameter, dwarfed forms usually being commoner than the giant forms. These variations in size and shape are sometimes termed "*poikilocytosis,*" and the dwarf and giant forms are called respectively microcytes and macrocytes.

Maragliano[1] has included the above changes, together with others about to be described, under the heading of

Necrobiosis in the red corpuscles, attributing them to a pathological condition of the serum.

The changes united under this heading may be divided for convenience' sake into:

(*a*) Endoglobular changes.

[1] XI. Cong. f. Inn. Med., Leipzig, 1892.

(b) Poikylocytosis and crenation.

(c) Changes in staining properties.

(d) Changes involving motility in the corpuscle as a whole, or in parts of it.

(e) Decrease in the average diameter of corpuscles with loss of the power to form rouleaux.

All these changes may be watched in normal blood outside the vessels, as necrosis gradually comes on from contact with the air. Under pathological conditions the same changes may

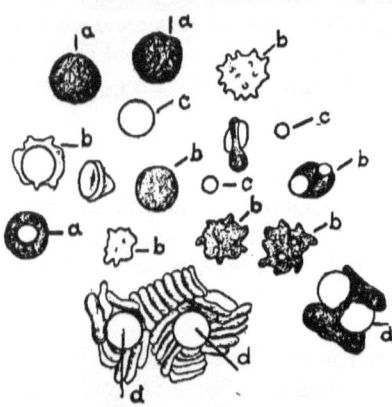

occur *outside the body*, but more quickly than usual (as other diseased tissues decompose more quickly after death than those of a sound man suddenly killed), or *inside the body*.

(a) *Endoglobular Changes* (see Fig. 27, a).—These consist in the appearance of clear hyaline spaces of various shapes within the corpuscle, round, triangular, rod-shaped, etc. In the fresh specimen they

FIG. 27.—Degenerative Changes in Red Cells.

change their shape rapidly and continually; in dried and stained specimens they appear as sharply outlined light spaces in the corpuscle. In normal blood these changes occur after thirty to seventy minutes outside the vessels. In some pathological conditions specimens show them the instant the blood is collected, and presumably they were present before it left the vessels.

(b) *Crenation and Poikilocytosis* (Fig. 27, b).—What we ordinarily know as crenation in the corpuscles is the same sort of process which, occuring within the vessels, we call poikilocytosis. A lump rises at one or more points in the corpuscle, becomes more pointed, and gradually the whole cell acquires amœboid motions, assuming in succession the various shapes with which we are familiar in poikylocytes.

(c) The pointed projections may break off and move about actively in the plasma. These motions, as well as the preceding amœboid movement of the whole corpuscle, are to be explained as irregular contractions of the necrobiotic protoplasm, similar in a general way to the actions of a hen after its head is cut off. These motions are not to be confounded with the finer Brownian or "molecular" movement to be seen in any healthy cell. The small bits broken off (Fig. 27, c) are doubtless the dwarf cells seen in dried and stained preparations. Curiously enough, these fragments tend again to assume the biconcavity character-istic of normal cells, as a drop of fat breaks into smaller but similar drops.

FIG. 28.—Elongated or Oval Corpuscles in a Case of Pernicious Anæmia.

(d) *Oval Shape.*—A great many cases of pernicious anæmia and some other diseases (see Epidemic Dropsy, page 240) show a marked tendency to oval shapes in corpuscles not otherwise considerably deformed. Even in normal blood I think there are a small number of oval forms, and in anæmia this number may be greatly increased till, as in Fig. 28, we get all the cells elongated. The same appearance can be produced by roughness in spreading the blood, but in such case the deformed corpuscles all point one way.

(e) *Changes in Staining Properties.*—Normal red corpuscles have affinity only for acid stains (eosin). The same degenerative changes that lead to the alterations in shape and size above described alter the staining properties of the cell as well, so that it takes up two or three colors (according to the number present in the stain), either as a diffuse mixture or irregularly, some parts of the cell taking color differently from others. This has been termed a "*polychromatophilic*" or degenerative change. Some observers have supposed it to be rather of the nature of *regeneration*, believing that the cells take color in this unorthodox way because they are half-developed, but the weight of evidence is that they are degenerative changes.

(f) In many secondary anæmias, especially in those associated with inflammations, the average diameter of the cells is lessened, and the rouleaux are not formed.[1]

(g) Cells may lose their hæmoglobin altogether, leaving only the shell of the corpuscle behind (see Fig. 27, d).

Now all these necrobiotic changes are characteristic of the severer grades of secondary anæmia such as occur in cancerous cachexia, phthisis, nephritis, etc.

The changes of staining affinity are less common than the others, and usually represent the severest grades of anæmia, but they have also been noted occasionally in smallpox, measles, scarlet fever, typhus, and purpura.

In pernicious anæmia they are, as a rule, much more common than in any other disease. Maragliano considers these degenerative changes to be due to toxic plasma. A lessened resistance to the ordinary plasma-environment on the part of the red cells would also explain them, and in such affections as paroxysmal hæmoglobinuria it seems the most probable cause. In syphilis the abnormal sensitiveness of the red cells to the influence of mercury seems another instance where the red cells are immature, decrepit, or weak. In syphilitic children, for instance, mercury easily gives anæmia, while in healthy children it does not. This will be discussed more fully under syphilis.

The necrobiotic phenomena above described have been observed by Maragliano in carcinoma, lead poisoning, leukæmia, pernicious anæmia, purpura, cirrhotic liver, nephritis, pneu-

---

[1] But in the severest forms of anæmia the diameters are apt to be increased (see below, Pernicious Anæmia).

monia, malaria, typhoid, erysipelas, and tuberculosis. Celli and Guarnieri (*Fortschritte der Medicin*, 1889, No. 14) found them in measles and scarlet fever. Weintraub (*Virchow's Archiv*, Vol. 131) noted them in epilepsy, pyæmia, and catarrhal jaundice.

A decreased resistance to pressure of electric currents and other influences has also been noted by v. Limbeck in some cases.

Such weakening of the red cells experimentally produced in animals by poisons has been found (Mya and Sanarelli, *Arch. ital. di Biolog.*, XVII., 1892) to increase the susceptibility to infectious diseases.

III. *Third Stage.*—Here the number as well as the quality of the red cells begins to suffer. So far I have mentioned only the qualitative changes in secondary anæmia and have purposely made these changes more prominent than the actual diminution in the count of red cells, because it is only comparatively rarely and in very marked cases that the diminution in red corpuscles is considerable. The blood characteristic of most cases of secondary anæmia is one in which the number of red cells is approximately normal.

The important exceptions to this rule are: 1. The anæmias of infancy and early childhood. 2. Large hemorrhages (soon after their occurrence). 3. Malaria. 4. Acute septicæmia.

The direct and rapid destruction of the corpuscles by the malarial organism or hemorrhage account for this. Of sepsis and the anæmias of infancy we shall speak later.

IV. *Fourth Stage.*—The blood of secondary anæmia shows often evidence not only of degeneration and destruction of the cells but also of regenerative changes, namely:

Nucleated Red Cells.

These are usually divided into three groups
    (*a*) Normoblasts.
    (*b*) Megaloblasts.
    (*c*) Microblasts.

Normoblasts.

(*a*) The first are normally present in moderate number in the bone marrow of healthy persons, and in great numbers in the marrow after hemorrhage. They are generally considered to be a younger stage in the life of the corpuscle than the non-nucleated forms seen in the circulating blood. Hence the appearance in the peripheral circulation of this form of nucleated cell is considered to mean that, in the comparatively plentiful reproduction of red cells called forth in the marrow by the anæmia, a certain number of red cells leave the nursery (the marrow) before they are grown up and circulate for a time in their immature state. A normoblast, then, represents an immature red corpuscle (see Plate IV.).

In size and color it is like an ordinary red cell except that we find, usually somewhat to one side of it, a round nucleus about one-half the diameter of the whole cell. With Ehrlich's tricolor mixture, this nucleus stains very deep blue, nearly black, and is sharply outlined against the pale yellow of the cell body around it.

The cell often looks as if it were pushing its nucleus out, i.e., in many instances we see the nucleus projecting over the edge of the corpuscle, or half out of it, and occasionally we find it lying beside the corpuscle from which it has just emerged; but this appearance is probably an artefact and not, as Ehrlich thought, the regular way of disposing of the normoblast nucleus.

Very frequently the nucleus has toward the centre a light spot, sometimes so brilliant that it looks like the reflection of light from the surface of a drop of ink or any dark liquid, what artists call the "high light." Occasionally there are several of these light spots in a nucleus, or it may be all light blue-gray except a dark blue rim. This is the commonest type of normoblast. But now and then we meet with one when the nucleus is more or less separated into two or more pieces. These pieces are usually connected by pale-staining "bridges," perhaps radiating from a centre so that the nucleus is "rosette-shaped," or it may take any one of a large number of different shapes. The parts of the nucleus which are nearest the periphery of the cell usually stain deeper than the "bridges" which join them.

Sometimes the nucleus breaks apart completely and we find two or more separate unconnected nuclei within the single cell.[1] Or one of the pieces may be outside the cell and the others inside.

[1] Apparently the nucleus is absorbed or degenerates (see Israel and Pappenheim: Virchow's Archiv, vol. 143).

Rarest of all is the appearance of true mitosis in the nucleus of a normoblast.

Megaloblasts.

(b) The typical megaloblast as usually described is so unlike the normoblast that we should not naturally think of them as near relations.

It does not occur anywhere in the healthy adult body, not even in the bone marrow. In the early fœtal marrow and in the marrow and circulating blood of grave forms of anæmia it is to be found, usually in company with a certain number of normoblasts.

Ehrlich described megaloblasts as the sign or product of a different type of blood formation, namely, the *fœtal type*, and considered those anæmias in which it occurs as tending to a return of the blood to the fœtal state. [This has been recently confirmed by the researches of Pappenheim, though Ehrlich's detailed theory of two methods of blood formation is now generally discredited. All nucleated red cells lose their nuclei by "absorption"; none by extrusion.] Ehrlich regarded the presence of megaloblasts as a bad prognostic sign, and believed that a pernicious or fatal anæmia was characterized by an excess of these cells over the normoblasts. He recognized that they might be found in various milder forms of anæmia; but here the *prevailing type* is the normoblast, and regeneration may be more active than degeneration. In his general conception of the prognostic import of megaloblasts Ehrlich has been supported by the weight of later clinical observation, although it has been shown that the anæmia due to intestinal parasites can be cured, despite the presence of the megaloblasts as the prevailing type of nucleated red cells. So far as I know this is the only exception to Ehrlich's rule.

The *typical megaloblast* is an abnormally large cell (11 to 20 μ in diameter, frequently showing marks of degeneration (polychromatophilia) in its protoplasm, which is therefore brownish or purplish with the Ehrlich-Biondi stain. Its nucleus is very large, filling most of the cell, and contrasts with the normoblast nucleus not only by its greater size but by the pale, even stain which it takes up. The commonest color of the nucleus with the Ehrlich-Biondi stain is pale green or robin's-egg color. It is not stained evenly but dotted over with purplish granules arranged in a fine mesh like the knots in a fish-net (see Plate IV.).

Outside the nucleus there is usually a narrow band of clear white, apparently an empty space, separating the nucleus from the encircling protoplasm. The protoplasm close round this colorless ring is usually stained more deeply than the rest of the cell. Cracks and "flaws" are sometimes to be seen in the protoplasm, giving evidence, as its purplish stain does, of the necrobiotic changes described by Maragliano.

The outline of the whole may be quite circular: oftener it is oval or somewhat irregular, but rarely much deformed.

Microblasts.

(*c*) Microblasts, which are rarer than either of the varieties just described, consist of a nucleus like that of a normoblast or smaller, and contained in a cell body *smaller* than the normal red corpuscle. In the writer's experience the cell body is usually reduced to a few shreds of discolored protoplasm hanging about the nucleus (see Plate IV.). Their clinical significance is usually supposed to be that of megaloblasts.

" Atypical Forms."

As a rule we find in a given specimen of blood only typical normoblasts, microblasts, or megaloblasts, and accordingly can easily reckon up the number of each kind and see which type of blood formation predominates. Sometimes there are a few cells present, about the classification of which we cannot come to a decision, and I have occasionally seen a specimen of blood containing a large number of nucleated red cells *no one of which* could strictly be classed *either* as a " normoblast," a " megaloblast," or a " microblast," as these are defined above.

The researches of Pappenheim have thrown much light on this difficulty. While insisting with Ehrlich that the megaloblast and the normoblast represent respectively the early fœtal and the post-uterine types of blood formation, and that there are no real "transitions" from the one to the other, he yet recognizes that the two varieties are not *absolutely* to be differentiated by any of the ordinarily accepted criteria such as size,

Examination of the Blood.

PLATE IV.

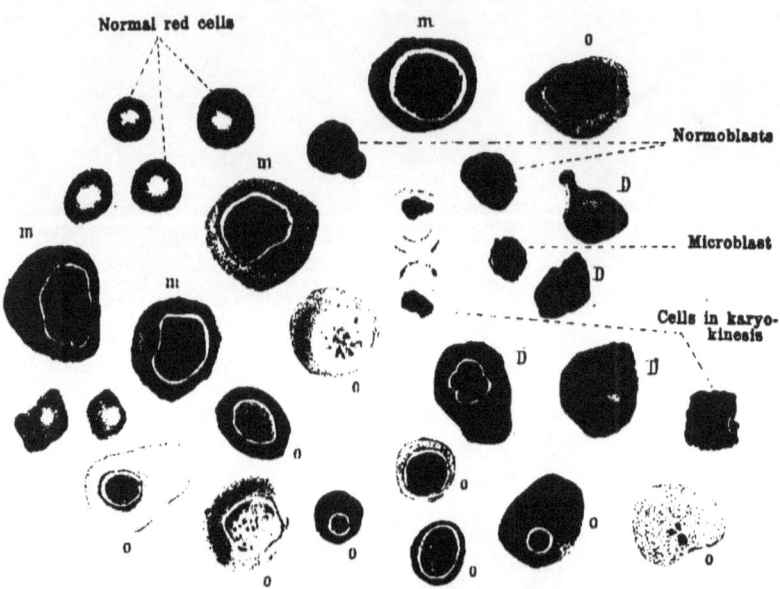

Varieties of Nucleated Red Cells.

m. m. m. m. = Typical megaloblasts.   D. D. D. D. = Cells with dividing nuclei.
o. o. o. o. o. o. o. = Other (unnamed) varieties of nucleated red corpuscles.

Scale of μ

Cells deformed in size or shape.

R. C. Cabot fec.

Lith. Anst. v. E. A. Funke, Leipsig.

PLATE IV.

(1) m, m, m, m— *Young megaloblasts.*

(2) D, D, D, D; the *upper two* are probably *old normoblasts* with degenerating nuclei, and the lower two old megaloblasts with nuclei is a similar condition.

(3) o, o, o, o, etc.—The two cells in the lower right-hand corner are probably *old megaloblasts* whose nuclei are nearly absorbed. The three cells immediately to the left of these are probably *young normoblasts*—the lowest one being the youngest. The other four cells marked "o, o, o, o" (those to the extreme left) are probably *middle-aged megaloblasts.* The two labelled "Normoblasts" are really *old normoblasts.* The appearance of extrusion of the nucleus on one of them is probably an artefact. The large cell on the extreme upper right-hand corner is probably a megaloblast with a "pyknotic" or œdematous (degenerating) nucleus.

(4) In the young or "typical" megaloblasts (m, m, m, m) note the white line around the nucleus, the variations in its tint, and, in two of them, the discolorations of the protoplasm (polychromatophilia), especially near the nucleus. The lower of the two cells in karyokinesis shows this best.

(5) In the *microblast* note the ragged edge of the protoplasm.

(6) In the lower portion of the plate ("*cells deformed in size or shape*") an actual field from a case of pernicious anæmia was copied. *Macrocytes* (or large cells), *microcytes* (or small cells), and misshapen cells or *poikilocytes* are shown.

(7) The "*polychromatophilic cells*" in the lower right-hand corner were stained with the same mixture as those to the left of them, but have taken up other colors besides the orange G, which alone is taken up by normal red cells.

color of nucleus, etc. *Most* "megaloblasts," he admits, are larger than *most* normoblasts, but there are occasional giant normoblasts and dwarf megaloblasts which by size alone are indistinguishable. The large, pale, delicately netted nucleus of the "megaloblasts" is simply a *young* nucleus. All young nuclei are relatively large and pale, while the small dark nucleus of the normoblast is simply an *old* or degenerating nucleus. The *real* criteria of the two varieties, according to Pappenheim, is not the size or color of nucleus nor of the whole cell, but the structure of the nuclear network. This is a point difficult to make out by ordinary staining methods and not easily appreciated. Luckily for us, most "megaloblasts" *are* larger than most "normoblasts;" and further, most of them as seen in the blood are *young* (*i.e.*, have large pale nuclei with delicate chromatin network), while most "normoblasts" are *old*, as shown by their small, dark, coarse-skeined nucleus, so that in the majority of cases Ehrlich's criteria for the two varieties are sufficiently correct for diagnostic purposes. Pappenheim of course wishes to abandon the terms "megaloblast" and "normoblast" altogether, but since size still remains the most easily recognized criterion of "megaloblasts" and "normoblasts" I shall continue to use the terms. On the chances, then, *any nucleated red cell over 10 μ diameter should be classed as a megaloblast whatever the appearance of its nucleus*, and *any nucleated red cell under 10 μ diameter is probably a normoblast* whatever the appearance of its nucleus. *Microblasts* simply represent degenerating forms (usually normoblasts) whose protoplasm is falling away. The clinical significance of the two varieties is just such as Ehrlich supposed. [These points will be made clearer by reference to Plate IV. and the remarks intended to explain it.]

In most cases of severe secondary anæmia we find a few normoblasts. In very severe forms, whatever the cause, we may or may not find an occasional megaloblast. But these are much rarer than the normoblasts, even in the severest types of secondary anæmia. The only exceptions to this rule are the anæmias due to intestinal parasites, in which, though secondary and curable, the megaloblasts in some cases predominate over the normoblasts.

Summing up the changes characteristic of secondary

anæmia, which includes almost all the important pathological appearances occurring in red cells, we have:

I. $\begin{cases} (a) \text{ Lack of hæmoglobin.} \\ (b) \text{ Lowered specific} \\ \quad \text{gravity.} \end{cases}$ Characteristic of mild cases.

II. The above and necrobiotic } Characteristic of moderate changes of Maragliano. } cases.

III. $\begin{cases} (a) \text{ Lack of red cells.} \\ (b) \text{ Presence of normo-} \\ \quad \text{blasts and the above} \\ \quad \text{(I. and II.).} \end{cases}$ Characteristic of severe cases.

IV. Megaloblasts and the above } Characteristic˜of very se-
(I., II., and III.). } vere cases.

The changes in the white cells will be discussed in the next chapter.

Among the commonest causes of secondary anæmia are: I. Infective and febrile diseases, acute or chronic. II. Malignant disease. III. Chronic suppurations, nephritis, chronic dysentery, cirrhosis of the liver. IV. Bad hygiene, pregnancy, and lactation. V. Intestinal parasites. VI. Poisons (lead, arsenic, etc.).

To discuss the way in which each of these influences acts in producing anæmia is tempting, but falls outside the plan of this book.

The following are good examples of the condition of the blood:

SECONDARY ANÆMIA.

Case.	Age.	Sex.	Red cells.	White cells.	Per cent. hæmo-globin.	Remarks.
1	23	F.	1,656,000	2,300	18	Post-malarial.
			2,048,000	2,600	24	After 7 days' treatment.
			1,808,000	3,200	30	" 14 " "
			1,568,000	1,300	58	" 24 " "
			4,248,000	2,300	60	" 34 " "
			....	......	72	" 43 " "
2	45	M.	2,208,000	......	50	Post-malarial.
3	9	F.	2,186,000	8,500	30	Post-hemorrhagic (8 hours).
4	41	F.	3,240,000	5,400	59	Post-hemorrhagic (b l e e d i n g fibroid).
5	32	F.	2,920,000	12,000	47	After abortion with hemorrhage.
6	40	M.	2,040,000	9,600	10	Chronic dysentery.

Differential count in case 6 showed polynuclear cells, 66.3; myelocytes, 1.4; 8 normoblasts, 5 megaloblasts—seen in counting 400 leucocytes.

2. HYDRÆMIA.

(a) Seen from the opposite point of view almost all cases of anæmia are hydræmic. That is, if the total volume of blood is to remain approximately constant (as it appears to do), any loss of solids (corpuscle substance) must be made up by water taken in from the tissues. Hence any anæmic person's blood is thin, watery, or hydræmic. Women's blood is somewhat more hydræmic than men's, because less rich in cells. Ordinary chlorosis and secondary anæmia show no more water than normal in the serum, but the cells are probably somewhat water-logged.

(b) In many conditions of dropsy, whether from heart or kidney, we may have more water than normal, both in the plasma and in the corpuscles themselves, which are capable of taking up considerably more than their normal amount of water.

(c) Any temporary dilution of the blood under the conditions mentioned above (ingestion of liquid, lowered blood pressure, etc.) is from one point of view a hydræmic condition.

No special clinical significance attaches to it other than that of anæmia, whose correlative it is.

CHAPTER VIII

Much confusion has been caused in the past by the failure
to see in leukæmic blood anything more than an extreme and
permanent form of leucocytosis, while leucocytosis was thought
of as a mild and temporary leukæmia.

We know now that they are totally different phenomena,
differing not in the number, but in the *kind* of cells present in
the increased numbers.

Definition.

There are many difficulties in defining leucocytosis. To my
mind the term is best used to mean: *An increase in the number
of leucocytes in the peripheral blood over the number normal in the
individual case, this increase never involving a diminution in the
polymorphonuclear varieties, but generally a marked absolute and
relative gain over the number previously present.*

(*a*) I say "in the peripheral blood" because certain observers hold that leucocytosis is not a real increase in the
total number of leucocytes in the blood, but only an affair
of distribution, the cells being drawn or attracted to the periphery and out of the internal organs. Whether this theory
be true or not, it is accurate to say that in the drop which we
draw (whether also in the internal organs or not), the leucocytes are present in increased numbers per cubic millimetre.

(*b*) In persons not usually to be considered sick, but simply
somewhat wizened or ill-nourished, the normal count of white
cells may be as low as three thousand per cubic millimetre.
For such an individual ten thousand cells per cubic millimetre
would be a decidedly pathological condition. On the other
hand, there are persons, usually those of notable vigor and
good nutrition, whose white cells rarely fall below ten thousand.

Obviously we must take account of these differences both in
our definition and in our practice if we are to reason correctly
from the data of blood examination.

(c) Further we must lay stress upon the varieties of leucocytes whose increase constitutes leucocytosis in distinction from either variety of leukæmia (splenic-myelogenous, or lymphatic).

For instance, given a count of eighty thousand leucocytes per cubic millimetre, we cannot tell without knowing the varieties of cells present whether the case is a genuine leukæmia or a merely leucocytosis symptomatic of pneumonia, suppuration, malignant disease, or other conditions.

(d) Thus defined leucocytosis is of two kinds. 1. That in which the relative proportions of the different varieties to each other is unchanged. 2. That in which the increase is made up solely or largely by a gain in the polymorphonuclear leucocytes.

The latter includes nearly all pathological leucocytoses, the former being confined chiefly to the physiological leucocytoses next to be described.

(e) Lastly, in order to be sure that the polymorphonuclear cells are not decreased, we must know what the normal percentage *for that individual* is. The normal percentage of these cells in infancy is from twenty-eight to forty per cent. In adults it is much higher, but varies like the total count, according to conditions of nutrition, etc. Thus the normal for adults is usually set at from sixty to seventy per cent, but no one individual's blood shows such variations in health, and if we include the obviously ill-nourished, but not actually sick, and also those in blooming health, we shall have to widen our normal limits considerably. From fifty to seventy-five per cent are within normal limits according to the above conception. But obviously we can make no absolute judgment by a standard so vague. It is much better, I think, to consider each individual as his own standard within these limits, his count of polymorphonuclear cells being a fair measure of the soundness and vigor of his metabolism. Thus, in an obviously debilitated individual, we should consider seventy-two per cent of these cells very high, while in a vigorous athlete it might not be so.

It is the endeavor to include all these limiting conditions that has made my definition so long and involved. It gives us, if it turns out to be true, some better way of classing individuals than as "sick" or "well" as regards their blood state. We find out *how* well or how sick their blood is (to a certain extent), (a)

7

by the total number of leucocytes present, and (*b*) by the proportion of polymorphonuclear neutrophiles in a given one thousand of these leucocytes.   These data tell us approximately *how* normal or *how* abnormal a given individual's blood is.   When a given disease like pneumonia occurs, we need to know, if possible, what is the ordinary leucocyte count and differential count of that case, on top of which a leucocytosis may (or may not) be built up.

Condition of stasis, temporary blood concentration, dilution, and vasomotor disturbances must, of course, be excluded or allowed for, since these may increase not only the total leucocyte count, but often the percentage of polymorphonuclear cells.   Whether or not differences of race make any difference in the normal count of white cells, I cannot say, but certainly the average of a group of college athletes would be higher than that of some country towns in New England where everybody is more or less under-nourished; and if one is to practise among all sorts and conditions of men, I think he cannot but expect to find people's leucocytes vary all the way *from 3,000 to 10,500 per cubic millimetre*, without there being more than malnutrition to account for the lower figures.

Into the theories of how leucocytosis is brought about I shall not enter; no one of them as yet commands general assent.

We may divide leucocytoses for convenience' sake into: 1. Physiological leucocytoses.   2. Pathological leucocytoses.

PHYSIOLOGICAL LEUCOCYTOSES.

1. Leucocytosis of the new-born.
2. Leucocytosis of digestion.
3. Leucocytosis of pregnancy.
4. Leucocytosis post-partum.
5. Leucocytosis after violent exercise, massage, and cold baths.
6. Leucocytosis of the moribund state.

The Leucocytosis as Affected by Digestion.

(*a*) Total abstinence from food lowers the leucocyte count. In the blood of the professional faster Succi, the number sank within his first week's fast to 861 per cubic millimetre.   After the first week it rose to 1,530, and remained there throughout his thirty days' abstinence (Luciani[1]). The polymorphonuclear cells and eosinophiles are said by Tauszk to be increased in chronic starvation.

Von Limbeck counted the blood of a melancholic patient who had fasted a week, and found 2,800 white cells per cubic millimetre. These facts support the idea that the number of leucocytes depends (within certain limits) on the individual's assimilation of food. In cancer of the gullet we find similar low figures.

(b) After a meal rich in proteids the leucocyte count rises about thirty-three per cent in most sound persons. Ten thousand cells may perhaps be considered the average, three to four hours after a proteid meal, but if the count before a meal is only 4,000 or 5,000, digestion will perhaps not raise it above 7,000, while vigorous adults may show 13,000. Digestion leucocytosis is always *relative* to the count of the individual's blood *when fasting*. This is to be obtained preferably before breakfast, as during the day the leucocytosis caused by one meal may not be gone before the influence of the next meal begins.

Occasionally we see sound persons with little or no digestive leucocytosis. Some of these cases are to be explained by habitual constipation (v. Limbeck); in others the reason is more obscure. But there is no doubt of its being the rule after meals of mixed or proteid diet. In herbivorous animals, and presumably in vegetarians, it is not found.

Any disease of the gastro-intestinal tract, whether functional or organic, may prevent the appearance of the digestion leucocytosis (see later under Diseases of the stomach, page 280). In anæmic and debilitated conditions it is frequently absent.

In children it is especially marked. Schiff[2] records a case of a healthy infant whose blood an hour after birth showed 19,500 (see next section), after its first meal 27,625, and after its fourth meal 36,000 white cells per cubic millimetre. After the second day this gradually diminished.

Food seems to call forth a greater leucocytosis in proportion as it is a *novelty* in the stomach. Cases of gastric ulcer who had been fed exclusively by rectum for some weeks show a

[1] "Des Hungern," German translation by O. Fränkel. Hamburg, 1890.
[2] Zeit. f. Heilk., xi., 1890.

greater leucocytosis after their first meal than later. Perhaps
the size of the digestion leucocytosis in the new-born is to be
similarly explained. In diabetics the digestion leucocytosis is
sometimes very large.

The leucocytosis can usually be observed one hour after a
meal, increases for two, three, or even five hours according to
the slowness of digestion, then falls again.

Burian and Schur[1] found an increase of the polymorphonuclear varieties in those cases in which an increase of the total
count took place at all. Eosinophiles show no regular changes.

Diagnostic Value.

1. When we wish to know whether a person is accurate in such
statements as that they have "eaten nothing for a week," we can
get evidence from the leucocyte count, which should be very low
if the assertion be true. Whenever we cannot communicate
with a patient and wish to know how much food he has taken of
late, we can form some idea from the blood examination. In
the case of a patient who spoke only Russian, I was led to
look for a stenosis of the gullet by the lowness of the leucocyte
count (2,700), and the probang confirmed the suspicion.

2. As suggested above, we can form some idea of a person's
general vigor, nutrition, and capacity to assimilate food by the
number of leucocytes and the proportion of mononuclear
cells, as compared with the average figures for that age and
locality. Persons *debilitated* from any reason are apt to
show it in their blood by the changes above mentioned, the
element of hysteria being sometimes recognizable by other
signs (see below: "Eosinophilia," page 116).

3. Slowness of digestion is indicated by a late appearance of
the digestion leucocytosis. The inferences to be drawn from the
blood in diseases of the gastro-intestinal tract will be discussed
later (page 274).

4. Perhaps the chief importance of digestion leucocytosis is
as a possible cause of false inferences, through being taken for a
pathological increase. Bearing this in mind, we must always
examine the blood as *near* a meal as possible, or better still
before breakfast.

[1] Wien. klin. Woch., February 11th, 1897.

Leucocytosis of the New-Born.

The following table is compiled from the best authorities on the subject (Schiff, Gundobin, Bayer, Hayem, and others):

Age.	Red cells.	Leucocytes.
At birth......................	5,900,000	17,000 to 21,000 (26,-000 to 36,000 after first feeding).
End of first day..............	7,000,000 to 8,800,000	24,000
" second day...........	Generally increased.	30,000
" fourth day...........	6,000,000	20,000
" seventh day..........	5,000,000	15,000
Tenth day....................	....	10,000 to 14,000
Twelfth to eighteenth day ...	....	12,000
Sixth month	....	12,000
Sixth year and upward	....	7,500

The increase is explained by Lepine, v. Limbeck, and others as a combination of blood concentration with large digestion leucocytosis. Gundobin and others are opposed to this theory. Certainly the influence of digestion on infant's blood is much greater than in adults. After a meal 30,000 leucocytes is never a very high count in infants under two years.

A fuller discussion of the subject will be found in the chapter on the blood in infancy.

The Leucocytosis of Pregnancy.

Most primiparæ show during the latter months of pregnancy a moderate increase of all varieties of leucocytes. Thirteen thousand cells per cubic centimetre is about the average count.

In multiparæ it occurs in only about fifty per cent of the cases. Digestion leucocytosis "on top of" the constant pregnancy leucocytosis, so to speak, does not occur.

As mentioned above, the relative percentage of the different types of leucocyte *remains unchanged*, so that all varieties must be equally increased (eosinophiles excepted). The fact that digestion does not increase the pregnancy leucocytosis, leads to the suggestion that the whole thing may be only a prolonged digestion leucocytosis—the mother having to eat for two. The swelling of the breasts may also account for part of the leucocytosis. In the last weeks of pregnancy the leucocytosis increases till at the beginning of labor it is often 16,000 to 18,000. It has no diagnostic value, as it is not present during the earlier months of pregnancy when diagnosis is difficult, and in the later months such conditions as hydatiform mole and fibroid tumors might raise the count of white cells as much as pregnancy.

Leucocytosis After Parturition.

The following charts illustrate the course of the leucocyte curve from the time of parturition till the end of the second week after it.

All were primiparæ excepting Nos. 5, 8, and 9. There was no sepsis in any case, and the temperature charts were practically normal after the second day. No reasons are known for the variations between the different cases. All were counted at the same hour of the day, and under the same conditions of nutrition. All nursed their children.

The only importance of this leucocytosis is that it might be confounded with a pathological leucocytosis in a case suspected of being septic. Just how long the leucocytosis is prolonged during lactation has not been studied so far as I am aware, but it certainly may go on several weeks.

Violent exercise, massage, and short cold baths have been shown to cause a temporary increase in the number of leucocytes in the peripheral blood, all varieties of the cell being equally increased. The explanation usually given is that the blood is concentrated by vasomotor contraction and rise of blood pressure.

Schultz (*Deut. Arch. f. klin. Med.*, 1893, page 234) found the *leucocytosis of exercise* amount to about the same as that of digestion, 11,000 to 13,000. He also noted that in dogs merely opening the peritoneum aseptically or breaking a leg caused leucocytosis.

Thayer studied twenty cases of typhoid and found an average of 7,724 white cells before and 13,170 after a Brand bath (*Johns Hopkins Medical Bulletin*, April, 1893). The increase took place equally in all varieties. Winternitz (Imperio-Royal Medical Society, Vienna, February, 1893) came to a similar conclusion and found also that prolonged cold bathing decreased

the number of white cells (dry cold does the same). A patient
was recently brought to the Massachusetts Hospital who had
fallen through a hole in the ice and been some minutes in the

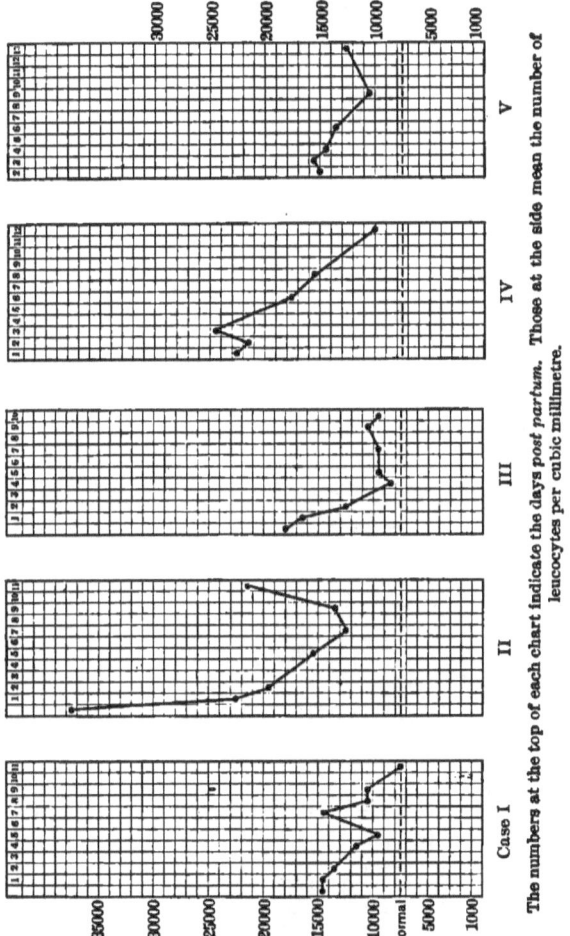

icy water. His temperature was 91.8° by the rectum. Blood
count showed 17,500 leucocytes per cubic millimetre. Next
day he was perfectly well. On the contrary, short hot baths
decrease and prolonged ones increase the number of leucocytes.

Local arm baths have a similar effect, raising the count of leucocytes in the blood of the immersed arm if cold and short, and lowering it if hot and short, while prolonged immersion has an opposite effect. In the other arm the counts go up when

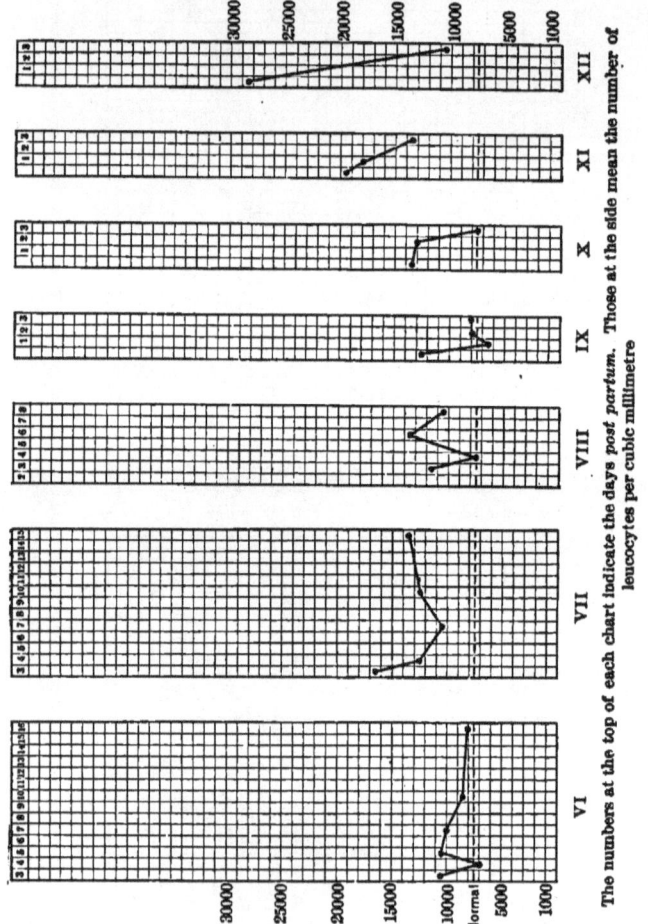

·those of the immersed arm go down, and *vice versa* (Rovighi).[1]
Mitchell[2] found that the leucocytes showed distinct increase (as

[1] Arch. Ital. d. Clin. Med., xxxii., 3, 1893.
[2] American Journal of the Medical Sciences, May, 1894.

well as the red cells and hæmoglobin) after one hour's general massage.

All these forms of leucocytosis are usually explained by changes in blood pressure, and vasomotor changes affecting the calibre of the peripheral vessels and consequently their contents.

Terminal Leucocytosis.

The leucocytosis of the moribund state, though by no means invariable, occurs in many cases, whether from the influence of a terminal infection or from stasis. Where death is sudden or rapid it does not occur. It seems to be analogous to the terminal rise of temperature seen at the close of many chronic non-febrile affections. The longer the patient is moribund the higher the count reaches. In pernicious anæmia the increase may be so great as to simulate lymphatic leukæmia. Such a case occurred in the writer's own experience. The patient had presented the signs and symptoms of pernicious anæmia, and the blood was typical of the disease in all respects except for the lack of nucleated red cells.

Slides taken on the day of death showed a ratio of one white to fifteen red cells, the small lymphocytes greatly predominating, but the autopsy revealed simply the lesions of pernicious anæmia. The differential count of one thousand leucocytes on the day of death showed: Lymphocytes, 91.7 per cent; polymorphonuclear cells, 7.7 per cent; eosinophiles, 0.5 per cent. Four megaloblasts were seen while counting these. The total leucocyte count was unfortunately not made.

In ordinary cases the differential count shows an increase in the polymorphonuclear leucocytes. Thus in a case reported by Rieder, in which the leucocyte count rose during the last two days of life from 7,800 to 59,300, the polymorphonuclear cells constituted 87.5 per cent of the whole 59,300.

PATHOLOGICAL LEUCOCYTOSES.

For convenience' sake these may be divided as follows:
1. Post-hemorrhagic leucocytosis.
2. Inflammatory leucocytosis.
3. Toxic leucocytosis.

4. Leucocytosis in malignant disease.

5. Leucocytosis due to therapeutic and experimental influences.

1. *Post-hemorrhagic Leucocytosis.*

Within an hour after a large hemorrhage we find commonly a considerable increase (16,000–18,000). In hemorrhage from the stomach this disappears again usually within a day or two, while in ordinary traumatic hemorrhage it persists longer. This last fact may perhaps be explained, as v. Limbeck suggests, by the local conditions in the wound rather than by the loss of blood in itself.

The polymorphonuclear leucocytes are usually increased relatively and absolutely as in other forms of pathological leucocytosis. Sometimes we have lymphocytosis (see page 114). The degree of increase in the white cells is parallel in a general way to the anæmia produced in the individual, *i.e.*, it depends on his powers of recuperation rather than on the amount of blood lost. Its duration follows the same rule.[1]

2. *Inflammatory Leucocytosis.*

I use the term "inflammatory leucocytosis" rather than "leucocytosis of infectious diseases" because there is a considerable number of infectious diseases in which no leucocytosis occurs, while it accompanies almost all forms and cases of inflammation. Nevertheless I shall class under this heading some diseases in which inflammation plays but a very subordinate rôle.

I. Although *purulent and gangrenous* processes usually cause a higher count of white cells than *serous* processes, the amount of the exudation is not a measure of the amount of leucocytosis. It seems to depend rather on the resultant of two forces, viz., the severity of the infection and the resisting power of the individual. These factors may interact in various ways:

1. Infection mild :   resistance good   = small leucocytosis.
2.   "   less mild :   "   less good = moderate leucocytosis.
3.   "   severe :   "   good   = very marked leucocytosis.
4.   "   "   "   poor   = no leucocytosis.

[1] Further account of the blood after hemorrhage will be found on page 126 et seq.

This will be illustrated later under "Pneumonia" and under "Sepsis." Experiments on animals show that whereas moderate sized doses of septic cultures, not sufficient to kill the animal, are followed by leucocytosis, larger doses after which death follows speedily, do not raise the leucocyte count at all. Animals weakened by any cause show less leucocytosis to a moderate dose than strong animals.

If the individual reacts from the shock his leucocytes are increased again and rise above normal. If reaction fails the leucocytes do not rise.

II. Inflammatory leucocytoses differ from physiological leucocytoses—

(a) In being usually of larger extent.

(b) In being almost always accompanied by a relative and absolute increase in the percentage of polymorphonuclear cells.

III. The course of the leucocytosis as regards both amount and duration shows, like the temperature chart, certain more or less characteristic differences in different diseases.

IV. In some cases in which the absolute number of leucocytes is not increased, we see a relative increase in the polymorphonuclear cells, pointing to the fact that influences are at work similar to those which produce an *absolute* increase.

V. That the amount of exudation is not of itself a measure of the amount of leucocytosis is shown by the fact that erysipelas or scarlet fever may be accompanied by as high a count as the average count in pneumonia or empyema.

That purulent exudations usually have more effect on the white cells than do serous ones is due, I suppose, to the fact that a purulent inflammation usually means a severer infection.

VI. No direct connection exists between leucocytosis and fever, many febrile affections running their course with a normal leucocyte count. When both leucocytosis and fever are due to the same causes they rise and fall together, but the correspondence is rarely accurate, and marked leucocytosis may exist without fever.

VII. Acute, rapidly spreading inflammations seem to produce a greater leucocytosis (other things being equal) than those in which the process is relatively chronic and stationary. For instance, an appendicitis, when well walled off and stationary, shows less increase in white blood cells than while its lesions are progressing. But peracute, overwhelming general sepsis may have no effect on the leucocytes, the reactive power of the organism being crushed.

VIII. Most inflammatory leucocytoses are preceded by a temporary diminution in the number of leucocytes. This occurs in animals from *shock* of any kind (blows on the head, tying to the etherizing board), and it seems not unlikely that the cause is the same in all cases.

The following is a list of the more important inflammatory or infectious conditions in which leucocytosis appears :

1. *Infectious diseases with comparatively slight local inflammatory processes :*

(*a*) Asiatic cholera.

(*b*) Relapsing fever.

(*c*) Typhus fever (according to the majority of observers).

(*d*) Scarlet fever.

(*e*) Diphtheria and follicular tonsillitis.

(*f*) Syphilis (secondary stage).

(*g*) Erysipelas.

(*h*) The bubonic plague.

(*i*) Yellow fever (some cases).

2. *Infectious diseases with more extensive local lesions :*

(*a*) Pneumonia.

(*b*) Small-pox (suppurative stage).

(*c*) Malignant endocarditis, puerperal septicæmia, and all pyæmic and septicæmic conditions.

(*d*) Actinomycosis.

(*e*) Trichinosis.

(*f*) Glanders.

(*g*) Acute multiple neuritis (febrile stages).

(*h*) Acute articular rheumatism.

(*i*) Septic meningitis and cerebro-spinal meningitis.

(*j*) Cholangitis, cholecystitis, and empyema of the gall bladder.

(*k*) Acute pancreatitis.

(*l*) Endometritis, cystitis (some acute cases).

(*m*) Gonorrhœa.

3. *Local inflammatory processes :*

(*a*) *Abscesses* of all kinds and situations, such as Felon.

Carbuncle, furunculosis.

Tonsillar and retropharyngeal abscess.

Appendicitis, phlebitis (some cases).

Pyonephrosis, perinephritic abscess and pyelonephritis.

Osteomyelitis, empyema.

Psoas and hip abscess when not simply tubercular.

Abscess of lung, liver, spleen, ovary, prostate.

Salpingitis and pelvic peritonitis, epididymitis.

(b) *Inflammations of the serous membranes* including:

Pericarditis, peritonitis, arthritis (serous or purulent, nontubercular), conjunctivitis.

(c) *Gangrenous inflammations*, as of the

Appendix, lung, bowel, mouth (noma).

(d) Many inflammatory skin diseases, such as dermatitis, pemphigus, pellagra, herpes zoster, prurigo, some cases of universal eczema, etc.

3. *Toxic Leucocytosis.*

Under this heading I have grouped most of the conditions not obviously to be explained as infectious or inflammatory (though some may turn out to be such) and not due to malignant disease or therapeutic agencies. This classification is chiefly for convenience' sake and represents only a guess at the real explanation of the leucocytosis:

(a) Leucocytosis of illuminating-gas poisoning.

(b) "   " quinine poisoning.

(c) "   " rickets (many cases).

(d) "   " the uric-acid diathesis, gout.

(e) "   " acute yellow atrophy of the liver.

(f) "   " advanced cirrhosis of the liver (some cases) especially with jaundice.

(g) "   " acute gastro-intestinal disorders (ptomains ?).

(h) "   " chronic nephritis, usually in uræmic cases.

(i) "   after injections of tuberculin and thyroid extract.

(j) "   after injection of normal salt solution (intravenous).

(k) "   after ingestion of salicylates.

(l) "   during and after etherization.

Possibly the leucocytosis of *acute delirium* belongs also in this group.

4. *Leucocytosis of Malignant Disease.*

Very likely this belongs more properly under one or another of the classes just mentioned. Some observers think that it occurs only from the inflammation excited in the periphery of some malignant tumors; others that it is due to absorption of morbid products from the tumor itself; others again that it is to be accounted for by the cachectic state associated with the growth of the tumors. The details and conditions of its occurrence will be discussed later (page 332).

5. *Leucocytosis Due to Therapeutic and Experimental Influences.*

Pohl[1] found that most of the so-called tonics and stomachics produce a slight increase in the white cells in animals, particularly the vegetable tonics like tincture of gentian, and oil of anise seed, while bismuth, bicarbonate of soda, and iron had no such effect. Quinine, caffeine, and ethyl alcohol gave likewise negative results. Von Limbeck found leucocytosis in men after oil of peppermint and oil of anise seed.

Binz[2] got the same results with camphor. In all these experiments the substances were given by the mouth.

Using subcutaneous or intravenous injections, Löwit experimented on animals with hemialbumose, peptone, pepsin, nucleinic acid, nuclein, extract of blood-leech, pyocyanin, tuberculin, curare, uric acid, urate of sodium, and urea. All but the last of these produce temporary decrease followed by increase of leucocytes.

Goldschneider and Jacob[3] used extracts of various organs. Extract of spleen, marrow, and thymus produced leucocytosis preceded, as in Löwit's experiments, by a brief diminution in the number of leucocytes, while extract of pancreas, thyroid, kidney, and liver had no effect.

Winternitz[4] injected a large variety of substances subcutane-

[1] Arch. f. exp. Path. u. Pharm., 1889, vol. xv.
[2] Arch. f. exp. Path. u. Pharm., vol. v., p. 122.
[3] Arch. f. Anat. u. Physiol., 1893, p. 567.
[4] Arch. f. exp. Path. u. Pharm., vol. xxxv., p. 77.

ously and found that the degree of leucocytosis was parallel to the degree of local reaction excited.

For example, neutral salts and weak acids or alkalies produced slight local inflammation and a leucocytosis of from forty to seventy-five per cent of the original count. But irritants like turpentine, croton oil, nitrate of silver, sulphate of copper, mercury, antimony, digitoxin, etc., produced local suppuration (aseptic) and much greater leucocytosis (two hundred to three hundred per cent).

Pilocarpine and antipyrin have been found by v. Jaksch and others to produce marked increase in the number of leucocytes when given subcutaneously. During the use of thyroid extract Richter (*Centralblatt f. inn. Med.*, 1896, p. 3) noted leucocytosis.

A large number of observations on the effects of injections of bacteria or their toxins agree in the following results.

1. Where the dose is very large the leucocytes are reduced, and the animal dies.

2. Where the dose is not sufficient to kill the animal the temporary diminution in the leucocytes is soon followed by leucocytosis.

3. Where the dose is slowly fatal the count of leucocytes oscillates up and down within wide limits.

4. Animals previously rendered immune to the poison injected show little or no leucocytosis.

5. Leucocytosis is more easily called forth and of greater extent in young animals.

6. Most pathogenic organisms act similarly, but bacilli and toxins of tuberculosis as a rule cause no leucocytosis.

7. There is no evidence that any one variety of leucocyte is attracted by any particular bacillus or toxin.

In the above sketch of therapeutic and experimental forms of leucocytosis no attempt has been made to give anything but the more interesting and important outlines of the immense amount of work done.

Cell Structure of the Leucocytes in Leucocytosis.

Hitherto we have spoken as if leucocytosis meant only an increased *number* of the normal cells, but one cannot study the cell forms in extensive pathological leucocytosis without noting

in many cases *qualitative* changes in the individual cells.   These
are chiefly :

   1. A greater or less approximation of the nuclei of polymorphonuclear neutrophiles to the appearances of the myelocyte
nucleus.   As will be mentioned later under leukæmia, we find in
every blood containing many myelocytes numerous cells whose
nucleus is on the border-line between the myelocyte and the
polymorphonuclear stage, so far as appearances go.   Now in
leucocytosis we find the same "border-line" cells in smaller

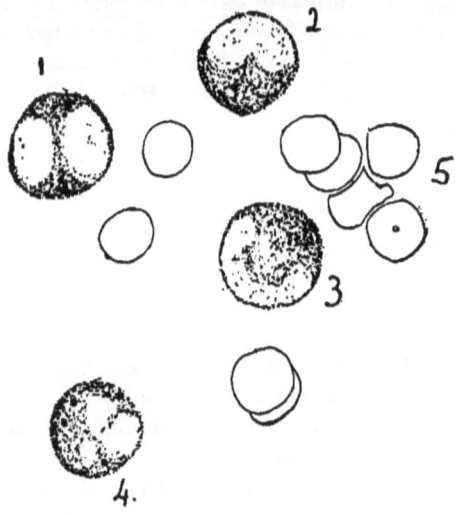

Fig. 29.—Atypical Leucocytes seen in Leucocytosis. 1, Leucocytes with polar arrangement of nuclei (mitosis?); 2 and 3, leucocytes with nuclei resembling those of myelocytes; 4, leucocyte containing two kinds of granules.

numbers, the *likeness* to the myelocyte sometimes passing into
identity in one to three per cent of the cells.

   2. A greater or less approximation of the appearance of the
large lymphocytes' protoplasm to that of myelocyte protoplasm,
i.e., a diffuse violet or purple color exactly as in the myelocyte
but non-granular.   Engel makes a separate variety of this cell,
giving it the useless name of "mononuclear cell."

   3. Other finer changes, such as the number, size, and staining power of the neutrophilic granulations, polar position of the
nuclei, etc. (see Fig. 29), require further study.

Changes like the above militate against the idea that leucocytosis is simply a matter of distribution in the peripheral or internal vessels.

Absence of Leucocytosis.

It is of fully as great a practical assistance to us to know that in certain infective diseases leucocytosis is regularly absent as to know those conditions in which it is to be expected. Among the most important diseases in which leucocytosis is conspicuously absent are:

(a) Typhoid fever.
(b) Malaria.
(c) Grippe (most cases).
(d) Measles.
(e) Rötheln and mumps.
(f) Cystitis.
(g) Tuberculosis, including—
    Incipient phthisis.
    Miliary tuberculosis.
    Tubercular peritonitis.
    "   ostitis and periostitis.
    "   pleurisy.
    "   pericarditis.[1]

In some of these affections, notably in miliary tubercle and the later weeks of typhoid, the leucocytes are diminished. Further details will be given under the special diseases.

LEUCOPENIA.

Definition.—A diminution in the number of white cells in the peripheral circulation as compared with the number normal for the given individual.

1. The effects of starvation and malnutrition in producing leucopenia have already been described. Such leucopenia is usually associated with lymphocytosis (see below). Cancer of the gullet is an example of this class.

2. Short hot baths or prolonged cold baths produce temporarily the same result (Winternitz, *loc. cit.*).

---

[1] Tubercular *meningitis* often does show leucocytosis (*vide infra*. page 266).

8

3. Most of the infective diseases in which there is no leuco-cytosis are sometimes characterized by leucopenia, e.g., grippe, measles, miliary tuberculosis, and other forms of pure tuber-cular infection, malaria, and especially typhoid, in the later weeks of which it is almost invariable, and is accompanied by lymphocytosis.

Where a case of leukæmia is complicated by an infective disease (pneumonia, septicæmia) the number of leucocytes may fall below the normal. In a case recently occurring at the Mass-achusetts General Hospital in which a lymphatic leukæmia was terminated by septicæmia from glandular suppuration, the white cells fell gradually from 40,000 three weeks before death to 419 per cubic millimetre on the day of death. I have never heard of a lower count than this. The differential count was unchanged (lymphocytes = ninety-eight per cent).

4. In pernicious anæmia the count is usually very low and may fall below 1,000 cells per cubic millimetre. Other forms of anæmia (rachitic, syphilitic) occasionally produce the same re-sult.

LYMPHOCYTOSIS.

Lymphocytosis is a relative increase in the lymphocytes in the blood, with or without an increase of the total leucocytes count The increase is relative to the percentage of lymphocytes normal for the individual. When lymphocytosis and an increase of the total leucocyte count are present we cannot distinguish the blood from that of lymphatic leukæmia, and the distinction must depend upon the course and symptoms of the case.[1]

1. Such a condition (relative to the adult) occurs *in healthy infant's blood* and in many diseases of infancy, the blood seem-ing to have a tendency to return to the infantile type. This is especially true of cholera infantum and any gastro-intestinal trouble. Anything that retards the infant's normal gain in weight or general development retards its blood development as well. Thus a child of three, convalescent from a summer diar-rhœa, may have fifty to sixty per cent of lymphocytes, which

---

[1] The lymphocytosis of chlorosis has been mistaken for lymphatic leukæmia (Schreiber) owing to too exclusive reliance on the results of the blood examination. The patient recovered. Such cases are very rare, and the difficulty hardly ever arises.

would be normal for an infant of a few weeks, but for three years old is very high.

2. *Hereditary syphilis* is perhaps the best-known cause of relative lymphocytosis in children. *Scurvy* may produce the same result. Dividing the anæmias of children into two groups, those that do and those that do not produce leucocytosis, it appears that the great majority of those whose total leucocyte count is normal show a relative lymphocytosis. This is the case irrespective of whether there is enlargement of the spleen or not.

Sometimes the smaller, sometimes the larger lymphocytes are in the majority. Often no division between the two kinds is possible.

3. In adults some forms of *debility* may be associated with relative lymphocytosis as above noted (page 97). It is most marked, however, *in chlorosis, pernicious anæmia*, and the anæmia secondary to *syphilis*, in the later weeks of typhoid fever and in lactation.

4. Certain cases of *Graves' disease* show marked lymphocytosis. How such cases differ from those that do not show it I have not been able to determine.

5. It occurs also in *hæmophilia, goitre*, in some cases of *cervical adenitis*, whether tubercular or lymphomatous, and in *tumors of the spleen*.

6. During the administration of thyroid extract a lymphocytosis has been recently noted by Perry (New York *Medical Record*, August 29th, 1896).

7. The larger forms of lymphocytes are increased in some splenic tumors (chronic "ague cake"), at the end of scarlet fever, in pneumonia with delayed resolution (some cases), in measles, certain forms of phthisis and in the non-suppurative stages of small-pox; also in many of the same diseases in which the small lymphocytes are increased.

8. So far I have referred chiefly to relative lymphocytosis. Absolute lymphocytosis is very rare outside of lymphatic leukæmia. One case occurred at the Massachusetts General Hospital in 1894—a child of six, who passed through an attack of bronchopneumonia with uneventful recovery, the only peculiarity of the case being the marked increase of white cells running up to 94,600, *sixty-nine per cent of which were lymphocytes*. During convalescence the blood became normal and the child

left the hospital well in all respects. The case will be referred to later in the account of the blood of pneumonia.

Diagnostic Value of Lymphocytosis.

1. I have already suggested that the degree of health in persons not organically diseased might perhaps prove to vary directly with the percentage of polymorphonuclear cells in the blood.

2. In children the same percentage is to a certain extent a measure of the child's degree of development—causes of leucocytosis being excluded, and the percentage normal for a child of the patient's age being taken as the standard.

3. The diagnosis of obscure syphilitic disease may be supported by the coincidence of lymphocytosis with eosinophilia.

4. Absolute lymphocytosis in the presence of glandular tumors is our mainstay in the diagnosis of lymphatic leukæmia.

EOSINOPHILIA.

Definition.—An increase in the percentage of eosinophiles in the circulatory blood, with or without an increase in the total leucocyte count.

The researches of Neusser, Zappert, Weiss, Klein, and others have brought the eosinophilic cells once more into the prominence which they lost when it became apparent that they were in no way peculiar to leukæmia.

1. Leukæmia is occasionally associated with eosinophilia (see below, page 167), but in the majority of cases this is not so. As in normal blood, from one to three per cent of them are to be found.

2. In infancy the percentage of eosinophiles is very often higher than in adults, so that in them eosinophilia may be considered physiological. In adults its presence is often unexplained. The eosinophiles are the most seemingly capricious of all blood cells. A certain amount of light has been thrown on them by the observations of Neusser and his pupils (Weiss, Schreiber, Klein, and others).

3. Neusser noticed that eosinophilia occurs—

(A) In many affections of the bones (sarcoma. leukæmia, osteomalacia).

(B) In many affections of the skin (pemphigus, pellagra, and others).

(C) In troubles involving the female genitals, especially the ovaries.

(D) In disturbances of the sympathetic nervous system.

That there is some relation between these seemingly unconnected sets of phenomena is shown by various *other* facts besides the presence of eosinophilia in them all.

(*a*) Bone and genitals.

Osteomalacia is most apt to occur in pregnancy and is cured in some cases by castration.

(*b*) Genitals and sympathetic nervous system.

The presence of all sorts of psychoses and vasomotor troubles associated with menstruation, pregnancy, and the climacteric, and the so-called "reflex" disturbances in connection with uterine or ovarian disease, are well known.

(*c*) The connection of the skin with both of the last-mentioned systems is seen in the trophic disorders and sympathetic dermatoses of hysteria and ovarian disease.

Working out the suggestions of this theory Neusser and his pupils have found relative eosinophilia in the following affections:

1. *Bones.*

Osteomalacia, malignant bone-tumors, pernicious anæmia (some cases), splenic-myelogenous leukæmia (occasionally). [The writer has seen slight eosinophilia in osteomyelitis.] Possibly the relative eosinophilia of normal infants' blood may be connected with the great activity of their bone growth.

2. *Diseases affecting the skin.*

Urticaria, pellagra, dermatitis herpetiformis, and pemphigus (constantly); some varieties of herpes, prurigo, eczema, lymphodermia perniciosa; after vaccination, in scarlet fever and syphilis (*not* measles or small-pox), ichthyosis, lupus, myxœdema.[1]

---

[1] I do not vouch for these or for any of Neusser's statements, which are frequently incorrect. In a single case each of pemphigus and prurigo I have found only four per cent and three per cent of eosinophiles. On the

3. *Genitals.*

Gonorrhœa, prostatitis, many ovarian tumors, before and during the early days of menstruation, puerperal mania, and the psychoses 'of menstruation, of the puerperium, and of the climacteric; in sexual neurasthenia, after coitus, and in lactation.

4. *Sympathetic Nervous System.*—The psychoses last mentioned, hysteria, Basedow's disease, and some of those given under the next heading.

5. Besides these general groups, Neusser has noticed another class of cases characterized by eosinophilia, namely, those in which some member of the group of *xanthin bases* is supposed to be in the system. In the so-called uric-acid diathesis the nuclein derivatives are transformed in the intestine into one of the xanthin bases, and their presence in the system appears to give rise to eosinophilia.

At any rate we regularly find eosinophilia (according to Neusser) in diseases thought to be characterized by an excess of these substances in the system. Examples of this are found in gout, bronchial asthma, emphysema, certain forms of migraine and epilepsy, oxaluria, uræmia, tetanus, some gastro-intestinal troubles, ankylostomiasis, after injections of nuclein, pilocarpine, tuberculin, iron preparations, and in most non-malignant liver diseases. All these Neusser believes stimulate the sympathetic nervous system and hence the bone marrow, through the production of xanthin bases. In asthmatic patients he succeeded in producing a paroxysm by injecting nuclein subcutaneously.

Possibly under this heading comes the eosinophilia after antipyrin, and that sometimes found in chlorosis, scurvy, nephritis, chronic malaria, and phthisical patients with cavities. In the latter cases it has been suggested that the patients may

other hand, in a case of dermatitis herpetiformis in which I lately examined, the differential count of five hundred cells showed :

Poymorphonuclear neutrophiles,	.	.	47 per cent.
Small lymphocytes,	.	.	.	.	25 "
Large "	.	.	.	.	8 "
Eosinophiles,	.	.	.	19 "
Myelocytes,	.	.	.	1 "

inoculate themselves with tuberculin absorbed from their lung cavities.

6. *Tumors of the spleen* are also accompanied by eosinophilia in some cases. Neusser does not explain this under the theory above sketched.

Many acute mental troubles show eosinophilia, while chronic cases do not.

Other causes of eosinophilia are phosphorus poisoning and injections of campherin.

In Osler's clinic there have recently been observed three cases of trichinosis in which the eosinophilic cells were from the first increased, and continued to increase till in one case at the time of death there was 68 per cent of eosinophiles in a leucocytosis of 17,000. I have had one similar case.

We also find eosinophilia in some cases of syphilis and syphilitic disease of the spinal cord (tabes dorsalis).

DIMINUTION IN EOSINOPHILES.

1. During digestion.

2. After castration.

3. In febrile stages of pneumonia, grippe, typhoid, diphtheria, sepsis, and most infectious diseases accompanied by leucocytosis. That this is not due simply to the presence of fever is shown by the fact that in malaria and scarlet fever, despite high fever, eosinophiles may be increased.

4. In the moribund state eosinophiles are diminished or absent.

In the post-critical stages of pneumonia and other infectious diseases the eosinophiles swing up above the normal.

4. Malignant disease, hemorrhage, and most of other causes of leucocytosis also diminish the eosinophiles.

DIAGNOSTIC AND PROGNOSTIC VALUE OF EOSINOPHILIA.

Neusser has suggested the following points:[1]

1. In the diagnosis between puerperal mania and puerperal sepsis, eosinophilia points to the former.

2. Between a tumor connected with the genital system and one not so connected, eosinophilia points to the former.

[1] For none of which I can vouch.

3. In determining whether a given case of hysteria, neurosis, or psychosis is likely to be benefited by castration, the presence of eosinophilia favors the operation.

4. In malignant disease an eosinophilia points to a metastasis in the osseous system (tumors of the spleen are not included in this rule).

5. In cases of doubtful syphilis eosinophilia combined with lymphocytosis (see above) speaks in favor of syphilis.

6. The diagnosis of any obscure form of "uric-acid diathesis" is helped by finding an increase of eosinophiles.

7. In distinguishing malignant liver disease from other liver disease eosinophilia points to the latter.

1. In the *prognosis* of chlorosis, eosinophilia is favorable.

2. In the prognosis of scarlet fever and scarlatinal nephritis the greater the eosinophilia the better the prognosis.

3. After hemorrhage increased eosinophiles show active regeneration of blood and good prognosis.

4. In pernicious anæmia eosinophilia is favorable for the same reason.

MYELOCYTES.

The occurrence of the myelocyte of Ehrlich in the circulating blood is always to be looked upon as pathological, that is, as the intrusion of a variety of leucocyte naturally a stranger to the circulating blood and a permanent inhabitant of the marrow. Although it is so close morphologically to other varieties of leucocytes that we should certainly suppose it to be an intermediate stage between the large lymphocytes and the polymorphonuclear neutrophiles, the fact that it does not occur outside the marrow in health speaks against the supposition.

Of the occurrence of the myelocyte in leukæmia and pernicious anæmia mention will be made under those diseases. The object of this section is to give a list of the other conditions under which it appears.

Neusser[1] has found small percentages of myelocytes in uræmia, carbonic-acid poisoning, diabetes, syphilis, puerperal mania, osteomalacia, Basedow's disease, and sarcoma, also during menstruation.

[1] Cited in Klein: Volkmann's "Samml. klin. Vorträge," December, 1893.

Capps found considerable percentages near death in general paralysis (see Book II., page 313).

J. J. Thomas found them in myxœdema.

The majority of other references to them in literature relate to different forms of grave anæmia. For example:

(1) Hayem[1] speaks of cells apparently myelocytes (he did not use Ehrlich's methods) in cases of extreme anæmia.

(2) E. Krebs[2] found them in severe anæmia.

(3) Loos[3] describes them in the anæmia of hereditary syphilis, and Rille[4] finds them in the anæmia of acquired syphilis.

(4) Neusser[5] mentions their presence both in pernicious anæmia and in chlorosis.

(5) Hammerschlag[6] made a similar observation.

(6) Engel[7] noted their presence in a case of what he cautiously calls "pseudo-pernicious anæmia ," and in diphtheria.

(7) Arnold[8] mentions them.

(8) Klein[9] gives a list of various diseases (besides leukæmia), in which they have been found, many of which are essentially anæmic conditions.

(9) Holmes[10] has found them in phthisis. I can confirm this observation.

(10) The writer[11] found them especially in the anæmia secondary to malignant disease (see page 351).

Besides these conditions the writer has found them occasionally in almost all the conditions in which leucocytosis or grave anæmia is present—for example, in pneumonia, malaria, sepsis, peritonitis, granulating wounds, osteomyelitis, phlebitis, rickets, Hodgkin's and Addison's disease, tuberculosis, and other diseases.

[1] "Du Sang," Paris, 1889, p. 382.
[2] Inaug. Dissert., Berlin, 1892.
[3] Wien. klin. Woch., 1892, p. 291.
[4] Loc. cit., 1893. No. 9.
[5] Loc. cit., 1892, No. 42.
[6] Berlin klin. Woch., August 20th, 1894.
[7] Virchow's Archiv, vol. cxxxv.
[8] Loc. cit., vol. cxl.
[9] Volkmann's "Sammlung klin. Vorträge," December, 1893.
[10] New York Medical Record. September 5th, 1896.
[11] Boston Medical and Surgical Journal, loc. cit.

The most curious example of their occurrence known to me is the following:

Mrs. W—— had been starving herself more or less for six months from motives of economy. Two weeks before I first saw her she began to suffer with cystitis. From both these troubles she made a rapid recovery, which has persisted now eighteen months. There was at the first count a leucocytosis of 15,100; partly due to cyanosis, as she had just been having a chill. The red cells were 7,300,000. Hæmoglobin, eighty-seven per cent. Differential counts were as follows:

Date. Number of cells counted.	May 2d 800. Per cent.	May 6th 1,000. Per cent.	May 7th 400. Per cent.	May 8th 400. Per cent.	May 13th 1,000. Per cent.
"Polynuclear neutrophiles"...	82.7	82.2	83.6	80.2	68.5
Lymphocytes..................	8.6	12.5	9.4	11.3	25.2
Large mononuclear	8.2	1.5	2.0	6.0	5.2
Myelocytes	.5	3.5	4.0	2.5	.6
Eosinophiles.................	.0	.3	1.0	.0	.5

What caused the presence of myelocytes I do not know. At that time I had never seen them in any curable disease and was alarmed by their appearing, but this case proves that they are not always of any importance.

In a general way their presence seems to have about the same significance as that of normoblasts, but they occur much more frequently. As a rule I think they indicate an acceleration of the function of those organs (marrow ?), by which red corpus-cles and granular leucocytes are furnished to the blood. Such an acceleration may be supposed to take place in leucocytosis, leukæmia, and pernicious anæmia, which are the chief conditions in which myelocytes appear in the blood.

CHAPTER IX.

HÆMOGLOBIN.

As stated above, the hæmoglobin may increase and diminish
in lines parallel to those of the red cells. In that case we suppose the amount of hæmoglobin per corpuscle to be normal and
the *color index* or *valeur globulaire* is said to = 1. Where the
hæmoglobin is diminished more than the count of corpuscles, we
say that the color index is less than 1. For example, if a man
has 5,000,000 red cells per cubic millimetre and only 50 per cent
of hæmoglobin, we estimate the color index by simply reducing
the count of cells to a stated percentage (5,000,000 cells = 100
per cent of cells) and dividing this percentage into the hæmoglobin percentage—*i.e.*, $\frac{50}{100} = 0.5 =$ the color index. Therefore 4,000,000 red cells (= 80 per cent) with 60 per cent of
hæmoglobin give a color index of $\frac{60}{80} = 0.75$.

The color index rarely goes above 1, except in pernicious
anæmia (see below). As a rule when the red cells are above the
normal the hæmoglobin rises equally, sometimes it lags behind
a little, but rarely if ever does it rise higher than the cells.

In most anæmias, as has been pointed out, the hæmoglobin
suffers markedly before any considerable loss of red cells takes
place. In other words, the corpuscles seem to get thin before
they die, and except in malaria, hemorrhage, and a few other
cases they are not destroyed while in the full vigor of health.[1]

The loss of hæmoglobin is loss of albumin, the chief constituent of the cells, and hence is usually loss of weight.

In general the changes in the hæmoglobin are best studied in
connection with changes in the count of red cells, and so far as
they have not already been mentioned will come in under the
various special diseases.

---

[1] This is of course not literal. There is no reason to suppose that good-
sized corpuscles get smaller. It is more likely that a smaller generation
is sent out by the blood-making organs.

FIBRIN.

The fibrin network to be seen in normal blood during coagulation (see page 54) is increased in a considerable number of conditions. Hayem has studied these minutely, and described several varieties of arrangement of fibrin fibres as characteristic of special diseases, that is, he studied fibrin qualitatively as well as quantitatively, and also as regards the rapidity of its formation.

The rate of fibrin formation is often not the same as the rate of coagulation. It is not parallel to the number of leucocytes or blood plates, at least not in all cases (malignant diseases, scurvy).

In a general way we expect increased fibrin in infectious and inflammatory diseases, but there are notable exceptions to this. The greater the exudation and the freer it is (in a cavity or on the surface) the thicker the fibrin network, while so-called interstitial inflammations or such conditions as parenchymatous nephritis show little increase in fibrin. The seat of the lesions has no considerable influence, except as it modifies the nature of the lesion. An abscess in one place has the same effect as an abscess elsewhere, provided it is equally free or equally confined, and of the same contents.

Tuberculosis does not increase fibrin if uncomplicated. Leucocytosis and fibrin behave alike in many respects, especially in relation to the vigor of resistance which the individual opposes to a given infection. When the individual is so weakened that he does not react well against the infection, the leucocytes and fibrin are but slightly increased, whereas in a vigorous individual the same infection would have markedly increased both fibrin and leucocytes. But neoplasms raise the count of leucocytes without changing the amount of fibrin.

In a general way fibrin increases and decreases as fever does, but often persists after fever is gone.

The most marked fibrin networks are seen in pneumonia, acute articular rheumatism, suppurative diseases, and in scurvy. In erysipelas it follows the leucocytes (increased in severe, not in mild cases). In the early days of grippe it is increased. The fever of hysteria or chlorosis shows no increase of fibrin and post-hemorrhagic anæmia with or without fever shows none.

Fibrin is diminished in pernicious anæmia, not increased in leukæmia, typhoid, malaria, malignant disease, non-suppurative diseases of liver, nephritis (except interstitial nephritis, where it may be increased), heart disease, purpura, hæmoglobinuria (sometimes decreased).

The most valuable point about the fibrin appears to be the absence of any increase in malignant disease, whereby a diagnosis between the affection and a suppuration may be helped. Otherwise the information given by it is chiefly confirmatory of impressions given by other features in blood examination.

LIPÆMIA.

The blood invariably contains small quantities of fat, especially during digestion (v. Jaksch [1]).

In the blood of persons suffering from a variety of diseases such as phthisis, diabetes mellitus, obesity, alcoholism, nephritis, and in some dyspnœic conditions, suppressed menses, pregnancy, icterus, typhus, malaria, mental disease, diseases of the heart and pancreas, as well as in health, fat is occasionally to be seen in considerable quantities. Grawitz [2] finds that if the blood is collected in a fine capillary tube and this is kept in a horizontal position for some time, fat rises to the surface like cream, and can be seen with an oil-immersion lens in the form of fine drops. Gumprecht [3] demonstrated it with osmic acid, which stains the fat drops black, and proved them to be fat by dissolving them in ether, xylol, etc.

Lipæmia has no special significance so far as is known, and is not characteristic of the diseases above mentioned. Its cause is unknown.

[In almost any preparation of the fresh blood fat drops are to be seen unless the patient's skin is washed with alcohol before puncturing. Even with these precautions a few drops may often be seen in healthy people's blood.]

[1] "Klin. Diagnostik," p. 75 (English translation).
[2] Loc. cit., p. 160.
[3] Deut. med. Woch., 1894, No. 39.

MELANÆMIA.

In malaria the occurrence of a black pigment in the leu-cocytes which have taken plasmodia into themselves, is gener-ally to be seen during and shortly after a paroxysm. Pigment free in the blood is only to be seen at the moment of seg-mentation among the new generation of parasites. The same condition has been observed in relapsing fever and in persons suffering from melanotic malignant tumors, the pigment being always in the white corpuscles. Presumably it must at some time be free in the plasma, but it is rarely if ever seen outside the cells.

In Addison's disease Tschirkoff [1] observed pigment in the leucocytes.

HEMORRHAGE.

Women can stand a greater hemorrhage and yet live than men can. Children, on the other hand, succumb to compara-tively slight hemorrhages (cf. Blood in Infancy, page 385). In-dividual differences make a great difference in the ability to survive hemorrhage, and no exact amount of blood can be stated as the maximum that any one can lose and yet survive.

Changes in the Blood Resulting from Hemorrhage.

The red cells and hæmoglobin of course suffer proportionally at first; later the hæmoglobin in the newly formed cells is always deficient (see below).

The striking point in the blood after hemorrhage is the evi-dence it gives us that even before the hemorrhage has ceased the other tissues begin to contribute fluid to make up the volume upon which life depends. The serum is markedly diluted by this fluid, but still serves to give the heart something to contract on and so prevents blood pressure from falling as fast as it otherwise would do. Were it not for such contributions from neighboring tissues the organism could sustain but slight hemorrhage without succumbing at once. We have then after hemorrhage a diluted or hydræmic blood, even though we do

[1] Zeit. f. klin. Med., vol. xix., 1891.

not assist the efforts of nature by contributing fluid by intra-venous or rectal injection. Behier reports a case due to trauma in which the count was only 688,000 per cubic millimetre.

Coagulation increases in rapidity the more blood is lost, so that after severe hemorrhage it takes place almost instantly.

BLOOD REGENERATION.

The regeneration of the blood after hemorrhage may be taken as typical of the same process in anæmia from other causes.

The length of time needed for full restoration to normal depends not merely on the (*a*) *amount* of blood lost, but also on the (*b*) age and nutrition of the patient as well as upon (*c*) the methods of *treatment* carried out and the existence of (*d*) other disease (typhoid, malignant disease, phthisis, etc.).

Allowing for these other conditions we may say that, other things being favorable, the loss of

I. Less than   1 per cent of the blood mass is made up in 2 to 5 days.
II. From   1 to 3   "   "   "   "   "   5 " 14 "
III.   "   3 " 4   "   "   "   "   "   14 " 30 "

The last amount means a very severe hemorrhage. Few surgical operations involve the loss of over three per cent, and after such accordingly we expect the blood to be normal again in two weeks, provided the individual is otherwise sound (see Malignant Disease, page 335).

Young, well-nourished persons are of course quicker in making up losses than the old and weak.

Blood Condition During Regeneration.

1. *Red Cells.*—(A) As previously mentioned, the hæmoglo-bin becomes relatively low as soon as the regenerative process is well established, and as recovery progresses the red cells are almost always normal in numbers for some time before the stat-ure, weight, and color of the individual cells is what it should be. A color index of 0.50–0.60 is not unusual—in short, what some call a "chlorotic" condition of the blood.

(B) Qualitative changes are those already described on page 72, namely: (*a*) Deformities in size and shape with an average diminution in size; (*b*) polychromatophilic cells; and (*c*) nucleated corpuscles. These latter are almost exclusively of the nor-moblast type, but an occasional megaloblast has been observed.

Blood Crises.—Von Noorden was the first to notice that in some cases nucleated corpuscles are to be found in the circulation in great numbers for a few hours only, the blood examination both before and after showing few or none at all. The name of "blood crisis" has been given to these sudden outpourings of nucleated red cells; they are to be observed during recovery from various forms of anæmia.

2. *White Cells.*—Immediately after a loss of blood we can usually find a decided *leucocytosis* despite the dilution of the blood (see above, Post-hemorrhagic Leucocytosis).

This leucocytosis is in no way different from those occurring from other causes. The percentage of polymorphonuclear cells is usually increased, and the eosinophiles often disappear. As pointed out by Stengel we may have a lymphocytosis after hemorrhage. A case of anæmia from bleeding piles, in which the red cells were 2,723,000 and the hæmoglobin 35 per cent, showed in a total leucocyte count of 4,200, 69 per cent of small lymphocytes and only 28 per cent of polymorphonuclear cells. Leucocytosis if present is rarely very high, seldom reaching over 30,000. It is not invariably present, or if present sometimes is of very short duration. Thus in a patient whose red cells were reduced to 3,200,000 by a profuse uterine hemorrhage the white cells counted next day were only 8,000; while in the next bed of the hospital was a woman crushed in a railroad accident whose red cells were 1,280,000, and the white cells 28,000, the usual state of things.

The leucocytes may be increased even by a *cerebral hemorrhage* which is not large enough considerably to affect the red cells in most cases. Ten apoplectic cases (with autopsy) observed at the Massachusetts Hospital showed such counts as the following:

1. Red cells 5,512,000, white cells 25,000, Hb. 85 per cent.
2. Red cells 5,560,000, white cells 15,600, Hb. 90 per cent.

Whether the leucocytes are here affected by any influence other than that of hemorrhage I do not know.

The effect of transfusion (intravenous saline solution) is apparently at first to increase the leucocytosis.

D——, a patient with traumatic rupture of the urethra, had

had severe hemorrhage for forty-eight hours before it was checked at 1 P.M., November 1st, 1895. At 4 P.M., his pulse being 165, the count showed: red cells, 3,304,000; white cells, 10,400. He was at once given a pint of sterilized normal salt solution by intravenous injection under the strictest asepsis. Ten minutes after the transfusion the leucocytes numbered 32,400. One hour later they were 24,700, and the red cells 3,632,000. Four hours later leucocytes, 31,900; red cells, 3,046,000. The later counts were as follows:

	Red cells.	White cells.
November 2d : good pulse	3,608,000	34,600
" 2d (5 P.M.) : good pulse	2,944,000	30,200
" 3d (4 P.M.) : good pulse	2,928,000	15,800
" 13th	3,360,000	16,600

A good recovery was made.

IMPORTANCE FOR SURGERY OF BLOOD COUNTING AFTER HEMORRHAGE.

Mikulicz, who as a surgeon should speak with authority and who always takes account of the condition of the blood in his cases, lays down (following Laker) the following rule: *Never operate on any case when the hæmoglobin is below thirty per cent.* The question of operating at once or waiting for recovery from "shock," is a very common one in the accident rooms of any hospital and is generally settled on general impressions of the patient's vigor. We know, say, that he has lost blood, but we have no way of ascertaining how much. If his "shock" is due to hemorrhage he may need transfusion; if it is due to cerebral concussion or compression, the transfusion will do more harm than good. The blood count can settle these questions, and could reveal much which is now obscure, if it were more frequently employed in surgical cases and a standard like that of Mikulicz worked out.

In cases of suspected ruptured tube in extra-uterine pregnancy, the question of whether the patient is suffering from internal concealed hemorrhage can be settled in many cases by the blood count, which will show a decided loss of red cells if

9

the hemorrhage is large, and thereby distinguish the condition from peritonitis, obstruction, or strangulated hernia, none of which affects the red cells. Any other concealed hemorrhage, as for instance from ruptured kidney or spleen or liver, may be indicated by the blood count when by other physical signs the diagnosis might be very difficult.

Summary.

The blood count is of importance after cases of supposed hemorrhage.

1. To ascertain whether such has taken place.
2. Its extent.
3. Whether operation is to be immediate or not.
4. Whether transfusion is indicated.
5. How soon the patient has got back enough blood to make operation worth while.

CHRONIC HEMORRHAGE.

Piles, uterine disease, hæmophilia, purpura, and other causes may produce a long-standing drain on the blood.

Some patients apparently can lose a little blood almost daily for years without acquiring any severe anæmia, and if the individual is otherwise sound and does not suffer from an underlying disease like phthisis, cancer, or nephritis, he can probably go on for a long time without showing any bad effects from the repeated small hemorrhages. *How* much he can stand we have no way of judging, for we cannot measure the amount of blood lost. When, however, such small repeated losses *do* produce an anæmia, regeneration is apt to be much slower than after a single large hemorrhage. The longer the drain has been going on the poorer the chance for recovery, and the slower the latter will be if it does take place.

Gain in body weight does not always mean gain in corpuscle substance as well (see Malignant Disease, page 335).

BOOK II.

SPECIAL PATHOLOGY OF THE BLOOD.

PART I.

DISEASES OF THE BLOOD.

CHAPTER I.

THE PRIMARY ANÆMIAS.

1. THE BLOOD IN PERNICIOUS ANÆMIA.

THE definition of the disease has been sufficiently explained before (see page 84) and we can proceed at once to the description of the blood.

1. Gross appearances.

(a) The drop as it emerges from the puncture is often excessively pale and watery, but not more so than may occasionally be seen in secondary anæmia or chlorosis. Sometimes it is not nearly so pale as in other cases with equally low counts, a fact which may be due to the increased color index sometimes present (see below). In one case (color index 1.2) I have seen the blood as red as normal.

Another appearance, which I have frequently observed in this and other anæmias, is an uneven, streaked color in the drop, as if the cells were unequally divided in the plasma.

(b) As striking as the color of the drop is its great fluidity; the rapidity with which it slips off the ear or finger often makes it difficult to suck it up in time. It is usually very slow in coagulating.

2. The fresh specimen in most cases shows no rouleaux formation, a diminution in blood plates and fibrin, and usually great variations in the size and shape of the corpuscles with a tendency to an oval shape and an increase in the average diameter. Not infrequently the deformed corpuscle shows active pseudoamœboid motions of its projecting points or of the cell as a whole. The great lack both of red and white cells is noticeable even in the fresh specimen.

Red Cells and Hæmoglobin.

(*a*) Quantitative changes (see Table I.). The average count of red cells in the sixty-eight cases of my table is about 1,200,000, which may be taken as the average count in patients seen at the stage of the disease at which they feel sick enough to seek medical advice.[1] We very rarely get an opportunity to examine the blood in the early stages of the disease, so that we have to judge of them chiefly from the evidence given during the remission so commonly observed. In the relapse following such a remission the blood count may fall from 5,000,000 to 1,000,000 in a period of from six weeks to six months. In the later stages of the disease 500,000 red cells per cubic millimetre is not rare, and if the diminution has been gradual, the patient may be up and about and able to do light work with a count no greater than this. I had an opportunity to observe such a case in the wards of Dr. F. C. Shattuck at the Massachusetts General Hospital five years ago, where for several weeks the blood count remained at or near 500,000, yet the patient was outdoors daily, read the papers, and seemed perfectly comfortable. Evidently it is not the anæmia itself which kills the patient.

The lowest count on record is that reported by Quincke— 143,000 per cubic millimetre.

TABLE I.

No.	(a) First Count.		(b) Highest Count.		(c) Lowest Count.		Total number of examinations.
	Red cells.	Per cent hæmoglobin.	Red cells.	Per cent hæmoglobin.	Red cells.	Per cent hæmoglobin.	
1	450,000	10	658,000	18	363,000	10	6
2	490,000	?	490,000	?	410,000	?	2
3	503,000	10	522,000	18	368,000	10	6
4	510,000	20	680,000	?	510,000	20	3
5	600,000	24	....	....	....	....	1
6	630,000	?	658,000	?	450,000	?	13
7	670,000	?	670,000	....	670,000	....	1
8	680,000	20	680,000	20	680,000	20	1
9	694,000	20	2,654,000	....	694,000	20	8
10	735,000	?	1,500,000	?	730,000	?	3
11	784,000	14	784,000	14	784,000	14	1
12	842,000	?	842,000	?	842,000	?	1
13	896,000	18	896,000	18	430,000	6	3

[1] Cf. Schaumann: Out of his 38 cases, 1 was over 2,000,000; 26 between 1,000,000 and 2,000,000; 11 below 1,000,000; average 1,290,000.

TABLE I.—(*Continued*).

No.	(a) First Count.		(b) Highest Count.		(c) Lowest Count.		Total number of examinations.
	Red cells.	Per cent hæmoglobin.	Red cells.	Per cent hæmoglobin.	Red cells.	Per cent hæmoglobin.	
14	896,000	17	3,800,000	70	608,000	15	20
15	962,000	15	1,028,080	15	962,000	15	3
16	963,000	38	....	....	....	....	1
17	984,000	28	....	....	....	....	3
18	988,000	?	....	....	....	....	1
19	992,593	34	1,080,000	?	992,593	34	2
20	1,018,000	20	....	....	....	....	1
21	1,096,400	12	1,096,400	13	624,000	13	4
22	1,064,000	23	1,430,000	25	1,064,000	23	5
23	1,060,524	35	....	....	....	....	1
24	1,092,000	25	1,150,000	39	893,000	....	5
25	1,111,000	?	1,111,000	?	756,000	?	3
26	1,113,000	18	2,820,000	?	1,038,000	?	8
27	1,126,000	?	1,126,000	?	1,100,000	?	2
28	1,137,000	· 20	1,137,000	20	550,000	15	4
29	1,140,000	20	1,140,000	20	622,160	25	3
30	1,150,000	?	2,802,000	....	1,150,000	....	16
31	1,150,000	30	....	....	....	....	1
32	1,176,000	29	....	....	....	....	1
33	1,200,000	15	....	....	....	....	1
34	1,226,284	25	4,450,000	65	762,000	?	12
35	1,270,000	16	2,700,000	30	....	....	2
36	1,280,000	24	1,328,000	29	664,000	22	16
37	1,288,000	?	1,910,000	?	1,288,000	....	3
38	1,289,000	32	1,628,000	34	1,121,000	34	5
39	1,296,000	25	1,296,000	25	1,248,000	25	3
40	1,300,000	28	1,300,000	28	970,000	30	2
41	1,336,000	28	1,336,000	28	956,000	20	3
42	1,344,000	23	1,344,000	23	758,000	17	3
43	1,364,000	35	....	....	....	....	1
44	1,493,000	32	1,500,000	?	....	....	2
45	1,498,000	20–30	....	....	....	....	1
46	1,500,000	35	3,700,000	53	1,460,000	30	8
47	1,516,000	35	1,916,000	35	1,516,000	35	3
48	1,582,000	20	4,760,000	52	1,624,000	30	12
49	1,583,000	20	1,768,000	40	1,500,000	20	4
50	1,600,000	25	4,032,000	80	1,288,000	23	10
51	1,627,000	?	....	....	....	....	1
52	1,632,000	28	1,632,000	28	1,180,000	30	7
53	1,755,000	20	1,755,000	20	1,117,000	20	2
54	1,768,000	?	2,458,000	?	1,768,000	?	6
55	1,800,000	28	2,868,000	41	1,508,000	31	5
56	1,800,000	25	....	....	....	....	1
57	1,800,000	30	1,800,000	30	1,768,000	22	3
58	1,819,000	34					
59	1,872,000	25	1,872,000	25	1,144,000	30	3
60	1,884,000	....	1,889,314	....	1,330,000	....	4
61	1,920,900	33	1,930,000	35	1,600,000	28	4
62	1,929,000	38	....	....	....	....	1

TABLE I.—(*Continued*).

No.	(a) First Count.		(b) Highest Count.		(c) Lowest Count.		Total number of examinations.
	Red cells.	Per cent hæmoglobin.	Red cells.	Per cent. hæmoglobin.	Red cells.	Per cent hæmoglobin.	
63	1,946,000	40	....	....	....	....	3
64	1,984,000	39	1,984,000	39	598,000	15	3
65	2,000,000	20	2,000,000	20	1,200,000	20	2
66	2,080,000	25	5,056,000	70	1,632,000	50 (?)	9
67	2.076,000	15	4,500,000	45	1,384,000	10	10
68	2,524,000	26	2,524,000	26	1,280,000	13	5
	Average = 1,200,000	26					293
							Average = 4+

The great but temporary improvements above alluded to,
followed by relapse, occur either with or without treatment.
In the course of a few months the count of red cells may rise

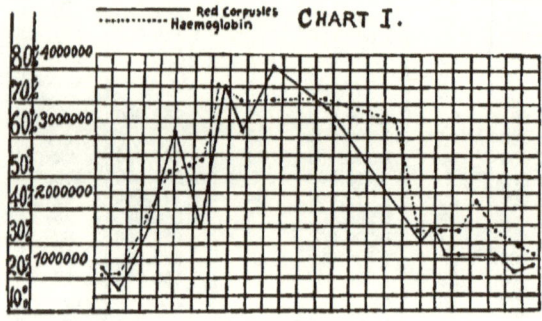

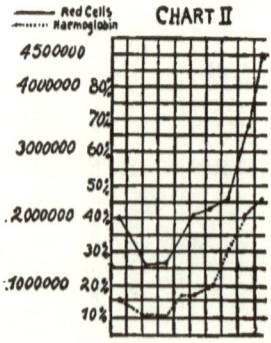

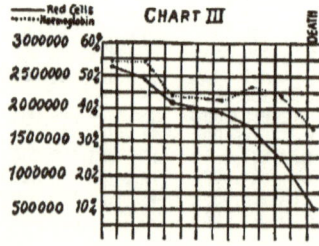

to normal, the nucleated corpuscles (see below) disappear, and the patient is apparently restored to health and goes to work with a laugh at the doctor. I have followed one case through five such relapses in a period of three years before the fatal issue came. Frequently the patient feels so well during one of these remissions that he goes to work and is lost sight of, and, under such conditions, the incautious are apt to report " cure."

The *accompanying charts* [1] show the three types usually met with; No. II. being, of course, only a fragment of a case similar to No. I., while the steady progression of No. III. may have been preceded by a rise from a former downfall, though no such history was obtained.

Looking over a considerable number of cases, one can hardly help being struck with the tendency of the count to remain near the figure 1,000,000. Cases rarely remain stationary at, say, 2,000,000, and often die without sinking below 1,000,000. It seems as if some self-applying mechanism tended to arrest the destruction of corpuscles at or near this point (see Table I.).

In counting the red cells some difficulty and error may result from the very small size of some of the cells. It is especially important that the diluting solution should be clean and freshly made, else without the aid of a stain it may be hard to distinguish the dwarf cells or microcytes from bits of extraneous substance.

Quantitative Changes.

White Corpuscles (see Table II.).—The rule is a very considerable diminution in the number of leucocytes. Thus of sixty cases which I have examined forty-two were under 5,000, the average of all being 3,800.

[I have excluded from this series counts made immediately after hemorrhages and counts in infants. The latter are very apt to show a leucocytosis in connection with *any* form of anæmia.]

As the disease progresses the leucocytes fall even more rapidly than the red cells, and counts as low as 500 white cells per cubic millimetre are not uncommon.

---

[1] The number of perpendicular lines represents the number of weeks.

Leucocytosis when present in the blood of adult cases is always due to some complication like hemorrhage or suppuration.

TABLE II.—WHITE CELLS—FIRST EXAMINATION.

No.	White cells.	No.	White cells.	No.	White cells.
1.........	400	21	2,900	41	4,828
2.........	500	22	3,000	42	4,900
3.........	800	23	3,000	43	5,000
4.........	1,000	24	3,200	44	5,200
5.........	1,000	25	3,200	45	5,300
6.........	1,000	26	3,300	46	5,500
7.........	1,500	27	3,400	47	5,600
8.........	1,600	28	3,500	48	6,000
9.........	1,800	29	3,600	49	6,000
10.........	2,000	30	3,700	50	6,000
11.........	2,000	31	3,704	51	6,400
12.........	2,000	32	4,000	52	6,500
13.........	2,000	33	4,000	53	7,000
14.........	2,000	34	4,000	54	7,200
15.........	2,300	35	4,000	55	7,500
16.........	2,600	36	4,200	56	7,600
17.........	2,800	37	4,300	57	9,000
18.........	2,800	38	4,400	58	9,600
19.........	2,800	39	4,500	59	10,000
20.........	2,800	40	4,720	60	10,100

Average = 3,800 +

As mentioned above, the blood plates and fibrin are much diminished.

In four cases in which Dr. Lindström, of Boston, was kind enough to give massage, we were unable to see the slightest gain either in corpuscles or hæmoglobin, such as can be produced temporarily in most healthy persons. The observations of J. Mitchell on this point we were unable to confirm.

Hæmoglobin.

The great majority of cases of pernicious anæmia have a relatively high percentage of hæmoglobin (*e.g.*, 1,000,000 red cells and 35 per cent. of hæmoglobin, or a color index of 1.75). In some cases this is not so, and in others we cannot tell whether it is so or not, owing to the unreliability of the v. Fleischl instrument when used for very low hæmoglobin percentages.

Of the 50 cases in the series on page 134, in which the hæmoglobin was tested, a color index of over 1 was apparently present in 29, or 58 per cent, and a color index of less than 1 in 21, or 42 per cent, of the cases.   How many of these hæmoglobin estimations may have been wrong I cannot say.

From the frequency with which we find the corpuscles well stained and larger than normal in pernicious anæmia (see below), we should expect that the hæmoglobin *would* be relatively high, and in a larger percentage of cases than the v. Fleischl instrument indicated.

An increased color index is probably a bad prognostic sign. In the remissions of the disease when the cells are increasing fast, the hæmoglobin lags behind and the color index is *low*. As the relapse follows, the color index in many cases progressively increases.   Cases *whose color index is low* and in which the average diameter of the red cells is normal *are apt to be gaining at that time*, while those with high color index are apt to be losing at that time.

The average color index in the cases in which the hæmoglobin and red cells were both tested was 1.04, the average percentage of hæmoglobin being 26 and of corpuscles 24 (=1,200,000).

QUALITATIVE CHANGES.

1. *Red Corpuscles.*

(a) *Increase in the average diameter* of the cells is a very constant and striking feature of the stained specimens in this disease.   In no other disease do so large cells or so many of them occur.

Out of forty-eight cases in which I have looked for this point, forty-one showed the increase, as far as could be judged without actually measuring any large number of cells.   This does not mean that every cell is larger than normal, but that those larger than normal outnumber those undersized; the "macrocytes" are more numerous than the "microcytes."   Occasionally we see cells over 20 μ in diameter, some with nuclei, some without.

(b) *Deformities in Shape.*—The eye soon gets used to the shapes assumed by the necrobiotic corpuscles and learns to distinguish them from the distortions due to technique or to crena-

tion.   Most of them fall under one or another of the types shown
in Plate IV.   Litten has laid particular stress on the horseshoe
forms, and thinks them peculiar to pernicious anæmia.   The
battledore and sausage-shaped forms are very common.   In
one case I found all the red cells of the latter shape, so that they
looked at first sight like a lot of gigantic bacilli.   That this appearance was not due to the technique (as I had at first supposed) is probable from the fact that the rod-shaped cells did
not point all in one direction as they would have done if pulled
out of shape by the process of spreading (see Fig. 30).   This ap-

Fig. 30.—Elongated or Oval Corpuscles in Pernicious Anæmia, resembling the blood of
lower animals.

pearance is only an exaggeration of what may be seen in most
severe anæmias, namely, a tendency toward an oval shape like
that of amphibian corpuscles.   This is usually true of those
cells (in pernicious cases) which are not more violently deformed.

Occasionally we see cases with no considerable deformities
whatever in the red cells.   In nine cases out of sixty in which

¹Some writers advise the use of less heat than usual in dealing with
cover-glass specimens of pernicious anæmia.   I have not found this so,
and heat as usual up to 150° C. and then stop.

this point was observed, little or no deformity was noted. I cannot make out that such cases have any better or worse prognosis than others. I have never seen cases whose red cells were all *undersized*, but a normal average diameter was present in somewhat under one-quarter of the cases in which I have looked out for this point.

(c) *Staining Properties of the Red Cells.*—The white spots or streaks described by Maragliano, Hayem, and others are very often seen in the red cells of pernicious anæmia despite good technique. Some corpuscles are so pale in the centre that we see only the narrow ring of stained protoplasm at the periphery, a mere shell. Others are swollen up so as to show no sign of central biconcavity, and stain deeply and evenly all over.

More common than in any other form of anæmia are the polychromatophilic red corpuscles (see Plate IV.) which with the Ehrlich-Biondi mixture stain brownish, purple, or gray, either as a whole or in parts. In the nucleated red cells the protoplasm is very apt to show this change, so that it is often difficult to distinguish them from lymphocytes. In difficult cases we have sometimes to fall back upon the appearances of the edge or periphery, which in most red corpuscles shows some thin place or crinkle characteristic of a *flat* cell, while the lymphocyte gives us the more solid-looking outline of the *spherical* cell.

All these microchemical changes can be better brought out with hæmatoxylon-eosin or eosin-methyl-blue stains, but all that is needed for clinical purposes can be made out with the ordinary Ehrlich-Biondi mixture.

Nucleated Red Corpuscles.

Nothing further needs to be said in description of these forms (see above, pages 89-94). We have no *exact* method of estimating the number of nucleated cells either in relation to the whole number of red cells or in a cubic millimetre. All we can do is to note the number seen in *such* an area of a cover-glass specimen as is covered while counting a given number of white cells, say 1,000. Knowing the ratio of red to white corpuscles, we can calculate from this number of nucleated red cells their approximate relation to the whole number of red cells.

Thus if the ratio of white to red be 1:1000 (1,000,000 red and 1,000 white) and we have seen two nucleated red corpuscles while making a differential count of 1,000 white cells, the total number of red cells passed over must be approximately 1,000,-000 and the number of nucleated corpuscles about two in 1,000,-000 red cells or two in a cubic millimetre. Of course where leucocytosis is present and the ratio is raised—say to 1:150 (10,000 white and 1,500,000 red)—finding two nucleated red cells while counting 1,000 white would mean that there were two nucleated cells in every 150,000 non-nucleated, or twenty in a cubic millimetre (or in 1,500,000 non-nucleated cells).

Such calculations are inaccurate because we are never sure that the red cells and white cells are distributed in the dried specimen exactly as they are in the blood. Part of the leucocytes may be accumulated at the edges of the cover-glass so that the ratio in the middle may be different from that in the circulating blood.

Nevertheless we can get some idea of how plentiful the nucleated corpuscles are, and as their significance in prognosis depends far more on their *kind* than on their *number*, greater accuracy as to the latter is not at present important. For instances, two megaloblasts per cubic millimetre mean a worse prognosis than twenty normoblasts, provided there are no other kinds present in either case. It is the *ratio* of megaloblasts to normoblasts and not the absolute number of each, that is of importance.

In all of the sixty cases of pernicious anæmia in which I have examined the blood, the number of megaloblasts has exceeded the number of normoblasts, and as the cases grew worse the megaloblasts grew relatively more numerous (often absolutely as well). Further, in several hundred cases of severe secondary anæmia I have never yet seen the number of megaloblasts exceed the number of normoblasts.

The range of variation in the number of nucleated cells present has extended in my series from 6 per cubic millimetre to 7,100 per cubic millimetre (see Table III.). The calculation can be made by using the following formula.

Let n = the number of white cells counted (by differential count).
" m =   "   "   nucleated red cells seen while counting these.
" p =   "   "   white cells per cubic millimetre (Thoma-Zeiss).

$p \times \dfrac{m}{n} = x =$ number of nucleated red cells per cubic millimetre.

The search for nucleated corpuscles in pernicious anæmia

is sometimes the most laborious undertaking in all blood examination, but it is also one of the most important. We may search two or three hours before finding one nucleated corpuscle, but on that corpuscle may hang the character of our prognosis. If it be a megaloblast and no other nucleated red corpuscles are seen, the prognosis is bad, and it is important that we should know it. This is particularly true when the case is seen during a remission, for under these conditions we might never suspect a case of pernicious anæmia but for the presence of megaloblasts. They are not always difficult to find; indeed, in one of my cases they were nearly as numerous as the white cells, but, as a rule, we do not get off with less than two hours' work.

The following table (Table III.) shows the number of nucleated corpuscles per cubic millimetre in thirty of the cases examined by the writer.

TABLE III.—NUMBER OF NUCLEATED RED CELLS PER CUBIC MILLIMETRE IN THIRTY CASES OF PERNICIOUS ANÆMIA.

Case Number.	Total nucleated red cells.	Megaloblasts.	Normoblasts.	Microblasts.
1...............	7,100	5,300	1,325	475
2...............	6,468	3,476	924	2,068
3...............	854	574	266	14
4...............	277	277	0	0
5...............	240	160	80	
6...............	229	123	106	
7...............	208	130	78	
8...............	200	134	66	
9...............	117	103	14	
10...............	116	80	36	
11...............	114	95	19	
12...............	112	96	16	
13...............	96	96	0	
14...............	96	84	12	
15...............	92	59	33	
16...............	46	26	20	
17...............	45	36	9	
18...............	39	33	6	
19...............	35	32	3	
20	28	26	2	
21...............	28	21	7	
22...............	28	28	0	
23...............	18	12	6	
24...............	14	14	0	
25...............	11	11	0	
26...............	11	10	1	
27...............	11	9	2	
28...............	9	6	3	
29...............	8	7	1	
30...............	3	2	1	

White Corpuscles.

Qualitative Changes.—Unless the cover-glasses are spread unusually thick, it may take a long time to find enough leu-

TABLE IV.—PERCENTAGES OF LEUCOCYTES IN PERNICIOUS ANÆMIA.

LYMPHOCYTES, LARGE AND SMALL.		EOSINOPHILES.		Number of counts.
No.	Per cent.	No.	Per cent.	
1............	79.	1...........	9.	1
2.................	77.	2...........	6.2	1
3................	71.	3...........	6.	1
4............·.....	61.6	4...........	4.7	2
5................	58.	5...........	4.6	2
6................	57.6	6...........	4.5	3
7................	57.2	7...........	4.4	1
8................	57.	8...........	4.3	1
9................	56.9	9...........	4.	1
10................	56.	10...........	4.	5
11................	53.9	11...........	4.	1
12................	53.8	12...........	3.7	2
13................	51.5	13...........	3.5	1
14................	49.5	14...........	3.4	2
15................	49.4	15...........	3.4	1
16.....	47.9	16...........	3.1	1
17................	47.9	17...........	3.	3
18................	47.	18...........	2.8	2
19................	46.	19...........	2.7	2
20................	45.9	20...........	2.6	1
21................	45.5	21...........	2.6	3
22................	44.7	22...........	2.6	2
23................	43.7	23...........	2.6	1
24................	42.2	24...	2.	1
25................	41.	25...........	2.	1
26................	40.8	26...........	2.	2
27................	40.5	27...........	1.6	1
28................	39.	28...........	1.6	1
29................	38.	29...........	1.5	5
30................	38.	30...........	1.5	2
31................	37.8	31...........	1.5	1
32................	36.1	32...........	1.5	1
33................	35.7	33...........	1.4	1
34................	35.6	34...........	1.2	3
35................	35.6	35...........	1.2	1
36................	34.	36...........	1.2	1

cocytes for an accurate differential count, so great is the leuco-penia in many cases. It is worth while, therefore, to spread some cover-glasses more thickly than would be advisable if we had only the red cells to examine. Such preparations should be dried at once by artificial heat.

Lymphocytosis is the chief feature (see Table IV.).

TABLE IV.—PERCENTAGE OF LEUCOCYTES IN PERNICIOUS ANÆMIA
(Continued).

LYMPHOCYTES, LARGE AND SMALL.		EOSINOPHILES.		Number of counts.
No.	Per cent.	No.	Per cent.	
37.	33.6	37.	1.	1
38.	33.1	38.	1.	2
39.	33.	39.	1.	1
40.	33.	40.	.8	1
41.	31.8	41.	.8	1
42.	29.4	42.	.8	1
43.	28.7	43.	.7	1
44.	28.4	44.	.6	1
45.	27.3	45.	.5	1
46.	27.2	46.	?	1
47.	26.5	47.	.3	1
48.	24.2	48.	.2	2
49.	22.	49.	.0	1
50.	21.2	50	.0	1
51.	19.8	51.	.0	1
52.	16.	52.	.0	

In 52 cases examined by myself the lymphocytes (large and small) averaged 45.4 per cent. About nine-tenths of these were small forms. As the fatal termination approaches, the percentage of lymphocytes rises. An extreme case of this change has already been recorded on page 90. Two other cases showed respectively 71 and 79 per cent of lymphocytes a few days before death. The polymorphonuclear cells suffer proportionately as a rule. On the other hand, Ewing has observed a marked rise in the percentage of the poly-nuclear cells near death, although autopsy revealed no complication.

Eosinophiles are occasionally increased, 9 per cent being present in one of my cases, 6.6 per cent in another. The average of 78 examinations in my 52 cases is 2.7 per cent.

Small percentages of *myelocytes* are the rule. They are present in 42 of my 52 cases. The following table shows the percentages:

10

TABLE V.

No.	Percentage of myelocytes.	No.	Percentage of myelocytes.	No.	Percentage of myelocytes.
1........	9.2	19........	1.8	37	0.6
2........	8.8	20........	1.5	38	.6
3	8.	21........	1.5	39	.5
4........	6.3	22........	1.5	40	.4
5........	6.	23........	1.4	41	.3
6........	4.6	24........	1.2	42	.2
7........	4.	25........	1.	43	.0
8........	4.	26........	1.	44	.0
9........	3.6	27........	1.	45	.0
10...ʌ.....	3.4	28.	1.	46	.0
11........	3.	29........	1.	47	.0
12........	3.	30........	.8	48	.0
13........	2.7	31........	.8	49	.0
14........	2.5	32.	.8	50	.0
15........	2.2	33........	.6	51	.0
16........	2.2	34........	.6	52	.0
17........	2.2	35........	.6	Average = 2 per cent.	
18........	2.0	36........	.6		

As has been explained above (page 121), the myelocyte is found in a great variety of affections, although very sparingly in most, but, so far as my observations go, its presence is more constant and the percentages run higher in pernicious anæmia than in any other disease except leukæmia. I am speaking now of percentages. With a leucopenia such as is usually present in pernicious anæmia, 2 per cent of myelocytes means absolutely a very small number per cubic millimetre.

Taking 3,800 leucocytes per cubic millimetre as the average for pernicious anæmia (see above, page 137) 2 per cent of myelocytes amounts to only 76 per cubic millimetre. In leukæmia the absolute number of myelocytes is seldom under 150,000 per cubic millimetre. '

The more important characteristics of the blood of pernicious anæmia are as follows:

1: *Red cells about 1,000,000 per cubic millimetre.*

2. *White cells much diminished.*

3. Hæmoglobin variable, *sometimes increased* relatively (= high-color index).

4. Deformities in size and shape of red cells in many cases.

5. *Increase in average diameter of red cells.*

6. Polychromatophilic red cells.

7. *Megaloblasts more numerous than normoblasts.*
8. Lymphocytosis.
9. Small percentage of myelocytes.

The items italicized are the most important and characteristic.

Diagnostic Value.

1: *Pernicious anæmia and chlorosis* may be indistinguishable without the examination of the blood. The pallor of the two diseases is not always different either in degree or in kind, and the symptoms and physical signs may be identical.

The differential diagnosis is easily made by the blood. The red cells rarely reach as low as 2,000,000 in chlorosis and the number and degree of degenerative changes are less than in pernicious anæmia. Megaloblasts have been seen in chlorosis (Hammerschlag) but have never constituted a majority of the nucleated red cells present. In the great majority of cases the pallor and other signs and symptoms of chlorosis are due to lack of hæmoglobin per corpuscle (for the corpuscles are not only pale but very small-sized), and not to a lack of corpuscles. The high-color index and large size of the scanty cells in pernicious anæmia constrast strongly with this.

The white cells are about the same in both diseases, though usually fewer in pernicious anæmia. Lymphocytosis is common to both diseases. Myelocytes are occasionally found in chlorosis, but much less commonly than in pernicious anæmia.

2. *Pernicious Anæmia and the Anæmia of Malignant Disease.* —Not long ago I examined the blood of a gentleman who had gradually and without assignable cause acquired a "lemon-yellow" pallor, without loss of flesh, vomiting, pain, or any localizing sign or symptom. The diagnosis of pernicious anæmia had been made. To my great surprise I found over 4,000,000 red cells, with only 38 per cent of haemoglobin, and 18,780 white cells, 86 per cent of which were polymorphonuclear neutrophiles. One normoblast was seen. Fibrin was not increased. · The anæmia was evidently secondary, and the autopsy ten months later showed cancer of the stomach.

Malignant disease may bring down the count of red cells to 1,000,000 or lower, but *in such cases* leucocytosis is usually present. As will be seen in the chapter on malignant disease,

leucocytosis is by no means invariable in the anæmia of cancerous growth, but *in those cases* which cause such an anæmia
as to resemble the counts of pernicious anæmia, leucocytosis is
the rule. This in itself is usually sufficient to exclude uncomplicated pernicious anæmia. Where an increase in the whole
number of leucocytes is not present in malignant disease,
there is often an increased percentage of polymorphonuclear
cells, contrasting strongly with the increased percentage of lymphocytes in pernicious anæmia. Normoblasts and not megaloblasts are the rule in malignant disease. If megaloblasts are
present they are in the minority, while in pernicious anæmia
they are in the majority. The average size and staining power
of the red cells is increased in most cases of pernicious anæmia
and decreased in most cases of malignant disease.

3. *Pernicious Anæmia and other Secondary Anæmias.*—Most
secondary anæmias which are severe enough to reduce the count
of red cells below 2,000,000 follow the type of malignant disease and show leucocytosis. The great pallor and dyspnœa
seen in connection with some cases of *tuberculosis* and *nephritis*
rarely mean a low count of red cells, but simply a loss of
hæmoglobin. I remember two cases in adjacent beds at the
Massachusetts General Hospital, both with extreme yellow pallor without emaciation; one had 1,020,000 and the other 4,100,-
000 red cells, the hæmoglobin in each being about thirty per
cent. The first was pernicious anæmia, the second nephritis.

Purpura, typhoid, lead poisoning, chronic malaria, and other
diseases may reduce the red cells to a point as low as that seen
in early stages of pernicious anæmia and may *not be accompanied by leucocytosis;* but the absence of changes most characteristic of the latter disease (a majority of megaloblasts, increased diameter and color index in the red cells) serves to make
the diagnosis clear.[1]

4. *Pernicious Anæmia and Leukæmia.*—Occasionally in infants these two diseases seem to approach very near each other
and are difficult to distinguish. In infancy, as is well known,
any anæmia (primary or secondary) is apt to be accompanied by

[1] Another point of difference emphasized by Grawitz is that the plasma
of pernicious anæmia has a relatively larger amount of solids than that of
anæmia secondary to the above diseases. This is hardly a clinically applicable test, but is said to be a valuable one.

leucocytosis and an enlarged spleen. Further leukæmia, which in adults usually causes a relatively slight anæmia, affects the red cells much more strongly in infancy, and may reduce them to a number decidedly suggestive of pernicious anæmia. Therefore in both diseases we may have enlarged spleen, great anæmia, and leucocytosis.

The one characteristic point of leukæmic blood—the abundance of myelocytes—usually enables us to distinguish the two diseases, for although present in both diseases the myelocyte is much more plentiful in leukæmia. Unfortunately we have no way of fixing just *how* numerous myelocytes must be in order to constitute leukæmia. It is only in infancy and very rarely then that this difficulty arises, but at that period I am inclined to believe that we sometimes see conditions intermediate between the two diseases, indicating the ultimate identity of the two. Their numerous clinical resemblances cannot here be discussed. (For further comment on this point see page 395.)

PROGNOSTIC VALUE OF THE BLOOD IN PERNICIOUS ANÆMIA.

The prognosis is always very bad, but the following scheme indicates the presence of a severe or of a mild type:

1. *Severe (rapidly fatal).*	2. *Less Severe (slower course).*
(*a*) Extreme progressive anæmia.	(*a*) Remissions.
	(*b*) Normal or low-color index.
(*b*) High-color index.	(*c*) Normal-sized or small cells.
(*c*) Increase in size of red cells.	(*d*) No degenerative change.
(*d*) Degenerative changes.	(*e*) Numerous normoblasts.
(*e*) Numerous megaloblasts.	(*f*) Few megaloblasts.
(*f*) Few or no normoblasts.	(*g*) Normal percentage of poly-
(*g*) Lymphocytosis.	morphonuclear cells.

It has been thought by some observers that the absence or great scantiness of nucleated corpuscles indicated lack of any effort at regeneration on the part of the blood-making functions and hence a peculiarly malignant type of the disease. I have never seen cases in which no nucleated corpuscles were present, but their scantiness has seemed to me as a rule to be associated with a more *slowly* fatal type of the disease.

No significance has seemed to me to attach to the presence of larger or smaller percentages of eosinophiles.

	Pernicious anæmia.	Chlorosis.	Secondary anæmia.	Leukæmia in infancy.
Red cells	About 1,000,000	Rarely under 2,-000,000.	May be 1,000,000 or less.	May be under 2,000,000.
White cells....	Usually decreased.	Usually normal....	Usually increased.	Usually more increased than in any other disease.
Hæmoglobin ..	Often relatively high.	Always relatively low.	Relatively low...	Relatively low.
Megaloblasts..	Constitute the majority of the nucleated red cells.	Rare.............	Rare; never more numerous than normoblasts.	Common.
Normoblasts ..	Less numerous than the megaloblasts.	Occasional; always more numerous than megaloblasts.	Common	Common.
Size of red cells	Increased..........	Diminished..	Various; not increased.	Various; not increased.
Lymphocytes..	Increased..........	Increased	Usually diminished.	Usually increased.
Polymorphonuclear cells.	Decreased	Decreased........	Usually increased.	Usually diminished.
Myelocytes....	Common.....	Rare..............	Rare	Usually more numerous than in other diseases.

To illustrate the different size of the cells in chlorosis and pernicious anæmia I have had photographs taken of the blood of a case of two of these diseases and of normal blood, *all on precisely the same scale.* See Figs. 31, 32, 33.

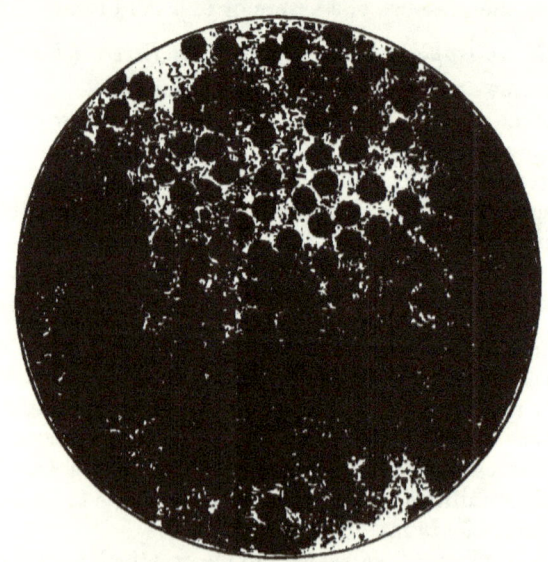

Fɪɢ. 31.—Normal Blood. Magnified 350 diameters.

Fig. 32.—Pernicious Anæmia. Magnified 350 diameters. Note the relatively large size and well-stained centres of the cells.

Fig. 33.—Chlorosis. Magnified 350 diameters. Note small size and pale centres.

2. THE BLOOD IN CHLOROSIS.

This has been already described for the most part under the heading of Secondary Anæmia. In many cases the two are indistinguishable by the blood examination alone, the changes consisting simply in the presence of light, small-sized, pale, more or less deformed red cells whose number may or may not be decreased, according to the severity of the case. Leucocytosis is rarely if ever present in uncomplicated chlorosis, but is often absent in secondary anæmia. Normoblasts may be present in both. The chief points of distinction are:

(a) The red cells are more apt to be uniformly undersized and under-colored in chlorosis, while in secondary anæmia we more often find normal cells among the diseased ones.

(b) The color index may be lower in chlorosis than is common in secondary anæmia, and this lowering is more constant in chlorosis.

(c) Lymphocytosis, which is very common in chlorosis, is not so common in secondary anæmia.

(d) Nucleated corpuscles are less common in chlorosis than in anæmia secondary to malignant disease.

(e) Coagulation is rapid, in contrast with the very slow clotting of pernicious anæmia and of many secondary anæmias. Yet fibrin is not increased.

The Blood in Gross.

The pallor of the drop is sometimes excessive, fully as great as in pernicious anæmia, and the liquid is very fluid and thin. Yet it coagulates very rapidly and our technique must be prompt.

RED CELLS AND HÆMOGLOBIN.

Quantitative Changes.

Hayem has recorded cases whose count was as low as 1,662,-000 and even 937,360 per cubic millimetre. Such figures are certainly rare in this country, and the striking fact is usually the *slight* numerical loss of red cells, considering the extreme pallor of the patients.

The lowest count in the Massachusetts Hospital series was 1,932,000, and in W. S. Thayer's 63 cases 1,953,000. The accompanying tables, from the Massachusetts Hospital records, show the range of red cells and hæmoglobin in 109 cases as counted when the patients first came under observation. The highest counts (7,100,000 and 5,884,000) are undoubtedly due to some temporary stasis or concentration of the blood.

The average of the 109 cases, 4,112,000 red cells per cubic millimetre, is remarkable in so nearly coinciding with Thayer's [1] series above referred to, the average of which is 4,096,544. The average hæmoglobin percentage of this series, 41.2 per cent, is also very close to Thayer's (42.3 per cent). This gives us on the average a reduction of the corpuscle substance to one-half the normal, or to the equivalent of 2,250,000 healthy red cells; 61 of the 109 cases have 4,000,000 or more red cells. These figures do not agree with those collected by v. Limbeck, in which only 99 out of 247 are over 4,000,000. But this probably means simply that in this country the patients seek medical advice before their disease has advanced very far, while in Germany they wait longer before resorting to a hospital. For, as above explained, in all anæmias the individual corpuscles suffer in quality first and only after some time begin to decline in number. This is especially the case in chlorosis, although by no means peculiar to that disease.

The color index is invariably low, as seen in the table, although it is rare to see it fall below .30. In only four cases of the present series did it go below that figure, the average being about .50.

v. Noorden [2] found that the color index was especially apt to be low in first attacks and less often in the recurrent or habitual cases, but Romberg [3] in a study of one hundred and seventeen cases has not found this true, and I agree with Romberg. One of the lowest color indexes in my series was in a woman over fifty who had a truly habitual chlorosis.

[1] See Osler's article on Chlorosis in the "American Text-Book of Medicine," vol. ii., 1894.
[2] Chlorosis: Wien, 1897 (Hölder).
[3] Berl. klin. Woch., June 28th, 1897.

TABLE VI.—CHLOROSIS.

Red Cells.	Cases.
Between 7,000,000 and 8,000,000............	1
" 6,000,000 " 7,000,000............	1
" 5,000,000 " 6,000,000............	17
" 4,000,000 " 5,000,000............	42
" 3,000,000 " 4,000,000............	33
" 2,000,000 " 3,000,000............	14
" 1,000,000 " 2,000,000............	1

Average of these 109 cases = 4,112,000

White Cells.	Cases.	White Cells.	Cases.
Between 15,000 and 14,000.....	2	Between 7,000 and 6,000.....	19
" 14,000 " 13,000.....	1	" 6,000 " 5,000.....	11
" 13,000 " 12,000.....	3	" 5,000 " 4,000.....	9
" 12,000 " 11,000.....	5	" 4,000 " 3,000.....	7
" 11,000 " 10,000.....	9	" 3,000 " 2,000.....	1
" 10,000 " 9,000.....	6	" 2,000 " 1,000.....	1
" 9,000 " 8,000.....	7		
" 8,000 " 7,000.....	23		104

Average, 7,400.

PER CENT OF HÆMOGLOBIN IN CHLOROSIS.

Between 10 and 19 =	7 cases.		
" 20 " 29 = 13	"		
" 30 " 39 = 28	"		
" 40 " 49 = 25	"		
" 50 " 59 = 24	"		
" 60 " 69 = 7	"		
" 70 " 79 = 1	"		

105

Average, 41 per cent.

The striking contrast is with pernicious anæmia, rather than with secondary anæmia. In the former the color index, as above mentioned, averaged 1.04 in 68 cases. In secondary anæmia it is almost always below 1, but does not *average* so low as in chlorosis, although in individual cases it may be very low.

For example, Osterspey quotes a case of gastric cancer with a blood count of 4,230,000 red cells, and only 22 per cent of hæmoglobin; a color index of .26.

Red Cells (Continued).

Qualitative Changes.

(a) The stained specimen shows a greater or less degree of *pallor of the corpuscle centres* corresponding so accurately to the diminution in hæmoglobin that a practised observer can tell approximately how low it is simply from the stained specimen. The pallor, however, is to be taken in connection with the *size* of the cells, for the diminution in hæmoglobin is not due simply to a bleaching out of the cells, but to their loss of size.   Hence,

(b) The *diminution in the average diameter* of the cells is a very important feature.   Both in this respect and as regards the bleaching of individual cells, many cases contrast with most secondary anæmias, in that a large proportion of the cells are affected alike, *i.e*, are small and pale, while in secondary anæmia there are apt to be well-stained and good-sized or oversized cells in every field.   These last occur also in chlorosis, but less frequently as a rule.   Hence the usually lower color index of chlorosis.   In certain cases this distinction does not hold and the two conditions are identical in so far as the size and color of the red cells are concerned.   It is to the white cells that we must look for help in differential diagnosis.

(c) *Deformities in size and shape* are very common in all advanced cases, but often absent in mild or moderate ones.   They present no special peculiarities except that macrocytes are relatively rare and microcytes relatively common.   In the severest cases, however, the macrocytes begin to get more numerous and we approach the picture of pernicious anæmia.

(d) *Degenerative changes* (Maragliano, see page 88) are not common but are occasionally present in severe cases.

(e) *Nucleated red corpuscles* are *very* scanty even in advanced cases.   Hayem never saw any, but most observers find them in small numbers after long search.   They are almost always of the normoblast type, but megaloblasts have also been found.

The scantiness of nucleated red cells is a point of contrast with the anæmia secondary to malignant disease, in which even in mildly anæmic states we readily find nucleated corpuscles, while in chlorosis, even in severe cases, a long search may show very few or even none at all.

Specific Gravity.

Chlorosis is usually agreed to be one of the diseases in which specific gravity and hæmoglobin run parallel, and as the inaccuracies and inconveniences of the v. Fleischl instrument are so great, it seems to the writer better to follow the specific gravity rather than the hæmoglobin. The tables on page 42 (Part I.) show how the inference from density to coloring matter can be made. A specific gravity of 1030 is not very rare.

WHITE CELLS.

A. Quantitative Changes.

Leucocytosis is absent in uncomplicated cases. In the series in Table VI. the occasional leucocytosis may be due to digestive or to a variety of other influences (uterine troubles, etc.), which could not be excluded.

The average in Thayer's 63 cases was 8,467; in the present series (see Table VI.) it is 7,485.

As in pernicious anæmia, the worst cases are apt to have leucopenia, and as improvement progresses the white rise even faster than the red corpuscles.

Thus in Romberg's careful study of 117 cases, 24 cases whose hæmoglobin was under 40 per cent had an average of 6,350 leucocytes per cubic millimetre, while 52 cases whose hæmoglobin averaged 60 per cent had an average of 9,250 leucocytes. He found the average in healthy girls of the same age 9,068 white cells per cubic millimetre.

The absence of leucocytosis is the most important point in ·distinguishing chlorosis from secondary anæmia due to cancer, suppuration, etc.

B. Qualitative Changes.

Lymphocytosis is usually present, as in pernicious anæmia, wherever the disease is well marked, and sometimes even in mild cases. Thus Rieder found in 12 cases an average of 33 per cent of lymphocytes, the highest percentages being 53.7, 43.5, and 41.7. Either the small or the large lymphocytes may predominate. In my own experience it has usually been the small forms.

The neutrophiles suffer proportionally, their low percentage contrasting often with that of secondary anæmia associated with leucocytosis. Eosinophiles are occasionally increased. In Rieder's 12 cases the average percentage was 3.5, the highest percentages being 9.6 and 7 per cent.

Myelocytes are rare but have occasionally been observed in small numbers.

Regeneration of the Blood.

As the patients begin to mend under the influence of treatment, the blood changes are just the reverse of those seen during the development of the disease. First the corpuscles gain in numbers, the hæmoglobin still remaining low; later and much more slowly the coloring matter, size, and weight of the cells are renewed. It seems as if the new-formed cells were of light weight and had to be replaced gradually by cells of normal stature. The nucleated corpuscles and deformities disappear and the leucocytes shoot up often a little above the normal.

Blood Plates.

Usually considerably increased.

Chlorosis without Known Blood Changes.

Romberg quotes the following facts: Three girls, nineteen, twenty, and twenty-five years of age, came to him with typical symptoms of chlorosis. Their blood counts showed:

I. Red cells, 5,246,000; Hb., 80 per cent.
II. "   "   5,376,000; "   83   "
III. "   "   4,408,000; "   87   "

All improved markedly under iron treatment.

I mention this because I have seen several similar cases and have heard of others from colleagues.

Summary.

1. Blood as a whole: Very pale in marked cases, very fluid, but coagulates rapidly. Fibrin not increased. Specific gravity usually low, running parallel with the hæmoglobin.

2. Red cells: Average 4,000,000 when patient is first seen,

very rarely go below 1,000,000. The majority of them are *small-sized, pale,* often deformed. Nucleated corpuscles are rare (normoblasts as a rule).

3. White cells, not increased.

Lymphocytosis, occasionally eosinophilia.

4. Blood plates increased.

Diagnostic Value.

1. The points of difference from pernicious anæmia have been discussed.

2. It is important to distinguish it from simple debility, and from cases whose skin only is anæmic; in both of these conditions the blood is normal.

3. From secondary anæmia it may be indistinguishable in case the latter be without leucocytosis. Where leucocytosis is constantly present and the percentage of polymorphonuclear leucocytes is increased, chlorosis (uncomplicated) can be excluded. Of course many of the complications which may occur in chlorosis are accompanied by leucocytosis.

Other Forms of Anæmia.

1. Cases of acute fatal anæmia following purpura or severe hemorrhage of any kind are sometimes classed as pernicious anæmia. The blood certainly differs in many respects from that of ordinary pernicious anæmia. Ehrlich describes such a case following metrorrhagia in which the red cells were reduced to 213,360 per cubic millimetre without much deformity of individual cells and with a decided *decrease* in the average diameter. Polychromatophilic forms numerous. No nucleated corpuscles whatever could be found even after many hours' search. The leucocytes were decreased to about 200 (!) per cubic millimetre. Eighty per cent of them were small lymphocytes, six per cent large lymphocytes, and only fourteen per cent polymorphonuclear. Eosinophiles and myelocytes absent. Autopsy showed no red marrow in the long bones except at the epiphysis, and an entire lack of effort on regeneration.

W. S. Thayer has observed two similar cases, and Bignami and Dionisi have seen cases of the same kind following the prolonged deglobularizing action of the malarial organisms. I have never seen just this type of anæmia.

2. Some cases of severe chronic chlorosis seem to belong in a separate category. Like the variety last described the blood is here of the *microcyte* type, the diameter of the corpuscles being greatly reduced. I have observed one case somewhat similar in a male of fifty-two, a carpenter whom I had noticed for several years at his work, the palest man I ever saw out of bed. About two years ago I had an opportunity to examine his blood, he feeling well, at work, and objecting to the bother of the

FIG. 34.—Chronic Secondary Anæmia due to Bleeding Piles. Magnified 350 diameters. Note the similarity to chlorotic blood (Fig. 33, page 151).

examination. His blood showed: Red cells, 2,530,000; white cells, 2,000; hæmoglobin, 32 per cent.

The red corpuscles were not at all deformed but were *very* small (see Fig. 34) and very pale in the centre. While counting 1,200 white cells 17 normoblasts were seen; no megaloblasts. The leucocytes showed: Polymorphonuclear neutrophiles, 54.5; small lymphocytes, 35; large lymphocytes, 9.4; eosinophiles, 1.1.

The man is still well and hearty, complains of nothing, but is as pale as ever. A few days ago he disclosed to me that he had had bleeding piles for ten years. He had been hitherto concealing this fact.

CHAPTER II.

I. LEUKÆMIA.

THE distinction between leukæmia and leucocytosis has been sufficiently dwelt on above.

The blood of the vast majority of cases of leukæmia falls clearly under one or the other of two distinct types, *myelocytæmia* on the one hand, *lymphæmia* on the other. Myelocytæmia is only found in cases with great hypertrophy of the spleen, marked marrow changes, and little or no enlargement of the other lymphatic tissue. Such cases are usually chronic (two to five years). Lymphæmia, on the other hand, may be associated either with acute or chronic forms of the disease, and while in all cases of lymphæmia we have some set of lymphatic glands enlarged there may be no externally *visible* glands enlarged, and the spleen may be as big as in cases associated with myelocytæmia. The diagnosis of leukæmia can easily be made by the blood alone, but we cannot say from the blood whether or not the spleen or visible lymph glands are the organs chiefly involved. In acute cases the lymph glands of the alimentary tract (cervical, faucial, gastro-enteric, mesenteric) may be the only set involved.

All of the thirty-one cases associated with myelocytæmia which have come under my observation have run a chronic course, while of the cases showing lymphæmia five were chronic, three acute, and two subacute. All showing myelocytæmia had very large spleens without enlargement of visible lymph glands, but two of the lymphæmias had spleens almost filling the abdomen.

The disease leukæmia, then, is associated with three types of blood.

1. Chronic myelocytæmia.
2. Chronic lymphæmia.
3. Acute lymphæmia.

1. MYELOCYTÆMIA.

(Splenic-myelogenous leukœmia.)

The drop as it emerges from the puncture looks somewhat opaque in color, but is neither whitish nor chocolate colored. It flows very sluggishly, however, and is difficult to spread between cover-glasses owing to the masses of white cells contained in it. Coagulation is slow.

RED CELLS.

In early stages of the disease there is no anæmia. Later the diminution in red cells is moderate, averaging about 3,120,000 in the thirty-nine cases of Table VII., A. The patients are *often not pale* and may feel perfectly well. The hæmoglobin is usually diminished, the color index being about 0.6 in my cases. It is difficult to read the v. Fleischl instrument in leukæmia, as the presence of so many leucocytes gives a muddy tint to the liquid, not easy to compare with the red of the glass.

TABLE VII.—LEUKÆMIA.

A			B		
No.		Red cells.	No.		White cells.
1....	Highest ...	5,000,000	1....	Highest ..	1,072,222
2....	....	4,877,000	2....	....	980,000
3....	....	4,800,000	3....	....	820,000
4....	....	4,592,000	4....	....	800,000
5....	....	4,288,000	5....	....	756,000
6....	....	4,016,000	6....	....	748,000
7....	....	3,760,000	7....	....	716,000
8....	....	3,635,570	8....	....	656,000
9....	....	3,605,000	9....	....	626,600
10....	....	3,400,000	10....	....	570,000
11....	....	3,292,000	11....	....	500,000
12....	....	3,200,000	12....	....	492,000
13....	....	3,080,000	13....	....	454,000
14....	....	3,078,000	14....	....	448,000
15....	....	3,010,000	15....	....	430,000
16....	....	2,996,000	16....	....	428,000
17....	....	2,960,000	17....	....	405,000
18....	....	2,938,000	18....	....	400,000
19....	....	2,921,600	19....	....	394,000
20....	....	2,868,000	20....	....	386,000
21....	....	2,792,000	21....	....	340,000

11

TABLE VII.—LEUKÆMIA (Continued).

A		B	
No.	Red cells.	No.	White cells.
22....	2,738,000	22....	320,000
23....	2,715,000	23....	290,000
24....	2,576,000	24....	260,000
25....	2,520,000	25....	220,500
26....	2,322,222	26....	213,000
27....	2,320,000	27....	188,000
28....	2,256,000	28....	183,000
29....	2,140,000	29....	175,800
30....	2,112,000	30....	170,000
31....	2,060,000	31....	189,600
32....	2,016,000	32....	138,000
33....	2,010,000	33....	134,400
34....	1,866,664	34....	132,000
35....	1,420,000	35....	111,000
36....	1,386,000	36....Lowest...	98,000
37....	1,358,000	Average = 428,000	
38....	1,200,000		
39....Lowest....	408,000		
Average = 3,131,000 +			

Qualitative Changes.

The striking point is the presence of *very numerous nucleated red cells* even in the absence of *any sign of anæmia*. With over 4,000,000 well-formed and well-colored red cells, we may have hundreds of nucleated ones in every cover-glass. They are as numerous in this form of leukæmia as in the worst forms of pernicious anæmia, even though the patient may be feeling nearly well.

Both normoblasts and megaloblasts may be seen, but in most cases the latter are in the minority. Many of the normoblasts show fragmentation in their nuclei, and occasionally true karyokinetic figures are to be seen. In the anæmic cases we find all the other changes in the red cells characteristic of anæmia, but the nucleated cells are always more prominent than in any other form of anæmia of a like severity. This shows that nucleated corpuscles are not to be thought of as evidence (like deformities in shape) of regenerative or degenerative conditions only. A special connection to the bone marrow is very clearly indicated, all the more so as in the lymphatic

PLATE II.

FIG. 1.—Both this and Fig. 2 are intended to be fac-similes of actual microscopic fields.

(a) Note the cell between those labelled 8 and 9—apparently a "mast cell." Such cells are often seen in this form of leukæmia. With Ehrlich's stain they present this appearance. Basic stains bring out coarse blue granules on the periphery of the protoplasm.

(b) Note also the cell at the extreme upper right-hand corner of Fig. 1, which it is almost impossible to classify either as a myelocyte or as a polymorphonuclear neutrophile, since it *appears* to be intermediate between the two varieties.

(c) Both the nucleated corpuscles are normoblast; 9 has polychromatophilic protoplasm. The red cells show scarcely any deformities and very slight deficiency in coloring matter.

FIG. 2.—(a) Note the deformities in size and shape of red corpuscles, owing to the anæmia present.

(b) No lymphocytes are figured, as they made up only two per cent of the white cells in this case. Eosinophiles were absent.

(c) Note that the contrast between this figure (leucocytosis) and the one above it (leukæmia) is not in the abundance of white cells but in the *kind* of white cell predominating among those present.

Examination of the Blood.

PLATE II.

Figure I = Splenic-myelogenous Leucaemia
Figure II = Leucocytosis (cancer of kidney)
Cells stained yellow = Red corpuscles
   1. 2. 3. 4 a. 5 = Polymorphonuclear neutrophiles
   6 = Lymphocyte
   7 a. 8. = Eosinophiles
   9 a. 10 = Nucleated red corpuscles
   All others = Myelocytes

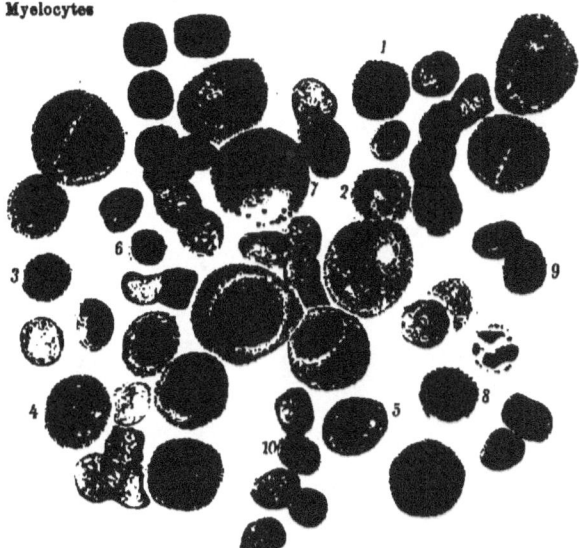

Figure I
Leucaemia.

Cells stained yellow = Red corpuscles
  All others =
  Polymorpho-
  nuclear-
  neutrophiles

Scale of μ

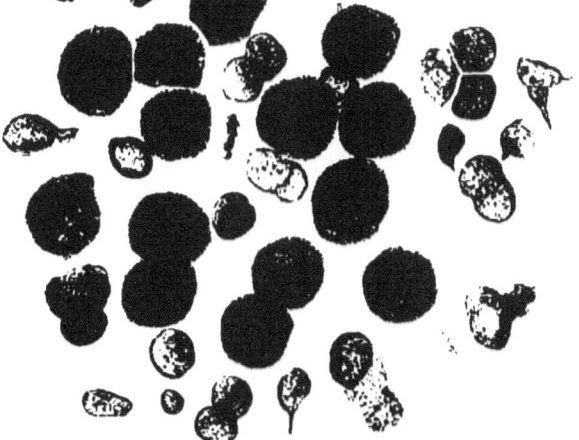

Figure II
Leucocytosis.

form of the disease in which the bone marrow is usually much less affected, nucleated corpuscles are much less numerous, appearing in relatively small numbers in the very acute anæmic cases and not at all in those who are not anæmic.

Other qualitative changes are not marked and correspond to the degree of anæmia present; often there are none at all.

As the count of the white cells rises, that of the red may fall, and *vice versa ;* or the red cells may remain at a comparatively high figure despite the progress of the white.

WHITE CELLS.

Quantitative Changes.

The average number per cubic millimetre in the thirty-six cases of Table VII., B (the lymphatic cases being excluded), was 438,000 at the time when the cases first came under observation. The highest count in this series is 1,072,222 and the lowest 98,000.

Cases are on record in which the white cells were actually more numerous than the red. The average ratio in my series is about one white to seven red. The highest ratio is 1: 2, and the lowest 1: 37. It is best to use the "red counter" with a dilution of 1: 200 in counting the white cells, otherwise they are often too crowded for convenience. The hæmatokrit is useful in this disease and in any condition where the white cells are much increased, not to supersede the Thoma-Zeiss or to give us the absolute number of cells, but for comparative observations as to the length of the column of white cells from day to day in a given case. Hayek [1] has shown that the count of leucocytes may vary enormously in a very few hours; *e.g.,* 10 A.M., 122,500; 4 P.M., 235,000; or again, 10 A.M., 730,000; 4 P.M., 547,500.

In the fresh specimen we notice that a large proportion of the white cells are not amœboid, a point of marked contrast with leucocytosis, in which nearly all the leucocytes are amœboid. This is due to the fact that the myelocytes which form so large a portion of the leucocytes in this disease possess little if any faculty of amœboid motion. We should expect therefore to find their nuclei free from the twists and distortions

[1] Hayek: Wien. klin. Woch., 1897, No. 20.

characteristic of the amœboid (polymorphonuclear) cells. And this is in fact the case (see below).

TABLE VIII.—MYELOCYTÆMIA (SPLENIC-MYELOGENOUS LEUKÆMIA).

No.	Red cells.	White cells.	Hæmoglobin.	Polymorphonuclear neutrophiles.	Small lymphocytes.	Large lymphocytes.	Eosinophiles.	Myelocytes.	Basophiles.	Intermediate forms.	Normoblasts seen while counting them.	Megaloblasts seen while counting them.	Date.
1	2,010,000	716,000	30	40	1	10	4	42	3.8	Many	Many	Many	Nov. 1st, 1897.[1]
	1,720,000	732,000	..	....									Nov. 3d, 1897.
		708,000		....									Nov. 12th, 1897.
2	4,125,000	253,900	55	....									July 16th, 1895.
		200,000		....									July 25th, 1895.
	4,016,000	846,000	..	56.5	7	4.5	4	28	Many	Many	3	1	Jan. 21st, 1897.
	4,592,000	448,000	60	46	1.5	14.5	1.5	33.5	"	"	2	0	Feb. 8th, 1897.
				46.6	1.4	10.4	2.2	36.7	"	"	3	0	Feb. 17th, 1897.
3	2,960,000	175,800	42	17	3	11	19	49	"	"	13	31	July 15th, 1897.
	3,184,000	264,000	38	....									July 29th, 1897.
	3,156,000	276,000	40	....									Aug. 5th, 1897.
4	3,400,000	111,000	35	27.2	10.5	26	3	25	Many	Many			
5	3,670,000	183,090	..	31	15	8	5	32	"	"			
6	3,100,000	430,000	48	....									Aug. 10th, 1896.
	3,080,000	405,000	40	72.2	2	3.6	2	17.4	Many	Many	5	9	Aug. 31st, 1896.
7	2,520,000	510,000	50	51	.6	2	4	42.4	"	"			Jan. 22d, 1896.
		528,000	..	....									Jan. 22d, 1896.[2]
		570,000	..	....									Jan. 23d, 1896.
		560,000	..	....									Jan. 24th, 1896.
8	4,016,000	800,000	58	55	5	4	4	34	Many	Many			June 4th, 1894.
		26,000											Aug. 10th, 1894.
9	2.792,000	139,600	..	50.4	18.9	0.2	6.1	24.4					April, 1898. Later
10	2,715,000	394,000	..	44	1.5	1	2.5	51					the count of
11	2,256,000	340,000	..	62.3	3.8	1.8	1.8	30.3					leucocytes was
12	4,288,000	213,000	37	53.8	2.2	2.8	14.4	18	8.8				normal for sev-
13	2,921,000	492,800	..	61	3	0	3	33					eral months.
14	3,010,000	188,000	..	37	23	6	8	26					
15	2,996,000	134,400	..	46	1.5	0.5	4	48					
16	4,800,000	220,500	..	62	1.5	1	2.5	33					Jan. 22d, 1896.
	3,060,000	274,000	41	33	10	11.5	3	42.5					June, 1897.
17	2,016,000	260,000	..	26	8	1	5	60					
18	2,576,000	748,000	..	46	2	0.5	1.5	50					
19	2,448,000	168,800	42	45	3	3	3	46					
	2,120,000	190,000											
	2,528,000	159,000	45										
20	5,120,000	134,000	78	74.2	4	4	2.8	15			4	1	Feb. 22d, 1896.
	5,000,000	137,800	..	....									Feb. 25th, 1896.
	4,800,000	138,000	..	61	6	2.2	2.5	28	...				Feb. 28th, 1896.
21	......	......	..	32	4	4	5	55					
22	....	......	..	49.6	3.6	2.2	6	38.6					
23	....	......	..	30	10	5	5	45	10				
24	....	......	..	54	8	0	5	34					
25	....	......	..	47.5	24.5	5	1.5	27.5					
26	....	......	..	36	4	4	28	28					
27	....	... ..	..	57.5	0	1.5	3.7	36	1.5				
28	....	......	..	42	5	3	1	47	2				
Av.	3,120,000	348,000	52	46	6	4.6	5.1	35	5				

[1] Many cells on border-line between large lymphocytes and myelocytes and between these and polymorphonuclear neurophiles.

[2] Cerebral hemorrhage. Death January 25th, 1896.

With or without the influence of therapeutic agencies the white cells may fall gradually to normal and remain there for some time, the patient feeling greatly improved. Such a case occurred under my observation, and the patient, a washerwoman, went back to work and afterward passed through an attack of lobar pneumonia in safety.

At such a time, when no increase in the white cells is present, we should never suspect leukæmia, seeing the case for the first time, unless we chance to make a differential count; then the characteristic qualitative changes (see below) would be seen.

QUALITATIVE CHANGES.

1. Myelocytes.

The enormous number of myelocytes is the chief point of interest. The average in my 28 cases was 35 per cent (see Table VIII.), rising in one case as high as 60 per cent and only twice falling lower than 20 per cent.

Taking the average total number of leucocytes as 428,000 per cubic millimetre, the absolute number of myelocytes would be over 150,000 per cubic millimetre. So far as I am aware the highest count of myelocytes in any other disease is that mentioned on page 306 in a case of malignant disease, namely, 4,514 per cubic millimetre. The contrast is sufficiently striking. I wish to insist upon this point, namely, that the blood of splenic-myelogenous leukæmia is absolutely peculiar and characteristic, and could not be confused with that of any other disease. Certain writers of late years have concluded that because myelocytes do occur in a great variety of diseases as well as in leukæmia, therefore there is nothing peculiar about the blood of the latter affection. It would be as logical to say that because albumin and casts occur occasionally in the urine of persons practically well, therefore there is nothing characteristic about the urine of acute nephritis.

Between the largest number of myelocytes ever recorded in any disease other than leukæmia, and the smallest number ever found in the latter disease, there is as great a difference as there is between the minute traces of sugar to be found in normal urine and the marked glycosuria of diabetes mellitus.

At the first glance the stained specimen of leukæmic blood seems to be composed mostly of myelocytes, but this is because they are on the average so much larger than the other forms of white cells, which, being packed away in the interstices between the large myelocytes, do not appear prominently at first sight.

Although (as just mentioned) the average size of the myelocytes is greater than that of any other kind of leucocyte, there is a great range of variation in their size, and some are hardly, if at all, larger than a red cell. (This is equally true of the myelocytes as seen in the bone marrow. See above, page 71.)

The individual characteristics and variations in the myelocytes have been already sufficiently described on page 69.

2. Polymorphonuclear Cells.

Although absolutely the number of these cells is greatly increased, the number in each 1,000 leucocytes is considerably diminished. The average percentage in the 28 cases of Table VIII. is 46, the figures ranging between 17 and 72 per cent.

The individual cells show a much greater range of variation in size, staining properties, and the size and shape of the nucleus than in any other condition. In most forms of leucocytosis, for example, one adult cell looks very much like another, but in this form of leukæmia we are often struck by—

(a) *Very small* cells or *very large* cells.

(b) *Dark stained* or very *pale stained* cells.

(c) Unusual shapes in the nuclei.

Besides these variations we often see cells apparently belonging to this type, but whose protoplasm shows no color whatever. Such a cell is figured to the right of Plate II., Fig. 1. Other cells show a few granules scattered about against a perfectly white background. The outer rim of the cell is usually stained faintly, so that we can hardly make out its outline. Such cells usually contain basophile granules beside the neutrophile.

(d) There are always some cells on the border-line between the polymorphonuclear and the myelocyte, and in regard to which decision must be arbitrary. We cannot help getting the impression that at any rate in *this* disease the two varieties are only different stages in the development of the same cell.

(e) More than one kind of granule is sometimes seen in the protoplasm, *i.e.*, eosinophilic or basophilic as well as neutrophilic.

3. *Lymphocytes.*

It is here that the greater relative *diminution* occurs, to make room for the incursion of the myelocytes. In percentages they are reduced from their normal, 20 to 30 per cent, to an average of 10.6 per cent, as in leucocytosis. But still their absolute number is always increased. Thus the lowest percentage present in Table VIII. (namely, two per cent) would mean 8,760 out of the average 438,000, the total leucocyte count per cubic millimetre, and 8,760 is three or four times as many lymphocytes per cubic millimetre as are present in normal blood.

The proportion of large and small forms among the lymphocytes varies a great deal. Sometimes the lymphocytes of this form of leukæmia do not differ from those of normal blood, but in most cases we find one or more of the following atypical varieties:

(*a*) Lymphocytes with a protoplasm so darkly stained that it is difficult to distinguish them from myelocytes. Indeed in some cases where hints of a granular look appear in the violet-stained rim we find it impossible to be sure whether we are dealing with a large lymphocyte or a myelocyte. The personal equation alone decides.

(*b*) Cells like lymphocytes except that they contain from three to ten widely separated granules of one or more varieties (basophilic, acidophilic, or neutrophilic).

4. *Eosinophiles.*

Like all the other varieties these are *absolutely* much increased. Relatively—by percentages—they may or may not be so. In my series they ranged from 1.5 to 28 per cent, averaging 5.1 per cent, a slight increase over the normal.

Many writers, wrongly interpreting Ehrlich's observations on this point, have stated that an increased *percentage* of eosinophilic cells was the distinguishing mark of leukæmia, and even recent writers (*e.g.*, Gilbert, Strümpell) continue to repeat this false statement.

The cell characteristic of splenic-myelogenous leukæmia is not the eosinophile but the myelocyte.

We distinguish several types of eosinophiles in leukæmic blood.

(*a*) Ordinary (polymorphonuclear) eosinophiles.

(*b*) Eosinophilic dwarf cells.

(*c*) Eosinophilic myelocytes.

(*a*) Needs no comment; (*b*) is simply a very small cell with eosinophilic granules; sometimes such cells are not over 5 µ in diameter. They are not uncommon in this form of leukæmia and are very rare in any other disease. The same is true of (*c*), the eosinophilic myelocytes which are very rare in any other disease, except pernicious anæmia, where they are occasionally seen.

These cells are like myelocytes except that their granules are eosinophilic instead of neutrophilic (see Plate I. and Plate II.). They are found in the marrow in considerable numbers and constitute the majority of the eosinophilic cells seen in this form of leukæmia. Occasionally we see eosinophiles with a few basophilic or neutrophilic granules as well.

5. *Basophiles.*

(*a*) The lymphocytes may contain basophilic granules as in any ordinary blood.

(*b*) Certain of the myelocytes contain fine basophilic granules in addition to their usual neutrophilic granules.

(*c*) "*Mastcellen*" or coarsely granular basophiles, usually with a trilobed nucleus, are almost always seen in specimens stained with dahlia or methylene blue. With the triple stain their protoplasm is nearly unstained, but usually a number of round *white* spots can be made out against a faintly stained background. These are the basophilic granulations. Mast-cells make up from one to ten per cent of the leucocytes in most cases of myelocytæmia.

6. Polymorphous Condition of the Blood.

Weiss has rightly insisted on the fact that in this type of leukæmia the blood preparations show a very *polymorphous* condition, that is, there are no fixed types, but every variety shades through intermediate forms into some other variety. No two cells are alike. Precisely the same conditions obtain in the normal marrow, and we can scarcely resist the impression that in this form of leukæmia we see in the blood unfinished cells of various kinds which usually do not appear in the circulating blood.

As Charcot-Leyden crystals have no diagnostic value and are not peculiar to any disease, no description of them will be given here. They appear to be present wherever eosinophiles are plentiful, *e.g.*, in asthma, gonorrhœa, in the bone marrow, etc.

Kanthack considers that a diminution in eosinophiles (progressive) is a bad prognostic sign. During remissions, when the leucocyte count may fall to normal, the percentage of myelocytes remains large and the diagnosis could usually be made even if we saw the case then for the first time. This I have observed in two cases, and Thayer has had the same experience.

II. LYMPHÆMIA.

(*Lymphatic Leukæmia.*)

Although Fraenkel once maintained that all cases of lymphatic leukæmia are acute, and that therefore the difference between the various forms of the disease rests simply on the rapidity of the process in the blood and clinically, there is no doubt that chronic lymphatic leukæmia exists.

Fraenkel was enabled to maintain his position only by extending the term *acute* to cover all cases whose symptoms last not more than four months. Six weeks is the limit agreed upon by most other observers.

The writer has watched five cases of typical lymphatic leukæmia for periods of from seven months to two years. One was as little sick as any case of leukæmia that I have ever seen, and came over thirty miles from time to time to report at the Out-Patient department. His blood showed little variation from the following figures: Red cells, 2,300,886; white cells, 112,000.

The differential count always showed the overwhelming majority (over ninety per cent) of small lymphocytes characteristic of the disease. The lymph glands were all much enlarged, the spleen just palpable. The patient kept about his work as a gardener for over two years. Grawitz has watched a similar case for over four years.

The blood of acute lymphæmia differs as a rule in many respects from that of chronic cases. These differences will be referred to later on.

RED CELLS.

The count of red cells is often somewhat lower than in the splenic-myelogenous form of the disease, averaging 2,730,000 in my cases. In acute cases it is usually very low and the anæmia progresses rapidly. In chronic cases the red cells behave about as in myelocythæmia, except as regards nucleated forms.

Here the point of interest is the *comparative rarity of nucleated red cells*, the abundance of which is so marked a feature of splenic-myelogenous leukæmia. They follow the grade of anæmia present. Cases occurring in children show more abundant nucleated corpuscles (the same is true of all leukæmia in children) than those occurring in adults; and the megaloblasts, usually scanty, may equal the number of normoblasts. In very acute cases the number of nucleated forms is greater and may be as great as in myelocytæmia. Two cases recently reported by Herrick [1] exemplify this.

WHITE CELLS.

Quantitative Changes.

As a rule the numerical increase is not nearly so marked as in the splenic-myelogenous form. The average ratio of white to red cells is about 1:50 instead of 1:7, and we rarely see counts reach the height common in the other form of the disease. The highest count of my series was 1,480,000 at the patient's first visit, and the lowest 30,000, the average being 141,000 as compared with 438,000 in the other form. These figures refer to uncomplicated cases.

[1] Journal of the American Medical Association, July 24th, 1897.

PLATE III.

(a) *Chronic Lymphœmia* with Excess of *Small* Lymphocytes.

One polymorphonuclear cell is present. All the rest are lymphocytes and exemplify the variations in the morphology of the cell occurring in this and other diseases as well as in health, *e.g.*, variations in the staining of the protoplasm and nucleus, indentation and even division of the nucleus.

Note that the scale of the whole of Plate III. is larger than in the other plates (see scale of μ).

(b) *Acute Lymphœmia* with Excess of *Large* Lymphocytes.

Note the lack of chromatin in both nuclei and protoplasm of large lymphocytes. The plasma around them or their extreme edge took most of the stain. The brown tint of the red cells is due to underheating. Compare the colors with those in the figure above (a) in which the preparation was properly heated.

PLATE III.

a

b

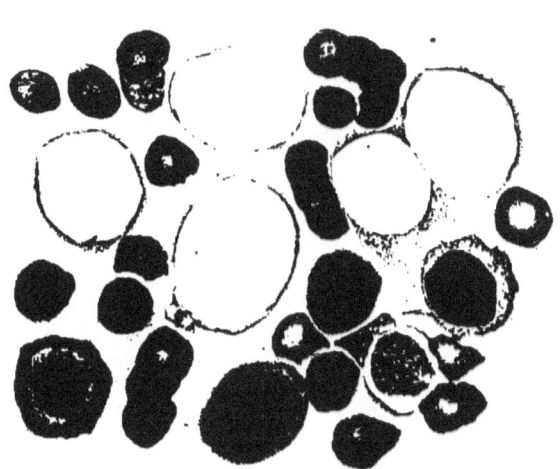

Lymphatic Leucaemia

a. Small Lymphocytes in excess
b. Large　　　„　　　„　　„

Scale of μ

R. C. Cabot fec.　　　　　　　　Lith. Anst. v. K. A. Funke, Leipzig.

Qualitative Changes.

1. *Lymphocytes* (small forms, large forms, or a mixture) make up usually over ninety per cent of all the leucocytes present. In some cases they are all nearly of one size, while in others we find every gradation from the smallest to the largest, so that it is absolutely futile to attempt to separate them into "large" and "small." Four of my cases were made up wholly of the small forms all under 10 μ in diameter, two were composed largely of forms over 15 μ in diameter, while six showed every intermediate size.

TABLE IX.—LYMPHATIC LEUKÆMIA.

No.	Red cells.	White cells.	Per cent haemoglobin.	Small lymphocytes.	Large lymphocytes.	Polynuclear neutrophiles.	Eosinophiles.	Myelocytes.	Normoblasts.	Megaloblasts.	Remarks.
1........	4,877,000	132,000	....	75.8	16.	4.6	1.6	2.	4	1	Subacute; ten weeks.
2........	912,000	23,000	17	15	82.	2.4	.1	.5	....	..	Jan. 24th, 1896.
	1,440,000	43,600	23	....	....	....	....	....	....	..	Jan. 26th, 1896. Acute; two weeks.
	1,336,000	92,000	20	25.4	73.2	.5	.1	.8	3	1	Jan. 27th.
	1,100,000	120,000	....	....	....	....	....	....	....	..	Jan. 28th. Death; autopsy.
3.	3,000,000	31,600	....	68.5	28.	3.2	.2	....	....	..	April 3d, 1896.
	3,500,000	31,500	55	78.	15.6	5.6	.2	.6	....	..	April 5th, 1896.
	3,608,000	28,500	55	95.3	*	4.3	.3	....	...	..	April 6th, 1896.
		40,000	....	....	....	....	....	....	....	..	April 7th, 1896. Acute: five weeks.
		31,500	...	95.5	*	4.	.5	....	2	2	April 8th, 1896.
	4,700,000	40,000	....	....	....	....	....	....	....	..	April 12th, 1896.
	3,100,000	3,400	....	39.	52.	9.	....	....	....	..	April 22d (sepsis—semicomatose).
		800	....	94.7	*	5.3	....	....	....	..	April 29th. Death.
4........	2,960,000	1,480,000	....	87.0	12.	.1	....	....	....	6	March 21st, 1897. Chronic.
5........	4,160,000	80,000	....	80.5	2.1	17.2	....	.2	....	..	Oct. 26th, 1896. Chronic.
	2,768,000	77,500	50	88.7	1.6	9.4	.2	.1	....	..	Nov. 5th, 1896.
		51,800	....	....	....	....	....	....	....	..	Nov. 7th, 1896.
				90.4	1.4	8.	.2	....	....	..	Nov. 15th, 1896.
		79,500	....	....	....	....	....	....	....	..	Nov. 17th. Died December, 1897.
6........	3,520,000	64,000	60	94.	....	6.	....	....	....	..	Chronic.
7........			....	94.	*	5.7	....	.37	....	..	Chronic.
8........			....	97.9	7.	1.4	.8	....	2	..	Acute.
9........			....	86.2	7.	9.8	....	....	....	..	History unknown.
10........			....	72.	28.	....	....	....	....	..	History unknown.
11........			....	99.6	*	.4	....	....	Few	..	History unknown.
12........			....	92.2	*	7.8	....	....	....	..	History unknown.
13........	700,000	600,000	10	99.8	*	.2	....	....	..	3	2,500 cells counted.
Average.	2,900,000+	59,000+	40	60.2	15.	4.2	.2	.4			

* Large and small forms counted together on account of the impossibility of differentiating them in these cases.

In acute cases, where the large cells usually predominate, the staining is often very faint throughout the nucleus and protoplasm (see Plate III., *b*), so that at first sight we should think something was wrong with our technique. Other forms of leucocytes in the same preparation, however, will stain normally, showing that the trouble is in the lymphocytes and not in the technique. These large lymphocytes are identical in their appearance with those found at the "germ centres" of all adenoid tissue, and probably are the mother cells of the small lymphocytes. Benda has termed them "lymphogonien." They have often been mistaken for myelocytes, from which they are to be distinguished by the absence of any neutrophile granulation. They often show evidences of degeneration (see above, page 63). The protoplasm may be entirely unstained as in most of the cells in Plate III., *b*, or it may stain pale gray or pink. In other specimens, especially those of the small-cell type (Plate III., *a*) the lymphocytes stain well. Their nuclei are frequently indented or even divided in two (this occurs also in normal blood, but less often).

Fraenkel believes still that lymphæmia, though not always acute, is usually so, and that if a chronic case takes on acute symptoms the blood becomes more lymphæmic, while if a case starts acute and becomes chronic the lymphocytes decrease. Thus in a case reported by v. der Wey[1] a chronic myelocytæmia six weeks before death began to have fever, hemorrhages, great increase in the total leucocyte count and in the anæmia. No complication. The lymphocytes increased 30 per cent, and the polymorphonuclear neutrophiles dropped from 30 to 3 per cent.

Gerhardt[2] watched a case which began acutely with a large percentage of *large* lymphocytes and then became chronic with a predominance of *small* lymphocytes.

In acute cases Litten[3] has noticed fatty degeneration in the leucocytes.

The following figures illustrate the influence of a septicæmia (from suppurating cervical glands) which ended the life of No. 3 in the above Table X.

[1] Deut. Arch. f. klin. Med., vol. 57.
[2] 15th Cong. f. innere Med., 1897.
[3] 11th Cong. f. innere Med., 1893.

Date.	Number of leucocytes.	Percentage of lymphocytes.
April 3d.	31,600	96.5
" 4th.	31,000	
" 6th.	28,505	93.6
" 8th.	44,000	
" 10th.	31,500	95.5
" 12th.	40,000	
" 13th.	Sepsis began.	
" 20th.	5,661	
" 21st.	4,000	
" 22d.	3,400	92.
" 24th.	3,222	
" 28th.	800	
" 29th.	471	94.7
Death on the 29th.		

Zeissl's case, also of the lymphatic form, showed the following:

Date.	White cells.	Percentage of lymphocytes.	Percentage of adult cells.
September 9th	80,000	96.	4.
" 24th	113,000		
" 26th	119,000		
" 29th	122,000	97.8	2.
October 6th	140,000		
" 9th	Pneumonia began.	99.	1
" 10th	119,000		
" 11th	98,000		
" 12th	68,500		
" 13th	43,500	88.7	11.3
" 14th	50,000		
" 15th	9,350	85.4	14.6
" 16th (A.M.)	133,200		
" 16th (P.M.)	172,000	75.	25.

Polymorphonuclear neutrophiles are often so scarce that one has to look through several thousand leucocytes before finding one. There is nothing abnormal about them. *Eosinophiles* and *myelocytes* are equally rare.

Summary.

The leading characteristics of leukæmic blood are as follows:
(a) *Myelocytæmia*.
1. Red cells about 3,000,000, nucleated forms very numerous.
2. White cells about 450,000, of which
3. Myelocytes form about thirty per cent.

4. Every possible form of cell *intermediate* between the ordinary varieties is to be seen. ("Polymorphous blood.")

(b) *Chronic Lymphœmia.*

1. Red cells about 3,000,000 or lower; nucleated forms rare.

2. White cells about 100,000 or lower, of which

3. Small lymphocytes usually form over ninety per cent.

4. Myelocytes and eosinophiles very scanty.

(c) *Acute Lymphœmia.*

1. Red cells *much* diminished; nucleated forms not infrequent.

2. *Large* forms of lymphocytes usually predominate; many of them often show signs of degeneration.

3. Neutrophiles and eosinophiles very scanty.

Diagnostic Value.

Leukæmia is distinguished by the blood examination from

1. Hodgkin's disease: (a) splenic, (b) glandular.

2. Tumors of the spleen and vicinity (e.g., kidney or retroperitoneal glands).

3. Enlargements of the lymphatic glands from tuberculosis, syphilis, malignant disease.

4. Hydronephrosis.

5. Huge leucocytosis from any cause.

6. Chronic malaria.

7. Amyloid disease.

1. *Leukæmia and Hodgkin's disease* (lymphadenoma or pseudo-leukæmia). The pathology of the two diseases is identical but for the blood count. In Hodgkin's disease the blood is normal, or shows only a moderate anæmia or leucocytosis (polymorphonuclear cells alone increased), and the diagnosis is easily made.

2. *Tumors of the spleen* and epecially of the *kidney* are very apt to be mistaken for leukæmia. Within a year I have been asked to examine the blood in three cases of "leukæmia," all of which turned out to be malignant disease of the kidney. In all of these there was a large tumor resembling the spleen in the left hypochondrium and a very large increase of white cells. In two of them the blood was examined fresh and the great number of white cells in the slide taken as evidence confirmatory of leukæmia. The stained specimen, however, showed only

marked leucocytosis with ninety per cent of adult cells of the ordinary type and no myelocytes. Other large tumors of this region showed similar results. Occasionally cases of leukæmia with numerous metastases are described as "sarcomatosis," and then it is asserted that the blood of leukæmia is identical with that of sarcoma. The source of the mistake is obvious.

3. *Adenitis* with hyperplasia due to tuberculosis shows usually normal blood[1] and is thus easily distinguished from leukæmia. Leucocytosis is often present in syphilitic cases and still more marked in those due to cancer or sarcoma, but the counts rarely reach 30,000 and myelocytes are absent or very scanty.

4. One case of *hydronephrosis*, in which the distention of the sac was so great that it presented as a hard, solid tumor on the right hypochondrium, was taken for leukæmia by a competent observer some years ago. The *normal* blood examination revealed the mistake, and excluded also malignant disease in all probability. The diagnosis was only reached, however, at the autopsy.

5. Huge leucocytosis in pneumonia or malignant disease may often cross the old boundary line of 100,000 white cells, beyond which none but leukæmic cases were supposed to venture. The differential count sets us right instantly, showing ninety per cent or so of the increase to be made up of ordinary polymorphonuclear leucocytes.

6 and 7. The large spleen and cachectic appearance associated with chronic malaria and long-standing suppurations may be easily distinguished from leukæmia by the absence of anything more than anæmia and leucocytosis in the blood.

	Red cells.	White cells.	Lympho-cytes.	Poly-nuclear leucocytes.	Myelo-cytes.	Nucleated red cells.
Leukæmia (splenic-myelogenous).	About 3,000,000	450,000 ±	About 7.6 per cent.	About 50 per cent.	About 87 per cent.	Very numerous.
Leukæmia (lym-phatic).	About 3,000,000	100,000 ±	About 96 per cent.	About 3 per cent.	Absent.	Rare.
Hodgkin's disease ..	About normal.	7,500 ±	Normal.	Normal.	Absent.	Absent.
Tumors of or near the spleen.	Usually diminished.	20,000 to 40,000 ±	Greatly decreased.	Greatly increased,	Few if any.	Few.
Leucocytosis in gen-eral.	....	May be over 100,000	Greatly decreased.	Greatly increased.	Few if any.	Few at times.
Chronic malaria....	Much diminished.	Somewhat increased.	Usually increased.	Usually decreased.	Few if any.	Few.
Amyloid disease....	Usually diminished.	Usually increased.	Usually decreased.	Usually increased.	Absent.	May be a few.
Hydronephrosis	Normal.	Normal.	Normal or decreased.	Normal.	Absent.	Absent.

[1] Sometimes marked leucopenia.

EFFECT OF INTERCURRENT INFECTIONS.

There are on record about thirty cases in which leukæmia (acute or chronic) has been complicated with some intercurrent infection, with marked effect upon the blood in all but one. This single case was an acute rheumatic arthritis reported by Richter in the discussion of Fraenkel's article in the *Deutsche medicinische Wochenschrift* for 1895 (Nos. 39, 43, and 45), p. 639. Here the blood remained unchanged.

Müller's [1] case of lymphatic leukæmia was complicated by a septicæmia, and the count of white cells *rose* from 180,000 to 400,000 per cubic millimetre, with a marked increase in the percentage of polymorphonuclear cells. Here was a genuine leucocytosis added to a leukæmia.

With the exception of these two cases, all those hitherto published have shown a marked progressive *decrease* in the total number of leucocytes without any change in the percentages of the different varieties in twelve, while eight showed like Müller's an increased percentage of the polymorphonuclear cells despite the decrease in the total leucocyte count.

Marischler [2] in a case of lymphatic leukæmia with cancer of the kidneys found:

	1. At First.	2. Later.
Red cells	3,450,000	2,400,000
White cells	96,000	48,000
Hæmoglobin	50 per cent.	30 per cent.
Polymorphonuclear cells	15.6 "	57.5 "
Small lymphocytes	83.3 "	40 "
Large lymphocytes	1.8 "	1.6 "
Eosinophiles	.18 "	.16 "
Myelocytes	....	.16 "

Various infections—miliary tuberculosis, pneumonia, grippe, erysipelas, abscess of kidney, septic lymph glands—alike decreased the leucocyte count. In one case a rise just before death was observed.

Thus in Henck's case the leucocytes fell from 400,500 to 89,000, in one of Müller's from 246,900 to 57,300, in Kovács' from 67,000 to 17,000, in Zeissl's from 140,000 to 9,350. I

---

[1] Müller: Deut. Archiv für klin. Med., 1892, vol. 50, p. 47.

[2] Wien. klin. Woch., July 23d, 1896.

have already mentioned a case of lymphatic leukæmia (page 173) in which the leucocytes fell from 40,000 to under 500, this last being on the day of death.   In this case the percentages of the different varieties of leucocytes remained entirely unchanged.

Herrick [1] reports a case complicated by acute streptococcus infection in which the white cells were 60,000 at the time of death.   How high they may have been earlier is not known.

It appears, therefore, that when an infection complicates leukæmia we may have—

1. No effect (see case of rheumatic fever as a complication, just mentioned).

2. A genuine leucocytosis on top, so to speak, of the leukæmia, with an increased percentage of polymorphonuclear cells.

3. A decrease in the leucocyte count with or without an increase of polymorphonuclear cells.   This decrease is by far the most common result and may go far below normal as death approaches.

Goldschneider [2] found that by the injection of splenic extract and other substances he could bring about a similar diminution in the number of leucocytes, but that, as in the case of intercurrent infections, this diminution was not accompanied by any improvement in the patient's condition and death followed as usual.

Abscesses occurring in leukæmic patients are filled with adult leucocytes as ordinary abscesses are, and do not contain myelocytes.

HODGKIN'S DISEASE.

(Pseudo-Leukæmia, Lymphoma).

The diagnosis of this disease is impossible without the blood count.   Its pathology is identical with that of leukæmia and even post mortem the two diseases are indistinguishable so far as the lesions outside of the blood are concerned.   Yet the blood is in no way peculiar, but presents in most cases all the characteristics of the normal tissue.   Its value is as negative evidence, telling us in a given case that leukæmia is absent even though all the other signs and symptoms may be those of leukæmia.

[1] *Loc. cit.*
[2] Discussion of Fraenkel's article.

12

(I.) Transitions from Hodgkin's disease to leukæmia are said to have taken place under the eyes of competent observers, but they are very rare. Only three such cases are on record so far as I know, that of Fleischer and Penzoldt,[1] that of Mosler,[2] and one reported by Senator,[3] where two sisters came under observation, both suffering form Hodgkin's disease. One died of it; in the other the blood changed to that of leukæmia before death.[4]

Doubtless many of the other cases supposed to exemplify a similar transition were really cases in which a leucocytosis arose owing to some inflammatory complication, as not uncommonly occurs (see below, Table X.).

From the existence of these very rare cases of a transition to leukæmia it has been supposed, especially by French observers, that Hodgkin's disease is simply an early stage of true leukæmia and that this would always become apparent were it not that the patients die of some intercurrent disease before the signs of leukæmia have time to show themselves in the blood. One difficulty with this view is that there occur chronic cases which last from eight to ten years without any change in the blood. Another difficulty is that the transition is in fact rare despite the relative frequency with which the disease is met with.

(II.) Undoubtedly many cases diagnosed as Hodgkin's disease are in fact cases of glandular hypertrophy due to syphilis or tuberculosis, and this fact has led many to the belief that *all* cases called Hodgkin's disease are in reality only syphilitic or tubercular adenitis. In a considerable number of cases, however, tuberculosis has been disproven by careful inoculation experiments with the glandular tissue, and there is no reasonable doubt that *some* cases at any rate are not due to tuberculosis or syphilis. Probably the diagnosis can never be made with absolute certainty during life.

(III.) The frequent occurrence of fever and other symptoms characteristic of an infectious disease has led some writers to class it as such. In a certain percentage of cases the disease

[1] Deut. Arch. f. klin. Med., vol. 17.
[2] Ziemssen's "Handbuch d. Path. and Therap.," vol. 8.
[3] Berl. klin. Woch., 1882, p. 533.
[4] It is noteworthy that all these cases are of some years' standing—before Ehrlich's methods were much used.

(like leukæmia) has run an acute course, lasting not more than six weeks from the first symptom to death. In some chronic cases the same sort of evidence of an infectious nature has been brought forward. Ulcerations occur in the mouth and intestine through which morbid products might gain admission. Various bacteria (pyogenic and others) have been found in the blood and tissues from time to time, but numerous negative examinations for micro-organisms are also on record, and the evidence is insufficient to establish the infectious nature of the disease. None the less, there is a growing tendency among the leading writers and observers in Germany and elsewhere, to believe that the disease will ultimately be shown to be infectious.

(IV.) Meantime most surgeons continue to regard it as a form of sarcoma'and to treat it like malignant disease.

The Blood.

Whatever the nature of the disease, we find in the earlier stages of most cases normal blood as will be seen in Table X. (cases 7 to 23 inclusive).

As the disease progresses the hæmoglobin soon begins to fall, later the red cells, until, as at the end of Case 10 of the present series, the blood may reach the severest grade of anæmia. In acute cases the anæmia may develop very rapidly. The usual qualitative changes characterizing severe secondary anæmia may be present.

TABLE X.—HODGKIN'S DISEASE.

No.	Age.	Sex.	Red cells.	White cells.	Per cent hæmo-globin.	Remarks.
1	28	F.	5,500,000	64,000	75	Polymorphonuclear cells, 95 per cent. Lymphocytes, 5 per cent.
2	....	M.	3,848,000	39,200	48	Acute. Diff.[2] 500. Polymorphonuclear cells, 95.2 per cent. Lymphocytes, 4.6 per cent.
3	24	F.	4,896,000	32,000	53	
4	19	F.	5,528,000 5,160,000	22,200 25,400	....	Diff. 200 cells. Polymorphonuclear cells, 86.5 per cent. Six weeks later. Lymphocytes, 12. per cent Eosinophiles, 1.5 "
5	19	M.	2,480,000	20,200	33	Stained specimens normal.

[1] There are no reliable differentia between sarcoma of lymph glands and "benign" lymphoma histologically.

[2] Diff. =Differential count of.

TABLE X.—HODGKIN'S DISEASE (*Continued*).

No.	Age.	Sex.	Red cells.	White cells.	Per cent hæmoglobin.	Remarks.
6	37	M.	5,990,000	13,500	....	Polymorphonuclear cells, 95 per cent. Lymphocytes, 5 per cent.
7	25	M.	5,440,000	9,500	59	Death; autopsy.
8	19	F.	5,724,000	6,800	42	Polymorphonuclear cells, 60 per cent. Lymphocytes, 40 per cent.
9	Adult.	M.	3,652,000	5,800	.. ..	Diff. 300. Polymorphonuclear cells, 50.0 per cent. Lymphocytes, 45.3 per cent Eosinophiles, 1.3 " Myelocytes, 1.7 " Big spleen, pallor, nosebleed, debility.
10	29	M.	5,210,000 3,840,000 1,000,000	5,000 5,600	....	Two months later. Three weeks "
11	58	M.	2,820,000	4,800	60	Polymorphonuclear cells, 80 per cent. Lymphocytes, 17 per cent. Eosinophiles, 3 "
12	21	M.	4,560,000	4,000 5,800	....	
13	23	M.	4,210,000	3,332	....	Myelocytes, 1 per cent. Big liver and spleen. Eosinophiles, 4 "
14	....	M.	3,800,000	1,440	67	Diff. 500. Polymorphonuclear cells, 71.25 per cent. Lymphocytes, 28.0 per cent. Eosinophiles, .75 " One normoblast.
15	....	...	....	No leucocytosis.	....	Diff. 200. Polymorphonuclear cells, 63.5 per cent. Lymphocytes, 36.5 per cent. Eosinophiles, 1 " Many of the lymphocytes have two nuclei.
16	......	...	....	No leucocytosis.	....	Diff. 300. Polymorphonuclear cells, 41.7 per cent. Lymphocytes, 48.4 per cent. Eosinophiles, 9.3 " Myelocytes, .6 "
17	4	M.	....	No leucocytosis.	....	Diff. 500. Polymorphonuclear cells, 60.2 per cent. Lymphocytes, 36 per cent. Eosinophiles, 5.6 " Myelocytes, 2. " Two normoblasts.
18	....	F.	....	....	....	Diff. 500. Polymorphonuclear cells, 92.6 per cent. Lymphocytes, 5.2 per cent. Myelocytes, 2.2 " No eosinophiles.
19	....	...	....	No leucocytosis.	....	Diff. 313. Polymorphonuclear cells, 62.3 per cent. Lymphocytes, 37 per cent. Myelocytes, .6 "
20	28	M.	5,218,000	11,800	85	Polynuclear, 51 per cent. Small lymphocytes, 35 " Large " 7 " Eosinophiles, 7 "

TABLE X.—HODGKIN'S DISEASE (Continued).

No.	Age.	Sex.	Red cells.	White cells.	Per cent hæmo-globin.	Remarks.
21	30	M.	5,280,000	6,800	55	Diff. Polymorphonuclear cells, 76 per cent. Lymphocytes, 22.3 " Eosinophiles, 1.4 " Myelocytes, .3 " No nucleated red cells.
22	32	M.	4,616,000	2,400	70	
23	.... ..	...	....	2,200	....	Diff. Polymorphonuclear cells, 69 per cent. Small lymphocytes, 19 " Large " 18 " Eosinophiles, 4 " Few normoblasts.

White Cells.

When inflammation arises in the glandular tumors and some-times when none is found, the white cells may be greatly in-creased, even up to a ratio of 1 : 80 red cells, as in Case 1 of the present series. There is, however, no more resemblance to leu-kæmia than in any other form of leucocytosis, the polymor-phonuclear cells alone being increased. There is no reason for supposing, as Reinert[1] does, that relative diminution of the lymphocytes is owing to the diseased condition of the lymph glands, for, unless some septic process gets a foothold in the glands, the lymphocytes present a normal number or even (as in Case 16) considerably increased percentages. Pfeiffer[2] has recently reported a case of the cutaneous form of the disease with sixty per cent of lymphocytes out of a total leucocyte count of 6,500.

As in any other cachectic condition, small numbers of mye-locytes may be found. They were seen in six of our cases out of eighteen in which a color analysis was made, the highest per-centage being two per cent. Eosinophiles are usually decreased when leucocytosis is present.

Summary.

Normal blood in early stages.
Later often marked anæmia.
Sometimes leucocytosis.

[1] "Die Zählung der Blutkörperchen," Berlin, 1891.
[2] Pfeiffer: Wien. klin. Woch., 1897.

Diagnostic Value.

The only help given us by the blood is in excluding leukæmia. Syphilis, tuberculosis, or malignant disease might cause similar blood changes or lack of changes.

EFFECTS OF SPLENECTOMY ON THE BLOOD.

Twenty-three cases are on record in which the blood has been studied after operation, but only some half-dozen of these are carefully recorded. They explain themselves:

TABLE XI.

Case.	Red cells.	White cells.	Per cent. haemoglobin.	Polymorpho-nuclear neutrophiles.	Small lymphocytes.	Large lymphocytes.	Eosinophiles.	Average diameter of red cells.	Remarks.
*1	4,570,000	8,000	63	..	..	..	..	....	Before operation.
	4,970,000	30,000	64	..	..	..	..	....	Three days after.
	5,180,000	65,000	77	..	..	..	..	....	Six days after.
	4,800,000	17,500	66	..	..	..	..	....	Forty-eight days after.
	4,353,000	11,700	85	..	..	..	..	....	Four months after.
	3,300,000	11,600	85	..	..	..	..	....	Five years after.
*2	3,200,000	53,000	65	..	..	..	..	....	(1893, for abscess.) Three weeks after.
	4,500,000	13,800	80	..	..	..	.	....	Four months after.
†3	1,634,000	12,000	45	61	16	20	3	8.1 μ	Operated (April 9th, 1893) for malarial hypertrophy with twisted pedicle. April 23d.
	2,460,000	20,000	87	49	18	32	1	....	May 6th.
	4,580,000	27,000	110	66	18	15	1	7.7 μ	May 13th, 1894.
	3,977,000	8,000	100	62	21	11	6	....	October 2d, 1895.
†4	4,850,000	30,000	108	83	8	8	1	....	Operation for hypertrophied, wandering spleen. Before operation.
	4,700,000	39,000	100	91	5	4	0	....	Seven days after.
	3,680,000	18,000	105	78	15	6	1	....	Two months after.
	2,750,000	20,000	63	84	5	10	1	....	Three years after.

* Czerny : Cited in Laudenbach ; Arch. de Physiol., 1896, p. 724.
† Hartman and Vaquez : Soc. de Biol., February 5th, 1895.

PART II.

ACUTE INFECTIOUS DISEASES.

CHAPTER III.

INFLUENCE OF FEVER ON THE BLOOD.

SOME of the blood-changes found in acute infections are to be regarded as due simply to the fever associated with the disease. It is worth while, therefore, to consider what fever *per se* can do to the blood.

Maragliano[1] and others have shown that during fever from any cause a *contraction* of the peripheral vessels occurs. When fever disappears, whether spontaneously or from the action of antipyretics (phenacetin, quinine, etc.), a *dilatation* of the vessels follows.

Following the laws to which we have so often alluded, the contraction of the vessels causes a concentration of the blood with rise in specific gravity and in the number of blood cells per cubic millimetre. This concentration is still further increased by the greater loss of water which the organism suffers during fever than under normal conditions.

The effect of these two influences in increasing the number of red cells per cubic millimetre is, however, counteracted to a considerable extent by the sharing of the blood in the general tissue destruction which goes on with increased rapidity during fever. Many corpuscles are thus destroyed, but until the temperature falls the anæmia is covered up by the concentration. When the fever leaves the patient there is a sharp fall in the number of cells per cubic millimetre, due partly to the destruction of corpuscles (hitherto masked by concentration) and partly to the *dilution of the blood* which is the result of the post-febrile dilatation of the peripheral vessels above mentioned. The sud-

[1] Zeit. f. klin. Med.. vols. 14 and 17.

denness of this fall in the count is proportional to the suddenness of the fall in temperature.

The alkalinity of the blood has been often said to be diminished in fever, but recent research tends to show that these results were obtained by faulty technique, and it is doubtful whether the reaction of the blood shows any constant changes in fever.

Leucocytes and fibrin show no constant changes, though in the majority of infectious fevers they are increased.

PNEUMONIA.

The Blood as a Whole.

(a) Bacteriology.—The diplococcus lanceolatus has been found in the blood of pneumonic patients repeatedly, especially in those in whom there has been some secondary diplococcus infection (e.g., diplococcus endocarditis); but such findings are rare and have generally been in fatal cases with very severe generalized infection.

For example, Sittmann[1] out of 16 cases found diplococci in the blood of 6, most of which were complicated with lesions in other organs, and 4 of which died, while of the 10 whose blood was sterile, 9 recovered.

Boulay[2] found the organism in 2 cases shortly before death. Belfanti[3] found it but 6 times out of a large number of cases, and of these 6, 5 died. Goldschneider[4] and Grawitz[5] got similar results. Cohn[6] in 32 cases found the organism in 9; 7 of these died. The other 2 had empyema and other evidences of metastatic action of the pneumococci. Fraenkel has obtained over 300 colonies from one puncture. Their virulence was less than that of those in the sputa, showing apparently the effects of the blood's antitoxic power. Nevertheless, it is obvious that the presence of pneumococci in the blood is a bad prognostic sign.

[1] Deut. Archiv f. klin. Med., 1894, p. 323.
[2] Paris Thesis, 1891.
[3] Riforma Medica. Naples, 1890, No. 37.
[4] Deut. med. Woch., 1892, No. 14.
[5] Grawitz: Charité-Annalen. vol. 10.
[6] Cohn: Deut. med. Woch., 1897, No. 9.

(*b*) Coagulation is remarkably rapid and in fresh specimens the fibrin network is very thick and appears within a few minutes.

(*c*) In cases with cyanosis the blood is often concentrated at the periphery so that its specific gravity is high and the number of corpuscles large.

(*d*) Monti and Berggrün[1] observed that in children the specific gravity was high throughout the course of the disease, falling with the temperature.

The toxicity of the blood is doubled (Albu: Virchow's *Archiv*, Vol. 149).

Red Cells.—During the fever the red cells are approximately normal (unless increased by cyanosis); but after the crisis there is often slight anæmia, due partly to the blood destruction evidenced by the frequent presence of hydrobilirubin in the urine. Grawitz considers also that a general relaxation of the peripheral vessels in the post-critical period causes a dilution of the blood with (apparent) lessening of the red cells.

Maragliano has noticed " degenerative" changes in the red cells in severe cases, but as a rule they do not appear much affected either in quantity or quality and our attention is chiefly directed to the

White Corpuscles.—1. Probably as early as the time of the chill, and certainly within a few hours after it, the leucocytes are greatly increased, and continue so throughout the febrile period.

2. There is no correspondence between the daily variations in temperature and the leucocyte curve. In cases in which a pseudo-crisis occurs (the temperature falling but quickly rising again), the leucocyte count remains high, while at the time of the true crisis and often a few hours before it the leucocytes *begin* to fall. This fall, however, is hardly ever by "crisis," but though starting perhaps a little before the temperature it is one to two days longer in reaching normal. When the temperature reaches normal by lysis the leucocytes fall with it but generally more slowly, and reach normal later.

3. When resolution is delayed the leucocytosis continues, sometimes for weeks, and very gradually sags down to normal in cases in which resolution eventually occurs without complica-

tion. If abscess, empyema, or gangrene follow, the leucocytes stay up.

4. The degree of leucocytosis is probably the resultant of the factors mentioned on page 106, and does not run parallel to the degree of fever or the amount of lung involved. Nevertheless cases with extensive signs in both lungs are more apt to have very high counts, provided the "reaction" of the patient against the infection is vigorous. The cases appear to fall into the following groups as regards the degree of leucocytosis present.

1. Mild infection, vigorous reaction = slight leucocytosis.
2. Severe or moderate infection, vigorous reaction = marked leucocytosis.
3. Severe infection, feeble reaction = no leucocytosis.

(a) The cases in Class 1 all recover, but they are very few in number. (b) Those in Class 2, which includes over nine-tenths of all cases, may or may not recover, according as the fight between patient and disease comes out one way or the other.

(c) Class 3 *almost invariably die;* there is not sufficient of a struggle to raise the leucocyte count.

Where either the patient or his disease *easily* gains the mastery there is no leucocytosis or a very slight one; but in the much larger class of cases in which the struggle is a fierce one, leucocytosis appears, *whichever way the struggle results.*

Pick [1] noted that pneumonia complicating cases of small-pox which were already very sick, caused no leucocytosis, and the same is often true in those whose power of resistance is reduced by age, alcoholism, typhoid, or by some chronic disease.

Von Jaksch, noticing the fatality of cases without leucocytosis, suggested that we should induce leucocytosis by injecting turpentine or other irritants so as to cause abscess; but this has not proved of any benefit to the patient, nor has the production of leucocytosis without abscess, as can be done with pilocarpine or nuclein, been any more successful. There is no difficulty in producing the leucocytosis by these means, but all observers are agreed that it does the patients no good.

Leucocytosis is checked by antipyretics (Hare [2]) but not by

[1] Arch. f. Dermat. und Syph., vol. 25, p. 63.
[2] New York Medical Record, May 9th, 1896.

cold bathing, which speaks in favor of the latter method of reducing temperature.

The general course of the leucocytes is seen in the accompanying charts from Billings, to whose excellent article I am greatly indebted.

CHART I.—PNEUMONIA, SHOWING FALL BY CRISIS (BILLINGS).

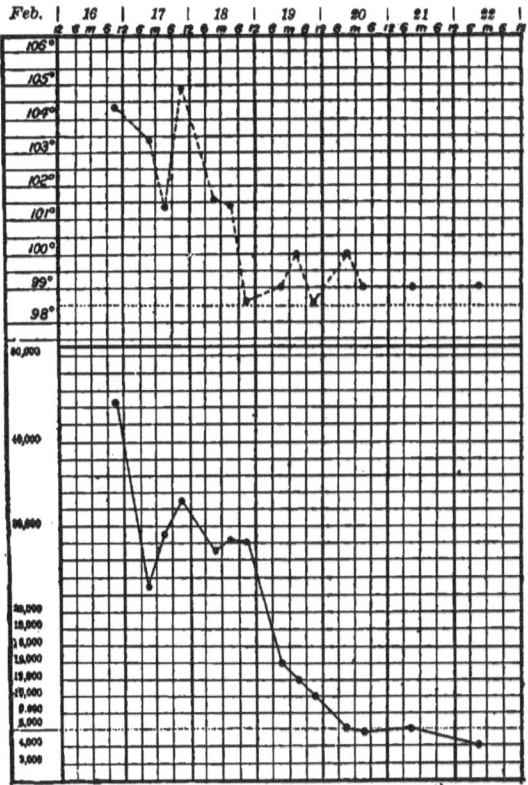

The upper chart shows the course of the temperature, the lower that of the leucocytes.

Qualitative Changes.—As in most forms of leucocytosis the polymorphonuclear leucocytes are enormously increased, often making over ninety per cent of all the white cells. Eosinophiles and blood plates disappear and the lymphocytes are much reduced. After the crisis this is reversed, the polymorphonuclear forms falling often below 60 per cent, while the eosinophiles and blood plates are above normal. As to the differential count

CHART II.—PNEUMONIA AND RHEUMATISM.

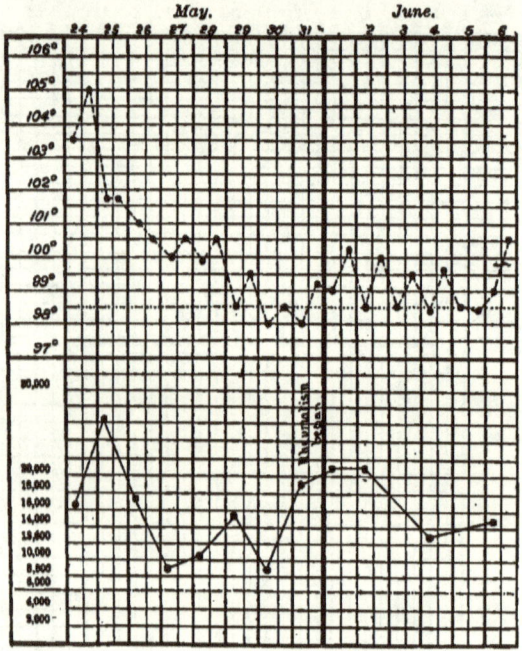

The upper chart shows the course of the temperature, the lower that of the leucocytes.

in the (fatal) cases in which leucocytosis is absent, data are scanty. Bieganski thought the polymorphonuclear varieties decreased, Rieder found them increased, while Billings finds them normal. No general law can be stated on this point as yet.

In one remarkable case occurring at the Massachusetts General Hospital in 1894, the conditions were entirely different from those just stated. The patient, a girl of six, had at entrance 72,100 leucocytes per cubic millimetre. Two days after the count was 94,600. A differential count made at the same time showed that the small lymphocytes made up 66 per cent of all the 94,600 leucocytes per cubic millimetre. The poly-morphonuclear cells were reduced to 30 per cent. Lymphatic leukæmia was thought of, but the leucocytosis was gone in ten days, and within a fortnight the patient left the hospital well. I have seen one reference to such a condition. "In a certain number of cases the leucocytosis is characterized by the great number of the youngest forms of leucocytes. This condition persists during convalescence."[1]

Diagnostic and Prognostic Value.

1. In cases of so-called "central pneumonia" in which the symptoms but not the physical signs of the disease are manifest, the presence of a well-marked leucocytosis is often of great diag-nostic value. It excludes malaria, typhoid, and uncomplicated grippe as causes of fever, and if scarlet fever and suppuration can be excluded by other evidence, it makes pneumonia very probable.

I have repeatedly seen the diagnosis of pneumonia made in the absence of physical signs and largely on the evidence of the blood count, the diagnosis being confirmed several days later by the appearance of typical signs of consolidation. In a case of Dr. F. C. Shattuck's, sick five days, yet showing no signs of consolidation of the lung, the presence of a marked leucocytosis excluded typhoid, the only other likely diagnosis, and led Dr. Shattuck to treat the case as pneumonia, the wisdom of which course was later demonstrated by the appearance of signs of consolidation.

2. Between pneumonia and capillary bronchitis the condition of the blood is of no help, as the latter also causes leucocytosis, and some cases affecting the larger tubes do the same.

3. In cases of pneumonia occurring in very old or very young people, in which the fever and symptoms may be very slight, the presence of leucocytosis may be the first thing to direct our attention to the lungs, dyspnœa and cough being ab-sent.

[1] Stiènon : Jour. de Méd., de Chirurg. et de Pharm., Bruxelles, 1895, t. iv., fasc. 1.

In *prognosis*, the important point is that *the absence of leucocytosis is a very bad sign, while its presence is neither good nor bad.* It must be remembered also that in the very mildest cases we may find the same absence of leucocytosis which in any other but the mildest would be almost surely fatal.

This last point, which appears to me of great importance, is illustrated by the following figures:

Halla reported 14 cases; 2 had no leucocytosis, and both died.

Billings reported 22 cases; 1 had no leucocytosis and died.

Laehr with 16 cases, and Rieder with 26, got similar results.

Ewing in 101 cases found leucocytosis absent in 6; 6 died.

Von Jaksch and Kilodse likewise maintain that the absence of leucocytosis is usually fatal.

In the Massachusetts General Hospital 329 cases have been studied. In general they entirely confirm the results obtained by Billings and summarized above; 32 of them presented no leucocytosis at any time, and of these 32, 30 died, another one seemed moribund but finally recovered, while the remaining case was a very mild one.

The evidence, therefore, is overwhelmingly in favor of the view that where leucocytosis is absent in any but the mildest cases the prognosis is almost fatal. *The presence of leucocytosis, on the other hand, is no guaranty whatever of a favorable issue.*

The series of cases at the Massachusetts Hospital is too large to exhibit in tabular form. Their results may be summarized as follows:

Cases with leucocytes under 10,000 = 32   (30 of these fatal)
"   "   "   between   10,000 to 15.000 = 38
"   "   "   "   15,000 " 20,000 = 72
"   "   "   "   20,000 " 25,000 = 65
"   "   "   "   25,000 " 30,000 = 37
"   "   "   "   30,000 " 35,000 = 22
"   "   "   "   35,000 " 40,000 =   4
"   "   "   "   40,000 " 45,000 =   7
"   "   "   "   45,000 " 50,000 =   4
"   "   "   "   50,000 " 55,000 =   5
"   "   "   but not accurately counted = 43
                                                      ‾‾‾
                        Average = 24,000 -̇   329

TYPHOID FEVER.

Bacteriology.

Although the bacilli of Eberth are occasionally to be found in the blood by culture, it is only in the marked cases that they occur, and then but rarely, so that at present we derive no help in doubtful cases by the bacteriological examination of the blood.

Kühnau, using 5–10 c.c. of blood, found the organism in 10 out of 41 cases, from 2 to 9 slow-growing colonies in each. Other observers have been successful in only 7 out of a total of 176 cases examined. Block has recently succeeded in isolating the organism twice during the life of a patient who sub sequently died. In 6 other cases he was unsuccessful. It has been asserted that when the bacilli enter the blood the serum reaction (*vide infra*) does not appear.

Toward the end of the disease, when the temperature is apt to be very irregular (so-called "period of steep curves"), pyogenic cocci are occasionally to be found in cultures made from the blood, and doubtless account for many of the recrudescences and temporary febrile attacks, with or without chills, which are so common in early convalescence.

The Blood as a Whole.—1. Coagulation and fibrin are normal.

2. Specific gravity follows the course of the hæmoglobin.

3. The general effects of fever (see above, page 183) are in part accountable for the changes next to be described, while some of them are more peculiar to typhoid fever.

Red Cells.—During the first two weeks there are no considerable changes, except in so far as a certain amount of concentration of the blood with apparent increase of cells may be brought about by diarrhœa or sweating. Baths have a like effect if the blood is examined just after the immersion.[1] In the third week the red cells usually begin to decrease and in extreme cases may get as low as 1,300,000 at the beginning of convalescence—*i.e.*, when body weight begins to increase. Hayem considers that the diminution begins rather suddenly in the middle or end of the third week of severe cases, but according

---

[1] Antipyrin and acetanilid have no effects on the red cells.

to Thayer the diminution is gradual, though at first sight, growing more rapid at the time of defervescence, and continuing
often into convalescence. The lowest point is reached about the
first week of convalescence.

The following figures (Thayer) illustrate this.

First week, 2 counts.	Second week, 10 counts.	Third week, 9 counts.	Fourth week, 6 counts.	Fifth week, 7 counts.	Sixth week.
5,636,000	4,960,599	4,951,535	4,038,333	3,856,786	4,364,250

His later counts show a gradual increase. He finds that the
amount of anæmia bears, *as a rule*, a direct relation to the
severity of the case, but in one of his cases a grave anæmia
(1,300,000) followed a mild attack. " The anæmia may be severe
enough to form of itself a dangerous complication of the process." Henry has likewise recorded counts as low as 1,306,000
and 804,000 in two convalescent typhoids.

Hæmoglobin.—The loss of coloring matter roughly parallels
that of the red cells, but is always relatively greater and is
slower in reaching normal. In the case just noted it was 20 per
cent, color index .7.

Leucocytes.—The absence of any increase of the white cells
is the most important point.

Starting with an approximately normal count, the number
falls during the fever, often below 2,000, according to Hayem,
and sometimes below 1,000 per cubic millimetre. Khetagurow
finds the lowest counts (2,500–3,000) about the end of the third
week.

Thayer's figures are as follows:

First week, 21 counts.	Second week, 50 counts.	Third week, 40 counts.	Fourth week. 28 counts.	Fifth week, 16 counts.	Sixth week, 5 counts.
6,984	6,468	6,260	5,877	6,621	7,000

In the four hundred and ninety-one cases counted at the
Massachusetts General Hospital, the course of the leucocytes
has unfortunately not been followed by weeks with sufficient
accuracy to make comparisons of value. In a general way,
however, they corroborate all of Thayer's positions. At the beginning of the cases the count was often high (11,000), owing
probably to concentration of the blood by starvation and diarrhœa. The high count of *red* cells confirmed this, the ratio of
red to white remaining normal. The counts of leucocytes then
gradually diminished, as in Thayer's cases.

The range of the counts was as follows:

Between 1,000 and 2,000 = 7 cases.
" 2,000 " 3,000 = 33 "
" 3,000 " 4,000 = 59 "
" 4,000 " 5,000 = 108 "
" 5,000 " 6,000 = 82 "
" 6,000 " 7,000 = 72 "
" 7,000 " 8,000 = 47 "
" 8,000 " 9,000 = 37 "
" 9,000 " 10,000 = 29 "
" 10,000 " 11,000 = 10 "
Over 11,000........ .. = 7 "

491 cases.

From these figures I have excluded all cases counted only under circumstances likely to concentrate the blood (cyanosis, after baths, after severe diarrhœa).

There is no doubt that leucocytosis *does* occasionally occur when no complication exists *so far as we can ascertain during life*. Four of the cases over 11,000 (see the above table) were counted repeatedly and complications were carefully sought for, but none were found. The most striking case showed the following counts:

October 3d............................. 13,100
" 4th............................. 13,000
" 5th............................. 16,500
" 7th............................. 13,300
" 8th........................ ... 11,200
" 10th............................. 10,600
" 13th 13,500
" 15th............................. 17,700
" 17th......................... 15,500, death ; autopsy.

The autopsy showed typical typhoid lesions and nothing else.' Another and much milder case showed 11,000–12,000 white cells constantly for over two weeks, and no cause could be found to account for it.

The great rarity of such cases and constant association of leucocytosis with any of the numerous complications which we can recognize, rather inclines me to the belief that in all the cases in which leucocytosis exists constantly, some complication

¹ Thrombosis of internal veins and osteomyelitis were not carefully searched for at autopsy and may have existed.

13

really *is* present though unrecognized.   The possibility of a secondary septic infection, of an osteomyelitis, or phlebitis of internal veins cannot be excluded without further evidence.

Examples of the effect of complications are as follows:

Perforation.—Case I.	(a) Five days before perforation,	8,300
	(b) At time of the perforation, .	24,000
Case II.	At time of perforation, . .	18,500
Phlebitis.—Case I.	(a) Two days before onset, . .	6,400
	(b) At time of the onset, . . .	12,900
	(c) One week later, ...	10,100
Case II.	(a) One week before onset, . .	4,800
	(b) At time of onset, ...	16,200
Otitis Media.—Case I.	(a) At entrance, ...	5,300
	(b) Mastoid abscess, ...	16,400
Case II.	(a) At entrance, ...	8,400
	(b) Two weeks later, after opening drum membrane (sero-pu r u l e n t discharge), ...	11,200
Case III.	(a) At entrance, ...	7,320
	(b) Otitis, ...	14,000

A freely discharging otitis soon ceases to cause leucocytosis, *e.g.*, a case of serous otitis media seven days after puncture, but still freely discharged, showed but 5,320 white cells per cubic millimetre.

An abscess of the buttock raised the count from 8,000 to 11,200, and a hemorrhage from 8,000 to 11,300.

General bronchitis has usually no effect in augmenting the leucocyte count unless the disease invades the smallest tubes (capillary bronchitis).   Thus two cases of this affection showed 9,000 and 8,000 leucocytes respectively.

Cystitis had no effect in two cases.[1]

In two cases whose symptoms simulated otitis (deafness, rise of temperature, pain in the head, and in one a convulsion) but whose blood counts were normal, the trouble turned out to be functional and nothing came of it, the symptoms disappearing within twenty-four hours.

[1] I have an impression based on rather fragmentary evidence that complications directly due to the Eberth bacilli, *e.g.*, Eberth cystitis or Eberth pneumonia, do *not* raise the leucocyte count.   I hope to investigate this point later.

Some observers [1] have noted a slight leucocytosis at the beginning of convalescence. Thayer did not find this, and I have been equally unsuccessful.

It occasionally happens in very exhausted patients that complications fail to produce any leucocytosis, the patient (as in some fatal cases of pneumonia or purulent peritonitis) being unable to react against the infection. For example, I have seen a large ischio-rectal abscess develop in a moribund typhoid patient without producing any effect on the leucocyte count. Von Limbeck has noticed the same lack of reaction in typhoid patients after a hemorrhage and bronchopneumonia, and Rieder in croupous pneumonia occurring as a complication.

These cases, however, are exceptional, and in many of them the percentage of adult leucocytes rises, though no increase in the total leucocyte count is present. This increased percentage of polymorphonuclear forms generally betrays the presence of the complication, since during most of the disease (if uncomplicated) the polymorphonuclear forms are *diminished*.

In normal cases the blood begins to return to normal as soon as the fever is gone and reaches the normal in the sixth or seventh week.

Qualitative Changes.

Red Cells.—The condition is either normal or shows the changes common to all varieties of secondary anæmia.

White Cells.—All observers are agreed upon the following changes:

1. The polymorphonuclear cells progressively diminish with a corresponding increase in the lymphocytes. This change is but slight in the first two weeks, but grows marked in the latter part of the illness, the polymorphonuclear cells falling below 50 per cent. Among the lymphocytes, the larger forms predominate.

2. It is not until after the disappearance of fever (from three to ten days after it, according to Ouskow) that the polymorphonuclear cells begin to increase again and their normal percentage

---

[1] *E.g.*, Aporti and Radaeli (11th Congress for Medical Science, Rome, March 29th, 1894).

is not reached until the tenth or eleventh week. Thayer's
differential counts show:

Second week, 5 counts.	Third week, 1 count.	Fourth week, 3 counts.	Fifth week. 1 count.	Sixth week, 2 counts.
71.7 per cent.	66.5 per cent.	65.3 per cent.	58.5 per cent.	53.4 per cent.

3. Eosinophiles are present in small numbers.

Summary.

1. Post-febrile anæmia, sometimes very intense.

2. No leucocytosis; in late weeks leucopenia.

3. Increased percentage of lymphocytes at the expense of
polymorphonuclear forms, especially marked in later weeks.

4. Most complications cause leucocytosis.

Diagnostic Value.

There are few diseases (outside of those known as diseases
of the blood itself) in which the blood count is so often of value in
diagnosis. The diagnosis of typhoid fever is to be made by exclusion—exclusion of other causes of fever and of local inflammatory processes in particular.

1. Now in this process of exclusion, the blood is a most
powerful adjuvant, inasmuch as almost all *local inflammatory
processes have leucocytosis, while typhoid* (uncomplicated) *does not.*
I have seen two cases in which the chart and symptoms pointed
to typhoid but in which the persistent marked leucocytosis
directed attention to the search for an inflammatory focus. Both
were at first unattended with pain, tenderness, or other localizing symptom, but later signs and symptoms began to point to
the *liver*, from which pus was evacuated by puncture. These
cases of *abscess of the liver* are typical of the value of blood examination for any deep-seated suppuration. I have seen good
clinicians puzzled for twenty-four hours over the diagnosis between appendicitis and typhoid, but the indication of the blood
count was always fulfilled. All pyæmic or septicæmic processes
are distinguishable from typhoid by the same test—the presence of leucocytosis in the former.

Of the value of the blood in distinguishing certain cases of
pneumonia from typhoid I have already spoken on page 189.

2. Aside from local or general pyogenic infections perhaps
the disease most often confounded with typhoid is *malaria*.

This is especially the case in the southern part of this country, where for want of proper blood examination the confusion of the two diseases is indicated in such a term as "typho-malarial fever." Malaria and typhoid are alike in having no leucocytosis, but the presence of the malarial parasite is an absolute test and in marked cases is always decisive. Very mild cases of malaria may show so few organisms in the peripheral circulation that without prolonged search they cannot be found, and in the severest types of all, the organisms are not very abundant. In the vast majority of cases, however, the organism can be readily found and our diagnosis made certain.

3. Tuberculosis, if uncomplicated by any pyogenic organisms, cannot be distinguished from typhoid by the examination of the blood alone, as neither disease shows leucocytosis.

A large proportion of lymphocytes is commoner in typhoid than in tuberculosis, but it may occur in either disease. In the majority of cases, however, tuberculosis is complicated with septicæmia from a secondary pyogenic infection, and is then easily distinguished by the existence of leucocytosis.

4. *Typhus fever* has not been well studied and the reports of its blood condition are contradictory. At present we cannot say whether or not it can be distinguished from typhoid by the blood examination. In most cases the absence of a serum reaction will exclude typhus.

5. Two cases of erythema nodosum with fever between 101° and 103° gave me trouble in diagnosis lately. In both the blood was normal and differed from typhoid only by the absence of a serum-reaction.

The occurrence of complications in typhoid may mask its characteristic blood changes so as to make the blood useless in diagnosis; but in most early cases, in which the diagnosis is especially important and difficult, the blood shows no leucocytosis and is therefore of great value in the exclusion of other diseases.

DIPHTHERIA.

Bacilli of diphtheria in the circulating blood are practically never to be found.

The specific gravity, according to Grawitz, is *above* normal at the height of the disease. He obtained the same result experimentally by injecting cultures of the Klebs-Löffler bacillus into dogs and rabbits. He concludes that the poison of the disease is lymphagogic and so concentrates the blood.

Red Corpuscles.—Morse's [1] investigations show an average of 5,100,000 in twenty cases counted during the first week of the disease and of 5,150,000 in 10 cases during the second and third week of the disease—practically normal figures.

These are the first systematic [2] investigations of the red cells in diphtheria and are confirmed by the reports of Ewing, Engel, and Billings. The latter observer in counts made in seven cases during the first five days of illness found an average of 5,600,-000+ red cells per cubic millimetre. During the first five to ten days after this, the same cases showed an average loss of 510,000 cells per cubic millimetre; five out of the seven showing considerable losses, two remaining about the same. These were cases treated without antitoxin. The two cases showing no loss of red cells were both very mild, one having no membrane at any time. The diminution ranged from 470,000 (third day) to 2,040,000 (sixth day). As a rule no diminution can be made out until after the third or fourth day.

Out of twenty-three cases treated with antitoxin and each counted several times over, only three showed any considerable diminution in the red cells and these lost less than 400,000 each, not much beyond the limit of error (200,000) allowed for by the investigator, and all of them severe cases. Six patients who were anæmic when admitted (average=4,640,000) showed a steady *rise* in the red cells as the disease (treated with antitoxin) progressed.

It is evident from these figures that antitoxin largely prevents the anæmia which usually develops in the first five to ten days. In cases not treated with antitoxin the regeneration from the resulting anæmia is slow. Healthy individuals injected with antitoxin showed a very moderate reduction in the red cells in about one-half the cases, the greatest loss being 932,-000 per cubic millimetre (fifteen cases counted by Billings).

Qualitative Changes.—Billings' careful study of stained specimens showed no deformities in size or shape and no nucleated red cells. Polychromatophilic red corpuscles were very few in

---

[1] Boston Medical and Surgical Journal, March 7th, 1895.
[2] Earlier reports are faulty as to technique.

the cases in which antitoxin was used, but more numerous where it was not used.

Hæmoglobin.—Here again the most thorough investigations are those of Billings. In cases treated without antitoxin there was an average loss of ten per cent, regained in part during convalescence, but as usual reaching normal later than the count of corpuscles. When antitoxin was given, the diminution of hæmoglobin was less marked, but where the decrease did occur the return to normal was slow compared to that of the red cells, even when the patients were up and about and apparently well.

White Corpuscles.—Leaving out the older observations in which the technique was probably faulty, the principal investigators are Morse, Ewing, Gabritschewsky, and Billings.

All agree that a considerable leucocytosis is present in most cases—34 out of 36 of Billings' cases, 26 out of 30 of Morse's (the latter made but one count in each case), 49 out of 53 of Ewing's. In a general way, the severest cases show the greatest leucocytosis, but it does not follow the pulse, temperature, nor the extent of the membrane, and "the ordinary clinical examination of the patient is of much greater value in . . . prognosis . . . than any information to be gained from the examination of the blood. The latter is simply confirmatory, never indispensable" (Billings). Morse's conclusions are the same, although he considers that with notable exceptions the amount of membrane is a rough measure of the degree of leucocytosis. He finds no correspondence between the glandular swellings and the degree of leucocytosis, though he noted that "in the fatal 'septic' cases with greatly enlarged glands," very high counts were present. Other cases with little or no enlargement of glands showed equally high counts, however.

Ewing's 4 cases without leucocytosis were all mild, but of Billings' 2 cases without leucocytosis one was the severest of his whole series, while the other was mild. Of Morse's 4 cases without leucocytosis 3 were mild and 1 severe. Gabritschewsky's 14 cases all showed leucocytosis.

Putting the results of these four observers together we see that when leucocytosis is absent the cases are *either* very mild or very severe, conditions analogous to those to be noted in pneumonia and septicæmia. The counts in recent epidemics range from normal to 48,000 (Morse) or to 38,600 (Billings). Felsenthal [1] found 148,229 per cubic millimetre in one case, and Bouchut's [2] counts are often over 75,000.

In a general way the counts rise while the disease progresses and fall gradually as improvement goes on, disappearing after the membrane. "The leucocytosis is well marked by the third day and very likely earlier" (Morse). Billings found an increase after one day's illness, but usually less than was present later in the disease; one of his cases, however, had a higher count on the first day of the disease than on any subsequent day, though no antitoxin was given.

The injection of antitoxin has apparently no effect upon the leucocyte count (strange to say) except in the first twenty-four hours after its use. Immediately, *i.e.*, within thirty minutes after an injection, the leucocytes are stated by Ewing to be considerably diminished, but the leucocyte curve does not reach normal any sooner than in cases in which no antitoxin is given, although it begins to fall in the majority of cases after the injection. The same thing (according to Billings) takes place without antitoxin.

The leucocytes of healthy persons are likewise unaffected by antitoxin injections.

Qualitative Changes.—All authors agree that in most cases the neutrophiles are increased. Morse found an average of 80 per cent in 26 of his 30 cases. Of the other 4, 1 was normal and 3 subnormal (58, 59, and 59 per cent); 2 of these were convalescent, the other had been sick a week and had 12,000 white cells per cubic millimetre. A similar lymphocytosis was present in 1 of Ewing's 53 cases, and in 1 of Rieder's during convalescence. Billings thinks such a lymphocytosis may be present in perfect health, mentioning cases with 32, 33, and 35 per cent of small lymphocytes in sound persons. Such a condition did not occur in any of his diphtheritic cases except in the single fatal case without leucocytosis. Here the polymorphonuclear cells were reduced to 55 per cent and the lymphocytes (large and small) made up the remaining 45 per cent, 28 per cent being large forms. [3] In the rest of his cases the polymorphonuclear

[1] Archiv f. Kinderheilk., vol. xv., p. 78, 1893.
[2] Comptes Rendus, 1877, lxxv., No. 3.
[3] In Rieder's case above referred to, aged three years, the lymphocytes rose from 19 per cent during the fever to 64 per cent in convalescence.

varieties averaged 80 per cent and the lymphocytes 19 per cent, the eosinophiles being reduced to 1 per cent on the average and often being entirely absent. With Morse eosinophiles averaged 2 per cent.

The proportion of polymorphonuclear cells is usually directly proportional to the total increase of leucocytes.

Ewing thinks that "the staining reaction of the leucocytes is an accurate measure of the severity of the diphtheritic infection," and this staining reaction he finds increased in favorable cases by the injection of antitoxin.

Billings did not find any such changes in "staining reaction," though he claims to have carefully followed out Ewing's procedures.

Engel[1] found that antitoxin at first slightly increased the percentage of lymphocytes, and sometimes this increase was very marked. In one case the lymphocytes increased from 24 to 65 sixty-five per cent after antitoxin.

The point on which he specially insists is the presence of considerable numbers of *myelocytes* in fatal cases.

Of the cases examined by him 17 died, and 9 of these had from 3.6 to 16.8 per cent of myelocytes in every one hundred leucocytes. Myelocytes were also present in some of the cases which recovered, but in smaller numbers (1.3 to 1.5 per cent.)

In one case he found on the third day of the disease 4.3 per cent of myelocytes, and from this point the percentage gradually rose to 13.8 per cent, and then fell, there being 1.7 per cent present at the time of death. An abscess occurring in the case showed only the usual polymorphonuclear leucocytes in its contents. He concluded that a large percentage of myelocytes is a bad prognostic sign in any case.

Myelocytes are not mentioned in any of the numerous differential counts made by Gabritschewsky, Ewing, Morse, and Billings, so that Engel's observation is so far unique.

Summary.

1. Moderate anæmia, especially in cases treated without antitoxin. Regeneration is slow.

2. Leucocytosis, very roughly parallel to the severity of the disease, unaffected by antitoxin treatment, gradually decreas-

[1] Gesellsch. f. innere Med., Berlin, July 6th, 1896.

ing the disease passes off, sometimes absent in very mild or very severe cases.

3. Polymorphonuclear leucocytes much increased during febrile stages, often diminished in convalescence.

4. Myelocytes numerous in some severe cases.

The blood examination has no diagnostic value so far as I can see; in prognosis the absence of leucocytosis (except in obviously mild cases) and the presence of many myelocytes are apparently bad signs.

CHAPTER IV.

SCARLET FEVER.

HEUBNER[1] noted hæmoglobinæmia in one case. Fibrin is not increased even at the height of the fever, provided inflammatory complications are absent.

Red Cells.—Very little is to be found in literature upon the subject. Kotschetkoff[2] noted a gradual diminution of the red cells to about 3,000,000, regeneration taking place in the course of not less than six weeks. Other observers have found little or no anæmia.

Hayem[3] estimates the average loss of red cells at 1,000,000. In mild cases he finds the lowest figures on the first day of normal temperature. In severer cases in which the fever comes down slowly, the red cells may not reach their minimum till twenty-four hours after reaching the normal temperature.

Felsenthal[4] in six cases found the count to be 4,500,000 to 5,500,000—no considerable variation from normal.

Zappert[5] in six cases found it to be from 3,920,000 to 4,-500,000, an average of 4,150,000.

White Cells.—Most observers are agreed that *leucocytosis is the rule*, contrasting in this respect with measles, in which no leucocytosis occurs. The increase may be present even six days before the rash appears and attains its maximum two or three days after the eruption. In light cases it may sink to normal even before the fever is gone, while in severer cases it may persist *several days after a normal temperature is reached.* Von Limbeck had a case in which the leucocytosis persisted for

[1] Déut. Arch. f. klin. Med., vol. 28.
[2] Ref. in Petersburg. med. Woch., 1892, 1.
[3] *Loc. cit.*, p. 914.
[4] Arch. f. Kinderheilk., 1892, p. 80.
[5] Zeit. f. klin. Med., 1893, p. 292.

twelve days after the temperature had become normal. Forty thousand per cubic millimetre is not unusual in well-marked cases. Rieder's ten cases averaged 17,500; Felsenthal's six counts were between 18,000 and 30,000. My own are similar.

In a general way the severest cases are apt to have the highest leucocyte counts; the figures have no direct relation to the amount of fever, glandular swelling, or to complications in the ear or kidney.

Qualitative Changes.—The polymorphonuclear forms are increased, often to 90 per cent, soon falling except in the worst cases. The peculiar characteristic of the disease is the persistence of eosinophiles in all but the severest cases despite the increase of polymorphonuclear forms. They may run as high as 5 per cent during the fever, and are still more numerous in convalescence, remaining increased for six weeks. According to Kotschetkoff, disappearance of eosinophiles is a bad prognostic sign except at the very beginning of the fever, when they may be temporarily absent in favorable cases. Presumably they have some connection with the exanthem, eosinophilia being so common in connection with skin lesions. They may number 15 per cent of the leucocytes in convalescence. Felsenthal's average is 5 per cent; Zappert's, 3 per cent. The lymphocytes are decreased proportionately to the severity of the case, the worst cases showing only 2 to 4 per cent.

An increase of eosinophiles during a scarlatinal nephritis is regarded by Neusser and his pupils as a favorable sign, and their absence as ominous. In ordinary cases without nephritis they reach their maximum in the second or third week and are not normal till the sixth.

Summary.

Moderate anæmia.

Leucocytosis beginning before the eruption and often lasting into convalescence.

Eosinophiles said to be increased in favorable cases, absent in bad cases.

Diagnostic and Prognostic Value.

1. The chief importance of the blood examination is in distinguishing the disease from measles and the eruptions of other diseases. Measles has no leucocytosis.

2. Whether the prognostic significance attached by Neusser and others to the percentage of eosinophiles is genuine or not cannot as yet be positively stated.

MEASLES.

In mild cases the blood shows no changes at all. Where bronchitis, coryza, and conjunctivitis are very marked, fibrin may be increased.

Red Cells.—In mild cases no change—never over 400,000 or 500,000 red cells are lost (Hayem). Felsenthal's eight cases showed counts of 5,000,000 to 5,500,000.

White Cells.—In most cases there is no increase. Felsenthal in eight cases found the count normal or diminished. Pée found but 4,000 in a case with a fever of 102.7°. Rieder's eight cases averaged 7,500, being *lowest* at the height of the disease and increasing as fever passed off. Complication with catarrhal pneumonia or a very bad bronchitis and coryza may slightly raise the count. The eosinophiles, contrary to the example of scarlet fever, are often absent during fever.

The Massachusetts Hospital records furnish the following counts:

TABLE XII.—MEASLES.

Age.	Sex.	Red cells.	White cells.	Per cent hæmo-globin.	Remarks.
38	M.	4,700,000	9,000	65	"Black measles" petechiæ.
8	M.	....	9,000	..	Differential count normal.
23	F.	....	8,000	68	104°; eruption out.
4	M.	5,000,000	7,000	60	Eruption just out.
10	M.	....	6,000	..	103°, three days before the eruption; differential count normal.
			6,000	..	Eruption out one day.
			6,000	..	Eruption out three days.
53	F.	....	3,500	..	
33	F.	....	3,500	67	

Felsenthal found the polymorphonuclear cells much increased and eosinophiles never over one per cent. In my own cases the differential counts were normal. The *value* of the blood examination is considerable in excluding scarlet fever, diphtheria, and syphilitic roseola, all of which show leucocytosis. It cannot apparently be distinguished by the blood count from *Rötheln* (German measles), in two cases of which, seen at the Massachusetts Hospital, the white cells were 6,000 and 8,000 respectively.

MUMPS.

Five cases of *mumps* under my care showed no leucocytosis.

WHOOPING-COUGH.

A girl of six recently seen showed at the height of the disease 12,600 leucocytes with 78 per cent of hæmoglobin.

SMALL-POX (VARIOLA).

Red Cells.—According to Hayem no other fever is so destructive of red cells. During the fever the count is normal or increased, but when the temperature falls permanently the number of red cells falls suddenly, whether because the blood is diluted (see above, page 158) or by a real destruction. From this time on the cells are slowly regenerated; even at the fifteenth day Hayem found them considerably below normal.

In hemorrhagic cases the anæmia comes on more quickly, its degree depending on the amount of hemorrhage. In one case, dying on the seventh day of the eruption, Hayem found but 2,000,000 red cells, in another at the same stage, 4,600,000.

Fibrin is not increased until the stage of suppuration is reached.

White Corpuscles.—Pick, who carefully studied 42 cases, found that the very lightest cases, such as occur in vaccinated persons, may cause no leucocytosis. In a woman of twenty-two on the third day of illness with a temperature of 105°, the count was only 4,200 and on the fifth day (temperature 99°) 3,600. This patient had been vaccinated.

Severe cases if without complication show no leucocytosis till the pus appears in the vesicles, and after this period the leucocytosis slowly sinks again. For example, on the fifth day of the illness, leucocytes 4,200; at the beginning of suppuration,

11,600 (eighth day); at the height of suppuration (tenth day), 17,200; at the thirteenth day, pustules drying up, leucocytes 7,600.

In the severest types, the leucocytes follow about the same course, there being no leucocytosis whatever in the initial or eruptive stages. Only when the infection with pus organisms begins do the leucocytes rise, the poison of variola itself having apparently no tendency to increase the count. The amount and duration of the increase at the stage of suppuration is in a general way proportional to the severity of the case. Widal[1] has recently found virulent streptococci in the blood in six cases of variola.

VARICELLA (CHICKEN-POX).

The only observation of which I am aware is that reported by Engel.[2] In a child of five he found during the height of the pustular stage a moderate leucocytosis, with 67 per cent of neutrophiles (high for a young child), and no eosinophiles. Three days later as the pustules were healing the neutrophiles had sunk to 47 per cent (normal for that age) and the eosinophiles had risen to 16 per cent.

The same conditions obtain after *vaccination*.

ACUTE ARTICULAR RHEUMATISM.

According to Hayem and Garrod[3] the blood constitutes as in syphilis a most valuable measure of the intensity of the sickness, which is parallel to the severity of the blood-changes rather than to the number of joints affected. The fever, the intensity of the lesions, and the state of the blood run parallel, in a general way, but the degree of anæmia is a more delicate index of the patient's condition than even the temperature chart (Garrod).

The Blood as a Whole.

Fibrin is greatly increased. In no other disease except in pneumonia is the network thicker or more rapid in formation. According to Maclagan, this is to be explained by an increase of

---

[1] Widal: Centralb. für. allg. Path., etc., 1896, p. 569.
[2] 15th Cong. für innere Med., 1897.
[3] British Medical Journal, May 28th, 1892.

tissue metamorphosis. Coagulation, on the other hand, is not quicker but slower than usual.

Lactic acid is present in excess, but cannot be clinically estimated, nor is its excess peculiar to this disease.

The alkalinity of the blood had been reported diminished, but the technique is not considered reliable by the best observers.

Red Cells.—Hayem [1] and Osler [2] state that the poison of acute rheumatism is a powerful and rapid destroyer of red cells. In acute cases, according to Hayem, the red cells lose at least 1,000,000 of their number and in cases which drag along and relapse the loss is from 1,500,000 to 2,000,000. When an attack is cut short by salicylate treatment the drain on the corpuscles is stopped.

So far as can be judged from the figures in Table XIII. of the Masachusetts Hospital cases this diminution does not seem to occur in all cases. Many of these cases had been sick some weeks before the time when the count was made, yet the counts are not very low. In the eight cases which have been sick over twenty days, the average of red cells is 4,462,000; in those sick between one and twenty days, 4,540,000; and in the whole group of cases, 4,400,000. The lowest count was 3,608,000. According to Hayem 4,000,000 is the usual count in acute cases and 3,000,000 to 3,500,000 in those which drag on and relapse.

Qualitative Changes.—Maragliano's so-called degenerative changes in the red cells have been observed in this disease, but are not very marked. Deformities and nucleated corpuscles appear only when the anæmia is very marked.

Hæmoglobin.—As in all secondary anæmias the corpuscles get thin and pale before they die, and hence the coloring matter is diminished more than the count. The average hæmoglobin percentage in this series is sixty-seven, and the color index .76. Hayem noted that, in some cases during convalescence, as the red corpuscles slowly increase the color index remains low or even goes lower still.

Leucocytes.—All observers agree that leucocytosis is the rule and that its degree is roughly parallel to the acuteness and severity of the attack (the individual's vigor of reaction is always a factor) and the amount of fever. The following tables illustrate the variations of the leucocytes in a fairly typical way:

[1] *Loc. cit.,* p. 917   [2] "Practice of Medicine," 1895.

TABLE XIII., A.—ACUTE ARTICULAR RHEUMATISM.

No.	Age.	Sex	Duration.	Degree of inflammation.	Red cells.	White cells.	Per cent hæmoglobin.	Remarks.
1	50	F.	17 days.	Red and hot.	?	39,000	65	
2	21	M.	5 weeks.	?	4,160,000	31,500	65	Knees and 1 ankle.
3	59	F.	?	?	5,476,000	27,000	94	Patient pale.
4	Adult.	M.	?			25,000	?	
5	33	M.	2 weeks.	Red and hot.	4,852,000	24,500	76	
6	20	F.	?	?	?	22,400	?	Acute endocarditis also.
7	Adult.	M.	?	?	4,216,000	21,000	56	
8	23	M.	4 weeks.	Tender and hot.	5,192,000	18,300	70	Temperature 102°.
9	28	M.	3 "	?	?	17,800	?	Many joints affected.
10	19	M.	4 days.	Red and hot.	?	17,400	?	
11	49	M.	?	?	4,800,000	17,700	?	Paronychia also.
12	49	M.	?	?		17,100	?	Dec. 2d.
13	21	F.	?	Red and hot.	3,944,000	17,000	45	Cheeks rosy.
14	24	M.	2 days.	?	4,600,000	16,000	68	
15	24	M.	?	?	4,670,000	15,500	68	
16	35	M.	....	......		15,200	45	
17	13	F.	1 day.	Red and hot.	4,840,000	15,200	65	Temperature 102°.
18	12	M.	2 weeks.	" "	4,400,000	15,000	56	
19	19	M.	4 days.	" "	4,780,000	14,500	75	Severe case.
20	9	F.	?	?	4,240,000	14,386	60	
21	9	F.	"	Red and hot.		14,050	?	
22	47	M.	1 day.	" "	4,750,000	14,000	72	One joint only affected.
23	25	F.	3 days.	Tender and hot.	4.850,000	14,000	75	
24	18	F.	2 months	No redness or heat.	4,156,000	14,000	54	
25	19	M.	?	?	4,172,000	14,000	70	
26	19	M.	?	?	4,580,000	13,500	64	Nov. 10th, 1895.
27	21	F.	1 day.	Red and hot.		13,500	?	
28	29	M.	?	?	4,820,000	12,750	68	
29	?	?	?	?	4,128,000	12,650	65	Dec. 1st, 1895.
30	37	F.	1 mouth.	Swollen, tender.	5,320,000	12,500	64	
31	24	M.	?	" "	5,000,000	12,500	65	
32	32	M.	?	?		12,100	?	Purpura also.
33	30	F.	?	?	4,160,0 0	12 000	?	
34	47	M.	4 weeks.	Very slight.	4,248,000	12,000	65	
35	27	F.	3 days.	Not " "	3,890,000	11,600	65	
36	17	M.	1 week.	" " "	4,600,000	11,500	70	Mild case.
37	27	M.	10 days.	Hot and red.	4,200,000	11,500	60	
38	33	M.	4 weeks.	?	5,480,000	11,000	80	Hands alone involved.
39	18	M.	?	Not red and hot.	?	10,000	....	One joint only affected.
40	28	M.	3 weeks.	" " "	3,608,000	7,000	40	
41	Adult.	M.	?	?	3,768,000	6,800	....	
42	29	M.	9 weeks.	Some joints hot.	4,104,000	5,500	58	Fourth relapse.
43	30	F.			3,440,000	4,700	26	Specific gravity 1040.
				Average =	4,400,000+	16,800+	67	

TABLE XIII., B.—SUBACUTE ARTICULAR RHEUMATISM.

No	Age.	Sex.	Red cells.	White cells.	Per cent hæmoglobin.
1	25	M.	4,750,000	15,000	60
2	30	F.	4,644,000	13,000	63
3	28	F.	?	10,600	?
4	28	F.	4,684,000	8,000	75
5	Adult.	M.	4,016,000	6,200	41
6	"	F.	4,188,000	5,750	73
	Average =		4,400,000	9,760	62

14

TABLE XIII., C.—CHRONIC RHEUMATISM, CHIEFLY ARTICULAR.

No.	Age.	Sex.	Red cells.	White cells.	Per cent hæmoglobin.	
1	78	F.	?	7,200	?	
2	19	F.	5,248,000	8,300	45	
3	82	F.	?	6,400	?	
4	58	M.	4,744,000	6,500	60	
5	30	F.	?	6,100	?	
6	20	M.	5,576,000	9,800	62	
			Average =	7,400		

TABLE XIII., D.—MUSCULAR RHEUMATISM.

No.	Age.	Sex.	Red cells.	White cells.	Per cent hæmoglobin.	Remarks.
1	46	M.	4,580,000	7,500	70	
2	54	M.	4,360,000	7,500	75	
3	38	M.	?	6,600	?	
4	54	M.	3,820,000	14,000	58	During febrile attacks.
5	27	F.	?	6,000	?	Lumbago.
6	35	M.	?	5,700	"	"
			Average =	7,500+		

The average leucocytosis in the acute cases is 16,800; in those mild and more chronic, so-called "*subacute*" cases the leucocytes range lower, averaging 9,760; while in chronic rheumatism, whether articular or muscular (including lumbago), there is no increase at all (average = 7,450).

In five cases of arthritis deformans treated at the Massachusetts Hospital the blood was normal except for a slight deficiency of hæmoglobin in two cases.

Summary.

Anæmia with leucocytosis, the degree of which is a measure of the severity of the infection. Fibrin much increased.

Diagnostic Value.

The blood tells us little if anything that could not be learned in other ways. It does not differ at all from that of a *septic arthritis*, or from that of acute *gonorrhœal arthritis*.

The only cases that I remember in which a blood examination has been valuable are the following:

CASE I.—The patient had muscular pains, fever, and a history of a malarial attack some months earlier. The question to be decided by the blood examination was between malaria and "rheumatism." The leucocytes were 23,600 per cubic millimetre, which made it clear that the case was *neither* malaria nor "rheumatism," since the former never increases the leucocytes and the latter could only give so high a count in case genuine *articular* inflammation were present. The case turned out to be croupous pneumonia which the high leucocyte count strongly suggested.

CASE II.—Patient presented symptoms and signs of acute polyarticular rheumatism with fever. The fever came down under salicylates, but soon rose again, and the man became wildly delirious. His delirium persisted after the salicylate was stopped. Several joints continued swollen and tender. The fever was very moderate, ranging between 99° and 101°. There were no rose spots and no spleen. The question arose as to whether it was a case of sepsis with localization in the joints, or whether it was a case of typhoid supervening on an arthritis of some kind. The blood count, which was repeated several times, always showed a perfectly normal blood except for a slight anæmia. The subsequent course of the case, during which he remained for nearly three weeks more or less delirious, made it clear to Dr. F. C. Shattuck, under whose care the patient was, that the diagnosis was typhoid.

Chronic rheumatism (muscular or articular) produces no constant blood changes appreciable by clinical methods (see Table XIII., C and D).

ASIATIC CHOLERA.

In no other disease so far as I am aware has an *acid reaction* in the blood been reported. This is at the end of life. All observers agree that the alkalinity is at least greatly reduced.

Our knowledge of the corpuscles is best summed up in Biernacki's [1] study of thirty-eight cases.

Red Cells.—In the *stadium algidum*, or stage of collapse, most of the symptoms are due to the great concentration of the blood from the loss of serous fluid in the stools. Hayem found the increase of red cells from this concentration to amount to from 1,000,000 to 1,500,000 per cubic millimetre.

Biernacki [1] found 7,662,500 in one case twenty-four hours

[1] Deut. med. Woch., 1895, No. 48.

after the beginning of the disease. The specific gravity may be as high as 1071 or 1072.

White Cells.—Leucocytosis is present, not merely as the result of concentration, but as a genuine increase to at least double the normal count. Biernacki found that cases with particularly high counts (40,000 to 60,000) were soon fatal, so that he considers a marked leucocytosis in the algid stage as a bad prognostic sign, although patients also die with low leucocyte counts in this period. Such a leucocytosis does not occur in ordinary diarrhœa or dysentery.

Leucocytosis is present as early as twelve hours from the first symptom and lasts at least as late as the sixth day. In the stage of reaction it usually decreases. In one very mild case reported by Biernacki there was not only no increase, but leucopenia (4,375 per cubic millimetre).

The differential count shows from eighty-two to ninety-five per cent of adult cells and a corresponding diminution of the young forms.

ERYSIPELAS.

Halla, Pée, Reinert, Rieder, and v. Limbeck agree that leucocytosis is usually present in well-marked cases. Von Limbeck finds the "leucocyte curve" to run roughly parallel with the temperature chart, sometimes beginning to fall a little before the latter. The counts rarely run very high, yet Reinert counted 39,627 in one case. Pée noted that the leucocyte count increases only while the process is spreading and that the size of the count was a tolerably accurate measure of the severity of the case.

Rieder found in seven cases an average of only 15,000 per cubic millimetre despite very high temperatures. In one case the leucocyte count remained high after the temperature had fallen, but in the others it anticipated the temperature. In one mild case he found no leucocytosis. Polymorphonuclear cells are greatly increased as in other forms of leucocytosis. Hayem noticed the same dependence of the leucocyte count upon the severity of the process.

In six cases at the Massachusetts General Hospital I found 17,000, 14,000, 13,000, 12,700, 7,250, and 6,200, the last two very mild cases. The count of leucocytes seemed proportional to the severity of the affection.

When the disease occurred in "scrofulous" cases, Hayem found only 7,000–8,000 leucocytes per cubic millimetre, while in cases with very extensive process and high fever 12,000–20,000 were present. He found also a loss of 500,000–1,000,000 in the count of the red cells, according to the severity of the case. This showed itself particularly just before the fall of the temperature. I have seen no reference by other writers to the condition of the red cells in this affection.

TONSILLITIS (FOLLICULAR).

Halla,[1] Pick,[2] and Pée[3] found leucocytosis as a rule in uncomplicated follicular tonsillitis; Rieder found it in a case complicated with acute nephritis.

The following table confirms these observations in the main, though in mild cases no leucocytosis was present.

TABLE XIV.—TONSILLITIS.

No.	Age.	Sex.	Red cells.	White cells.	Per cent hæmo-globin.	Remarks.
1	22	F.	4,368,000	19,200	35	
2	21	F.	....	18,000		
3	27	M.	....	18,000		
4	21	F.	....	16,800		
5	25	F.	... .	16,200		
6	30	F.	4,750,000	16,000	80	Temperature 101°.
7	27	M.	4,556,000	15,500	67	Six days; slight.
8	Adult.	F.	4,860,000	14,000	..	Follicular.
9	30	M.	4,730,000	13,500	76	Convalescent.
10	24	F.	5,000,000	13,500	68	Follicular.
11	Adult.	M.	....	13,500		
12	....	M.	4,952,000	12,250	94	
13	24	F.	5,816,000	11,900	65	Streptococcus; slight articular rheumatism.
14	....	M.	5,000,000	11,800	90	Follicular.
15	19	F.	4,552,000	11,600	52	
16	18	M.	5,150,000	11,500	83	Chronic recurrent; out in two days.
17	22	F.	5,016,000	9,600		
18	Adult.	F.	4,200,000	5,800	60	Follicular.
19	23	F.	....	7,925	52	Follicular; slight; temperature 99° next day.
20	45	F.	....	6,800		

[1] Zeitschrift f. Heilkunde, 1883, p. 198.
[2] Prag. med. Woch., 1890, p. 303.
[3] Pée: Inaug. Dissert., Berlin, 1890, p. 8.

The blood examination has no diagnostic value so far as I am aware. It is worth knowing that a simple tonsillitis can cause leucocytosis, to the end that if such is discovered on blood examination we need not suppose that some other process is present to account for the increase.

GRIPPE.

The references in literature to the blood of grippe are very scanty. Orion (*Archiv. d. Méd. milit.*, 1890, p. 280) found fibrin increased during the early days of the disease. Rieder (*Münch. med. Woch.*, 1892, XXXIX.) found no leucocytosis in grippe and but little in the "catarrhal pneumonia" following it.

The following table shows that the leucocytes are normal in at least five-sixths of the cases. Only eleven of the sixty-seven cases showed leucocytosis, and in one or more of these some complication was very possibly present. This is of importance in excluding *pneumonia* and *local inflammatory* conditions. The leucocyte count does not help us to distinguish the disease from *typhoid*. In this decision the serum reaction is our mainstay (see below, page 400). From malaria it may be distinguished by the absence of malarial organisms. In one case after an operation for traumatic epilepsy, the temperature rose to 104°, with a chill, and the question of meningitis was considered. The absence of leucocytosis excluded the meningitis, and the attack turned out to be grippe, which was just then very prevalent.

TABLE XV.—GRIPPE.

White cells.

Between	2,000 and	3,000 =	1	case.
"	3,000 "	4,000 =	3	cases.
"	4,000 "	5,000 =	6	"
"	5,000 "	6,000 =	5	"
"	6,000 "	7,000 =	14	"
"	7,000 "	8,000 =	5	"
"	8,000 "	9,000 =	6	"
"	9,000 "	10,000 =	9	"
"	10,000 "	11,000 =	7	"
"	11,000 "	12,000 =	3	"
"	12,000 "	14,000 =	8	"

. 67   "

TABLE XV.—GRIPPE.

Red cells.

Between 3,000,000 and 4,000,000 =   2 cases.
"   4,000,000 " 5,000,000 =   9   "
"   5,000,000 " 6,000,000 = 14   "

.   ‾‾
                               25   "

SEPTICÆMIA.

Puerperal septicæmia, infected wounds, septic arthritis, septic endocarditis, general infections with pyogenic bacteria, "pyæmia," are all identical so far as their effects on the blood are concerned, and will be considered together under the general head of Septicæmia.

Bacteriology of the Blood.

Cocci can be demonstrated in cultures from the blood of septicæmia more frequently than in any other class of infections. Rosenbach[1] in 1884 found streptococci and staphylococci in sepsis. Garré[2] in 1885 found the last-named coccus in a case of osteomyelitis. In 1890 v. Eiselsberg[3] found staphylococci in ten cases of septic wounds and one case of osteomyelitis, and streptococci and staphylococci together in five more cases whose wounds had become septic.

Czerniewsky,[4] Stern and Hirschler[5] found the same organisms in puerperal fever, the former observer in five cases.

Brunner,[6] Hoff,[7] and Blum[8] found pyogenic staphylococci in pyæmia and sepsis, and Saenger,[9] Roux and Lannois,[10] Cantu,[11] and Bommers[12] had equal success, each in a single case.

[1] "Microorganismen b. d. Wundinfectionskrankheiten," etc.. Wiesbaden, 1884.
[2] Fortsch. d. Med., 1885, No. 6.
[3] Wien. klin. Woch., 1890, No. 30.
[4] Archiv f. Gynäkol., 1888, No. 33.
[5] Wien. med. Presse, 1888, No. 28.
[6] Wien. klin. Woch., 1891, No. 20.
[7] Dissert., Strassburg, 1890.
[8] Münch. med. Woch., 1893, No. 16.
[9] Deut. med. Woch., 1889, No. 8.
[10] Revue de Méd., 1890, No. 12.
[11] Rif. Med., 1892, No. 96.
[12] Deut. med. Woch., 1893, No. 16.

Canon[1] and Sittman[2] investigated large numbers of cases with many positive results, and Grawitz[3] and Petruschky[4] and Cohn[5] were successful in finding pyogenic cocci in the blood of cases of ulcerative endocarditis as well as in other septic infections. Herschlaff[6] found them in erysipelas, acute tuberculosis, perforated typhoid ulcer, etc. Kühnan,[7] on the other hand, was unable to find anything in the blood of twenty-three severe pyæmic cases, and was successful in only one out of twelve cases of ulcerative endocarditis.

Taking the results of all these investigators together, it seems evident that in many cases of septicæmia, blood cultures, taken according to the directions on page 35, show the presence of pyogenic organisms, and that in many obscure septic cases the diagnosis may be greatly facilitated by such an examination. Negative results are of course very far from excluding septicæmia, but positive ones are sometimes of great value if proper precautions are taken in the technique of the examination. In the diagnosis of malignant endocarditis, often a most difficult one, Grawitz thinks blood cultures are especially important and likely to prove positive when the disease is present (see Diseases of the Heart, page 293).

Almost all observers agree that the finding of pyogenic cocci (except the staphylococcus albus) in the blood makes the prognosis almost surely fatal. The *toxicity* of the blood is doubled.

Red Cells.—All observers agree that very marked anæmia is present in severe cases. Roscher's[8] investigations tend to show that the diminution in red cells in septicæmia is greater than in any other infective disease, and appears in a shorter time. He found such a diminution present no longer than a few hours from the beginning of the illness. He finds the amount of anæmia proportional to the severity of the case, and (reckoning by means of the estimated solid residue) concludes that whenever the blood has lost one-quarter of its substance or more, death follows.

[1] Deut. Zeit. f. Chirurg., 1893, p. 571.
[2] Deut. Arch. f. klin. Med., 1894, p. 573.
[3] Charité-Annalen, 1804, vol. 10.
[4] Zeit. f. Hygiene, 1894, pp. 59 and 413.
[5] Deut. med. Woch., 1897, No. 9.
[6] Sem. Méd., 1897, p. 105.
[7] Deut. med. Woch., 1897, No. 25.
[8] Inaug. Dissert., Berlin, 1894.

He considers, therefore, that help as to prognosis is given us by the blood examination in septicæmia.

The serum becomes very watery, partaking of the general atrophy of the blood tissue. In a case of intensely acute puerperal sepsis Grawitz found the red cells reduced to 300,000 (!) although the patient had been sick less than twenty-four hours. The case seems almost incredible, but is reported in great detail in the author's recent text-book, to which reference has so frequently been made. He accounts for it by the combination of blood destruction and dilution.

In the nine cases of puerperal sepsis seen at the Massachusetts General Hospital in recent years the red cells averaged 3,780,000, which is very low, considering the shortness of the illness in most cases. (The influence of hemorrhage during parturition must of course be taken into account.)

In most of the septic wounds which I have seen the counts have not been low. But in one case of septicæmia from a suppurating fibroid of the uterus the red cells numbered only 1,800,000. In a case of puerperal sepsis of only a few days' duration, in a woman not previously anæmic, Hayem[1] recently reports the following figures:

> December   3d—Red cells 1,450,000
>   White cells......... 7,500
>   Hæmoglobin........ 20 per cent.
> December   6th—Red cells 2,578,000
>   White cells......... 8,000
>   Hæmoglobin .... 40 per cent.
> December 24th—Red cells 4,231,000
>   White cells......... 7,200
>   Hæmoglobin .... 65 per cent.
> (Recovery.)

Such cases are the best examples we have of an *acute anæmia* (hemorrhage excepted).

The *hæmoglobin* is usually diminished about as much as the corpuscles. According to Bond it tends to crystallize about the edge of a slide and cover-glass preparation of the fresh-blood.

Deformities in the shape and size of the corpuscles are not usually present except in the severest cases.

[1] La Méd. Moderne, January 13th, 1897.

TABLE XVI.—PUERPERAL SEPTICÆMIA.

No.	Age.	Sex.	Red cells.	White cells.	Per cent hæmoglobin.	Remarks.
1	31	F.	....	77,500	..	Autopsy.
2	21	F.	2,300,000	26,000		
3	29	F.	3,900,000	23,900	68'	Two days before delivery.
				21,000	..	Day of delivery.
				9,500	..	One day after delivery.
				15,500	..	Five days after delivery; breasts caked.
				15,000	..	Ten days after delivery.
				11,800	..	Twenty-six days after delivery.
4	28	F.	3,784,000	22,000	55	Miscarriage five days before; septic; curetted.
				13,600		Three days later, temperature falling.
				8,300		Seven days later, temperature normal.
				15,800		Fourteen days later, temperature up; curetted again.
				14,900		Fifteen days later, temperature falling.
				15,000		Sixteen days later, temperature falling.
				9,500	..	Thirty-two days later, temperature falling.
5	25	F.	....	20,800	55	
6	34	F.	....	15,900	..	September 2d, 1897.
				35,600	..	September 9th, chills.
				33,000	..	September 13th.
				35,600	..	September 16th. Recovered.
7	25	F.	2,936,000	20,000	50	April 1st, 1894.
				21,000	..	April 3d, 1894.
8	32	F.	4,904,000	19,300		Curetted.
				9,300	..	One week later, well.
9	24	F.	3,556,000	18,400		
10	..	F.	....	Marked increase.		Polymorphonuclear cells, 94%; lymphocytes, 6%.
11	26	F.	5,368,000	5,600	..	Died.

TABLE XVII., A.—SEPTIC WOUNDS.

No.	Age.	Sex.	Red cells.	White cells.	Per cent hæmoglobin.	Remarks.
1	37	F.	5,880,000	48,400	....	Sloughing breast; bedsore.
2	28	M.	7,600,000	25,400	....	Septic wound of foot.
3	31	F.	5,680,000	15,300	......'.	Sloughing breast after cancer operation.
				6,700	....	
			5,840,000	23,200	....	One month later; wound clean.
4	27	M.	4,450,000	10,500	....	Septic hand.
5	..	M.	5,600,000	8,800	....	Septic finger.

TABLE XVII., B.—SEPTICÆMIA WITH ARTHRITIS.

No.	Age.	Sex.	Red cells.	White cells.	Per cent hæmo-globin.	Remarks.
1	8	M.	....	25,000	....	Pus in elbow joint; no injury.
				43,000	....	Two days after operation, vent not free; opened further.
				24,000	....	Seven days after operation.
				20,700	....	Eight days after operation.
				6,700	....	Sixteen days after, well.
2	34	M.	4,520,000	19,000	65	Gonorrhœal, pus in knee.
3	59	M.	....	18,500	....	Pus in shoulder joint, no trauma.
4	22	M.	....	13,800	....	Gonorrhœal ankle.
5	39	M.	....	8,940	....	Gonorrhœal ankle; cultures negative.

TABLE XVII., C.—GENERAL STREPTOCOCCUS SEPTICÆMIA.

No.	Age.	Sex.	Red cells.	White cells.	Per cent hæmo-globin.	Remarks.
1	Adult.	M.	5,248,000	41,400		
2	"	F.	1,800,000	46,000	....	Suppurating fibroid.
3	22	F.	3,776,000	25,800	52	A fatal case, yet *no fever!*

Hæmoglobinæmia with reddish staining of the serum is often noticeable in the dried and stained cover-glass specimen where the plasma is deeply stained.

Leucocytes.—Considerable controversy has taken place as to the changes in the white cells effected by septicæmia; some observers finding leucocytosis, while others find none.

The results of experimental infections referred to above (see page 110) and the parallelism of the leucocyte changes in pneumonia, peritonitis, and diphtheria fully explain these apparent divergences, which perfectly exemplify the rules stated on page 106.

Leucocytosis occurs only when the struggle between the patient and his disease is intense, and whichever is victorious. When either side wins without any difficulty, *i.e.*, in the mildest and in the severest cases, leucocytosis is nearly or entirely absent; indeed, leucopenia may be found (as for instance in a case of septic endometritis reported by v. Limbeck—only 3,000 leucocytes). Von Limbeck and Krebs [1] found no leucocytosis in cases of perpetual septicæmia, but these were all fatal cases or very mild ones. Rieder, on the other hand, and the great majority of other observers (Sadler, [2] Roscher, [3] Kanthak, [4] Grawitz, etc.) find leucocytosis. This means that in most cases observed by these writers the infection was of moderate severity.

Only two of the twenty-one cases in Tables XVI. and XVII. showed no leucocytosis. One was very mild, the other died on the day of the count.

Summary.

1. Rapid development of severe anæmia.
2. Leucocytosis marked, except in very mild or very severe cases.
3. Blood cultures often contain pyogenic cocci.

Diagnostic Value.

The advantage of a positive bacteriological examination is obvious. Of the value of the blood count in distinguishing septic from non-septic wounds and estimating the degree of sepsis and the importance or needlessness of operative interference, not much is known. The subject deserves to be carefully worked out from a surgical point of view. The following cases, however, tend to show that we might utilize blood counting far more than we do to determine questions of this sort:

CASE I.—Frank B—— was a case of appendicitis operated on by Dr. M. H. Richardson at the end of an attack. A little pus was found, the appendix was excised, and the wound nearly closed, a small strand of gauze, however, being left in. Several days after the operation, there being at the time no external discharge, the temperature rose. The wound seemed perfectly clean. The man was very nervous about himself, and much

---

[1] Krebs: Dissert., Berlin, 1893.
[2] Sadler: Loc. cit.
[3] Roscher: Dissert., Berlin, 1894.
[4] Kanthak: Brit. Med. Journal, June, 1892.

stirred up at each dressing; and as the temperature never went higher than 101°, there seemed to be considerable doubt as to what the cause of the temperature was. The blood count in this case showed 52,000 leucocytes. On opening the wound a large amount of broken-down blood clot was evacuated, and the temperature came down to normal.

CASE II.—Mrs. S—— was a case of pus tube shelled out and sewed up tight. Ten days after the operation the temperature began to look as if pus were present. Here again the patient was exceedingly nervous; and, as so often happens, the question was asked and re-asked, whether she was keeping up her own temperature by the state of her mind. The blood count, however, showed marked leucocytosis, which led to a careful ether examination, revealing a fluctuating mass behind the uterus, from which pus was obtained by puncture.

CASE III.—Mr. R—— entered the Massachusetts General Hospital in December, under the service of Dr. C. B. Porter, with a compound fracture of the thigh. Some days after it had been put up, the temperature began to suggest the presence of pus, the wound, however, remaining perfectly clean. I counted the blood, and found a marked leucocytosis. A more thorough exploration of the wound revealed a pocket of pus, the evacuation of which brought down the temperature. I was not sure in this case whether the absorption of the blood clot, such as takes place, I suppose, after any compound fracture, would be sufficient to cause leucocytosis. I therefore counted several cases in which there was fever and presumably blood-clot absorption, namely, a hæmothorax, a pelvic hæmatocele, two compound fractures, and a crushed foot; in none of these was any leucocytosis present.

CASE IV.—Mr. S—— was operated on by Dr. J. C. Warren for traumatic epilepsy. Nothing special was found, and the wound was closed. Ten days after the operation the temperature rose to 104°, and the patient complained of severe headache and pain in the back. I counted the blood, and found no leucocytosis. Next day the temperature was down. The patient apparently had the grippe.

Several cases in which an old malaria was supposed to be "brought out" by a surgical operation, the patient having irregular fever and chills after the operation, have shown, on examination of the blood by the writer, no malarial organisms but marked leucocytosis. In these cases the symptoms of "malaria" ceased when the wound was more thoroughly drained, and I have no doubt that many cases of "malaria" after surgical operations are really wound sepsis.

It is difficult to make inferences from a leucocytosis in such cases, because no one, so far as I know, has thoroughly investigated the blood condition during the normal healing process of wounds. But there are certainly many cases in which we need the kind of information about the condition of a wound which the blood might give us, if the changes in connection with wounds were better known.

How often the questions are asked: Is this patient septic? Does this temperature mean anything of importance? Is this wound well drained? Is this complaint of pain hysterical or does it mean something operable?

How often the blood count would help us to answer such questions without leaving it for time to settle them after the most urgent need of settling them is gone, we do not yet know.

In puerperal cases, the fact that leucocytosis is always present for several days after delivery makes it harder to judge from the blood whether a given case is septic. I doubt if the blood count will give any information on this point not to be more easily obtained in other ways. Blood cultures, if positive, are of far greater importance, but take more time.

ABSCESS.

Goldberger and Weiss [1] have recently described a reaction to iodine in the leucocytes of the blood in cases of local suppuration. A syrupy mixture of the following elements is made:

> Iodi sublim 1
> Pot. iodati 3
> Aq. dest........................ 100
> Gummi ad syrupam.

This is painted on a slide and the unstained cover-glass preparation is pressed down into it. So treated normal blood or that of non-suppurative diseases shows the following: red cells dark yellow; white cells light *yellow* with very refractile, citron yellow nuclei.

In purulent affections the protoplasm of the leucocytes stains *brown*, either diffusely or in a granular or network distribution.

[1] Wien. klin. Woch., 1897, No. 25.

After an abscess is opened the brown color is at first confined to the periphery of the cell and soon disappears altogether. "Cold" abscesses, no matter how large, do not produce the reaction, but acute felons with only a thimbleful of pus have shown marked iodine reaction.

The reaction occurs also in pneumonia and in the moribund state.

The effects of abscess upon the blood are, I suppose, due to septicæmia. Nevertheless septicæmia *with* abscess formation differs enough from septicæmia *without* abscess formation, both clinically and hæmatologically, to make a separate description convenient.

The most easily studied variety of abscess is that connected with appendicitis, inasmuch as the frequency of operations in such cases gives us opportunity to verify what we suppose to be indicated by the blood count and see how far our suppositions are true.

At the Massachusetts General Hospital, most patients with other varieties of abscess go straight to the surgeon and their blood is not examined, but many cases of appendicitis come first to the medical wards, and hence we have records of over eighty cases whose blood has been examined.

I shall therefore begin the description of the blood in abscess by an account of appendicitis, which may probably be considered a typical case of abscess formation.

APPENDICITIS.

After excluding all cases in which the diagnosis was not sure we have left seventy-two cases.

TABLE XVIII.—APPENDICITIS.

No.	Age.	Sex.	Red cells.	White cells.	Per cent hæmo- globin.	Remarks.
1	43	M.	3,400,000	52,000	....	Question of typhoid; pus found at operation.
2	40	M.	6,800,000	43,000	....	Chronic case; 96 per cent. of adult leucocytes.
3	30	F.	....	39,900		
4	..	....	5,184,000	36,800		
5	..	....	4,800,000	36,000		
6	50	M.	4,290,000	35,000		
7	..	....	6,000,000	34,000	....	Three days after operation.
8	..	....	6,500,000	34,000	....	Seven " " "
9	?	M.	5,072,000	28,000		
10	..	....	....	24,200	....	Second attack; operation at 11 P.M. November 5th, count at 5:30.
				16,850	...	Serous peritonitis found. November 6th, 5 P.M.
				15,500	....	November 7th, 3 P.M.
				10,700	....	" 8th, 4 "
				15,100	....	Temperature still up. November 9th, 5 P.M.
				14,800	....	November 10th, 5:30 P.M.
				11,800	....	" 11th, 8:30 "
				17,850	....	" 12th, 8:30 "
				18,200	....	" 13th, 8 A.M.
				13,100	....	" 13th, 8:30 P.M.
						Recovery complete ten days later.
11	..	....	....	24,000	....	24° September 1st; operation, free turbid fluid without adhesions.
				12,500	....	September 10th.
				19,500	....	" 12th ; pocket of pus found.
12	23	M.	5,200,000	24,000		
13	..	....	5,144,000	23,000	82	January 14th.
				16,100	....	" 15th; before operation, ℥ v. + pus.
14	..	M.	....	22,500	....	Not operated; entrance.
				13,000	....	Second day.
				9,500	....	Third "
15	..	M.	....	22,300	....	12:20 operated; belly full of pus.
				9,500	....	8:30 moribund; blood dark and hard to get.
16	35	F.	....	22,000	....	July 6th.
				19,400	....	" 8th.
				14,900	....	" 10th, 104°; recovery.
17	..	M.	....	21,900	....	Appendicitis eight to nine days; operation; post-cæcal abscess.
18	..	....	....	21,700	....	November 5th, first operation.
				21,400	....	" 10th.
				16,000	....	" 13th.
				24,400	....	" 15th.
				20,200	....	" 16th.
				47,700	....	" 19th, second operation (pus pocket).
				16,700	....	" 20th.
				13,000	....	" 21st.
				10,700	....	" 22d.
				30,300	....	" 26th, third operation (pus pocket).
				20,900	....	" 27th.
				17,700	....	" 28th.
				25,100	....	" 29th.
				28,100	....	" 30th.
				20,400	....	December 1st.
				15,400	....	" 2d.
				25,000	... .	" 3d.
				11,900	....	" 4th.
				15,000	....	" 5th.
				21,900	....	" 6th.
				19,000	....	" 7th.
				11,000	....	" 8th.
				12,800	....	" 9th.
				11,700	....	" 10th.
				12,300	....	" 11th.
				15,600	....	" 12th.
				13,400	....	" 13th.
				14,700	....	" 21st.
				16,500	....	" 25th.
				11,300	....	" 26th
19	31	M.	... .	20,540	....	October 5th.

TABLE XVIII.—APPENDICITIS (*Continued*).

No.	Age	Sex	Red cells.	White cells.	Per cent haemoglobin.	Remarks.
19	31	M.	....	33,000	....	October 6th.
				14,640	....	" 8th.
				9,200	....	" 9th; moved bowels.
				21,000	....	12th ; tender still and tense.
				24,900	....	99° to 100° temperature.
				13,700	....	Normal; still sore.
20	..	M.	....	......	....	Appendicitis twenty-four hours; resistant belly.
				20,100	....	October 23d.
				14,000	....	" 24th, 9 A. M.
				12,400	....	" 24th, 4 P.M.
				13,250	....	" 24th. 11 P.M.; not operated.
				8,750	....	" 25th. 8 A.M.; liquids every two hours.
				9,600	....	" 25th, 3 P.M.
21	24	F.	....	20,000	....	May 24th.
				19,000	....	" 25th.
22	..	....	.. ..	20,000	....	June 5th ; temperature, 101.4°; pain and vomiting.
				9,000	....	June 7th; no pain.
				10,000	....	" 8th; no pain ; temperature, 100.6°; discharged.
23	..	....	4,800,000	20,000	....	Operated; pus.
24	..	....	5,564,000	20,000	....	
25	..	....	4,670,000	19,750	.. ....	January 13th.
			5,296,000	15,000	....	" 15th.
26	20	F.	....	19,600	....	" 29th.
			4,680,000	12,000	....	February 1st.
			4,688,000	8,933	....	" 5th; after operation.
27	..	....	....	19,500	....	No operation.
28	58	M.	5,120,000	19,000	....	Purulent peritonitis.
29	20	M.	5,680,000	18,930		
30	14	M.	....	18,000		
31	..	....	....	17,500	....	Accident case; operation; pint of pus under pressure.
32	25	M.	....	16,250	....	Fifth day. November 7th.
				17,450	....	November 8th.
				12,000	....	" 11th; not operated; well on 17th.
33	25	M.	....	16,200	....	
34	..	....	....	16,200	....	Eighth day; operation; large abscess cavity.
35	40	F.	....	16,051	....	Operated.
36	..	....	....	16,000	....	Entrance.
				8,000	....	Same evening; no operation.
				7,500	....	Next day.
				6,800	....	" "
37	..	....	6,160,000	16,000	....	General peritonitis.
38	..	....	....	16,000	....	November 12th, noon.
				8,000	.... ..	" 12th, 8: 30 P.M.
				7,500	....	" 13th, 8 A.M.; not operated.
				6,600	....	" 13th, 8 P.M.
39	..	....	3,300,000	16,000	....	
40	17	M.	4,380,000	15,600	66	March 25th, 9 P.M. ; vomiting, pain, tenderness.
				19,500	....	" 27th ; comfortable, no vomiting; signs more localized.
				22,900	.. ....	" 28th ; slight tenderness only.
				35,300	....	" 29th ; bowels move well; no symptoms.
				32,800	....	" 30th ; operation; large amount of pus.
41	27	M.	4,330,000	15,523		
42	23	M.	5,910,000	15,330		
43	22	M.	....	14,800	....	20th ; general peritonitis.
				10,000	....	21st ; " "
44	..	..	....	14, 700	....	Five days ; third attack; operation; free turbid fluid, no perforation; prompt recovery.
45	36	F.	4,250,000	14,700	70	27th, 8 P.M.
				13,150	....	28th ; symptoms less; no operation.
46	23	F.	....	14,400	....	February 23d, } ℥ ij. foul pus.
				10,300	....	" 24th, }
47	..	....	4,050,000	14,000	....	Catarrhal.
48	..	....	.. ..	13,400	....	3 P.M., November 9th; appendicitis twenty-four hours.
				11,200	....	5 P.M., November 10th; temperature, 98.8°.
49	..	....	5,000,000	13,000		
50	..	....	....	13,000	....	Visible tumor. March 27th.
				17,000	....	" " April 26th, operated; pus.
51	..	....	4,626,000	12,000		

TABLE XVIII.—APPENDICITIS (Continued).

No.	Age	Sex	Red cells.	White cells.	Per cent haemo-globin.	Remarks.
52	..	M.	....	12,000	....	Appendicitis cake. August 3d, operation; gangrenous appendix with adhesions.
				16,900	....	August 6th, fæcal fistula.
53	..	M.	....	11,900	....	No symptoms except pain for twenty-four hours; not operated.
54	31	M.	....	11,800	....	Very slight tenderness; no resistance or dulness. July 6th.
				19,900	....	Temperature up; tenderness and resistance. July 7th, operation; pus found.
55	..	M.	4,860,000	11,700	58	December 28th, 4 P.M.
				17,600	....	" 30th, 10 A.M.
				16,670	....	" 31st, 11 "
				11,950	....	January 1st, 9 P.M.
				10,800	....	" 5th.
				10,875	....	July 27th; nine days pain and vomiting.
56	22	F.	4,664,000	21,000	....	July 28th; more pain, tenderness and vomiting; operation showed pus.
				10 700	....	November 7th, appendicitis six days.
57	..	M.	....	9,000	....	Operation; abscess with considerable pus; gangrenous perforated appendix with concretion in it. Not operated till later.
				10,500	....	
58	12	F.	3,690,000	10,400	....	February 6th, 1½ M.; slight pain and tenderness.
59	46	M.	....	9,800	....	" 7th, 3 P.M.; temperature dropping.
				10,400	....	Catarrhal.
60	..	...	5,600,000	10,500		
				10,140	....	One week, fourth attack; no cake, no acute symptoms; operation; no pus.
61	..	M.	....			
				10,040	....	Sixth day, operation; abscess, ℥i. pus.
62	..	M.	....	9,000	....	Operated; no pus; catarrhal.
63	..	M.	....	8,400	....	December 1st.
64	24	F.	....	10,000	....	" 6th.
				7,200	....	" 15th.
				7,600	....	" 16th.
				7,760	....	No pus.
65	..	....	5,106,000	7,600		
66	..	....	5,600,000	7,600	....	No operation.
67	..	....	6,500,000	7,600	....	No pus.
68	..	..	6,500,000	7,050	....	Catarrhal appendix; five days in hospital.
69	31	M.	....	7,000	85	Catarrhal appendix.
70	47	M.	6,000,000	6,600	....	" chronic; nearly well; operation; no pus.
71	56	M.	....	6,000	....	" or very slight.
72	22	F.	4,320,000			

From the seventy-two cases of the adjoining table, together with forty-one other counts not here recorded, the following conclusions are to be drawn:

1. Red cells: no changes except in chronic cases with long-standing abscess.

2. Coagulation often slow, but fibrin always increased in suppurating cases.

3. As in most infections the mildest and the severest cases show no leucocytosis. *Four cases with general purulent peritonitis showed no leucocytosis*, its absence being confirmed by repeated examinations. The total absence of leucocytosis in a case not obviously mild is a very bad prognostic sign as in pneumonia and diphtheria.

4. Catarrhal appendicitis is rarely accompanied by leucocytosis (only once in this series—14,000).

5. *An increasing leucocytosis means a spreading process and may be the only evidence of the fact.* In Case 40 of this series, the patient entered with vomiting, localized pain and tenderness. The leucocytosis was 15,600. Three days later he was comfortable, had no vomiting and very little tenderness, and in all respects seemed to be improving, yet the white cells had risen to 22,900. Operation was postponed owing to the lack of all unfavorable symptoms *except the blood count.* Next day the bowels were moving well and the patient *had no fever and no bad symptoms of any kind,* but his leucocytes had risen to 35,300. On the following morning the surgeon was finally persuaded to operate and found a large amount of pus.

A steadily increasing leucocytosis is always a bad sign and should never be disregarded even when (as in this case) other bad symptoms are absent. It is of far more significance than a larger count which does not increase.

6. The size of the leucocytosis is of comparatively little significance. A low count (8,000–11,000) means one of three things:

(*a*) A mild case.

(*b*) A very severe case.

(*c*) An abscess thoroughly walled off.

After the abscess has ceased to spread and has become well walled off, the leucocyte count remains stationary or decreases. If it bursts into the general peritoneal cavity the count may rise sharply or it may fall to normal or subnormal, its movement depending on the degree of resistance which the system offers.

7. In the majority of cases the pus is neither completely walled off nor free in the belly, and such cases are accompanied by a moderate and fluctuating leucocytosis, which rises and falls according to a variety of conditions which cannot be accurately interpreted.

It usually increases in the first three or four days of the illness, and then becomes stationary or declines if the case is taking a favorable course (*i.e.,* if the pus is being absorbed or walled off), while it continues to increase when the case is going on from bad to worse.

Case 20 illustrates the course of the leucocytes in a favorable case not operated on; the leucocytes fell gradually but steadily from hour to hour so that in two days the count came down from 20,100 to 8,750, the tumor and tenderness simultaneously disappeared, and the patient was well in a few days more.   Case 38 dropped in eight hours from 16,000 to 8,000 and quickly recovered.   In Case 19, the leucocytosis fell in three days from 33,000 to 9,200, but rose again when the bowels were moved by enema, and took some days to reach normal again.   Evidently the peristalsis injured the abscess wall so that the process began to spread again and had to be walled off afresh.

8. When a leucocytosis of 18,000–25,000 is maintained for a number of days it usually means a large abscess pretty well walled off.

9. The majority of cases as seen at the Massachusetts General Hospital on the second, third, and fourth day of the illness show leucocytosis of 15,000–24,000, thirty-three of the present series falling within these figures.   Counts larger than this have always been proved to mean a large amount of pus or a general peritonitis.   Of the cases below 15,000 (fifteen in all) twelve did not come to operation, or if operated showed no pus.   This statement excludes the four cases of general purulent peritonitis without leucocytosis mentioned above.

10. Case 18 illustrates several points.   After the first operation the leucocyte count did not fall so rapidly as usual, and the cause of this soon turned out to be a pus pocket, after the evacuation of which the count fell in twenty-four hours from 47,700 to 16,700, only to rise again for another accumulation of the same kind.

After this last (third) operation the case progressed slowly but favorably, and yet the leucocyte count remained more or less above normal for a month.   The wound was healthy, freely discharging, and had healed satisfactorily at the time of the last count recorded.

Whether all wounds follow this course as regards the leucocytes I do not know.   It is an important point which needs working out, namely : What is the normal behavior of the blood count during the healing of granulating wounds?   If this were known, we might get valuable information as to whether a wound is doing well or not, by means of the blood count, which, if septic, would probably behave differently from its wont in wounds which do well. As it is, all these questions are not answerable. It is to be hoped that surgeons will investigate them.

Differential Diagnosis.

1. The presence of a marked leucocytosis excludes simple *colic with or without constipation*, and excludes certain forms of intestinal obstruction (if uncomplicated). Such cases of intestinal obstruction as are complicated with ulceration or gangrene or due to cancer may raise the leucocyte count.

Between general peritonitis from an appendicitis and intestinal obstruction, the presence of marked leucocytosis points to the former; but its absence may accompany either affection. I remember a case in which the diagnosis lay between these two affections, and operation was delayed because the absence of any leucocytosis was thought to rule out peritonitis, and it was hoped to get the bowels started by enemata, etc. When finally the abdomen was opened stinking pus gushed out and the patient died the same day.

2. Treves[1] has reported several cases in which it was hard to decide whether the diagnosis was *typhoid* or appendicitis. A blood examination would probably have decided the matter as it has in three cases in the writer's experience. Most cases of appendicitis of any severity show leucocytosis; typhoid almost never does if uncomplicated. Curtis[2] reports a case of typhoid with a tumor and tenderness in the right iliac region which closely simulated appendicitis but turned out to be a floating kidney. The blood count would have decided the matter.

3. Between *appendicitis and pus tube* the blood gives no help, as both affect it alike.

4. *Ovarian or pelvic neuralgia* (uncomplicated) never causes leucocytosis and may be excluded by its presence. The same is true of floating kidney, which has been sometimes confounded with appendicitis.

5. *Gall-stone colic*, and *renal colic* if uncomplicated by inflammatory disturbance, cause no leucocytosis, and can therefore be distinguished from appendicitis in most cases. If

[1] Medico-Chirurgical Transactions, 1888, lxxi., p. 165.
[2] "Twentieth Century Practice of Medicine," vol. viii., p. 461.

cholangitis, cholecystitis, pyelitis, or severe cystitis compli-
cate the colic, the examination of the blood will be no help
to us.

6. *Impaction of fæces* in the cæcum will not cause any leucocytosis and may be excluded when such is present. The count
may be of use, it seems to me, in deciding us whether an enema
ought to be given. It is sometimes desirable to give an enema
in cases simulating appendicitis, to help clear up the diagnosis,
but some physicians are afraid to do so for fear of causing a
walled-off abscess to break into the general peritoneal cavity.
In such cases, if no leucocytosis were present, we might go
ahead with a clearer conscience.

Mr. B—— entered the Massachusetts General Hospital September 20th, 1893, with a diagnosis of appendicitis. For twenty
days he had been having pain and tenderness in the region of
the appendix, pain being controlled by morphine. The bowels
had been loose, he said. There was dulness, tenderness, and a
distinct tumor in the region of the appendix, with slight pyrexia.
The blood count showed only 8,000 leucocytes. He was given
a compound cathartic pill, had a large movement of the bowels,
and all symptoms and signs disappeared.

7. *Extra-uterine pregnancy* and pelvic hæmatocele may cause
leucocytosis like appendicitis, but *do not increase fibrin* unless
peritonitis is present, and are likely to *show a marked diminution
in red corpuscles* if the hemorrhage is severe. The red cells
are normal in appendicitis except in chronic cases with abscess.

8. *Floating kidney* has been already mentioned in Curtis' case,
where in combination with typhoid it closely resembled appendicitis. Even without the presence of typhoid, the same difficulty of diagnosis may arise between appendix and floating
kidney. The presence of leucocytosis could not be accounted
for by the latter.

One of the next most common forms of abscess seen in
medical wards is pyosalpinx, which I shall call by the English
name of "pus tube." As this produces the same effect on the
blood as pelvic abscess or pelvic peritonitis, I shall consider the
three processes together.

PUS TUBE, PELVIC ABSCESS, AND PELVIC PERITONITIS.

Almost all that has been said of appendicitis applies equally well to these conditions.

TABLE XIX., A.—PUS TUBE AND PELVIC ABSCESS.

No.	Age	Sex	Red cells.	White cells.	Per cent haemo-globin.	Remarks.
1	36	F.	....	43,000	....	Double pus tube; too weak to operate. December 15th.
				31,000		December 22d.
				45,900		December 29th; abscess burst per vaginam.
				20,200		January 4th, abscess opened in groin.
				15,200		" 8th.
				12,200		" 11th.
2	..	F.	5,400,000	34,000	......	Pelvic abscess.
3	38	F.	....	34,000		Pus tube. June 18th.
				34,600		June 19th.
				35,000		" 20th.
				40,000		" 27th, fever and vomiting just before catamenia.
				17,300		July 1st, temperature normal.
				11,500		" 8th, mass decreasing.
				12,000		" 14th, slight thickening still.
4	34	F.	4,202,000	32,500	60	Pus tube; septic arthritis; jaundice.
5	..	F.	4,880,000	30,000		Pus tube.
6	23	F.	....	29,200		Double pus tube.
7	29	F.	4,544,000	28,800		General purulent peritonitis.
8	20	F.	....	27,300		Pus tubes.
9	26	F.	3,800,000	27,000	65	Double pus tube. November 17th.
				23,000		November 19th, operated.
10	48	F.	5,210,000	26,000		Pus tubes.
11	28	F.	5,120,000	24,400		Pus tube.
12	..	F.	....	24,400		Pus tube four weeks' duration.
13	24	F.	5,376,000	24,000		Pus tube.
14	..	..	3,760,000	23,000		Pelvic abscess (fetid pus).
15	45	F.	....	22,000		Pus tube.
16	..	F.	5,200,000	22,000		Pus tube.
17	..	F.	5,200,000	22,000		Pus tube; operation; pus found.
18	35	F.	3,704,000	21,100	65	Pus tube operated.
19	19	F.	....	20,200		May 1st.
				23,800		" 11th, mass the same; pus tube.
20	26	F.	5,021,000	20,000		Pus tube.
21	..	F.	4,400,000	19,800		Pus tube.
22	21	F.	....	19,000		Pus tube. Temperature 99°. April 26th.
				21,100		No fever. May 2d.
				10,000		May 4th.
				18,600		" 9th.
				19,600		No fever.
				21,600		May 18th, flow of pus from os started by manipulation.
				18,200		
				16,300	......	Out doors.
23	54	F.	3,940,000	19,000	60	Pus tube and ovaritis; operation; pelvis full of foul pus; recovery after hysterectomy.
24	25	F.	3,860,000	18,800		Pus tubes.
25	?	F.	4,592,000	18,800		" tube.
26	18	F.	3,840,000	18,500	55	" tube; three hours after food.
27	32	F.	5,776,000	18,000		" tubes.
28	28	F.	5,000,000	18,000		" tube.
29	30	F.	3,410,000	18,000		" tube, etc.
30	21	F.	5,088,000	16,400		" tube; syphilis. October 7th.
			5,184,000	18,000		October 12th.
31	22	F.	4,300,000	16,000	80	Pus ear.
32	..	F.	3,800,000	16,000		Pus tube.
33	35	F.	....	15,600		Pus tube. May 8th.
				18,200		May 18th, transferred.
34	36	F.	4,656,000	15,000	60	Pus tube; large amount of pus found.
35	19	F.	....	15,300		Pelvic peritonitis.

TABLE XIX., A.—PUS TUBE AND PELVIC ABSCESS (*Continued*).

No.	Age	Sex	Red cells.	White cells.	Per cent haemo-globin.	Remarks.
36	36	F.	8,696,000	14,975	48	Pus-tube. July 21st, chills and delirium.
				12,600	....	July 23d.
						" 25th; operated.
37	20	F.	4,310,000	14,800	30	Pus tube; chlorosis.
38	38	F.	3,008,000	13,853	22	Pus tube.
39	..	F.	4,700,000	12,500	70	Pus tube (double); operated.
40	35	F.	....	12,200	....	Pus tube; slight.
41	21	F.	....	12,200	.. ....	Pus tube. June 2d.
				12,300	....	June 10th.
42	19	F.	3,910,000	12,000	....	Pus tube.
43	..	F.	4,736,000	11,850	63	Pus tube. January 5th and 6th.
				13,750		
44	33	F.	4,240,009	11,000	55	Pus tube. Not operated; very slight.
45	47	F.	....	10,600	....	Chronic salpingitis. June 21st.
				11,000	....	June 25th, better.
				11,500	. ...	" 29th.
46	21	F.	3,800,000	10,400	64	Pelvic peritonitis.
47	..	....	7,000,000	10,000	....	Pelvic abscess (?).
48	38	F.	4,125,000	10,000	60	Pelvic abscess. August 28th.
				17,000	....	September 3d, temperature up.
				13,400	....	" 6th, normal temperature.
49	24	F.	....	9,000	....	Salpingitis, 9 A.M.; 99.4°.
				9,200	....	4:15 P.M.; five days in hospital.
50	23	F.	472,000	7,500	....	Pus tubes (small; size of finger).
51	..	F.	5,840,000	7,200	....	Pus tube.

From these data together with nineteen other counts not here recorded I conclude that: Increasing counts of leucocytes usually point to the need of an operation; stationary leucocytosis to a well walled-off abscess. The size of the count is a rough measure of the size of the abscess, and cases *without* leucocytosis rarely need operation and usually recover under palliative treatment, as also do many *with* leucocytosis.

Differential Diagnosis.

Pelvic pain and soreness may be as great in various non-suppurative conditions (ovarian neuralgia, etc.) as when abscess is present, but the leucocyte count is raised in none of the pelvic disorders of women except abscess, septicæmia (puerperal, after abortion, etc.), and hemorrhage (menorrhagia, metrorrhagia, ruptured tubal pregnancy). Endometritis and cystitis usually cause no leucocytosis. The application of these rules will not infrequently help in the diagnosis of pelvic disease and in deciding how much importance to attach to the complaints of pain, tenderness, etc., in a doubtful case. The absence of leucocytosis makes us rightly confident that no abscess of any considerable size exists.

OTITIS MEDIA.

Most cases, if purulent, show leucocytosis both before and after paracentesis. If serous (see Table XIX., B, cases 5, 10, 11, 12) the count is usually lower, and we can predict with moderate certainty whether serum or pus will be found on puncturing the drum. When the mastoid is involved the count runs higher. If the case drags on, the hæmoglobin may get low, otherwise the red cells are not affected.

In some cases the blood alone enables us to distinguish otitis and its effects from typhoid. In a case recently examined which several excellent clinicians pronounced typhoid, though there was a marked leucocytosis and no serum reaction, the autopsy showed pus in the jugular and lateral sinus but no typhoid.

TABLE XIX., B.—OTITIS MEDIA.

No.	Age.	Sex.	Red cells.	White cells.	Per cent hæmo-globin.	Remarks.
1	6	F.	....	36,700	...	Nephritis acuta. April 30th.
				27,300	...	May 7th.
				34,400	...	May 14th, otitis only.
				27,000	...	May 22d.
				21,000	...	May 28th, slight discharge still.
2	2	M.	....	23,000	55	
3	6	M.	....	18,600	20	
4	45	M.	....	14,500	...	With cerebral abscess.
5	Adult.	M.	4,786,000	16,800	...	Serous.
6	47	F.	4,168,000	16,600	65	Double purulent; vent not free; mastoid sore.
7	19	F.	5,120,000	16,480	88	April 28th.
				8,800	49	May 5th, well.
8	Adult.	F.	5,942,000	15,200	...	Pus.
9	Adult.	F.	4,472,000	14,750	60	December 7th, hysteria.
			5,416,000	9,750	46	December 25th (during dyspnœic and cyanotic attack).
10	27	F.	4,850,000	8,500	69	Serous.
11	7	F.	4,416,000	6,400	...	Catarrhal.
12	Adult.	F.	4,100,000	4,000	...	Serous.
13	4	M.	....	Marked leuco-cytosis.	...	Purulent; chronic right, acute left. Diff. 116 cells; polymorphonuclear cells, 57 per cent; lymphocytes, 31; eosinophiles, 3.

OSTEOMYELITIS.

In four cases in which no external opening was present, the patient complaining only of pain in the bone, the counts of leucocytes were 29,600, 25,600, 24,310, and 18,000; in each the prediction that pus would be found was verified at operation. Three differential counts in chronic cases with sinuses showed nothing remarkable, no increase of eosinophiles and no myelocytes.

The diagnostic value of the blood in osteomyelitis seems to me considerable, inasmuch as it is difficult by the symptoms alone to feel sure enough of the existence of pus to be willing to operate. "Rheumatic pains," "growing pains," and neuralgia can be excluded by the presence of leucocytosis.

OTHER ABSCESSES.

(1) *Felon.*—It is striking to see how small a collection of pus can raise the leucocyte count. Felons containing less than one-half drachm of pus may have a leucocytosis of 15,000 to 22,000. I have counted the blood in three such cases. The element of septicæmia must be considerable. It seems to make no difference whether or not the pus is under great *tension*. The leucocyte count does not fall sharply after the felon is opened, but gradually diminishes during the next seven to ten days. Even a

(2) *Gum boil* raised the white cells to 27,000 in one case. An

(3) *Abscess of the vulva* showed 23,500 leucocytes per cubic millimetre, and an

(4) *Abscess of the vagina*, 12,800. Other varieties are:

(5) *Parotid abscess*, 45,500 leucocytes per cubic millimetre.

(6) *Subpectoral abscess*, 16,000 leucocytes per cubic millimetre.

(7) *Abscess of the neck*, 22,200 leucocytes per cubic millimetre. *Carbuncle*, 41,000 leucocytes per cubic millimetre.

(8) *Psoas abscess* (infected), 50,000 leucocytes per cubic millimetre.

(9) *Abscess of ovary*, 26,000 leucocytes per cubic millimetre.

(10) One case of *perinephritic abscess* was watched for some days while the patient was getting up strength for an operation. It was an abscess of several months' standing, not increasing in

size during the last month, and the counts, as we should expect, did not rise or fall considerably but showed a steady well-marked leucocytosis.

July 29th, white cells, 21,400
" 30th, " " 21,200
August 8th, " " 22,400
" 11th, " " 23,000
" 24th, " " 22,200. (Operation.)

A second case counted only showed 16,000. Both abscesses contained over a quart of pus.

A third case, evidently tubercular in origin and probably not much infected with pyogenic cocci, showed only 10,000 white cells per cubic millimetre.

(11) *Abscess of the Lung.*—Five cases following pneumonia have occurred at the Massachusetts Hospital within the last three years; the counts are as follows: Case I., 16,800; Case II., 16,000; Case III., 16,400; Case IV., 30,000; Case V., 5,100.

(12) *Subphrenic abscess,* four cases.

Case.	Red cells.	White cells.	Per cent hæmoglobin.	Remarks.
1	4,450,000	53,267		
2	....	25,600	....	May 16th.
		15,500	....	May 17th.
		17,600	55	May 20th.
3	3,200,000	22,000	38	
4	....	15,300	....	October 20th. Supposed typhoid for first week.
		13,800	....	October 23d.
		16,600	....	October 27th.
		18,000	... .	November 5th.
		22,500	....	November 10th. Operation; a quart of pus; recovery.

Diagnostic Value.

1. The case of vulvar abscess was so morbidly modest that she complained of all parts of her body except the one diseased and gave a train of symptoms which utterly failed to account for the leucocytosis. The presence of this leucocytosis called for a much more searching physical examination than would have otherwise been made, and the seat of real trouble was discovered.

2. (a) The diagnosis between perinephritic abscess and cyst of the kidney is materially assisted by the fact that the former causes leucocytosis, while the latter (see page 305) does not.

(b) Both cancer of the kidney and perinephritic abscess cause leucocytosis, but if fibrin is not increased cancer is the more likely of the two. This differential mark has served me well in two cases.

(c) Hydatid of the kidney and pyonephrosis are not to be distinguished from perinephritic abscess by the blood examination. In abscess of the lung the blood gives no information that cannot be more easily gained in other ways.

3. Subphrenic abscess may be confounded with malignant disease, both of which may cause leucocytosis; but the absence of any increase of fibrin speaks against the existence of an abscess.

GONORRHŒA.

The red cells are not affected, but in acute cases a moderate leucocytosis is present and fibrin is increased. Qualitatively, the white cells have been said by Neusser and others to show an increased percentage of eosinophiles corresponding to the large proportion of these cells in the urethral discharge, but Vorbach has carefully studied twenty cases with reference to this point and finds the eosinophiles in the blood to vary from 0.5 to 11.5 per cent—averaging 4.2 per cent—within normal limits.

YELLOW FEVER.

Jones [1] found coagulation slow, the red cells *not* much diminished but showing decided degenerative changes; hæmoglobinæmia is common. He makes no observations as to the white corpuscles. Pothier of New Orleans, studying the epidemic of 1897, found the following: "Never less than 4,500,000 red cells per cubic millimetre, an average of 8,000-10,000 leucocytes. The hæmoglobin, on the other hand, was never over 80 per cent, and in some cases as low as 60 per cent. Neither fresh nor stained specimens showed anything abnormal about the corpuscles."

A case recently observed at the Massachusetts Hospital showed two days before death 7,800 leucocytes, 92 per cent of

[1] Journal of the American Medical Association, March 16th, 1895.

hæmoglobin, with an absence of the typhoid serum reaction. Through the kindness of Dr. Pothier I have been able to study cover slips from twelve cases of yellow fever from the Charity Hospital of New Orleans. The differential counts of leucocytes are as follows:

	I.	II.	III.	IV.	V.	VI.	VII.	VIII.	IX.	X.	XI.	XII.
Polymorphonuclear neutrophiles	77	74	93	86	87	88	97	84	86	84	77	73
Small lymphocytes	18	22	15	11	8	4	3	5	4	6	4	20
Large lymphocytes	5	2	2	2	5	8	..	11	10	6	18	6
Eosinophiles	..	2	..	.5	..	..	..	..	..	..	1	1
Myelocytes	..	..	..	.5	..	..	..	..	..	4		

Red cells showed nothing except in Case VIII., where there were marked deformities and a few normoblasts. In some cases there was a marked leucocytosis, in others none. (For serum reactions, see page 425).

TYPHUS FEVER.

Ewing[1] in four cases found no leucocytosis. Tumas[2] found no leucocytosis, as the following case shows:

Date.	Day of disease.	Temperature. A.M.	Temperature. P.M.	Red cells.	Per cent hæmoglobin.	White cells.
January 4th	4th.	......	40.0			
" 5th	5th.	39.2	39.6	4,440,000	80	9,600
" 6th	6th.	39.0	39.5	4,220,000	77	4,800
" 7th	7th.	39.0	40.0			
" 8th	8th.	39.2	39.3	4,280,000	.77	3,200
" 9th	9th.	39.0	39.5			
" 10th	10th.	38.8	39.2	4,440,000	77	3,200
" 11th	11th.	38.3	39.3			
" 12th	12th.	39.0	39.2	4,380,000	80	1,600
" 13th	13th.	38.8	39.5	4,780,000	80	3,200
" 14th	14th.	38.7	39.0			
" 15th	15th.	38.0	38.7	4,960,000	80	1,600
" 16th	16th.	38.1	38.8			
" 17th	17th.	38.7	38.6	4,160,000	70	4,800
" 18th	18th.	37.7	38.2			
" 19th	19th.	36.6	38.5	3,820,000	67	1,600
" 20th	20th.	38.1	38.3			
" 21st	21st.	37.5	38.1	3,450,000	62	3,280
" 22d	22d.	38.1	37.8	3,450,000	60	3,200
" 23d	23d.	37.5	38.0			
" 24th	24th.	37.4	38.0	3,130,000	50	3,200
" 25th	25th.	37.4	39.3			
" 26th	26th.	39.2	......			
Died on the 26th.						

[1] Ewing: New York Medical Journal, December 16th, 1893.
[2] Arch. f. klin. Med., vol. 41, p. 363.

On the other hand, Everard and Demoor,[1] and Wilks[2] found leucocytosis.

MALTA FEVER.

According to the article in Allbutt's recent "Text-book of Medicine" the red cells fall gradually in the course of the fever from 5,000,000 to about 3,500,000. Bruce finds the leucocytes normal in most cases. (See also page 424.)

RELAPSING FEVER.

(See Blood Parasites, page 425).

GLANDERS.

Christol and Kiener (*Comptes Rendus de l'Acad. des Sciences*, November 23d, 1868) reported leucocytosis in glanders. In a fatal case of acute glanders with autopsy which was recently studied at the Massachusetts Hospital the following counts were recorded:

October 24th, 1897.   Leucocytes, 13,600 ; hæmoglobin, 100 per cent.
October 31st, 1897.   Leucocytes, 11,600.
November 4th, 1897.   Leucocytes, 13,000.
November 9th, 1897.   Leucocytes, 12,600.
November 12th, 1897.   Leucocytes, 12,400.
Serum reaction absent ; fibrin increased ; pure culture of glanders bacilli from abscesses ; 86 per cent of the leucocytes were polymorphonuclear ; eosinophiles absent.

The bacilli of glanders can occasionally be cultivated from the blood.

THE BUBONIC PLAGUE.

In 1895 Aoyoma, a Japanese observer, studied the blood of this disease.[3] He found the bacilli peculiar to the disease by cover-slip preparations from the blood. The *red corpuscles* were not altered except that their number per cubic millimetre was at times increased (*e.g.*, 7,600,000, 8,190,000). The cause of this I do not know, but it accounts for part of the leucocytosis. The

[1] Annales de l'Institut Pasteur, February, 1893.
[2] Ref. in Sajous' Annual, 1895.
[3] "Mittheilungen aus d. Med. Fac. d. Kaiserlich Japanischen Universität," vol. iii., No. 2. Tokyo, Japan, 1895.

white corpuscles showed a marked increase—20,000 to 200,000 (!) per cubic millimetre. This leucocytosis was made up almost wholly of polymorphonuclear leucocytes; the eosinophiles were markedly diminished, and the blood plates were increased.

ACTINOMYCOSIS.

Ewing (*loc. cit.*) reports leucocytosis (21,500) in a single case. In a case of actinomycosis of the liver (autopsy) which occurred at the Massachusetts General Hospital in 1897 the following counts were recorded:

June 18th, leucocytes................................. 31,700
June 19th, leucocytes............................. 28,400
June 25th, leucocytes............................. 28,200

TRICHINOSIS.

At the International Medical Congress at Moscow (1897) Thayer reported two cases of trichinosis in both of which trichinæ were demonstrated in the muscle. The blood was of the greatest interest. Both cases showed an enormous relative and absolute increase of eosinophiles as the following counts show:

	Case I.		Case II.
	March 8th, 1896.	April 28th, 1896.	
Red cells................	4,232,000	....	5,000,000
White cells	16,500	17,000	13,000
Polymorphonuclear neutrophiles..............	50 per cent.	6.6 per cent.	37 per cent.
Small lymphocytes.......	5 "	19.5 "	11 "
Large lymphocytes.......	7 "	5.2 "	5 "
Eosinophiles.............	38 "	68.2 (!) "	44 "

In the second case it was the blood examination that suggested the diagnosis, the symptoms being rather those of typhoid or malaria.

I have recently had a case strongly resembling these. In a patient who had just returned from Germany where he had suffered from a severe gastro-intestinal attack, tender spots appeared in various muscles, and swelling of the face and hands, weakness, and anæmia were present. His blood showed:

	September 30th, 1897.	November 4th, 1897.
Red cells.....................	5,120,000	4,900,000
White cells	11,000	7,000
	Per cent.	Per cent.
Polymorphonuclear neutrophiles	39	36.5
Small lymphocytes.............	28	38
Large lymphocytes.............	3	8
Eosinophiles..................	28	17
Basophiles ("mastcellen")......	2	.5

This patient is unwilling to have a bit of muscle excised so that the diagnosis of trichinosis, which I regard as probable, cannot be verified. He is recovering rapidly.

EPIDEMIC DROPSY.

(Acute Anæmic Dropsy.)

MacLeod in Vol. III. of Albutt's "System of Medicine" describes under this title a disease not uncommon in India and other tropical countries. The blood shows a marked and con-

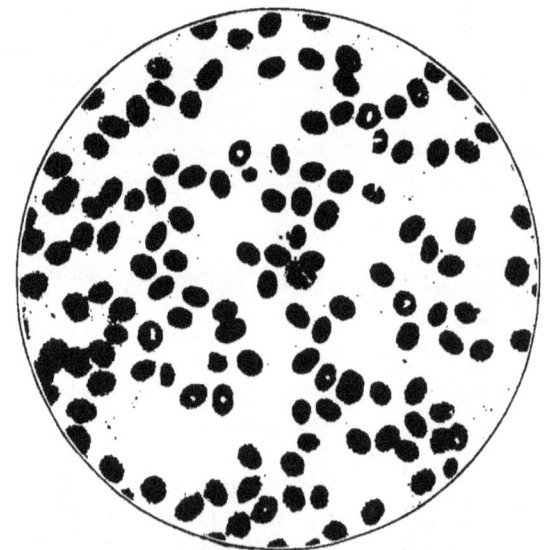

FIG. 35.—Blood in Epidemic Dropsy. Note oval shape of corpuscles. Magnified 350 diameters.

stant anæmia with leucocytosis and an "increase of granular or molecular matter in the serum." Dr. Greene, of the United States Marine Hospital service, recently wrote me an account of two cases strongly resembling MacLeod's description of epidemic dropsy; these cases were observed by Dr. Greene at Key West, Florida. One was fatal and the other recovered. The blood of both cases was notable in that the corpuscles were almost invariably oval instead of round, reminding him of the blood of amphibia. He was good enough to send me preparations of the blood; a microphotograph of one of them is here reproduced. Rouleaux formation was absent, another point in common with amphibian blood. There was no apparent increase of the leucocytes when I saw the blood, late the convalescence of the second case. (On the significance of oval forms, see page 87.)

TETANUS.

In a single (fatal) case of tetanus treated with antitoxin I observed the following counts:

	White cells.	Hæmoglobin.
June 21st, 1897	11,100	70 per cent.
June 23d, 1897	11,900	

The eosinophiles do not decrease as in most fevers.

BERI-BERI.

In a single afebrile case seen at the Massachusetts Hospital the following is recorded: Red cells, 3,896,000; white cells, 7,800; hæmoglobin, 48 per cent.

The eosinophiles are said to be much increased in the acute stages. Spencer (Lancet, January 2d, 1897) states that there is no leucocytosis.

16

CHAPTER V.

DISEASES AFFECTING THE SEROUS MEMBRANE.

1. SEROUS effusions, representing probably a milder type of infection than purulent effusions, have less effect than the latter upon the blood.

2. The serous effusions, however, must be subdivided into the tubercular and the non-tubercular. The former, like most forms of tuberculosis (see page 255), rarely raise the leucocyte count, while the latter may do so, though in a lesser degree than purulent processes.

Tubercular affections of serous membranes have been dealt with elsewhere (page 264); but an exception was then made of pleurisy, for although there is reason to believe that the majority of cases of serous pleurisy are due to tuberculosis, we rarely have proof of it, and most observations upon the blood of pleurisy have not been accompanied by bacteriological examination of the effusion. Tubercular cases have not been distinguished from non-tubercular. Hence the two are necessarily considered together here. .

SEROUS PLEURISY.

Von Limbeck finds in non-tubercular cases from 13,000 to 15,000 leucocytes per cubic millimetre. The red cells and hæmoglobin are not much affected except in chronic cases.

Rieder finds in non-tubercular cases during the stage of fever moderate leucocytosis, 13,000 in one case in which the bacteriological examination showed the presence of Fraenkel's diplococcus in the exudation. After the fever has subsided the leucocytosis falls to, or nearly to normal, so that cases examined for the first time some weeks after onset would show no increase at all. This he thinks explains the results of Halla and others who found no leucocytosis in serous pleurisy. According to Rieder the presence or absence of leucocytosis depends not so much on whether the product is serum or pus as on whether the trouble is stationary or advancing.

In tubercular pleurisy despite fever Rieder found but 4,600 white cells in one case, and Pick got similar results in two cases.

Hayem makes no clear distinction of tubercular and non-tubercular cases and states that "acute inflammatory" pleurisy has from 7,500 to 12,000 leucocytes per cubic millimetre. The fibrin network is much less dense than in pneumonia; in most of the tubercular cases it is not increased at all.

In ninety-nine cases examined at the Massachusetts General Hospital the average count of leucocytes was 6,130.

TABLE XX.—PLEURITIC EFFUSION (SEROUS).

Between	3,000 and	4,000	3 cases.
"	4,000 "	5,000	5 "
"	5,000 "	6,000	14 "
"	6,000 "	7,000	17 "
"	7,000 "	8,000	10 "
"	8,000 "	9,000	13 "
"	9,000 "	10,000	14 "
"	10,000 "	11,000	9 "
"	11,000 "	12,000	4 "
"	12,000 "	15,000	7 "
Over 15,000.			3 "
		Total	99 "
		Average	6,130.

Here tubercular and non-tubercular cases are not distinguished, and a majority of them were not seen till the trouble had been going on two or three weeks. The patients did not seek advice until the effusion was large enough to cause dyspnœa. Of the ninety-nine cases all but fourteen had *no leucocytosis*. Most of the cases were afebrile or nearly so, and very likely tubercular, but no cultures were taken in any. Eight cases reacted to injections of tuberculin. None of these eight had leucocytosis.

The cases *with* leucocytosis were mostly those seen in the febrile stage, near the beginning of the sickness. No differential counts were made.

In chronic cases the red cells are said to be considerably diminished, but this has not been the case in our series: no

count of under 4,000,000 was recorded,   and the coloring matter
was not much diminished.

Summary.

1. Red cells and hæmoglobin show no important changes.
2. White cells not increased in most cases except in febrile
stages, and not often over 13,000 then.   Tubercular cases if uncomplicated probably never have leucocytosis.

Diagnostic Value.

The blood count may help a good deal in doubtful cases by
excluding empyema, pneumonia, and malignant disease of the
lung, all of which are accompanied by higher leucocyte counts.
Compare the average count in serous pleurisy, 6,130, with the
average in pneumonia, 24,000, or in empyema, 18,300.   The few
counts I have seen of malignant disease of the lung have been
still higher.

Hayem insists, rightly it seems to me, that clinicians could
get real help from blood examination in almost every case of
doubtful diagnosis in which the lung and pleura are in question.
In children the leucocytes are considerably increased by even a
serous inflammation, their blood reacting always more strongly
than that of adults to any morbid influence, and in them it
may be impossible to distinguish serous from purulent pleurisy.

PURULENT PLEURISY (EMPYEMA).

The counts in nineteen cases observed at the Massachusetts
Hospital are as follows:

Case.	Red cells.	White cells.	Per cent hæmo-globin.	Remarks.
1	5,440,000	49,200	51	
2	....	41,500	60	
3	....	35,200		
4	6,000,000	32,000		
5	....	22,800	45	
6	....	22,600	......	Pneumococcus.

Case.	Red cells.	White cells.	Per cent hæmo-globin.	Remarks.
7	....	22,800	......	June 5th.
		34,700	......	June 7th.
		29,800	......	June 8th. Tapped turbid serum.
		17,700	......	June 9th.
		22,000	......	June 10th.
		22,100	......	June 12th.
		21,800	......	June 14th.
		17,200	......	June 22d.
		27,300	......	June 24th.
		30,100	......	June 29th.
		25,800	......	July 8th.
8	....	20,600	......	January 5th.
		14,700	......	January 7th.
		11,400	......	January 23d.
		11,700	......	January 26th. Tapped.
		18,000	......	January 30th. Re-accumulation.
		26,000	......	February 3d. Operated; pneumo-cocci and streptococci.
9	4,192,000	10,800	48	December 20th.
		18,500	......	December 22d. Broke into lung ; cul-ture sterile.
		14,500	......	January 2d.
		18,300	......	January 4th.
		10,000	......	January 9th.
10	....	16,200	50	Pneumococcus.
11	....	15,500		
12	....	15,200		
13	4,500,000	14,000		
14	4,850,000	12,650	85	
15	....	12,450	60	
16	4,000,000	12,000		
17	....	11,700	44	Culture sterile.
18	....	10,900		
19	....	7,600	......	Operated ; several pints of pus ; strep-tococci.

This is in marked contrast with serous pleurisy as above noted. Von Limbeck noticed the same thing.

PERITONITIS.

A patient with serous pleurisy (non-tubercular) is hardly ever in danger, while if the general peritoneal cavity is the seat of a like inflammation, recovery is almost out of the question. This clinical difference is parallel to the difference in the blood condition. Any inflammation of the peritoneum (non-tubercular), whether serous or purulent, calls very large numbers of leucocytes into the peripheral blood. The only exceptions to this rule are those cases in which the organism is so over-whelmed by the disease that it offers no resistance. We have seen that this same effect is produced in the severest cases of pneumonia and diphtheria, and presumably it is true of many other infectious diseases in which the blood has been less carefully studied.

Almost all cases of general septic peritonitis show very marked leucocytosis, and the spreading of a localized process is always indicated by an increasing leucocytosis. But here and there it happens that the patient cannot react against the disease at all, and then the leucocytes are normal or diminished. This never occurs in empyema because the system is never so overwhelmed by a septic process in the pleura. The fibrin network is increased in almost all cases. The following counts, all in fatal cases, illustrate these points:

TABLE XXI.—GENERAL PERITONITIS.

No.	Age.	Sex.	Red cells.	White cells.	Per cent hæmoglobin.	Remarks.
1	34	F.	4,860,000	54,000	....	Abscess of spleen (?).
2	Adult.	F.	7,000,000	32,000	......	Purulent; from appendix—myelocytes, 2 per cent.
3	27	M.	5,317,000	24,000	75	Dysentery, with perforation.
4	Adult.	F.	4,000,000	22,000	......	Chronic, purulent.
5	31	M.	....	19,000	......	Ruptured bladder.
6	Adult.	M.	....	16,000	......	Moribund.
7	Adult.	M.	6,000,000	6,000	....	Purulent; operation. Death.
8	52	F.	....	5,328	......	Obstruction; died in three days; autopsy.
9	Adult.	M.	5,760,000	5,300	......	Purulent. Death within 24 hours.
10	41	F.	6,840,000	4,600	95	" " " 24 "
11	....	..	....	Marked increase.	....	After appendix operation. Diff. 1,000 cells: Polymorphonuclear cells, 90.5 per cent; lymphocytes, 9.5; eosinophiles, 0; myelocytes, 1.
12	21	M.	....	42,200	....	June 30th.
				9,000		July 2d. Autopsy.
13	38	F.	....	1,700 !	......	August 2d. Autopsy.
				2,100 !	......	August 3d.

Diagnostic Value.

1. When a diagnosis rests between peritonitis and (a) obstruction (non-malignant); (b) malignant disease; (c) hysteria, phantom tumors or malingering, the presence of marked leucocytosis with increase of the fibrin network speaks strongly in favor of peritonitis.

Obstruction or malignant disease may increase the number of leucocytes, but rarely increases the amount of fibrin.

Hysterical or malingering patients have normal blood.

2. We cannot distinguish serous from purulent peritonitis in septic cases, but *tubercular peritonitis* can always be excluded if leucocytosis is present.

3. As to the "chronic granular peritonitis," non-tubercular and non-septic, I have seen no reference in hæmatological literature and have no first-hand knowledge.

4. In the *worst* cases leucocytosis may be absent, as in the most virulent type of pneumonia.

PERICARDITIS (WITH EFFUSION).

As in most other inflammations of serous membranes we can distinguish the tubercular cases which have no leucocytosis from the rheumatic or septic cases which always increase the white cells. The tubercular cases are discussed under tuberculosis (see page 267). The following counts illustrate the rheumatic form of the disease:

Case.	Red cells.	White cells.	Per cent hæmo-globin.	Remarks.
1	....	42,400	......	November 3d, 1895.
		32,600	......	November 7th, 1895.
		19,200	......	November 11th, 1895.
		17,500	......	December 8th, effusion nearly gone.
2	2,632,000	21,600	45	December 24th, endo - pericarditis, chronic nephritis.
		27,100	......	December 26th.
		36,600	......	December 29th, no fever.
		26,700	......	May 1st.
		19,200	......	May 3d.
		24,800	......	May 4th.
		28,600	......	May 7th.
		20,100	......	May 8th.
3	4,568,000	26,000	67	December 14th.
		19,400	......	December 20th, effusion subsiding.
4	....	24,000		
5	4,168,000	19,447	67	
6	....	15,400		
7	....	14,600	65	Autopsy.
8	....	12,000	63	Tapped.

Hayem has noted that pericarditis is far more apt to produce leucocytosis than is endocarditis.

Diagnostic Value.

In excluding cardiac hypertrophy or simple dilatation with ruptured compensation, both of which may occasionally simulate a pericardial effusion, the presence of marked leucocytosis is absolutely decisive. When we are sure that effusion exists, the absence of leucocytosis points strongly to a tubercular process as its cause.

MENINGITIS.

Leucocytosis is usually well marked. Von Limbeck considers that tubercular meningitis can be distinguished from purulent by the absence of leucocytosis in tubercular cases, but Osler [1] states that many cases of tubercular meningitis *do* have leucocytosis throughout their course, and my own observations in several cases tend to confirm this. Of Rieder's cases, one had leucocytosis and one did not. Zappert's case had 11,130 white cells, and Ziemke one with 17,500. It seems, therefore, that we sometimes have here an exception to the rule that tubercular processes do not produce leucocytosis. Certainly some cases do follow this rule. But however this may be, it is certain that purulent meningitis, whether secondary or of unknown origin, is characterized by high leucocyte counts (Table XXII.), and if in a case evidently of meningitis of some kind leucocytosis is absent, the case is probably tubercular in origin.

TABLE XXII.—MENINGITIS.

No.	Age.	Sex.	Red cells.	White cells.	Per cent hæmo-globin.	Remarks.
1	Adult.	M.	5,900,000	40,000	....	Diff. 1,000 cells: Adult cells, 93 per cent.; young cells, 7; eosinophiles, 0.
2	....	M.	6,400,000	33,000	....	(Otitis?) question of typhoid.
3	23	M.	6,000,000	27,500	95	March 16th; cerebro-spinal.
				16,500	....	" 18th.
4	15 mos.	F.	5,020,000	19,500	73	
5	7	M.	....	16,000		
6	26	M.	....	16,000		
7	20	F.	....	15,784	....	Autopsy; cerebro-spinal.
8	2	M.	....	14,200	....	Basilar; no tuberculosis in family; had pneumonia.
9	22	M.	4,356,000	14,000	72	
10	35	M.	....	11,700		
11	26	M.	5,040,000	11,200	....	Specific.

Cerebro-spinal meningitis (see Cases 3 and 7, Table XXII.) shows the same characteristics in the blood as do cases limited to the cerebral meninges. A case reported by v. Jaksch [2] had 4,800,000 red and 24,000 white cells.

[1] "Practice of Medicine," 2d edition.
[2] Zeit. f. klin. Med., 1893, p. 187.

EPIDEMIC CEREBRO-SPINAL MENINGITIS.

Williams finds leucocytosis in about two-thirds of his cases. The following cases were seen during the epidemic of 1897. The red cells are not markedly affected. Leucocytosis is the rule, but is not invariable. In a general way the higher the count the severer the case, and the count usually rises as the case gets worse and falls with improvement, though often very slowly.

TABLE XXIII.—EPIDEMIC CEREBRO-SPINAL MENINGITIS.

Age.	Sex.	Red cells.	White cells.	Per cent haemo-globin.	Remarks.
60	M.	....	51,200	100	Polynuclear cells, 95 per cent.
2	M.	....	43,800	....	April 26th.
			14,600	....	April 28th.
			16,800	....	May 7th, convalescent.
45	F.	....	40,000	....	Polynuclear cells, 94 per cent.
28	M.	....	35,600	....	November 18th.
			26,400	....	November 20th.
			27,000	....	November 22d.
			14,000	....	November 24th.
			13,600	....	November 27th.
			14,400	....	November 29th.
			10,300	....	December 4th, well.
5	M.	....	35,000	57	March 13th, polynuclear cells, 72 per cent.
			36,300	....	March 14th.
			24,400	....	March 18th.
			23,100	....	March 23d, recovery.
40	F.	....	35,000	....	Polynuclear cells, 93 per cent.
40	M.	5,360,000	32,000	....	Polynuclear cells, 82 per cent.
42	M.	....	30,000		
4	M.	....	28,800	69	September 24th.
			15,800	....	October 1st.
			12,000	....	October 10th, well.
9 mos.	F.	....	26,600	....	July 4th.
			20,200	....	July 13th.
			28,000	....	July 18th.
			17,800	....	July 22d, normal.
			27,400	....	July 28th, temperature 104°
			16,000	....	August 2d.
			11,700	....	August 13th, temperature normal.
27	M.	....	26,000	48	July 12th.
			31,200	....	July 17th.
13 mos.	M.	....	27,200	....	July 6th.
			22,300	....	July 7th.
7	F.	....	25,300	....	March 26th.
			21,400	....	March 30th.
			26,300	....	April 4th.
			12,900	....	April 13th.
					April 15th, discharged well.

TABLE XXIII.—EPIDEMIC CEREBRO-SPINAL MENINGITIS (*Continued*).

Age.	Sex.	Red cells.	White cells.	Per cent hæmo-globin.	Remarks.
25	F.	....	25,000	....	Polynuclear cells, 91 per cent; supposed grippe.
22	M.	....	24,200	100	September 6th.
			11,800	....	September 10th.
			11,300	....	September 13th, recovery.
24	F.	....	23,600	76	October 2d.
			10,600	....	October 18th
			9,600	58	November 15th.
			7,000	....	November 27th, recovery.
33	M.	....	20,600	60	
31	M.	....	19,500	55	Autopsy.
12	F.	....	19,000	....	March 13th.
			22,400	....	March 16th.
			26,400	....	March 23d.
			23,900	...	March 31st.
			20,900	....	April 5th.
			23,400	....	April 12th.
			14,600	....	May 24th, recovered.
40	F.	....	19,000		
5	M.	....	18,800	....	March 18th.
			16,400	....	March 30th.
			21,000	....	April 3d.
31	M.	....	18,000	62	
26	M.	....	17,700	68	
21	M.	....	16,200	60	October 3d.
			19,100	....	October 4th.
			10,000	....	October 15th.
			11,400	....	October 28th, became chronic.
10	M.	....	15,300	....	October 5th.
			16,900	....	October 7th.
			14,500	....	October 9th.
			16,400	....	October 13th.
			14,400	...	October 15th.
			17,200	....	October 17th ; 18th discharged well.
26	M.	....	14,600	75	
20	F.	....	14,800	73	Died.
29	F.	....	13,800	....	November 18th.
			20,700	....	November 21st.
			14,600	....	November 26th, recovery
23	F.	....	12,800	80	
9	M.	....	12,400	80	October 10th.
			17,900	....	October 11th.
			14,600	....	October 12th.
32	F.	....	12,400	....	September 16th.
			14,000	....	September 19th.
25	M.	....	12,100	80	Autopsy : serum reaction absent.
18	M.	....	11,700	....	October 3d.
			22,300	....	October 4th.
			18,100	....	October 5th, autopsy.
26	F.	....	10,700	95	June 14th.
			14,400	....	June 24th, died.

TABLE XXIII.—EPIDEMIC CEREBRO-SPINAL MENINGITIS (*Continued*).

Age.	Sex.	Red cells.	White cells.	Per cent hæmo-globin.	Remarks.
24	M.	....	10,000	....	June 6th.
			7,600	....	June 8th.
			15,600	....	June 9th.
			16,200	....	June 10th, temperature rising with count.
			12,300	...	June 11th.
			16,700	....	June 13th.
			18,800	....	June 15th.
			17,800	....	June 17th.
			17,800	....	June 18th.
			12,100	....	June 19th, temperature down.
			18,300	....	June 21st.
			16,800	....	June 22d, temperature up.
			16,400	....	June 23d.
			10,700	....	June 25th, temperature normal.
			11,700	....	July 1st.
22	M.	... .	6,500	60	Autopsy.

Flexner and Barker, investigating a large epidemic at Lonaconing, Maryland, found leucocytosis in every case (12,000 –32,000 per cubic millimetre). The epidemic studied by Williams and myself was apparently due to the diplococcus intracellularis of Weichselbaum.

Diagnostic Value.

Meningitis is the only intracranial disease (except abscess and apoplexy) which shows leucocytosis, and this fact may be of great help in excluding other causes of coma.

1. Brain tumor, hysteria, lead encephalopathy, diabetic coma, sunstroke,[1] and narcotic or alcoholic intoxication do not cause leucocytosis and hence can be excluded by its presence.

2. Uræmia, apoplexy, and post-epileptic coma may have leucocytosis and cannot be distinguished from meningitis when leucocytosis is present; but the absence of leucocytosis excludes meningitis.

3. Some cases of typhoid, when seen for the first time and

[1] In a case of heat exhaustion (temperature 104°) without coma, a leucocyte count of 27,200 is recorded at the Massachusetts Hospital.

without a history of the previous illness, may be difficult to distinguish from meningitis, but typhoid never has leucocytosis if uncomplicated and meningitis always has.

4. From pneumonia we cannot distinguish meningitis by the blood count.

PART III.

CHRONIC INFECTIOUS DISEASES.

CHAPTER VI.

TUBERCULOSIS.

RED CORPUSCLES AND HÆMOGLOBIN.

(a) Quantitative Changes.

I. THE striking fact is the absence of such anæmia as we should expect, judging from the pallor of the patients and the nature of the disease. It is common to find a normal or even increased number of red cells in pale cachectic-looking consumptives. We cannot help wondering whether our methods of examination are at fault, that is, whether the drop we examine is typical. (For discussion of the subject see page 81.) However this may be, it is undoubtedly the fact that in most cases of tuberculosis, even in advanced stages, the count of red cells is approximately normal. Often the hæmoglobin is also high.

II. In a smaller number of cases the hæmoglobin is much diminished, although the count of red cells is normal—in other words, we find the blood characteristic of a moderately severe secondary anæmia. The red cells are numerous enough, but only because their numbers have been recruited by the influx of "half-baked" or decrepit corpuscles, small-sized and pale, poor in albumin and hæmoglobin.

The condition differs from that of chlorosis mainly in that some of the red cells are normally developed and nourished, while in chlorosis all, or nearly all, are feeble. Such blood occurs in the severer and more cachectic sufferers from tuberculosis, just often enough to make us wonder that it is not *always* to be found.

III. In a small percentage of cases both red cells and hæmoglobin are considerably diminished (*vide* Table XXIII., case 32), the latter usually suffering more than do the actual number of cells, that is, the color index is usually below 1.

Von Limbeck[1] has recorded a case in which in the course of a tubercular process (acute miliary) the red cells fell as low as 730,000 (white cells, 4,300; hæmoglobin, twenty-five per cent). But the account of the blood is not sufficiently explicit in this case to enable us to exclude a true pernicious anæmia in the course of which the tuberculosis may have been only the last incident. No other such case is on record, so far as I am aware.

IV. *Fibrin* is not increased unless extensive secondary infection is present.

(b) *Qualitative Changes.*

I. There may be none whatever.

II. There may be only a pallor of some of the individual corpuscles with slight changes in size and shape.

III. In very severe cases the poikilocytosis may be extreme, but this is much rarer than in many other cachexias of the same severity (*e.g.*, malignant disease).

IV. An important point is the usual absence of nucleated red cells. Even after hemorrhages it is rare to find any nucleated red cells, and this is in marked contrast with cancer cases, in which nucleated red cells are the rule.

V. The degenerative changes described by Maragliano are sometimes found in severe cases with mixed infection (*vide infra*).

As regards the influence of the different seats of tubercular disease (meningeal, pulmonary, genito-urinary, acute miliary, etc.) upon the red corpuscles and hæmoglobin the following are the probabilities.

Pure tubercular disease itself, whatever its seat, has little or no effect upon the blood. The widely different conditions of the blood found in different cases depend probably on the presence or absence of various other organisms (diplococcus lanceolatus, pyogenic cocci) associated with the tubercle bacillus, and on whether there is some drain on the body albuminoids (diarrhœa, peritoneal effusion, starvation, prolonged suppuration). When the infection is a mixed one, the blood shows the ordinary effects of septicæmia (for then the case *is* practically one of septicæmia) in lessening the number and quality of the red

[1] *Loc. cit.*, p. 336.

cells. When there is drain on the fluids and proteid constituents of the body, the red cells may not seem to be diminished, owing to the concentration of the blood from loss of fluid. Under such circumstances they may even seem increased, but the individual corpuscles are sure to be lacking in hæmoglobin and the other nitrogenous bodies of which they largely consist.

Fever may be present without there being any changes in the red cells that we can detect. It is only septic fever, and not the fever of pure tuberculosis that drains the corpuscles of their vitality and lowers their numbers.

LEUCOCYTES.

(a) Quantitative Changes.

Here, as with the red cells, the striking fact is the absence of changes in pure tuberculosis. It makes no difference whether we are dealing with tuberculosis of the bones, serous membranes, or internal organs. So long as the infection remains unmixed the white cells are not increased. In certain localities (lungs, kidneys) the opportunities for a secondary infection and septicæmia are so great that we frequently find evidence of it in the blood. On the other hand, psoas abscesses before they are opened often contain only tubercle bacilli, and the blood of such cases shows no considerable changes.

So much more is known of the numerical variations of the leucocytes in tuberculosis than of the other blood constituents, that I shall give a separate account of them in phthisis, in tubercular bone disease, in tubercular meningitis, acute miliary tuberculosis, genito-urinary tuberculosis, and tubercular peritonitis.

I. PHTHISIS.

I. In *incipient phthisis* the leucocytes are normal except after hæmoptysis.

II. After attacks of *hæmoptysis*, there is usually leucocytosis, subject to wide variations according to the amount of the hemorrhage and the resisting power of the patient.

This follows the laws of ordinary post-hemorrhagic leucocytosis (*vide supra*) and disappears quickly when the hemorrhage ceases.

III. *Cavities.*—Very constantly accompanied by leucocytosis. Indeed the absence of leucocytosis in any case proves the absence of any cavity of considerable size.

IV. *Extensive infiltration* ("tubercular pneumonia") may cause marked increase of white cells, sometimes as great as in croupous pneumonia, but this is not invariable.

V. *Fibroid Phthisis* (chronic interstitial pneumonia).—As a rule the leucocytes show no increase, but if, as sometimes occurs, we have the combination of this condition with cavity formation, the latter may increase the count of white cells.

VI. *Fever.*—When the temperature is normal the leucocytes are normal, but a febrile state may or may not be accompanied by leucocytosis (according, presumably, as the fever is or is not due to pyogenic organisms).

VII. *Tuberculin Injections.*—At the height of the reaction fever the leucocytes almost always rise, the lymphocytes and eosinophiles being relatively increased.

In a general way, the worse the case the higher the leucocyte count, yet the signs may be advanced without causing any leucocytosis if cavities are absent.

The following tables give some idea of the range of the counts in average hospital cases of phthisis.

PHTHISIS—RED CELLS.

Between 2,000,000 and 3,000,000 = 1 case.
"   3,000,000 "   4,000,000 = 18 cases.
"   4,000,000 "   5,000,000 = 25 "
"   5,000,000 "   6,000,000 = 16 "

Total .... 60 "

PHTHISIS—HÆMOGLOBIN.

From 10 to 20 per cent = 1 case.
"   20 "   30   "   = 0 "
"   30 "   40   "   = 4 cases.
"   40 "   50   "   = 6 "
"   50 "   60   "   = 19 "
"   60 "   70   "   = 23 "
"   70 "   80   "   = 16 "
"   80 "   90   "   = 6 "
"   90 "   100   "   = 5 "

Total................ 80 "

PHTHISIS—WHITE CELLS.

Between	3,000	and	4,000	=	5 cases.
"	4,000	"	5,000	=	4 "
"	5,000	"	6,000	=	9 "
"	6,000	"	7,000	=	9 "
"	7,000	"	8,000	=	10 "
"	8,000	"	9,000	=	9 "
"	9,000	"	10,000	=	14 "
"	10,000	"	11,000	=	5 "
"	11,000	"	12,000	=	7 "
"	12,000	"	15,000	=	25 "
"	15,000	"	20,000	=	16 "
"	20,000	"	30,000	=	8 "
"	30,000	"	40,000	=	3 "

Total............... 124   "

The number of those showing leucocytosis is slightly greater than those without it, probably because incipient cases rarely think themselves sick enough to come to a hospital. On the other hand, some of the cases which appear to have been going on for months have normal leucocyte counts. The duration is less important than the nature and severity of the process. It is rare to see extensive signs in the lungs without leucocytosis— fibroid phthisis excepted.

Qualitative Changes in the White Cells.

1. Many cases show none at all.

2. When the leucocyte count is normal we may find an increased percentage of large and small lymphocytes, such as is commonly found in any blood poor in nutritive qualities (see page 96).

3. When leucocytosis is present, we usually find the ordinary marked increase in the percentage of polymorphonuclear cells at the expense of the lymphocytes.

For example: C. D——, male, thirty-two years old. Tuberculosis of lungs, with cavities; leucocytes, 17,580. Differential count of 1,000 cells shows:

Per cent.

Polymorphonuclear 83.4
Lymphocytes (small)................................ 8.2
Large lymphocytes (large and transitional) 8.4
Eosinophiles..................... .... 0.

17

4. Eosinophiles are increased during the reaction from an injection of tuberculin, and also in some cases with cavities in which possibly the individual inoculates himself with tuberculin manufactured in the cavities of his own lungs.

Otherwise the eosinophiles are increased only at certain physiological seasons—menses and coitus. In most cases associated with leucocytosis they are absent.

5. Myelocytes were found by Holmes, W. R. May, and myself in many cases of advanced phthisis. They averaged .3 per cent.

Perinuclear Basophilia.[1]

Neusser and his followers have advanced a theory that the occurrence of perinuclear basophilia during tuberculosis is a favorable sign and marks a system capable of resisting the 'tubercular infection. The researches of Futcher and my own attempts to verify Neusser's theory have not confirmed his findings.

Holmes, of Denver, has studied the leucocytes in phthisis with great care and considers that he finds therein means not only of diagnosing tuberculosis by the blood alone, but of measuring the degree of advancement of the process and the amount of resisting power in the patient.

I have carefully followed out Holmes' procedures with stains seen and approved by him. I can verify most of his statements of fact, but some of the inferences which he draws therefrom are, I think, wholly unwarranted. The blood changes in pulmonary tuberculosis are mainly such as he describes, but they have no diagnostic value, as similar changes are found in a great variety of other diseased conditions. The increase of polymorphonuclear forms in advanced cases, the increased amount of "débris," the degenerating forms, etc., are all characteristic not of tuberculosis alone but of any severe suppurative process. The increase of "débris" is probably the same datum which Watkins interpreted as an increase in blood plates and Goldberger and Weiss as "extracellular glycogen." (With Holmes' "undeveloped nuclei" in the leucocytes, compare page 121)

[1] See Appendix.

II. BONE TUBERCULOSIS.

Brown[1] has studied seventy-two cases, Dane[2] forty-one. Dane's study of the blood in forty-one cases of hip disease and Pott's disease is a very careful one. Whenever abscesses appeared in connection with the disease, cultures were taken when the abscess was first opened and again later on, and the coincidence of low counts with absence of pyogenic cocci and with high counts of secondary pyogenic infection is very notable. Dane's conclusions are as follows:

1. "High leucocyte counts, especially in hip disease, point to the probability that there is, or soon will be, abscess formation; but low counts do not preclude the presence of abscess, especially in long-standing cases.

2. "If abscess is present, a low count of white cells indicates the absence of secondary pyogenic infection (proved by cultures).

3. "Cases of traumatic origin are generally accompanied by a high leucocyte count.

4. "The leucocyte count bears no direct relation to the temperature; one case with 30,980 leucocytes (five-year-old girl) showed a temperature of only 99.4° at the time of the count. In another girl of three years whose temperature ranged between 101° and 104°, the leucocytes were only 7,224, or subnormal for that age (*vide infra*, page 336).

5. "Cases where at the primary operation the pus proved sterile show an increase in the leucocyte count when the wound becomes infected with pyogenic organisms" (as it always does).

6. "The red cells are rarely diminished, but the hæmoglobin is usually relatively low (mild secondary anæmia in these cases). This absence of a diminution in the red cells in these cases is the more remarkable because they were almost all in young children whose blood is much more sensitive to any deleterious influence than that of adults."

Brown dissents from several of Dane's conclusions. He thinks that a case may go on to abscess formation without any increase in the leucocyte count. When an increase *does* take

[1] Transactions of California Medical Society, 1897.
[2] Boston Medical and Surgical Journal, May 28th, 1896.

place he thinks it due either to a secondary infection or to an increased activity of the tubercular process itself without any secondary infection. The latter process, however, in Brown's experience causes only a moderate increase (2,000–3,000), while if a marked increase suddenly or gradually occurs he thinks it "most significant of secondary infection." With Dane's fifth conclusion he wholly agrees and adds: "After the infection (produced by the operation) the leucocytosis is very high for a time, and if the sepsis is acute and threatens life it remains high until the crisis is passed." Otherwise it gradually falls after the first few days, and if the patient progresses well, it disappears. If the pyogenic matter overcomes the recuperative power, the leucocytes fall as in peracute pneumonia or peritonitis. In such cases the anæmia increases as well.

Qualitative Changes.

(a) As in other forms of tuberculosis there may be none at all. (b) The cell changes in purely tubercular cases is illustrated well by Case 17 of Dane's series, a boy of seven whose blood on the day of operation for hip disease with large abscess showed 8,932 leucocytes. The differential count was as follows:

	Per cent.
Polymorphonuclear neutrophiles	40
Small lymphocytes	49
Large lymphocytes and transitional forms	8
Eosinophiles	3

Eight ounces of pus were evacuated, in which cultures showed the absence of pyogenic organisms.

This case demonstrates that some cases of tubercular suppuration have no tendency to produce leucocytosis or to increase in the neutrophiles, but influence the blood only by producing what might be termed a functional debility of the blood through lack of nutritive substances in the plasma. This condition is by no means peculiar to tuberculosis, but occurs in a great variety of debilitated or cachectic conditions, as already stated.

(c) But when a septicæmia complicates the tuberculosis, cell metamorphosis appears to be accelerated, and we get with the quantitative increase of leucocytes such qualitative changes as the following:

	Per cent.
Polymorphonuclear neutrophiles	84
Lymphocytes (small)	9
Lymphocytes (large and transitional)	6
Eosinophiles	1

This was a case (No. 33 of Dane's series) in which the abscess, sterile when first opened, had become inoculated with the staphylococcus aureus.

(d) Not every case with leucocytosis shows qualitative changes as the above. One of Dane's cases (No. 22, a boy of seven) showed a leucocytosis of 23,387, but only sixty per cent of these were polymorphonuclear, and two per cent eosinophiles.

In a case recorded by Dane (No. 32), *tubercular osteomyelitis* showed 6,083 white cells (subnormal, as the child was only two years old) with sixty-four per cent of polymorphonuclear cells. The pus from the bone cavity showed no pyogenic organisms on culture. Ordinary septic osteomyelitis gives very different results (see page 234). Dane's cases were almost exclusively hip and spinal affections.

The following cases from the Massachusetts Hospital records illustrate tuberculosis of other bones:

Case.	Diagnosis.	Red cells.	White cells.	Per cent hæmo-globin.
1	Tuberculosis of the knee joint......	6,472,000	9,400	63
2	" " " "	2,704,000	8,000	?
3	Metatarsal tuberculosis............	4,650,000	6,500	61
4	Tubercular rib....................	5,016,000	5,800	73

III. ACUTE MILIARY TUBERCULOSIS.

Probably there are no important changes in the red cells or hæmoglobin. The number of cases on record is too small to enable me to speak positively on this point, but the acuteness of the disease would lead us to expect the normal or approximately normal conditions recorded in the few published cases.

About the leucocytes we know more.

Quantitative Changes.

Normal or subnormal counts are the rule. When occasionally there occurs a leucocytosis it may be inferred that the miliary process accompanies a suppurative one, and that the latter and not the former is responsible for the increased number.

Warthin[1] reports a case with autopsy in which he made over thirty counts of the white corpuscles, verifying the more remarkable results by repetition. Autopsy showed, besides miliary tuberculosis, a cavity in the lower lobe of the right lung and a suppurating focus about the seminal vesicles containing four ounces of pus rich in tubercle bacilli. Whether pyogenic organisms were also present is not stated. The leucocyte counts were as follows:

Day.	Hour.	Leuco-cytes.	Remarks.
December 6th	10 A.M.	3,500	
" 12th	8 A.M.	5,000	
" 18th	5 P.M.	3,500	
" 22d	10 A.M.	5,625	
" 22d	11 : 30 A.M.	4,725	
" 22d	3 P.M.	5,000	
" 22d	5 P.M.	3,125	
" 24th	8 : 30 A.M.	3,750	
" 24th	11 : 30 A.M.	3,750	
" 24th	2 P.M.	2,500	
" 24th	4 : 30 P.M.	2,500	
" 25th	8 A.M.	1,875	[80 per cent.
" 28th	5 : 30 P.M.	3,750	Red cells, 4,125,000; haemoglobin,
" 29th	10 A.M.	1,250	
" 29th	2 P.M.	1,250	
" 29th	5 : 30 P.M.	3,750	
" 31st	12 M.	1,250	
" 31st	6 P.M.	2,500	
January 2d	11 A.M.	1,250	
" 2d	5 P.M.	2,500	
" 3d	2 : 30 P.M.	600	Severe chill. Count repeated several times.
" 5th	8 : 30 A.M.	3,750	
" 5th	11 A.M.	3,137	
" 5th	4 P.M.	8,125	Moribund.
" 6th	9 A.M.	10,000	
" 6th	10 A.M.	5,625	
" 6th	11 A.M.	2,500	
" 6th	12 M.	5,625	
" 6th	12 : 50 P.M.	Death.	

[1] Medical News, 1895.

In another case he found also a subnormal count. Rieder found normal counts in two cases. Von Limbeck states that the leucocytes are normal, but gives no counts.

The following cases from the Massachusetts Hospital records illustrate these points:

ACUTE MILIARY TUBERCULOSIS.

Age.	Sex.	Red cells.	White cells.	Per cent hæmo-globin.	Remarks.
28	M.	2,448,000	550	35	March 8th.
			1,200	....	March 11th.
			1,100	....	March 11th, gave protonuclein gr. xv. t.i.d.
					March 13th, differential count (see below).
			1,300	.....	March 14th, glands rapidly diminishing.
					March 18th, died. Autopsy.
52	F.	....	3,500	90	
18	M.	....	3,600	....	Autopsy.
40	M.	....	3,750	....	Autopsy.
14	F.	3,720,000	4,400	45	Autopsy.
51	M.	4,664,000	4,800	....	Autopsy. Chronic phthisis also.
23	M.	....	4,900	....	Autopsy. Differential count normal
18	F.	....	5,400	80	September 21st.
			7,400	....	September 24th, no serum reaction.
20	M.	....	5,600	64	Autopsy. No serum reaction.
12	F.	....	6,100	....	Autopsy.
19	F.	....	6,600	....	Autopsy.
37	F.	....	7,500	71	Autopsy.
20	F.	....	7,800	....	May 14th.
			7,200	....	May 22d. Autopsy.
36	M.	....	7,600	....	Healed phthisis also. Autopsy.
30	M.	....	9,250	....	April 18th.
			9,450	....	April 20th. Autopsy.
45	M.	5,237,000	10,000	....	Autopsy.
22	M.	....	12,700	....	Phthisis also. Autopsy.

Case I. of the above table is a striking example of the remarkably low leucocyte count sometimes seen in this disease. The counts were carefully verified by several competent observers. The differential count made on the 13th showed:

Polymorphonuclear neutrophiles........... 78 per cent.
Lymphocytes (small)..................... 12 "
Lymphocytes (large) .... 9 "
Eosinophiles........................... 1 "

Qualitative Changes.

In Warthin's case above quoted, he repeatedly made differential counts of the leucocytes by Ehrlich's methods with this average result:

Per cent.

Polymorphonuclear neutrophiles....................91.49
Lymphocytes (small)............................... 5.52
Lymphocytes (large and transitional).............. 3.09
Eosinophiles...................................... 0.
Myelocytes.. .2

IV. TUBERCULOSIS OF SEROUS MEMBRANE.

1. TUBERCULAR PERITONITIS.

The blood condition is exactly as in other forms of tuberculosis, except in so far as it is modified by the drain exerted on the blood by diarrhœa or by transudation or exudation into the peritoneal cavity. Such events concentrate the blood by withdrawing water and albumin from it and may give us a normal number of red cells per cubic millimetre, when in reality a considerable anæmia is present. As a rule, the blood shows a mild secondary anæmia without leucocytosis or with leucopenia. This is exemplified in the following tables from the Massachusetts Hospital records:

Age.	Sex.	Red cells.	White cells.	Per cent hæmo-globin.	Remarks.
26	F.	3,120,000	2,240	58	
33	F.	2,900,000	3,800	48	
24	M.	5,360,000	3,800	......	January 6th, 1896.
		5,760,000	5,600	85	April 13th, 1896.
25	F.	....	3,900	......	Tubercular tube.
21	M.	....	4,400		
27	M.	....	4,900	64	March 1st.
			5,500	......	March 9th.
43	M.	....	5,000	......	December 18th, 1895.
		4,560,000	3,250	76	January 10th, 1896.
30	F.	....	5,183	......	Tubercular tube.
20	F.	5,936,000	5,400		
44	M.	2,974,000	5,530	......	Pleuritic effusion also.
16	F.	3,840,000	6,000	56	
33	F.	4,000,000	6,000		
50	F.	5,240,000	6,400		
37	M.	....	6,700	......	May 22d, 1896.

Age.	Sex.	Red cells.	White cells.	Per cent hæmo-globin.	Remarks.
			7,000	.....	May 30th, 1896.
30	M.	5,560,000	6,800		
44	F.	....	7,000	73	
26	M.	4,368,000	7,400	45	
17	M.	4,904,000	8,000	75	
32	F.	....	8,200		
20	F.	4,200,000	8,500	58	Tubercular tube.
29	F.	3,400,000	8,600	30	
50	F.	4,600,000	10,000	50	
41	M.	5,200,000	10,000		
38	F.	4,816,000	11,200		
21	F.	3,555,000	11,500	65	
27	F.	....	16,900	76	Pelvic abscess also.
			18,300		

I know of no differential counts of leucocytes in tubercular peritonitis. Presumably the sluggish metabolism of the cells found in other forms of pure tuberculosis exists here and causes an excess of the mononuclear elements.

2. TUBERCULAR MENINGITIS.

Remarkably few counts are on record so far as I can ascertain. Von Limbeck gives but a single case (with autopsy). Four counts, the last on the day of death, showed the following:

> May 22d, 1889: Leucocytes...................... 8,000
> " 23d, 1889: " 8,000
> " 24th, 1889: " 6,000
> " 26th, 1889: " 7,500

Rieder records two cases, in one of which the leucocytes were "normal or subnormal; in the other increased." In both diagnosis was confirmed by autopsy. The counts in these cases were as follows:

> Case I.—February 26th, 1891: Leucocytes....... 7,800
> March 2d, 1891: Leucocytes............. 5,900
> Case II.—May 30th, 1891: Leucocytes. 14,400

Pick[1] saw two cases:

> Case I.—February 28th, 1890: Leucocytes......... 6,500
> · March 5th, 1890: Leucocytes............. 8,000

In the second case there was also no leucocytosis. Autopsy in both. Sorensen's ' two cases showed respectively 8,300 and 9,400 leucocytes. My own results in seven cases are as follows:

TUBERCULAR MENINGITIS.

Age.	Sex.	Red cells.	White cells.	Per cent hæmo-globin.	Remarks.
2½	M.	....	28,000	63	July 8th.
			34,300	......	July 9th. Autopsy.
2	F.	....	25,900	......	May 30th.
			23,800	......	June 4th. Tubercular perito-nitis also.
			32,800	......	June 8th.
			27,800	......	June 10th.
			23,600	......	June 12th.
			16,500	......	June 14th.
			21,000	......	June 16th.
			19,800	......	June 18th.
34	M.	....	21,500	......	Autopsy.
35	M.	....	14,700	68	Pleurisy also.
22	M.	....	14,400	......	January 25th.
			19,400	......	January 30th.
			13,200	......	February 2d.
			19,300	......	February 6th. Autopsy.
45	M.	....	8,000	......	Autopsy.
24	F.	4,590,000	6,600	46	Autopsy.

These are, so far as I can ascertain, the only cases of uncomplicated tubercular meningitis with autopsy in which blood examinations are recorded and in all but one of these nothing is said about red cells or hæmoglobin. Rotch mentions a single case complicated by an appendicitis in which the following count is recorded (girl of eleven years):

Red cells.................................... 5,298,750
White cells.................................. 37,500
Hæmoglobin (per cent)........................ 68

Whether the leucocytosis was due wholly to the appendicitis or not we cannot tell.

I have examined no other cases of uncomplicated tubercular meningitis in which autopsy confirmed the diagnosis. In two cases in which *clinically* the diagnosis was tubercular meningitis I found moderate leucocytosis, in one with ninety-one per cent polymorphonuclear cells. Two of the cases of miliary tuberculosis above mentioned had marked meningeal symptoms and

¹ Cited by Rieder.

plenty of tubercles in the meninges, but being a *general* and not a local process no conclusions as to the blood of tubercular meningitis can be drawn from the absence of leucocytosis in these cases.

On the whole, it seems that pure tubercular meningitis differs markedly from other pure tubercular processes, in that it has in most cases a strong tendency to raise the leucocyte count. Osler's results point to the same conclusion.[1] Ziemke[2] has recently reported a case with 17,500 leucocytes per cubic millimetre. The red cells and hæmoglobin show probably the same changes as in other forms of tuberculosis.

3. TUBERCULAR PERICARDITIS.

In one case in which tubercle bacilli were repeatedly demonstrated in the fluid obtained by tapping the pericardial sac I found no leucocytosis. I have not met with any other reports on the blood in this condition.

4. TUBERCULAR PLEURISY.

No doubt a large proportion of all pleuritic effusions are tubercular in origin, but, so far as I have seen, no counts are recorded in cases proved by culture or inoculation to be tubercular. The low leucocyte counts in most pleurisies (see above, page 211) tend to show that they are tubercular and not due to pyogenic organisms.

Pick mentions that he finds no leucocytosis in tuberculous pleurisy when uncomplicated by phthisis, but reports no actual counts.

5. GLANDULAR TUBERCULOSIS.

In cases of so-called scrofulous glands, whether in children or adults, the blood shows no important changes except that in children the hæmoglobin may be considerably diminished.

---

[1] Text-book of Medicine, 3d edition.
[2] Deut. med. Woch., April 8th, 1897.

GLANDULAR TUBERCULOSIS.

No.	Age.	Sex.	White cells.	Per cent hæmoglobin.
1................................	20	F.	5,600	75
2................................	28	M.	10,900	65
3................................	7	F.	11,000	

Leucocytosis is absent unless an abscess has been opened and infected. Whether or not tuberculosis of the abdominal or other internal lymph glands affects the blood, I am unable to say.

6. GENITO-URINARY TUBERCULOSIS.

Here the opportunities for a secondary pyogenic infection are so good that in well-marked cases we find the blood of septicæmia present. The following cases, all involving the bladder, kidney, and the external genitals, illustrate this point:

No.	Age.	Sex.	Red cells.	White cells.	Per cent hæmoglobin.
1	30	M.	3,796,000	14,452	44
2	41	F.	3,588,000	10,400	55
			3,000,000 +	14,452	
3	22	F.	....	10,200	
4	35	F.	5,808,000	8,800	65
5	22	F.	....	8,400	70
6	31	M.	....	7,600	57
7	31	F.	....	6,900	60
8	42	M.	....	7,000	December 18th.
				8,700	December 26th.
				8,300	January 11th.

SYPHILIS.

Reiss, in an article in the *Archiv f. Dermatologie und Syphilis*, 1895, Heft 1, says that the general constitutional influence of the poison of syphilis is best indicated by the condition of the blood. In one hundred cases he has arrived at the following conclusions regarding the

Red Cells and Hæmoglobin.

During the time between the chancre and the secondary symptoms, the red cells are slightly decreased, but this is much more

marked after the appearance of secondary symptoms and continues for a time even after treatment has begun. The hæmoglobin sinks steadily from the time of the primary lesion on,
but is not especially affected by the eruption. Even under
treatment the hæmoglobin *never* gets quite up to normal and prolonged mercurial treatment lowers it, although mercury has at
first a beneficial effect on the hæmoglobin as well as on the other
constituents of the blood.

Konried[1] goes further into detail. According to him, in the
first four to seven weeks after infection, the number of red cells
remains normal, but the hæmoglobin begins to fall off, losing
from ten to twenty per cent in that time. Afterwards it sinks
steadily unitl treatment is begun, the number of corpuscles also
falling slightly.

Newmann and Konried,[2] reporting in 1893 on two hundred
cases, say that up to the time of the secondary symptoms from
twenty-five to thirty per cent of hæmoglobin is generally lost,
without much change in the red cells, which sink considerably in
number after the outbreak of secondary lesions. Lezius'[3] likewise finds no diminution in the *number* of red cells until the outbreak of secondary lesions.

All these changes, like those about to be described, are apt
to be more marked in women than in men. In cases going on
to the secondary stage untreated, the hæmoglobin may sink to
as low as twenty-five per cent. In the tertiary stages and in
hereditary and so-called "constitutional syphilis" the red corpuscles are much more seriously affected, diminishing considerably in number as well as in weight and color. The
hereditary syphilis of infancy may indeed produce fatal
anæmia and very low counts are common, with large numbers of nucleated red cells and great deformities in shape
and size.

The effect of mercurial treatments on the red cells is interesting. Gaillard[4] found that the count of red cells increased during the first fourteen days and the hæmoglobin during the first
twenty-four days of treatment. After that time, if mercury was

[1] International Dermatological Congress, 1892.
[2] Wiener klin. Woch., 1893. No. 19.
[3] Inaug. Dissert. Dorpat, 1889.
[4] Gaz. des Hôp. 1885, No. 74.

still given, the hæmoglobin and later the number of corpuscles began to decline.

Konried (*loc. cit.*) found the hæmoglobin to rise during the administration of the first twenty-five to thirty-five inunctions, after which it began to go down. This was in cases in which treatment was begun just after the onset of secondary symptoms. In the worst cases it sank even as low as forty-five per cent despite treatment, and this usually means a bad prognosis and severe tertiary symptoms to come. In one of my own cases the hæmoglobin was only thirty-seven per cent, though the red cells were 4,988,000 (color index, .37).

Potassic iodide increases the red cells and hæmoglobin, but has no special effect on the leucocytes.

Cases often show spontaneous improvement in their anæmia as well as in other symptoms.

Justus[1] in three hundred cases claims to have observed a peculiar reaction of the hæmoglobin in syphilis, which does not occur in any other disease, and which he considers of much diagnostic value.

According to him, if in cases in which secondary symptoms have not yet appeared, we test the hæmoglobin and then give an inunction or a subcutaneous injection of mercury, we find that within twenty-four hours a very marked fall in hæmoglobin has taken place (ten to twenty per cent), owing to the action of the mercury on the weakened corpuscles. This sudden fall is followed by a gradual rise until within a few days the coloring matter is at a point slightly higher than before the mercury was given. In diseases other than syphilis this sudden drop does not occur. After the advent of secondary symptoms the peculiar reaction to mercury does not occur.

No evidence for or against this observation has as yet been brought forward by others. In view of the large number of cases in which Justus has tried the experiment it is certainly an interesting observation and deserves to be followed up. If true, it might give valuable assistance in the diagnosis of doubtful cases before the appearance of the "secondaries."

White Cells.

1. Here the changes are very characteristic. In the first stage the leucocytes are either normal or slightly increased, but

[1] Verhandl. d. 5. Cong. d. Deut. dermatolog. Gesellschaft, September, 1895.

the percentage of polymorphonuclear forms is almost always notably low, and that of the lymphocytes high. If mercury is given at this stage, the polymorphonuclear forms begin to increase toward normal and the lymphocytes proportionately to decrease. [Mercury given to healthy persons has just the opposite effect, increasing the lymphocytes at the expense of the polymorphonuclear forms.] Iodide of potash works exactly like mercury in this respect, increasing the polymorphonuclear leucocytes in syphilis, while it diminishes them in healthy persons.

2. As the eruption breaks out leucocytosis (12,750 and 16,800 in two of my cases) generally appears, the proportion of lymphocytes and of eosinophiles usually being increased. Engel describes a syphilitic child in whom the percentage of polymorphonuclear cells steadily rose as the child got worse. In such cases Engel considers these cells to be of prognostic importance. P. K. Brown has made a similar observation in bone tuberculosis. Treatment with mercury and potassium iodide tends to bring down the count of lymphocytes, while it raises the count of red cells; and among the white cells to increase the polymorphonuclear forms.

In the *tertiary stages*, with the severe anæmia which is often present, there occur occasionally leucocytosis, not uncommonly with small percentages of myelocytes, and a marked lymphocytosis. Müller[1] has described four cases of anæmia in syphilis so severe as to simulate pernicious anæmia very closely. In one the red cells sank to 720,000. Laache[2] mentions a similar case.

There are no constant changes in the blood plates. Specific gravity follows pretty closely the hæmoglobin percentage.

Diagnostic Value.

Justus' reaction of syphilitic blood to mercury, if true, might be of great value in distinguishing early syphilis from various other causes of debility.

The occurrence in adults of leucocytosis with increased percentages of lymphocytes and of eosinophiles, is very suggestive of syphilis as against tuberculosis, typhoid or malignant disease. In children, rickets and other diseases may give similar

[1] Charité-Annalen, vol. xiv.   [2] *Loc. cit.*

blood changes. The chief value of the blood examination, however, in syphilis is not for diagnosis but as a measure of the stage and severity of the infection. Low hæmoglobin and high percentages of the lymphocytes are characteristic of severe types. Leucocytosis usually means that the case has got beyond the primary stage, while in the tertiary stage the presence of myelocytes with a marked anæmia is of serious import.

Certain cases of this last type may closely resemble pernicious anæmia, from which, however, they are to be distinguished by their low color index, the frequent presence of leucocytosis, and the relative infrequency of megaloblasts as compared with the normoblasts, in case nucleated red cells are present.

LEPROSY.

Winiarski (*Petersburger medicinische Wochenschrift*, 1892, page 365) gives a careful study of seventeen cases of leprosy, and P. K. Brown[1] has watched sixteen cases. They find in young persons with mild cases no changes from the normal blood.

In severe cases, especially in old people, the anæmia may be severe (2,290,000 red cells with fifty-four per cent of hæmoglobin) and even comparable to pernicious anæmia (1,989,000 red cells with sixty-three per cent of hæmoglobin). In anæmic cases the color index is apt to be high, in one case 1.7 (!). Such severe types are associated with an increase of the average diameter of the red cells which explains the high color index. The hæmoglobin was *not* relatively low in any case.

Leucocytes.

No increase was present in any case. Four cases were subnormal. The percentage of lymphocytes, as in other debilitated conditions, is often high (forty-five to forty-seven per cent).

Bacteriology of the Blood.

Brown has succeeded in demonstrating the leprosy bacillus in the blood of one-half of his cases. The bacilli appear for the

[1] San Francisco County Medical Society, July 13th, 1897.

most part within the leucocytes, and here they accumulate in large numbers. It is especially in the tubercular form of the disease that Brown has found them. He was unable to cultivate the bacillus.

Streker[1] has likewise found the bacillus in the blood of four cases.

[1] Münch. med. Woch., 1897, Nos. 39, 40.

18

PART IV.

DISEASES OF SPECIAL ORGANS.

CHAPTER VII.

DISEASES OF THE DIGESTIVE APPARATUS.

1. Mouth.

In a case of thrush complicating chronic nephritis the following counts were recently recorded at the Massachusetts Hospital: October 16th—Red cells, 5,000,000; white cells, 16,200; hæmoglobin, 52 per cent. October 24th—White cells, 13,800; hæmoglobin, 55 per cent.

2. Œsophagus (see Malignant Disease, page 345).

3. Stomach.

The conditions existing in the stomach may influence the blood profoundly in three ways:

(a) They may be such as to prevent the normal absorption of nitrogenous material on which the blood, like all tissues, is absolutely dependent. Then the blood becomes starved. The extreme of this condition is the so-called "atrophy of the gastric tubules" which may produce a fatal anæmia. In lesser degrees the same process is at work in many forms of chronic dyspepsia, gastritis, or chronic starvation.

(b) They may lead to severe and repeated hemorrhages.

(c) They may lead to an auto-intoxication which poisons the blood as well as other tissues.

On the other hand, it is probably through the influence of an altered blood serum on the duodenal mucous membranes that ulcer of the duodenum is a sequel to severe burns of the surface of the body.

For an account of the influence on the blood of digestion, ingestion of liquid, and starvation, see page 99.

DISEASES OF THE STOMACH.

ANOREXIA NERVOSA.

From pure starvation the red cells may get as low as 900,000 as in the case mentioned by Martin. In the early stages the blood is normal. A recent hospital case showed 8,900 leucocytes with 87 per cent of hæmoglobin.

GASTRIC CANCER.

(See Malignant Disease, page 333.)

GASTRIC ULCER.

Red Cells and Hæmoglobin.

A severe anæmia is common. Out of the 28 cases in Table XXV., 13, or nearly one-half, had less than 50 per cent of hæmoglobin, and of the 21 in which the red cells were counted, 5 had under 3,000,000 red cells per cubic millimetre. The average count of red cells at the time when treatment began was 3,800,-000. There is no single disease, so far as I am aware, in which the red cells are so apt to be so low, except pernicious anæmia. Even cancer, as a rule, does not fall so low. This is due mostly, I think, to the frequency of *hemorrhage* from the ulcer; it is uncommon to see marked anæmia in patients who had never had a hemorrhage.

This anæmia is all the more striking when we remember that the frequent vomiting from which most patients suffer tends to concentrate the blood, *increase* the number of cells in a drop and so to make the blood seem less anæmic than it really is. This tendency to concentration is probably effective in some of the cases observed especially by Oppenheimer,[1] in which despite great pallor he found normal counts of red cells and hæmoglobin.

It is in such cases that the estimation of the dry residue of the blood serum would be of real value could it be made short and simple enough for clinical work. Grawitz, who is the prophet of this branch of blood examination, gives an interesting case illustrating this point.

A girl of twenty-five, suffering with peptic ulcer, and exceedingly

[1] Deut. med. Woch., 1889, No. 42.

pale, showed on counting the corpuscles 4,140,000 per cubic millimetre (no considerable reduction), and ninety per cent of hæmoglobin. A second count showed 4,340,000 corpuscles and ninety-one per cent of hæmoglobin. But the dry residue of the serum was reduced to three-fourths its normal amount. The serum suffers in anæmia as much as the corpuscles do. Any influence which deprived the serum of one-fourth of its normal solids (œdema being absent) must have really affected the corpuscles very much. Therefore the corpuscles must actually have been reduced to about 3,800,000, the reduction being masked by the concentration of the blood from vomiting. Lymph cannot have run into the vessels and diluted the serum, for (owing to the vomiting) the tide is all the other way. If then the serum is reduced a quarter the corpuscles must be so likewise. Unfortunately, to test the dry residue of the blood serum requires more time, skill, and apparatus than clinicians are apt to have. It is valuable whenever we wish to know whether or not an anæmia is being masked by concentration of the blood.

In severe cases the usual *qualitative evidences* of secondary anæmia (deformities, scanty normoblasts) are to be found.

TABLE XXV., A.—GASTRIC ULCER WITH HEMORRHAGE.

Age.	Sex.	Red cells.	White cells.	Per cent hæmo- globin.	Remarks.
23	F.	1,672,000	6,000	40	One pint of blood vomited on previous day ; blood in stools ; recovery.
29	F.	1,676,000	14,750	36	Large hemorrhage ; recovery.
25	F.	1,750,000	4,000	...	Recovery.
24	F.	1,892,000	7,000	30	January 16th, after hemorrhage.
		2,304,000	....	27	January 22d.
		3,064,000	3,500	35	January 31st.
		3,920,000	....	48	February 10th.
		4,680,000	....	55	February 20th.
				63	February 28th.
				67	March 5th.
29	F.	1,972,000	4,000	38	Recovery.
52	F.	2,031,000	17,200	30	Hemorrhage and perforation.
42	F.	2,216,000	13,500	32	
26	F.	2,968,000	5,300	45	November 9th, exclusive rectal feeding till 17th.
		2,788,000		30	November 16th.
				34	November 21st.
		2,296,000	....	34	November 29th.
		3,208,000	....	40	December 3d.
30	F.	3,432,000	7,820	45	Hemorrhage previous day.
		4,222,000	10,600	75	Two weeks later.
		4,392,000	6,700	70	Three weeks later.
25	F.	3,664,000	14,700	45	
48	F.	4,900,000	6,200	40	

TABLE XXV., B.—GASTRIC ULCER WITHOUT HEMORRHAGE.

Age.	Sex.	Red cells.	White cells.	Per cent hæmoglobin.
19	F.	5,856,000	10,650	90
21	F.	5,100,000	......	70
40	F.	4,400,000	9,000	53
39	F.	....	11,100	68
23	F.	....	9,300	90
22	F.	....	8,300	75
30	F.	....	6,800	70
25	F.	....	6,550	85
35	F.	....	6,500	50 April 27th. 45 June 6th.
47	F.	....	6,300	57
38	F.	....	5,800	60
19	F.	....	5,600	68
20	F.	....	4,300	57

Hæmoglobin.

As a rule the color index is low. Only one examination in the cases of the Massachusetts Hospital series showed an increased amount of hæmoglobin per corpuscle, and as this was not repeated or verified, it may have been a mistake. In all the other thirty examinations the color index was low (*e.g.*, Case 5, color index = .39).

Yet Osterspey records 1,900,000 red cells with 31 per cent of hæmoglobin (color index = .81); 3,296,000 with 70 per cent hæmoglobin (color index = 1.09); 4,048,000 with 84 per cent hæmoglobin (color index = 1.05). Such cases are certainly rare.

White Cells.

Leucocytosis is practically never seen except after hemorrhage and during digestion. When patients who have been fed for some time by the rectum are first given food by the mouth, the digestion leucocytosis may be very great, as in Case 11 of the above series, in which the cells increased from 4,000 to 15,500! The presence of a leucocytosis, when the influence of bleeding and digestion are excluded, is against the diagnosis of ulcer of the stomach.

DUODENAL ULCER.

No.	Age.	Sex.	Red cells.	White cells.	Per cent hæmo- globin.	Remarks.
1	30	M.	3,776,000	Normal	50	
2	47	M.	2,100,000	12,000	35	July 24th, much coffee grounds.
				7,650	....	July 29th (five days fasting).
				11,600	....	Four hours after meals.
				11,000	....	Constant feeding, July 30th.
			2,480,000	6,000	38	August 8th.
			2,630,000	6,500	36	August 21st, operation.

These figures are given simply to show that the blood in duodenal ulcer undergoes much the same changes as in gastric ulcer, and need no further comment.

ACUTE GASTRITIS AND DYSPEPSIA.

Acute gastritis or gastro-enteric attacks (Hayem's "*embarras gastrique*") do not affect the red cells or hæmoglobin, but are very often accompanied by leucocytosis (see Tables XXVI., A

TABLE XXVI., A.—ACUTE GASTRO-ENTERITIS.

Age.	Sex.	Red cells.	White cells.	Per cent hæmo- globin.	Remarks.
31	M.	7,000,000	18,000	....	Temperature 104°. Well next day.
8	F.	4,800,000	17,800	50	Temperature 101°.
50	F.	....	15,100	70	
13	F.	5,184,000	15,000	85	Well next day.
28	M.	....	14,400	....	September 17th, temperature 103°.
			12,800	....	September 18th.
			9,100	....	September 21st, temperature normal.
30	F.	4,860,000	14,200	80	Well in three days.
20	M.	....	12,000	67	
36	F.	....	11,600	68	
23	F.	6,244,000	11,600	86	Well in two days.
17	F.	4,600,000	11,000	70	
29	F.	....	11,000	....	Temperature 101°.
70	F.	4,632,000	10,000	90	
37	M.	4,186,000	9,200	68	
28	M.	....	6,900	90	Temperature 102°.
23	F.	3,860,000	6,400	65	
57	F.	....	6,000	....	Temperature 101°.
23	F.	5,144,000	5,400	95	
32	F.	....	5,200	50	Temperature 100°.

and (B). Where this is the case, it may help us to exclude typhoid fever, which has no leucocytosis. Even a twenty-four hours' dyspeptic attack may increase the leucocytes notably, as in Cases 1 and 2 in Table XXVI., A, and the presence of such an increase need not make us suspect anything behind the dyspepsia. It is probably to be classed as a toxic leucocytosis due to absorption of morbid products from stomach or intestine. Fibrin may be increased during the period of leucocytosis.

TABLE XXVI., B—DYSPEPSIA AND GASTRITIS.

No.	Age.	Sex.	Red cells.	White cells.	Per cent hæmo-globin.	Remarks.
1	24	M.	6,280,000	22,700	....	Gastralgia ; constipation ; whole belly tender.
				12,800	....	Three days later ; well in a week.
2	27	F.	4,750,000	14,000	74	At mealtime, 11,200 ; four hours later, 12,150.
3	26	F.	4,920,000	11,000	55	Dyspepsia.
4	23	M.	....	11,000	....	Acute gastritis.
5	....	...	5,016,000	8,924	86	
6	37	M.	....	7,326	77	Chronic gastric catarrh.
7	30	F.	3,678,000	7,000	75	Nervous dyspepsia.
8	41	M.	4,524,000	6,000	68	Before meal, November 1st, 6,000; November 2d, 6,300. After meal, November 1st, 6,800; November 2d, 7,400.
9	49	F.	4,200,000	4,000	80	Chronic gastritis.
10	18	F.	5,016,000	3,200	45	Dyspepsia.
11	60	M.	3,504,000	2,800	50	Chronic gastritis.

CHRONIC GASTRITIS.

(See Cases 6, 9, and 11, Table XXVI., B.)

Here the conditions are different and we never find an increase of the white cells, but often a decrease due to malnutrition. Digestion may produce no leucocytosis, or the increase may be very slight and late in appearing (four to five hours after a meal instead of two to three hours). It was present in nine out of twelve cases in our series.

Anæmia is very often present and may be extreme. It is believed by very high authorities that a *pernicious* anæmia may be caused by chronic gastritis with atrophy of the gastric tubules. The writer has never had the good fortune to see such cases.

The practical points about the blood of chronic gastritis are: (a) The not infrequently severe anæmia.

(b) The not infrequent absence of digestion leucocytosis as in gastric cancer, from which therefore the *absence* of digestion leucocytosis does not distinguish it.

The presence of a leucocytosis militates against the diagnosis of chronic gastric catarrh, and, if hemorrhage is excluded, points toward cancer.

HYPERACIDITY AND HYPERSECRETION.

The leucocytes average higher in these conditions than in chronic gastritis or dyspepsia with normal or decreased secretions (see Table XXVII.). Otherwise the blood is not remarkable.

TABLE XXVII.—HYPERACIDITY AND HYPERSECRETION.

No.	Age.	Sex.	Red cells.	White cells.	Per cent hæmo-globin.	Remarks.
1	Adult.	M.	5,024,000	12,300	82	
2	30	F.	5,768,000	10,800	82	Chronic gastritis.
3	40	M.	5,300,000	10,000	85	Slight digestion leucocytosis: 12,270 before meal, 14,300 three hours later.
4	40	M.	3,340,000	7,780	?.	Dilated stomach; no digestion leucocytosis.
5	28	F.	4,016,000	5,994	76	
6	57	M.	4,160,000	3,600	84	Lead poisoning and dilated stomach.

DILATED STOMACH.

No.	Age.	Sex.	Red cells.	White cells.	Per cent hæmo-globin.	Remarks.
1	22	F.	6,216,000	10,400	83	
2	51	M.	4,184,000	9,600	55	
3	47	M.	4,720,000	8,000	....	Nervous dyspepsia.
4	30	F.	5,000,000	6,000	75	Movable kidney.
5	64	M.	5,264,000	4,600	70	

DILATED STOMACH.

In many cases proteid absorption is so faulty that the blood is severely starved, but the *anæmia* may be concealed by the con-

centration of the blood brought about by the constant vomiting of large amounts of fluid. Kussmaul has shown that patients *often vomit more fluid than they ingest*, and it is obvious what must be the drain of this process on the fluids of the blood and all other tissues.

Digestion leucocytosis is often absent, as in cancer or chronic gastritis.

CORROSIVE GASTRITIS.

The blood was examined in a case of this kind in 1895 at the Massachusetts General Hospital with the following result: Red cells, 3,792,000; white cells, 32,500; hæmoglobin, fifty-three per cent.

DISEASES OF THE INTESTINE.

INFLUENCE OF SALINE CATHARTICS ON THE BLOOD.

Hay[1] gives the following figures, showing the effect of sulphate of sodium in concentrating the blood: Healthy man of thirty-three, 3:35 P.M. Red corpuscles, 5,025,000; given 85 c.c. of a concentrated solution of sulphate of sodium in water; thirty-five minutes later blood count showed red corpuscles, 6,540,000; sixty-five minutes later blood count showed red corpuscles, 6,790,000; four hours later blood count showed red corpuscles, 4,930,000. Evidently much fluid was drawn out of the blood-vessels and then within four hours the tissues had supplied the loss and the blood had returned to its normal density.

Hay also showed that dilute solutions of the same salt had far less effect in concentrating the blood. Farther he demonstrated that if the blood is *already concentrated* when the saline is given, no purgative effect follows.

Grawitz confirms these results; he found also that common salt still further concentrates the blood (hence its production of thirst), and considers that (as this concentration accelerates *coagulation*) the household use of salt water as a remedy to stop hemorrhage is well founded.

[1] Hay: "The Action of Saline Cathartics." Journal of Anatomy and Physiology, 1882. p. 430.

TABLE XXVIII.—ENTERITIS, COLITIS, AND DYSENTERY.

No.	Age.	Sex.	Red cells.	White cells.	Per cent hæmo-globin.	Remarks.
1	45	M.	3,840,000	17,000	50	Chronic dysentery. August 26th.
				14,300	....	September 3d.
				7,700	....	" 5th, dysentery ceased.
				8,800	....	" 20th.
2	25	F.	....	17,000	....	Chronic entero-colitis.
3	Adult.	M.	3,624,000	13,000	58	Chronic entero-colitis.
4	Adult.	M.	4,320,000	12,400	....	Ulcerative colitis.
			2,732,000	10,600	....	Two weeks later.
			4,488,000	6,000	....	Three weeks later; much improved.
5	39	F.	6,776,000	8,900	100	Acute febrile dysentery; bloody movements every hour.
6	3	F.	4,800,000	7,900	....	Ulcerative colitis.
7	Adult.	M	4,100,000	7,560	72	Chronic enteritis.
8	27	M.	4,872,000	7,000	....	" diarrhœa and tetany.
9	20	M.	5,008,000	6.460	39	" diarrhœa (tubercular?).
10	26	M.	4,900,000	5,300	80	Bloody stools ten days.
11	65	M.	....	5,200	80	Catarrhal entero-colitis.
12	40	F.	2,996,000	5,000	37	Chronic colitis.
13	27	F.	4,500,000	5,000	70	Diarrhœa.
14	34	F.	3,920,000	4,200	71	Chronic colitis.

ACUTE ENTERITIS.

Practically the great majority of cases of acute enteritis are part of a gastro-enteric attack, and in Table XXVI. (see page 278) the two have been lumped together. What was said of that table (page 279) need not be here repeated. Besides the slight leucocytosis there mentioned, we may find in cases in which the stools are very watery, a temporary concentration of the blood with increased specific gravity and red corpuscles.

CHRONIC DIARRHŒA.

(See Table XXVIII.)

In acute diarrhœa the other tissues respond to meet the loss of fluid sustained by the blood, and the blood is soon normal again. But when this process goes on long, the body becomes so wasted that the blood must share in the starvation and the albuminoids are drained out of it, leaving it watery and poor in corpuscles. A patient of Grawitz after years of chronic dysentery had but 1,880,000 red cells per cubic millimetre, while the serum had twice the normal amount of water and half the normal amount of solids. I have seen the count fall as low as 1,928,000 in a case of prolonged colitis, with final recovery. In another case the red cells reached no lower than 2,440,000, but the hæmoglobin was but ten per cent. A differential count of this man's blood showed the following:

Polymorphonuclear neutrophiles .... 66.3 per cent.
Lymphocytes (small) .... 24.9 "
Lymphocytes (large) ... . 6.0 "
Eosinophiles............................ 1.4 "
Myelocytes .... 1.4 "

While counting 400 leucocytes I saw 8 normoblasts and 5 megaloblasts. The total leucocyte count was 9,800 per cubic millimetre.

Cases 1, 3, 4, 12, and 14 of the series in Table XXVIII. show similar conditions. The hæmoglobin, however, usually suffers most, and the color index is low.

Leucocytosis is rare, but does occasionally occur, possibly owing to some complication or auto-intoxication.

TABLE XXIX.—INTESTINAL OBSTRUCTION.

No.	Age.	Sex.	Red cells.	White cells.	Per cent hæmoglobin.	Remarks.
1	....	...	3,120,000	20,800	....	Cancer.
2	52	M.	5,568,000	18,860	....	9th of May, cancer.
				18,800	....	17th of May, cancer.
3	Adult.	M.	....	14,666	....	No fæces three days.
						No urine two days.
				12,400	....	One day later, no fæces; urine drawn by catheter.
				4,100	....	Three days later, bowels moved six times.
4	35	M.	3,504,000	12,000	....	Chronic obstruction with hemorrhage.
5	21	M.	5,150,000	12.000	....	Obstruction (by a band).
6	56	F.	4,440,000	12,000	52	Cancer.
7	57	F.	4,272,000	11,000	75	Cancer.
8	Adult.	M.	5,800,000	6,800		
9	72	M.	4,850,000	6,000		
10	Adult.	M.	5,200,000	4,000		
11	"	M.	5,540,000	4,000		

Cholera is discussed on page 211.
For *appendicitis* see Abscess, page 222.

INTESTINAL OBSTRUCTION.

The only point brought out by Table XXIX. is that the white cells may be increased, especially where the obstruction is cancerous. Hence the blood count cannot be relied on to help us in the diagnosis between obstruction and peritonitis. It is more likely that the examination of the amount of fibrin will be useful, as it is said to be increased in peritonitis and not in obstruction.

DISEASES OF THE LIVER.

CATARRHAL JAUNDICE.

The serum is colored yellow or greenish-yellow and contains bile pigments in solution. It has been asserted that jaundice can be recognized here before it shows in the skin or urine. In mild cases, i.e., where some bile goes to the intestine and the obstruction is not long standing, *the blood is practically normal*, as the cases in Table XXX. show. No

TABLE XXX.—CATARRHAL JAUNDICE.

Age.	Sex.	Red cells.	White cells.	Per cent hæmoglobin.
21	M.	....	10,500	81
44	M.	....	10,200	
25	F.	4,310,000	10,000	77
			10,000	90
			8,000	
30	F.	....	9,600	68
42	M.	2,896,000	8,775	47. Alcoholic gastritis
26	M.	....	7,500	
21	M.	4,800,000	7,500	65
30	M.	....	7,400	64
30	M.	....	7,300	
53	M.	4,240,000	6,793	79
29	M.	....	6,200	82
	M.	4,996,000	6,000	78
35	M.	4,350,000	4,900	85
29	F.	....	4,200	85
			9,600	
19	F.	....	4,000	

one of these cases shows any leucocytosis, and the red cells and hæmoglobin have not suffered except in the alcoholic case in which other causes for anæmia were present. This is contrary to the observations of Grawitz, who found constantly leucocytosis, but agrees with those of v. Limbeck and Hayem, who never found any increase of leucocytes or any other changes in the blood count. Coagulation and the amount of fibrin are normal. Von Limbeck noticed an *increased resistance* of the red cells to the influence of distilled water and dilute saline solutions which in normal blood dissolve the hæmoglobin. He noticed also that the *size* of the red corpuscles was *greater than normal*, their volume in a given amount of blood being seventy-seven to eighty-one per cent (*i.e.*, they take up seventy-seven to eighty-one per cent of the room occupied by the drop) while the normal is about forty-four per cent. This was in cases with only from 4,000,000 to 5,200,000 red cells per cubic millimetre, so that it was evidently due not to an overcrowding of the drop with red cells but to a true increase of size in the individual cells. The same fact has been attested from a different point of view by the investigations of v. Noorden, who found the solid residue increased, and of Hammerschlag; and Grawitz has noted an increase in the specific gravity of the whole blood, though that of the serum remained normal. Normal red corpuscles put into the serum of icteric patients increase their diameter considerably, so that apparently the serum is responsible for the change.

Qualitative Changes.

Grawitz noted in severe cases that crenation took place much more rapidly than usual in freshly drawn blood, and that the rouleaux formation did not take place. This latter point was also noticed by Hofmeier[1] in icterus of the new-born. Silbermann[2] noticed in the same disease great deformities in the size and shape of the cells. In severe febrile icterus Weintraud noted in the red cells the white spots and streaks with active (molecular) movements described by Maragliano (see page 87) as endoglobular degenerative changes.

Summary.

Normal blood, except for increased size of the red cells and some degenerative changes in severe cases.

[1] "Die Gelbsucht der Neugeborenen," Stuttgart, 1882.
[2] "Die Gelbsucht der Neugeborenen." Arch. f. Kinderheilk., 1887, p. 401.

Diagnostic Value.

The constant presence of leucocytosis excludes an uncomplicated "catarrhal" jaundice, and points to the probability of malignant disease or inflammation (cholangitis, abscess). Syphilis and cirrhosis of the liver might show the same condition of the blood unless the characteristics of syphilitic blood were very marked (see page 269). From a severe cholæmia the absence of any marked anæmia distinguishes a purely catarrhal case. (For the changes in cholæmia see page 290.)

CIRRHOSIS OF THE LIVER.

1. ORDINARY (ATROPHIC) CIRRHOSIS WITHOUT JAUNDICE.

In the early stages (according to Hayem) neither the red cells nor the hæmoglobin fall considerably. Most other observers (perhaps thinking chiefly of the later stages) report marked anæmia. Wlajew[1] counted from 3,000,000 to 4,000,000 red cells; v. Limbeck had a case with only 1,500,000. He noted that the count might be increased after a tapping in cases with ascites, owing to the concentration of the blood from the rapid refilling of the belly with serum. Grawitz, on the other hand, noticed precisely the opposite effect in a case whose blood before tapping had been concentrated by cyanosis, the heart's action being embarrassed by the ascites. After tapping, when the heart's action had become easier and stronger, the cyanosis disappeared and the blood count fell from 4,700,000 to 4,300,000. In v. Limbeck's case it rose from 4,680,000 to 5,160,000. The moral is that we should draw no inferences from the count of red cells soon after a tapping.

The fifty-two cases in Table XXXI., A., were all advanced and their red cells averaged only 3,580,000 + per cubic millimetre. They steadily decrease as the disease progresses, one case getting as low as 1,300,000; but the anæmia may be concealed by cyanosis and concentration.

Qualitative Changes.

Hayem noticed a curious stickiness of the red corpuscles, a great tendency to adhere to each other. Von Limbeck looked

[1] Ref. in Petersburger med. Woch.. 1894. No. 43

for it, but could never find it. Hayem and Maragliano noticed degenerative endoglobular changes in the red cells ("*état cribriforme*").

TABLE XXXI., A.—CIRRHOTIC LIVER WITHOUT JAUNDICE.

Age.	Sex.	Red cells.	White cells.	Per cent. hæmo-globin.	Remarks.
53	F.	2,950,000	16,000	..	Recent hemorrhage.
41	M.	4,300,000	12,750	55	Liver enlarged ; ascites.
48	M.	4,992,000	9,000	62	Recent hemorrhage.
53	M.	2,120,000	9,000	23	March 15th.
		1,800,000	7,500	22	April 8th.
				15	April 18th.
				15	April 29th.
		2,350,000	6,000	20	May 10th.
		2,375,000	5,300	26	May 12th.
		2,450,000	5,200	20	June 10th.
		4,500,000	7,800	25	June 16th.
50	M.	3,440,000	8,320	46	Liver enlarged.
34	M.	....	7,900	95	
56	M.	....	7,500	68	
53	M.	....	6,200	60	
38	F.	....	5,700	65	
		5,720,000	5,200	46	Differential count normal.
54	M.	....	5,400	64	
56	M.	4,680,000	5,000	48	Liver atrophic, July 12th.
		4,312,000	4,000	62	July 25th.
42	M.	2,920,000	4,500	56	October 30th.
			13,400	..	November 7th, during digestion.
			15,300	..	November 11th, during digestion.
53	M.	....	3,800	72	
54	F.	....	3,300	65	
63	M.	3,844,000	3,000		
50	M.	3,568,000	2,400	50	
52	M.	3,440,000	2,400	50	

Hæmoglobin.

Usually the color index is low; the average was .66 in the ten Massachusetts Hospital cases.

White Cells.

Except after recent hemorrhage none of our cases showed any leucocytosis, and the average count was 7,240, some cases having notably low figures (2,400, 3,000, 4,500).

Hayem's results agree with this. Von Limbeck makes no definite statement on this point. Rosenstein and Wlajew found leucocytosis, the latter 12,000 to 17,000. Possibly their cases include the forms of cirrhosis *with* jaundice in which (see Table XXXI., B) the white cells are more often increased.

The forms of hypertrophic cirrhosis *without* jaundice (fatty infiltrated liver) are here classed with the atrophic cases whose blood has just been described.

TABLE XXXI., B.—CIRRHOTIC LIVER WITH JAUNDICE.

No.	Age.	Sex.	Red cells.	White cells.	Per cent hæmo-globin.	Remarks.
1	42	M.	1,024,000	19,600	36	Autopsy.
2	38	M.	3,400,000	19,500	50	
3	45	M.	4,568,000	14,000	65	Liver enlarged.
4	35	M.	5,016,000	12,000	..	Liver enlarged.
5	57	F.	....	......	..	Adult cells, 83 per cent; young cells, 17 per cent.
6	36	M.	2,064,000	4,300	50	Jaundice only transient.
7	50	M.	2,904,000	2,400	54	Autopsy (hypertrophic cirrhosis).

2. HYPERTROPHIC CIRRHOSIS WITH JAUNDICE.

Red Cells.

True (biliary) hypertrophic cirrhosis *with* jaundice has according to Hayem an intense anæmia in many cases. In others it has no more effect on the blood than ordinary atrophic cirrhosis. The six cases in Table XXXI., B, averaged a little lower in the count of white cells than the ten atrophic cases, 3,200,000 as contrasted with 3,580,000.

Hæmoglobin.

In a single case of this variety of cirrhosis Hayem found in four successive blood examinations a color index of more than 1. His counts are as follows:

Date.	Red cells.	White cells.	Per cent hæmoglobin.	Color index.
January 9th	1,599,600	....	41	1.27
" 11th	1,884,000	21,803	50	1.39
" 12th	1,798,000	18,082	50	1.46
" 15th	1,971,000	15,500	53	1.40

Dried specimens showed an increased average diameter of the cells as in pernicious anæmia. The patient died January 15th and the autopsy confirmed the diagnosis of hypertrophic cirrhosis.

The observations of v. Limbeck of the increased volume of the red cells in *jaundice* may perhaps be another example of the condition here noted by Hayem. The presence of bile in the blood makes all hæmoglobin estimations unsatisfactory.

Only one of our six cases showed this same condition—Case 5 in Table XXXI., B. The corpuscles numbered 2,064,000, or forty per cent, and the hæmoglobin fifty per cent, a color index of 1.25. This case was jaundiced at the time of the examination.

I have seen no confirmation of Hayem's observation by any other writer.

White Cells.

Leucocytosis is commoner in this than in the other variety of cirrhosis. Hanot and Mennier found from 9,000 to 21,800 leucocytes per cubic millimetre in five cases of hypertrophic cirrhosis and an average of 6,600 in ordinary cirrhosis. Leucocytosis was present in four of the six cases of the Massachusetts Hospital series, the average of all six being 9,000.

Diagnostic Value.

The blood of either form of cirrhosis has no diagnostic value, so far as I know, except to exclude abscess and hydatids. If no leucocytosis is present, abscess and hydatid cyst can usually be excluded.

HYDATID CYST OF THE LIVER.

The only observations which I have met with are those of Hayem and Neusser. Hayem states that the blood shows leucocytosis and increased fibrin. Neusser considers that the increase of eosinophiles which he finds in hydatids serves to distinguish them from hydronephrosis, dilated gall-bladder, etc.

ACUTE YELLOW ATROPHY OF THE LIVER.

Grawitz records a case with 5,150,000 red cells and 16,000 white cells.

A single case with autopsy was studied at the Massachusetts General Hospital in 1894, the blood showing 5,520,000 red cells, 12,000 white cells, and sixty per cent of hæmoglobin.

19

PHOSPHORUS POISONING.

Taussig,[1] v. Jaksch,[2] Badt,[3] and v. Limbeck[4] note an *increase* in the normal number of red cells per cubic millimetre. Taussig found 8,650,000 per cubic millimetre; Badt, 6,400,000, 6,500,000, and 6,800,000 in three successive cases; v. Limbeck, 6,500,000 and 7,900,000. That this increase is not due to concentration of the blood through vomiting of liquid is proved by v. Limbeck's last case, in which no vomiting whatever took place.

The count usually falls to normal within a few days. All these changes were verified in thirty-three cases at the Stockholm Hospital in 1892 (see Stockholm Hospital reports for 1892).

The white cells in v. Limbeck's second case were increased to 12,500. In v. Jaksch's five cases the counts were 58,750. 48,000, 8,000, 4,070, and 3,400.

CHOLÆMIA.

When jaundice is intense and long standing, as in complete obstruction of the bile ducts by gall-stones or tumors, the blood is weakened very notably, and hæmoglobin and the count of corpuscles fall steadily. Very little is to be learned upon the subject from the literature, but the qualitative changes mentioned under catarrhal jaundice are much more marked, and leucocytosis is apt to be present. I have studied the blood in a case of fatal chronic jaundice without fever and for which at autopsy no cause was found. The leucocytes ranged between 12,000 and 14,000.

GALL-STONES.

Netter[5] and Sittmann[6] have found pyogenic organisms in cultures from the blood of patients with gall-stones, as have also Gilbert and Girode.[7]

[1] Arch. f. experiment. Path. und Pharm., vol. xxx.
[2] Deut. med. Woch., 1893, p. 10.
[3] Dissert., Berlin, 1891.
[4] *Loc. cit.*, p. 34.
[5] Progrès Médical, 1886, No. 46.
[6] Deut. Arch. f. klin. Med., 1894, p. 323
[7] La Semaine Méd., 1890, No. 58.

Of the 22 cases of this disease examined at the Massachusetts General Hospital 2 were complicated with cholangitis (see Table XXXII., A). Excluding these 2, leucocytosis was present in only 4 of 20 cases. The red cells were low in 2 cases (2,800,000 and 3,900,000).

The absence of leucocytosis helps us to distinguish the disease from peritonitis and appendicitis, and excludes suppurative cholangitis.

TABLE XXXII., A.—GALL-STONES.

Age.	Sex.	Red cells.	White cells.	Per cent hæmo-globin.	Remarks.
39	F.	4,768,000	24,400	..	Cholangitis also.
30	F.	4,820,000	20,000	..	Cholangitis. Autopsy.
63	F.	4,610,000	18,800		
29	M.	....	16,200		December 16th.
			13,200		December 18th.
			10,000		December 21st.
40	F.	4,520,000	13,000		
60	F.	....	12,500	72	Temperature, 100.5°.
			11,500	70	
40	M.	....	10,250		
49	F.	....	10,000	90	Jaundice.
47	M.	....	9,800	85	
45	F.	....	9,200	100	
38	F.	....	8,900	60	Distended gall-bladder.
25	F.	5,072,000	8,800	..	Jaundice.
22	M.	3,288,000	8,000	..	Jaundice.
25	F.	4,900,000	8,000		
54	F.	....	7,600	80	
29	F.	2,844,000	7,400		
57	F.	....	7,400	85	
37	F.	....	7,300	..	October 1st.
			8,200	..	October 5th.
58	M.	....	6,000	64	
57	F.	....	5,400	68	
51	F.	....	5,300	63	
24	M.	4,320,000	4,000	..	Recurrent pain and jaundice.

CHOLANGITIS.

Here the leucocytosis is well marked whenever the inflammation has got beyond the catarrhal stage (see Table XXXII., B) and helps us to exclude simple impacted gall-stone, with or without colic. Cancer may or may not produce leucocytosis, but does not usually increase the fibrin network; it is said by Hayem that cholangitis does increase it.

TABLE XXXII., B.—CHOLANGITIS.

No.	Age.	Sex.	Red cells.	White cells.	Remarks.
1	....	F.	4,800,000	50,000	Suppurative cholangitis.
2	....	F.	6,400,000	30,000	
3	....	F.	4,960,000	22,000	
4	21	M.	4,976,000	14,800	Jaundice and cholæmia.
5	65	M.	....	14,186	Gall-stones; chills.
6	....	....	....	11,000	October 20th. Operation October 22d. Abscess of liver.
7	28	M.	6,640,000	9,000	Catarrhal.
			5,592,000	6,800	
8	34	F.	4,770,000	4,400	Catarrhal.

ABSCESS OF THE LIVER.

In all but one of the cases seen by the writer (see Table XXXIII.) the leucocytosis has been very marked. I have never been able to account for its absence in that case.

The blood does not differ from that of cholangitis with suppuration. From cancer it may often be distinguished by the absence of increased fibrin network in cancer, while it is always increased in suppurations.

TABLE XXXIII.—ABSCESS OF THE LIVER.

Age.	Sex.	Red cells.	White cells.	Per cent hæmo-globin.	Remarks.
20	M.	4,533,000	33,200	..	January 11th.
			48,000	..	January 14th. Operation.
15	F.	3,750,000	26,800	..	Operation.
60	F.	4,460,000	18,000	..	Operation.
28	M.	....	12,600		
33	F.	....	11,000	..	November 3d.
			17,500	..	November 4th, 11 A.M.
			19,200	..	November 4th, 2 P.M.
			20,600	..	November 5th, 10 A.M. Operation; autopsy.
26	M.	2,664,000	10,200	33	October 19th.
			12,000	..	October 20th.
			15,000	..	October 21st. October 25th, autopsy; streptococci.
51	F.	3,440,000	9,600		

CANCER OF THE LIVER.

(See Malignant Disease, page 346.)

GUMMA OF THE LIVER.

Von Jaksch in a single case found red cells, 2,756,000; white cells, 6,100.

DISEASES AFFECTING THE HEART.

PERICARDITIS.

(See Inflammation of Serous Membranes, page 247.)

ENDOCARDITIS.

In many cases of acute endocarditis the blood shows no changes. In others, whatever alterations there may be are covered up by those involved in the *rheumatic* arthritis associated with the endocarditis.

ULCERATIVE ENDOCARDITIS.

In *ulcerative or malignant endocarditis*, we may find the signs of a pyogenic infection (see page 216). Sometimes pyogenic cocci can be cultivated from the blood and if present *may be of the greatest value in a diagnosis* always difficult to make.

Grawitz goes so far as to say that in doubtful cases repeated negative results of cultures from the blood make it unlikely that ulcerative endocarditis is present.

Sittmann [1] considers that important help may be given as to the position of the primary focus of infection by the nature of the organism present in blood cultures—*i.e.*, the pneumococcus pointing to the lung, the colon bacillus to the intestine, etc.

Red Cells.

As in all forms of septicæmia marked anæmia rapidly develops, more rapidly probably than in any other disease. The hæmoglobin loses about equally with the corpuscles, according to most observers—that is, the blood destruction is so rapid that the red cells do *not* get thin before they die, as is usually the case, but are cut off in the prime of health.

Further evidence of rapid blood destruction is seen in the hæmoglobinæmia often present.

[1] *Loc. cit.*

Roscher (*loc. cit.*) records counts of 4,400,000 and 2,750,000, both fatal cases. In one casê seen by the writer the count was 3,792,000 with fifty-eight per cent of hæmoglobin.

White Corpuscles.

Rieder reports a single case showing these variations:

			Temperature.	White cells.
January	2d,	1891	105°	17,000
"	3d,	1891	99°	13,700
"	8th,	1891	103°	15,500
"	10th,	1891	101.5°	18,000
"	12th,	1891	101.5°	21,300
"	18th,	1891	101°	18,800
"	22d,	1891	104.5°	.13,000

February 11th, patient died.

Pée found leucocytosis. Roscher in two cases found: Case I.: 8,800 leucocytes; patient died in two days. Case II.: 16,-800 and 12,000. Krebs in one case found: October 27th, 15,-500; October 28th, 44,200; the patient died same day.

Nine cases were counted at the Massachusetts Hospital with the following results. In three only the fresh blood was examined and showed marked leucocytosis; in the others:

ULCERATIVE ENDOCARDITIS.

Case.	Red cells.	White cells.	Per cent hæmoglobin.	Remarks.
1		30,100	....	May 27th.
		15,800	....	May 30th.
		18,100	....	June 17th.
2		25,700	....	May 22d.
		27,840	....	May 24th.
		18,100	....	May 26th.
		22,000	....	May 28th.
3		20,400	....	Autopsy.
4		12,600	....	January 13th.
		14,500	....	January 14th.
		20,400	....	January 16th.
		24,000	....	January 18th ; died.
5	3,792,000	10,000	58	
6		8,900	55	Autopsy.

Practically the same are the counts in the following cases of apparently "benign" endocarditis with fever and rapidly shifting murmurs, the first complicating chorea in a boy of thirteen, the other in an adult.

"BENIGN" ENDOCARDITIS.

Age.	Sex.	Red cells.	White cells.	Per cent hæmoglobin.	Remarks.
13	M.	....	20,600	62	May 26th. Temperature 102°–104°.
			17,900	....	May 29th.
			18,700	....	May 31st.
			16,800	....	June 3d.
			21,200	....	June 4th.
			27,400	....	June 8th.
			22,700	....	June 11th.
			24,200	....	June 13th.
			21,900	....	June 15th.
			26,100	....	June 17th.
			26,800	....	June 19th.
			17,400	....	June 23d.
			28,700	....	June 26th.
			21,200	....	July 2d (outdoors).
			21,300	....	July 4th. Left the hospital July 19th.
56	F.	....	50,100	....	November 24th.
			35,800	....	November 27th.
			36,600	....	November 30th.
			22,800	....	December 7th.

Diagnostic Value.

(a) Blood cultures should never be omitted in cases of suspected malignant endocarditis. When positive they are of great value. (b) In excluding typhoid the presence of leucocytosis is important. I saw within a few months a case in which several consultants had made the diagnosis of typhoid, but in which the presence of marked and persistent leucocytosis and the absence of a typhoid serum reaction convinced me that the case was one of ulcerative endocarditis. This has since been verified.

MYOCARDITIS.

Whenever stasis and disturbance of the circulation result from weakness of the heart wall, blood changes identical with those described under Valvular Heart Disease are present. Otherwise the blood is normal.

VALVULAR HEART DISEASE.

Grawitz divides valvular heart disease into three stages with corresponding blood conditions:

1. Stage of full compensation: blood normal.
2. Stage of *acute* failure of compensation: blood diluted (Oertel's "plethora serosa").
3. Stage of chronic stasis and cyanosis: blood concentrated for the most part; at times diluted as well.

1. A valvular lesion *per se* has no effect on the blood.

2. When compensation fails and blood pressure is lowered, we find (*especially in the venous blood*) that the fluid from the surrounding lymph spaces has made its way into the vessels and dilated the blood. The specific gravity falls, red cells and hæmoglobin are lower than before, while the white cells are un-altered, and the plasma is shown to be more watery than before as well as of increased quantity per cubic millimetre. All these changes are less marked in capillary blood, and hence are *rarely observed.*

3. If the heart adjust itself partially to the increased work it has to do, and to the chronic passive congestion of the internal organs and at the periphery, the blood is concentrated, probably in part by transudations into serous cavities and lymph spaces, and in part by the increased excretion of moisture by the lungs. The specific gravity and the number of red cells are increased, *especially in the capillaries*, and to a lesser extent in the venous blood (the conditions being just the reverse of those in acute heart failure, stage No. 2). This is the condition usually found in heart disease with chronic venous stasis (passive congestion).

But this concentrated condition of the blood may be offset from time to time by fresh weakening of the heart and lessen-ing of blood pressure, and the combination of the two conditions may result in a normal blood count.

The condition of concentrated peripheral blood with the count of red cells above normal, is that most commonly seen in chronic heart disease with stasis.

Von Limbeck finds that aortic lesions are more apt to show a normal or diminished blood count, while mitral disease is more apt to be accompanied by the temporary dilutions and long-standing concentration above described. He does not explain the cause of this. One of his patients with double mitral lesion showed a decrease of 1,170,000 red cells (from 7,500,000 to 6,330,000) after exertion. When the patient was quiet, the lesion was compensated; on exertion compensation temporarily failed, blood pressure was lowered, and the blood diluted.

Sadler[1] found considerable anæmia in three out of four cases of aortic disease, while only two of seven patients with mitral lesions showed anæmia.

Schneider's[2] results were similar in that he found the red cells normal in the aortic cases and increased in the mitral ones.

Hayem found anæmia most common in aortic regurgitation, especially in young people.

In the Massachusetts Hospital records out of twelve cases of mitral disease five had less than 4,000,000 red corpuscles per cubic millimetre. Of three cases of aortic disease all were over 4,000,000. I think these figures simply mean that the mitral cases are more apt to come to the hospital in the stage of acute failure of compensation—therefore (see above) with diluted blood—while the aortic cases often come while compensation is still good and therefore with practically normal blood.

White Corpuscles.

Almost all writers whom I have consulted agree that the leucocytes are normal unless some complication occurs. Yet in a certain number of the Massachusetts Hospital cases mostly (but not exclusively) those with cyanosis, the leucocytes were *increased*, the counts ranging sometimes as high as 15,000, while the red cells were normal. I suppose this is to be accounted for by the fact that in any case in which the circulation is feeble and slow, the white cells accumulate at the periphery even more plentifully than the red. This is evidently so in the cases of congenital heart disease next to be mentioned, in which the red cells are increased only about forty per cent, while the white are often one hundred per cent more numerous than normal.

The apparently normal count of red cells in some of our cases was probably due to the covering up of an anæmic or diluted condition of the blood by concentration, the resultant of the two forces being an apparently normal count.

[1] *Loc. cit.*, p. 33   [2] Inaug. Dissert., Berlin, 1888.

Koblank (*loc. cit.*) gives the following cases illustrating this condition:

	Red cells.	White cells.
1. Mitral leakage	5,461,250	28,000 + ; autopsy.
2. Aortic leakage	4,716,600	13,000 +

This leucocytosis must be taken into account in making inferences from cases whose circulations are feeble, and no deeper underlying cause (*e.g.*, abscess, cancer) need be assumed to account for the increase.

Œdema and diuresis have in themselves little or no constant effect upon the blood, as a recent observation of Petrowsky's has demonstrated.

CONGENITAL HEART DISEASE.

In the cyanosis accompanying this affection very high blood counts are reported.   Gibson found:

Case.	Red cells.	White cells.	Per cent hæmoglobin.
1	8,470,000	12,000	110
2	6,700,000	12,000	92

Carmichael reports, red cells, 8,100,000, white cells, 16,000, in a single case, and Toeniessen counted 8,820,000 and 7,540,000 in two similar cases.   In one case entirely without evidence of any stasis I counted 8,431,000 red cells per cubic millimetre. How such cases are to be explained I do not know; the ordinary explanation of concentration of the blood will not hold in cases in which no stasis or lack of compensation exists, yet the skin is blue and the blood counts are enormous.

There is no doubt that the peripheral capillaries always contain more corpuscles per cubic millimetre than do the veins. Numerous reports from various observers agree upon this. Whether this is on account of the loss of water by perspiration and consequent drain of blood from the skin capillaries is uncertain, but in congenital heart disease both capillary and venous blood is overcrowded with corpuscles and the explanation is difficult.   Hayem in a case of this sort reports 7,000,000 red cells with a *decrease* in the average diameter.

The most important practical deduction from these data is that a blood count in a patient suffering from poorly compensated heart disease has no value in determining whether or not anæmia is present. The actual number of corpuscles in the body is not measured by the number contained in a drop of peripheral blood, since anæmia may be effectually masked by concentration or simulated by dilution.

This holds good equally for any condition involving *general* stasis and cyanosis either from embarrassment of the heart's action or otherwise (for instance, pneumonia in certain stage, emphysema, displacement of the heart by serous effusions, or tumors), or *local* stasis of the part from which blood is taken. Penzoldt [1] noted that in old hemiplegic cases, the blood from the affected side contained more corpuscles than that from the sound side, and the writer has noticed the same thing in a variety of vasomotor affections involving local asphyxia.

ANEURISM.

As a rule I have found the blood entirely normal, but in the following case it might have thrown light on the diagnosis. A patient was recently admitted to the Massachusetts Hospital with an acute affection of the chest, supposed to be pneumonia in spite of the slightness of the fever and the irregularity of the physical signs. At autopsy a ruptured aortic aneurism was found. The blood count had showed 3,324,000 red cells, 20,800 white, and 33 per cent hæmoglobin. The low percentage of hæmoglobin and red cells was really inconsistent with an acute pneumonia in a man previously well, and might have hinted strongly toward the correct diagnosis had attention been directed more carefully to the blood.

DISEASES OF THE KIDNEYS.

Many factors other than the disease itself may influence the blood of nephritic cases. For instance, in scarlatinal nephritis the long-standing leucocytosis is probably due largely to the scarlatinal poison, rather than to the nephritis. The occurrence of large quantities of blood in the urine has the same influence as any other hemorrhage upon the blood.

Œdema as such has apparently very little effect upon the

[1] Berliner klin. Woch., 1881, p. 457.

blood, but the *loss of albumin* in the urine tells both on the corpuscles and on the serum, thinning both with consequent lowering of the specific gravity of the blood.

ACUTE NEPHRITIS.

1. *Red Cells and Hæmoglobin.*

Whether largely from the loss of blood from the kidneys or from other causes, the red cells are often much diminished, but the hæmoglobin suffers still more. Laache reports an average loss of nineteen per cent of the red cells and twenty-six per cent of their coloring matter.

Hayem found no considerable loss of red cells unless the urine was hemorrhagic. The following cases illustrate his results.

CASE I.—Acute nephritis, ending in recovery.

	Red cells.
March 17th, 1882	3,069,000
March 31st, 1882	2,759,000
April 7th, 1882	2,821,000
May 1st, 1882, albuminuria ceased.	
May 17th, 1882	3,038,000
May 31st, 1882	3,689,000

CASE II.—Acute (puerperal) nephritis; recovery.

	Red cells.
April 6th, 1881	2,945,000
" 9th, 1881	2,976,000
" 12th, 1881, no albumin in urine.	
" 13th, 1881	3,137,500
" 20th, 1881	3,310,000

CASE III.—Nephritis (chronic ?) with hæmaturia.

Red cells .... 2,821,000.

(It should be noted that Hayem's counts are low on the average, and the instrument used by him not very reliable.)

Grawitz in acute nephritis records 3,400,000 red cells at the beginning of the third week, and 3,100,000 ten days later.

Koblank[1] counted 5,168,700 in a case of acute nephritis with œdema.

[1] Inaug. Dissert., Berlin, 1889.

Sadler (*loc. cit.*) in six cases of acute nephritis found in two cases 3,590,000 and 2,262,000 red cells; in the other four practically normal counts.

TABLE XXXIV.—ACUTE NEPHRITIS.

Age.	Sex.	Red cells.	White cells.	Per cent hæmo-globin.	Remarks.
56	F.	....	22,200	....	Temperature 102.5°.
			14,000	....	Sixth day.
			11,900	....	Ninth day, temperature falling.
			12,200	....	Nineteenth day.
11	F.	4,068,000	14,000	52	
45	M.	3,532,000	13,200	43	
3	F.	....	12,000		
23	M.	....	11,700	50	
24	F.	....	11,100	85	
33	M.	3,904,000	9,300	50	Purpura also.
22	M.	4,300,000	8,300	48	
22	M.	....	7,600	60	
44	F.	....	7,500	65	
37	M.	....	6,800	78	
20	M.	5,000,000	6,000	58	Acute parenchymatous.
22	F.	4,944,000	5,400		
			5,100	....	Acute parenchymatous.

In none of the few cases examined at the Massachusetts Hospital were the red cells much diminished, but in two cases the hæmoglobin was very low, the color index being .62 in one and .61 in the other.

The blood plates are much increased (Hayem) and fibrin slightly increased.

2. *White Cells.*

Leucocytosis is usually stated to be the rule, lasting often for weeks at a time and gradually diminishing in convalescence. Hayem gives counts of 14,973, 12,400, 15,000, and 13,000.

Koblank (*loc. cit.*) and Grawitz each in a single case found *normal* counts (7,300 and 5,600).

Sadler found an increase in only one of his six cases, and then the highest point reached was 13,312.

Of the thirteen cases of Table XXXIV. leucocytosis was present in six, in one of which it was followed for three weeks and still persisted, but it is my own belief that the leucocytosis of acute nephritis is due either to loss of blood by the kidney or to uræmia. Where these conditions are absent I have not found any leucocytosis.

CHRONIC DIFFUSE AND CHRONIC PARENCHYMATOUS NEPHRITIS.

Red Cells.

In advanced stages the counts may run very low, but more often it is chiefly the hæmoglobin that suffers through the drain of albuminoids from the blood into the urine.

Hayem gives the following figures:

CASE I.—Chronic parenchymatous nephritis.

	Red cells.	Per cent hæmoglobin.
June 20th	4,309,000	43
July 4th	4,216,000	44
October 18th	2,945,000	34

CASE II.—Same diagnosis.

	Red cells.	Per cent hæmoglobin.
March 6th	2,619,500	36
" 8th	2,836,500	36
" 23d	2,464,500	27

Koblank (loc. cit.) in the same disease found 3,291,700 red cells in a single case with much œdema.

Reinert found 4,050,000 with 50 per cent of hæmoglobin and 3,604,000 with 62 per cent hæmoglobin.

Sadler:

	Red cells.
Case 1	4,120,000
" 2	2,405,000—November 19th.
	1,100,000—January 14th.
	1,500,000—January 17th.
" 3	4,300,000
" 4	4,300,000
" 5	3,737,500—June 28th.
	3,593,700—July 3d.
	2,187,500—August 15th.
" 6	3,200,000—July 7th.
	3,257,000—July 22d.
	3,137,000—August 21st.

Grawitz in an acute exacerbation of a chronic parenchymatous nephritis found 1,928,000 red cells.

The Massachusetts Hospital cases show a considerable anæmia in nine out of the thirty-five, or one-quarter of the series. Great concentration is probably the cause of the very high counts in certain cases. The majority of cases are not far from normal so far as the number of red cells goes, and the hæmoglobin is also very little diminished.

CHRONIC NEPHRITIS.

Red cells.		Cases.
Between 1,000,000 and 2,000,000	1
" 2,000,000 " 3,000,000	2
" 3,000,000 " 4,000,000	11
" 4,000,000 " 5,000,000	12
" 5,000,000 " 6,000,000	6
" 6,000,000 " 7,000,000	3
	35

Color index averages about .7.

White Cells.

Hayem records 25,000, 19,000, 13,000, 10,000, and 6,000 and concludes that the counts vary much not only in different cases but in the same case at short intervals.

Koblank found 14,700 in a single case.

Sadler in one case found 6,300 in November and 16,000 in the following January; 12,000 in another case; 8,800, 7,700, and 1,916 in others.

TABLE XXXV., A.—LEUCOCYTES IN CHRONIC NEPHRITIS WITH URÆMIA.

Age.	Sex.	White cells.	Remarks.	Age.	Sex.	White cells.	Remarks.
32	F.	44,000	Eclampsia.	23	M.	12,500	
29	F.	22,600		58	M.	12,400	
29	M.	18,650	Polynuclear cells, 83 per cent.	50	F.	12,300	
				59	M.	12,100	
49	F.	16,800		44	M.	11,300	
20	F.	15,800	Differential count normal.	31	M.	11,200	
				45	F.	6,600	
38	M.	15,000		34	F.	4,600	
45	M.	15,000		30	M.	4,200	
37	M.	14,200					
15	F.	13,800			19 cases average 14,495.		
25	M.	13,400					

TABLE XXXV., B.—CHRONIC DIFFUSE AND CHRONIC PARENCHYMATOUS
NEPHRITIS. NO URÆMIA.

Age.	Sex.	White cells.	Age.	Sex.	White cells.	Age.	Sex.	White cells.
41	M.	3,000	50	F.	7,300	43	F.	10,300
30	M.	4,500	34	M.	7,400	56	M.	10,700
58	M.	4,800	55	M.	7,400	47	F.	10,800
30	M.	5,000	17	M.	7,500	10	F.	11,000
27	M.	5,100	25	M.	7,600	25	M.	11,200
30	F.	5,200	28	M.	7,600	16	F.	12,700
41	M.	5,500	15	F.	7,700	11	M.	13,000
20	F.	6,250	14	M.	7,750	27	M.	13,000
7	M.	6,400	33	M.	7,900	66	M.	14,000
39	M.	6,500	27	F.	8,300	56	F.	14,000
8	M.	6,500	30	M.	8,300	43	M.	14,500
8	M.	6,800	24	F.	9,000	45	M.	16,300
41	M.	6,800	52	F.	9,800			
28	M.	7,000	20	F.	10,000	40 cases average 8,657.		

The same wide range is seen in Tables XXXV., A and B,
in which I have divided the uræmic and the non-uræmic cases
into separate tables.   It will be seen from these that fourteen out
of nineteen uræmic cases showed leucocytosis, while thirty-one
out of forty non-uræmic cases showed no leucocytosis.   It is
difficult to suppose that this is mere coincidence.

CHRONIC INTERSTITIAL NEPHRITIS.

Hayem found the fibrin more increased in this form of nephritis than in any other, and the anæmia less pronounced.

Grawitz distinguishes two stages:

I. As long as the heart is strong enough to overcome the increased resistance at the periphery and the disturbances of circulation are not marked, the blood is normal.

II. When compensatory hypertrophy is no longer sufficient
to do the work of forcing the blood through the system, the
usual effects of failing compensation (see Heart Disease, page
296) appear (dilution and subsequent concentration of the
blood).

The *white cells* are normal.

TABLE XXXVI., A.—CHRONIC INTERSTITIAL NEPHRITIS.

No.	Age.	Sex.	Red cells.	White cells.	Per cent hæmo-globin.	Remarks.
1	39	M.	6,040,000	19,381	80	Uræmic coma; moribund.
2	......	F.	4,548,000	15,000	50	Uræmic; mitral stenosis.
3	Adult.	M.	4,244,000	12,000	67	Three and one-half hours after a meal.
4	46	M.	....	9,724	....	Uræmic; moribund.
5	20	M.	4,088,000	6,000	66	March 23d.
					52	" 30th.
6	34	F.	3,536,000	8,300	57	
7	69	M.	....	8,500	87	
8	32	M.	....	6,000	65	

TABLE XXXVI., B.—PYELO-NEPHRITIS.

No.	Age.	Sex.	Red cells.	White cells.	Per cent hæmo-globin.	Remarks.
1	24	F.	3,056,000	21,200	41	March 10th. Uræmia.
			2,976,000	15,200	38	" 13th.
			2,696,000	18,800	33	" 27th.
			3,272,000	25,200	33	April 14th.
2	26	F.	4,200,000	16,800	....	Perinephritic abscess too.
3	33	M.	4,536,000	15,550	36	Cystitis also.
4	26	F.	2,356,000	7,280	65	" "

TABLE XXXVI., C.—CYSTIC KIDNEY.

No.	Age.	Sex.	Red cells.	White cells.	Per cent hæmo-globin.	Remarks.
1	55	M.	3,664,000	6,400	....	Adult cells, 72 per cent. Supposed cancer. Enormous firm tumor on each side. Autopsy.

The cases recorded in Table XXXVI., A, are probably not inconsistent with these rules. Of the four cases with leucocytosis three were uræmic, and in the fourth the influence of digestion is seen. The hæmoglobin is lower than we should expect from Grawitz's account.

Uræmia, it would appear from these tables, may cause leucocytosis or at any rate is not infrequently associated with it. Aside from uræmia and hemorrhage, nephritis probably does not cause leucocytosis.

20

PYELO-NEPHRITIS.

Table **XXXVI.**, B, speaks for itself. The *anæmia* is often severe and leucocytosis is the rule.

STONE IN THE KIDNEY.

(See Table **XXXVII.**, A.) The state of the blood depends on the amount of ulceration caused by the stone; when this is considerable we have leucocytosis.

TABLE **XXXVII.**, A.—STONE IN THE KIDNEY.

No.	Age.	Sex.	Red cells.	White cells.	Per cent hæmo-globin.	Remarks.
1	..	..	....	22,800	85	Tender in loin.
				16,200		
2	19	M.	....	15,200	..	Much pus in urine.
3	..	M.	4,350,000	14,750	78	
4	25	F.	4,160,000	9,000	65	
5	48	M.	....	8,990		
6	58	M.	5,680,000	8,000		
7	..	..	4,340,000	8,000	..	Much pus in urine.
			6,100,000	16,500	..	Two weeks later.
8	52	M.	3,048,000	7,500	30	
9	45	M.	....	7,500	95	
10	51	M.	....	6,000	95	Uric acid stone passed.
11	30	M.	....	4,980	85	

TABLE **XXXVII.**, B.—FLOATING KIDNEY.

No.	Age.	Sex.	Red cells.	White cells.	Per cent hæmo-globin.	Remarks.
1	37	F.	5,056,000	9,200	75	
2	41	F.	4,684,000	9,000	75	
3	23	F.	5,400,000	6,000	69	
4	43	F.	4,700,000	2,400	76	
5	38	F.	....	....	75	Aneurism of arch also.
6	24	F.	....	....	80	
5	38	F.	4,416,000	5,800	67	
6	24	F.	....	7,600	80	

A large number of similar counts might be quoted.

Diagnostic Value.

Cancer would also cause leucocytosis, but would not increase fibrin as a rule, while most cases of stone with ulceration do increase fibrin.

FLOATING KIDNEY.

The blood is normal. This fact has some diagnostic value; for example, when we confound appendicitis with floating kidney, as has been done (see page 230). The presence of leucocytosis excludes the latter and favors the former. Most tumors or abscesses with which a floating kidney might be confused could be distinguished by the same criterion.

PYO-NEPHROSIS.

CASE I.—Female, 36; leucocytes, 16,200, of which 85 per cent are neutrophiles. Half a pint of pus found at operation.

CASE II.—July 25th—red cells, 3,856,000; white cells, 9,800; hæmoglobin, 45 per cent. July 29th—Red cells, 3,450,000; white cells, 9,000; hæmoglobin, 55 per cent. August 3d— White cells, 6,650. August 6th—Operation. Pint of foul pus. Death.

DISEASES OF THE LUNGS.

BRONCHITIS.

"Acute catarrhal and chronic purulent bronchitis have relatively little leucocytosis in most cases" (v. Limbeck).

Except for this and a few other passing references, there is hardly anything in literature on the blood in bronchitis, so that I shall be forced to base my statements chiefly on the few counts recorded at the Massachusetts General Hospital.

1. ACUTE BRONCHITIS.

Aside from "capillary bronchitis," cases are not infrequently seen in which the signs are simply those of general bronchitis of the finer tubes, yet the symptoms are much more like pneumonia. Whatever may be the real conditions in the lungs of such patients, their blood is not infrequently exactly like that of pneumonia and does not help at all in the differential diagnosis between the two diseases (see Cases 1 and 2, Table XXXVIII., A).

TABLE XXXVIII., A.—ACUTE BRONCHITIS.

Age.	Sex.	Red cells.	White cells.	Per cent hæmoglobin.	Remarks.
70	F.	4,420,000	41,000	70	
56	M.	4,800,000	26,000	65	Temperature, 103°.
22	M.	....	23,450	67	Temperature, 101°.
41	F.	4,192,000	15,000	65	November 5th.
			11,300	..	November 16th.
			17,600	..	November 25th.
26	M.	....	14,200	70	Temperature, 101.5°.
28	F.	6,196,000	12,000	65	
46	M.	....	11,800	..	Temperature, 104°.
20	M.	....	10,600	65	Temperature, 104°.
40	M.	....	10,300	..	Temperature, 101°.
42	M.	....	9,300		
50	F.	5,260,000	8,000	72	
50	M.	5,952,000	7,900	50	
52	M.	....	7,000	70	
25	M.	....	7,000	74	Temperature, 103°.
59	F.	....	6,800		
36	M.	4,392,000	6,000	72	October 31st.
			8,600	..	November 3d.
29	M.	....	4,000	80	Temperature, 102°.

TABLE XXXVIII., B.—CHRONIC BRONCHITIS.

No.	Age.	Sex	Red cells.	White cells.	Per cent hæmoglobin.	Remarks.
1	Adult.	M.	3,680,000	18,500	63	
2	48	M.	....	15,000	....	Chronic febrile, with laryngitis. Recovery.
3	27	F.	5,384,000	8,800	73	Constipation; neurasthenia; two weeks afebrile.
4	61	M.	4,300,000	8,000	63	Five months.
5	20	F.	....	7,925	78	
6	18	M.	....	7,792	....	Keratitis, conjunctivitis. No symptoms.
7	26	F.	4,700,000	6,700	70	Asthma.
8	29	F.	4,100,000	5,500	61	Empyema of the antrum.
9	20	M.	....	5,062	....	One month.

In the majority of acute cases, however, the blood shows no changes unless concentration due to cyanosis be present (see Cases 4 and 7, Table XXXVIII., A).

In chronic cases (Table XXXVIII., B) leucocytosis is very uncommon, more so, I think, than the table represents. If more counts were added, nearly all, I think, would be normal.

The red cells and hæmoglobin show no changes to speak of in either acute or chronic cases.

The blood has no diagnostic value so far as I know except that when pneumonia is in question a normal count of white cells speaks against it and in favor of bronchitis. If emphysema is also present it sometimes produces a different blood condition from that of simple bronchitis.

EMPHYSEMA AND ASTHMA.

Grawitz reports an increase in the number of red cells in *emphysema*, which he believes to be due to cyanosis and to cover up the really anæmic condition of the blood of many patients. Practically the same conditions are present as in the cyanosis of heart disease (see page 296) and the concentration of the blood is brought about in the same way. Leichtenstern[1] noticed a diminution in hæmoglobin at the time when the heart first fails, due probably to the diminished blood pressure which allows the lymph from neighboring tissues to flow into the vessels and dilute the blood.

In both asthma and emphysema it has been noted by Müller,[2] Gollasch,[3] Gabritschewsky[4] and others that *eosinophiles* are very numerous in the sputum, and Fink[2] also noted an increase of the same cells in the blood, running as high as 14.6 per cent instead of the normal one to two per cent. This increase is present only at the time of the paroxysm and for a short time before and after it. Billings[5] reports the following counts:

	January 26th.	February 4th.	February 11th.
Red cells.	3,911,000	4,221,000	4,630,000
White cells.	8,300	7,500	7,600
Hæmoglobin	68 per cent.	75 per cent.	86 per cent.
Polymorphonuclear cells	36 "		
Lymphocytes (small) . .	5 "		
Lymphocytes (large) . .	5.2 "		
Eosinophiles.	53.6! "	38.2 per cent.	33.9 per cent.
	Few normoblasts	. . . .	No nucleated red cells.

[1] "Ueber das Hb-Gehalt des Blutes," etc., Leipzig, 1878.
[2] Ref. in Fink, "Beiträge z. Kennt. des Eiters," Dissert., Bonn, 1890.
[3] Fortschritte der Med., 1889.
[4] Arch. f. exp. Path. und Pharm., 1890, p. 83.
[5] New York Med. Journal, May 22d, 1897.

Their presence in increased numbers before a paroxysm makes it possible to predict its coming (v. Noorden, Schwerskewski). As this applies only to pure *bronchial asthma* and not to cases secondary to disease of the heart or kidney, Schreiber states that we are enabled to distinguish bronchial from cardiac or renal asthma by the increase of eosinophiles in the blood and sputa in bronchial cases, which does not occur in asthma due to cardiac and renal trouble.

ASTHMA.

Age.	Sex.	Red cells.	White cells.	Per cent hæmo-globin.	Remarks.
26	M.	....	32,500	..	Fifth. Temperature 100°. Bronchitis and emphysema.
50	F.	....	19,200 19,800	.. 50	Seventh. Temperature normal. Typical bronchial asthma during paroxysm.*
70	M.	5,500,000	13,000		Chronic asthma and emphysema in paroxysm ; polynuclear cells, 79 per cent.
29	M.	....	9,750		

For Pneumonia, see page 184.
For Phthisis, see page 255.
For Abscess of Lung, see page 235.

SYPHILIS OF THE LUNG.

In a case of syphilitic infiltration of the lung (autopsy—Drs. Councilman and Wright) recently observed at the Massachusetts Hospital the leucocytes rose rapidly from. 8,700 to 27,400 as death approached.

PART V.

DISEASES OF THE NERVOUS SYSTEM, CONSTITUTIONAL DISEASES, AND HEMORRHAGIC DISEASES.

CHAPTER VIII.

DISEASES OF THE NERVOUS SYSTEM.

NEURITIS.

In a single case of multiple neuritis, febrile and apparently of an infectious nature, the following counts are found in the records of the Massachusetts General Hospital:

Date.	Temperature.	Red cells.	White cells.	Per cent hæmoglobin.
July 10th........	101°...............	4,816,000	25,000	42
" 13th........	....	....	24,800	
" 16th........	....	....	18,700	
" 20th........	....	....	21,000	
" 25th........	....	4,320 000	16,000	60
" 31st	(No fever.)........	....	28,700	
August 7th	" "	....	19,500	
" 20th	" "	....	23,200	

The patient, a boy of eleven, recovered and left the hospital well.

But these changes occur also in alcoholic (afebrile) neuritis, as the following counts show.

Case.	Red cells.	White cells.	Per cent hæmoglobin.
1	3,608,000	15,000	75
2	3,260,000	14,000	64
3	....	13,700	60
4	... .	11,200	68
5	....	7,700	80
6	....	6,700	82

In all cases the counts were made just at mealtime, so that the leucocytosis is not due to digestion. Gastritis was not present in either case.

One case of post-diphtheritic neuritis in a child of eight showed the presence of anæmia only: Red cells, 3,850,000; white cells, 7,393; hæmoglobin, 70 per cent.

Neuritis in lead poisoning does not affect the count of leucocytes, as twenty-five cases studied at the Massachusetts Hospital have shown.

Neuralgia, whether facial, intercostal, sciatic, or ovarian, showed normal blood in numerous cases examined at the Massachusetts Hospital.

DISEASES OF THE BRAIN.

Meningitis (see Inflammation of Serous Membranes, page 248).

Zappert in one case of *brain abscess* found only 4,000 white cells.

In *pachymeningitis hæmorrhagica* and *cerebral syphilis* (one case of each) v. Jaksch found leucocytosis. My own experience has been the same.

Cerebral and cerebellar tumors have no effect on the blood as far as could be judged from nine counts in the former and three in the latter disease. Von Jaksch found slight leucocytosis in two cases of brain tumor and one of *cysticercosis*. Zappert found normal blood in one case of cerebral tumor.

Fresh cerebral hemorrhage usually causes leucocytosis, as the following table shows:

Age.	Sex.	Red cells.	White cells.	Per cent hæmo- globin.	Remarks.
42	M.	....	31,000	95	Autopsy.
52	M.	....	30,000	....	Polynuclear cells, 92 per cent.
		5,512,000	25,000	85	Autopsy.
47	M.	....	19,400	....	Autopsy.
70	F.	....	16,800	68	Hemorrhage four days before count. Autopsy.
		5,560,000	15,600	90	
37	M.	....	12,300	70	
38	M.	....	10,400	58	Conscious; recovered.
37	M.	....	10,300	90	Autopsy.
65	M.	....	10,200	60	

CHOREA AND TETANY.

Chorea showed in twelve cases normal blood except for increased percentages of eosinophiles, as in Zappert's two cases, which Louga confirms.

Burr has made a careful study of the blood in thirty-six cases and arrived at the following conclusions: There is usually a slight diminution in red cells and a moderate diminution in hæmoglobin. Any severe grade of anæmia is due to some complication. He did not record the leucocytes. Tetany shows no blood changes.

DISEASES OF THE SPINAL CORD.

Chronic diseases of the spinal cord, such as tabes dorsalis, syringomyelia, spastic paraplegia, diffuse myelitis, paralysis agitans, and progressive muscular atrophy, are found to produce no changes in the blood.

For Spinal Meningitis, see page 249.

GENERAL PARALYSIS OF THE INSANE.

Capps [1] has made a careful study of the blood in nineteen cases and comes to the following conclusions:

1. Red corpuscles and hæmoglobin are always slightly diminished, the averages being 4,789,900 and 85 per cent.

2. Most cases show a slight leucocytosis—22 per cent above the normal on the average. Early cases may have no leucocytosis.

3. The differential counts show that the blood is slightly *older* than that of normal adults. The polymorphonuclear leucocytes average nearly 74 per cent and the smaller forms of lymphocytes only 14.2 per cent, while the larger forms of lymphocytes are relatively numerous, averaging 7.8 per cent. In a few cases the eosinophiles were very numerous [2] (8.7 and 6.4 per cent).

4. At the time of *convulsions* the red cells and hæmoglobin are apparently increased (due no doubt to the violent muscular

---

[1] American Journal of the Medical Sciences, July, 1896.

[2] Roncoroni (Archiv. di Psichiat. Scien. 1894, p. 293) finds eosinophiles increased even to twenty-five per cent in the agitated and violent cases.

contractions which raise blood pressure and concentrate the blood, or to cyanosis).

There is a sudden and pronounced increase in the leucocytes during and after convulsions or apoplectiform attacks. That this is not due to concentration of the blood or to stasis Capps thinks is shown by the fact that not only the number but the differential count of white cells show changes, the *"large mono-nuclear" cells being relatively increased,* sometimes as high as 25 per cent. *Myelocytes* were seen in one case after the convulsions, and especially just before death when in a leucocytosis of 18,250 11 per cent were myelocytes.[1]

HYSTERIA AND NEURASTHENIA: HYPOCHONDRIASIS.

A large number of cases have been counted at the Massachusetts General Hospital, with a view to excluding other diseases. The blood count is always normal except that in a certain number of the hysterical cases eosinophiles are relatively increased, and that many of the neurasthenics show the increased percentage of lymphocytes which I have alluded to above (page 97) as characteristic of a variety of debilitated conditions.

Marked anæmia is seldom present, although the hæmoglobin is not infrequently as low as 65 per cent. Reinert[2] found the hæmoglobin under 60 per cent in only 4 out of 48 cases of hysteria, and in *none* of 36 neurasthenics.

The value of the blood examination in such cases, like that of the urine or the lungs in hysteria, is as negative evidence, and in this respect it is important. When the discrepancy between complaints and signs is great, we want to be doubly sure that nothing hidden escapes our notice, and the blood examination is one of the most valuable adjuvants we have in the discovery of deep-seated inflammation or malignant disease, as well as in giving us a general measure of the patient's degree of bodily health as distinguished from nervous force. The former may be high when the latter is low, or both may be low, and the dis-

---

[1] Leucocytosis has been repeatedly noticed in convulsions from various causes. Probably the irritant which causes the motor discharge also acts on the leucocytes by chemotaxis.

[2] Münch. med. Woch., 1805, No. 14.

tinction marks out two classes of cases in which somewhat different treatment is appropriate. There is no use in undertaking to make "blood and fat" when the patient has already plenty of each, though it may be well to carry out the same *régime* as a matter of suggestion.

MENTAL DISEASES.

The association of anæmia with insanity is too frequent to be a mere coincidence, though it is hard to make either serve as a cause for the other. Very possibly they should both be looked upon as symptoms of a common underlying (unknown) cause.

This form of anæmia has been noticed by Houston[1] in melancholia and general paralysis, and by Smith[2] in various forms of insanity. -

Krypiakiewicz[3] noticed an increase of eosinophiles in acute forms of insanity but not in the chronic forms. The *leucocytosis of acute delirium*[4] is exemplified by the following case from the Massachusetts Hospital records:

A girl of fifteen; acute delirium; leucocytes, 12,750; no food for eight hours; red cells, 4,510,000; hæmoglobin, 63 per cent.

Puerperal mania is to be distinguished from the delirium of puerperal sepsis by the fact that the latter shows leucocytosis with increased percentage of polymorphonuclear cells, while the former has no leucocytosis (if uncomplicated) and the eosinophiles are apt to be increased [5] (diminished in sepsis).

A case of puerperal mania seen by the writer showed: Red cells, 5,210,000; white cells, 6,500; hæmoglobin, 84 per cent; eosinophiles, 8 per cent.

CONSTITUTIONAL DISEASES.

OBESITY.

Oertel distinguishes a plethoric and an anæmic form of obesity not merely clinically but by the evidence of post-mortem

[1] Houston : Boston Med. and Surg. Journal, January 11th, 1894.

[2] Smith : Jour. of Ment. Sc , October, 1890.

[3] Krypiakiewicz: Wien. med. Woch., 1892, No. 25.

[4] Ref. in Klein-Volkmann's "Sammlung klin. Vorträge," December 1893.

[5] Neusser : *Loc. cit.*

examinations. He believes that there is a real over-filling of
the vessels in the first. The second form occurs most often in
women.

Kisch examined (with v. Fleischl's instrument) the hæmoglobin of 100 obese patients; 79 showed over 100 per cent of
hæmoglobin, 1 reaching 120 per cent, while the other 21 were
anæmic.

DIABETES.

There is nothing characteristic about the blood except the
increased amount of sugar to be detected (.57 per cent as against
.1 normally); but this is not a clinically applicable test.

Two simple tests for diabetic blood have recently attracted
attention:

1. Bremer's test: Heat thick-spread blood films to 135° C.;
cool and stain with one-per-cent aqueous solution of Congo red for
two minutes. The blood if diabetic looks *yellow* (to the naked
eye). Normal blood similarly treated looks *red*. Staining with
methyl blue also shows a difference between normal blood and
diabetic blood. The normal is blue, the diabetic yellowish
green.

2. Williamson's test: Make a mixture of

Blood, ... 20 c.mm. (2 drops).
Aqueous methyl blue (1 : 6,000),   .   .   . 1 c.c.
Liquor potassæ, 60 per cent (sp. gr., 1.058), . 40 c.c.
Water, ... 40 c.c.

Let the mixture stand three to four minutes in boiling water.
With diabetic blood the mixture turns yellow, with normal blood
it does not. Williamson has found this test positive in eleven
diabetics and negative in one hundred cases of other diseases.
Bremer claims that by his method cases of diabetes can be
recognized before sugar appears in the urine or after it has
(temporarily) disappeared. Le Goff confirms the value of the
test. Eichner and Folkel find Bremer's reaction to be as stated,
but find similar color changes in leukæmia, Hodgkin's disease,
and Graves' disease, and changes something like it in a variety
of cachectic conditions. Badger has studied the blood of diabetics, leukæmics, cases of Graves' disease, and other cases at
the Massachusetts Hospital. Only in Graves' disease did he
find reactions like those of diabetic blood.

The alkalinity has been said to be greatly diminished, especially in the fatal coma, but v. Noorden thinks the tests are unreliable.

Fat is often increased in the blood, up to about twelve times the normal, so that the serum is milky, and glycogen has been demonstrated microchemically in the corpuscles.

Red Cells.

Sugar in the blood draws water from the tissue into the vessels, thereby *diluting the blood;* but in a short time the blood frees itself of the excess of sugar and fluid through increased diuresis so as to *concentrate the blood.*

These two alternating influences serve to explain the widely different counts of different observers.

Toward the end of the disease a decided *cachexia* often develops, the anæmia of which may be temporarily covered up by the concentration above noted, or accentuated by the *dilution* which sometimes occurs. Accordingly we may find the corpuscles increased, normal, or diminished in different cases or at different times with the same case.

Grawitz counted 4,900,000 red cells in a patient in comparatively good health, and three weeks later, when the patient had just been seized with the fatal coma, the count showed 6,400,000 per cubic millimetre.

The white cells show no constant changes, except that. v. Limbeck has noted in several cases that the digestion-leucocytosis is unusually large even without previous fasting. Von Jaksch found leucocytosis in one of his eight cases, but on this point as on many others his results are almost unique. The only similar observation is that of Habershon,[1] who reports moderate leucocyosis, decreased by strict diet. In thirteen cases I have never seen leucocytosis. A single case of diabetic coma showed 4,200 leucocytes per cubic millimetre.

GOUT.

A few cubic centimetres of serum from gouty blood made acid with acetic acid (six drops of a twenty-eight-per-cent solution to every drachm of serum) deposit crystals of uric acid on a

[1] St. Bartholomew Hosp. Rep., 1890, p. 153.

thread in from eighteen to forty-eight hours; but this is not always to be found, and is by no means peculiar to gout.[1] Uric acid is to be found in the blood in pneumonia, cirrhotic liver, nephritis, grave anæmia, leukæmia, and gravel; also in health and after a meal of calf's thymus or any food containing much nuclein.

The red corpuscles show no special changes except in severe chronic cases which are sometimes anæmic. The white cells are increased according to Neusser, while v. Limbeck and Grawitz found the blood wholly normal.

It is particularly in this disease that Neusser supposed the "perinuclear basophilic granulations" to exist in the white cells, which he believes to be characteristic of any "uric-acid diathesis." Futcher has conclusively disproved this. Fibrin is increased in acute cases.

MYXŒDEMA.

Le Breton[2] examined the blood in one case before and after thyroid treatment and found after forty days' treatment that the red cells had risen from 1,750,000 to 2,450,000, the white from 4,500 to 9,600, and the hæmoglobin from 65 to 68 per cent.

The remarkably high color index in this case before treatment (nearly 2.!) corresponds with the observations of Le Breton in the dried specimen, which showed a decided increase in the size of the red corpuscles. He also noticed before instituting the thyroid treatment the presence of nucleated red cells and an excess of the polymorphonuclear form of leucocytes. Under treatment the nucleated red cells disappeared and the lymphocytes rose to their normal per cent.

Putnam[3] has watched a similar case in which the red cells rose from 3,120,000 to 5,700,000 under thyroid treatment.

Murray[4] has collected 23 cases with blood examinations. Of these 7 showed normal blood, 10 were anæmic, 4 had leucocytosis, and 2 had both anæmia and leucocytosis.

[1] It is important to evaporate the serum at a temperature not above 70° F., otherwise crystals will not form.

[2] Le Breton: Ref. in Wien. med. Blätter, 1895, p. 49.

[3] Putnam: Ref. in Murray's article in "Twentieth Century Practice of Medicine," vol. iv.

[4] Murray: "Twentieth Century Practice of Medicine," vol. iv., p. 710.

Kraepelin · noticed (like Le Breton) a marked increase in the average diameter of the corpuscles in three cases, even when the count and the hæmoglobin were normal.

I have had an opportunity to examine the blood in three cases of this disease, but did not find anything remarkable in any of them.

Case.	Red cells.	White cells.	Per cent Hæmoglobin.
1	4,670,000	6,000	87
2	4,460,000	8,800	..
3	4,856,000	5,200	80

Differential counts were made in three cases and no increase in the size of the corpuscles, such as Le Breton and Kraepelin saw, was present in these cases. The count showed:

Case.	Polymorphonuclear cells.	Lymphocytes.	Eosinophiles.
1	67	28	5
2	67	27.8	4.4
3	74	26	

The increase of eosinophiles in two of these cases may perhaps be due to the skin troubles present in the disease.

J. J. Thomas found a few myelocytes in a case of Putnam's.

CRETINISM.

Koplik[2] records the following in two cases of sporadic cretinism:

CASE I.—Fifteen months old; advanced stage of disease. Hæmoglobin, 18 per cent.

CASE II.—Red cells, 3,026,000; white cells, 13,500; hæmoglobin, 105 per cent. This high hæmoglobin corresponds to *normal fœtal* blood. The child was nine weeks old, but its backward development is mirrored in the blood. As the case improved under thyroids the hæmoglobin came down.

[1] Kraepelin : Deut. Arch. f. klin. Med., vol. xlix., p. 587.
[2] New York Medical Record, October 2d, 1897.

GRAVES' DISEASE (BASEDOW'S DISEASE; EXOPHTHALMIC
GOITRE).

The blood is normal, except for an occasional associated
chlorosis and sometimes a marked lymphocytosis. In one case
I found 51.3 per cent of lymphocytes and 1 per cent of myelocytes in 1,000 leucocytes, the polymorphonuclear cells being
only 48 per cent; but in fourteen other cases I have never found
this again. The same fact has been noticed by Neusser (cited
in Klein, *loc. cit.*).

Oppenheimer[1] found the red cells and hæmoglobin normal in
two cases. Von Jaksch[2] in one case "complicated with myxœdema" found 3,818,000 red and 8,000 white cells.

The association of Graves' disease with chlorosis is illustrated by two cases from Zappert:[3]

Case.	Red cells.	White cells.	Per cent hæmoglobin.
1	2,858,000	3,800	32
2	2,738,000	3,800	30

The same writer found eosinophiles much increased (8.5 per
cent) in one out of four cases.

ADDISON'S DISEASE.

Some, but not all, cases are accompanied by marked anæmia.
Neumann[4] observed a case in which the symptoms came on
acutely and the red cells sank to 1,120,000 per cubic millimetre.
During the convalescence which followed the cells ran up above
normal, reaching 7,700,000.

Tschirkoff[5] reports two cases in which the red cells were respectively 3,230,000 and 2,933,000 at the lowest, but whose
hæmoglobin was extraordinarily high, over 100 per cent in one
case. This he found on spectroscopic examination to be due to
a great increase of reduced hæmoglobin in the corpuscles.
Methæmoglobin was also noted.

The white corpuscles showed no changes, quantitative or

[1] Deut. med. Woch., 1889, p. 861.
[2] Zeit. f. klin. Med., 1893, p. 187.
[3] Zeit. f. klin. Med., 1893, p. 266.
[4] Neumann: Deut. med. Woch., 1894, p. 105.
[5] Zeit. f. klin. Med., 1891, vol. xix., Suppl. Heft 87.

qualitative, except that they contained black pigment granules. Three cases have been examined at the Massachusetts Hospital. The first, a woman of thirty, showed 6,240,000 red cells with 14,000 white, and 90 per cent of hæmoglobin. The differential count of 900 leucocytes showed the following figures: Polymorphonuclear cells, 53.4 per cent; lymphocytes, 41 per cent; eosinophiles, 4.5 per cent; myelocytes, .9 per cent.

The eosinophiles were very large, some of them eosinophilic myelocytes.

The second, a man of forty-two, was very anæmic and weak at entrance and showed: Red cells, 2,196,000; white cells, 7,500; hæmoglobin, 20 per cent. Differential count of 200 leucoctyes showed: Polymorphonuclear cells, 65 per cent; lymphocytes, 31.5 per cent; eosinophiles, 3.5 per cent; five normoblasts; marked poikylocytosis.

Under suprarenal extract his blood improved in a month till his red cells numbered 4,700,000; white cells, 9,000; hæmoglobin, 65 per cent.

The third a man of fifty-two, showed: October 20th—Red cells, 2,848,000; white cells, 4,800; hæmoglobin, 45 per cent. December 10th—Red cells, 2,624,000; white cells, 7,100; hæmoglobin, 45 per cent. Differential count: Polynuclear, 74 per cent; small lymphocytes, 22 per cent; large lymphocytes, 4 per cent; eosinophiles, .4 per cent. No nucleated red cells.

A fourth patient, kindly sent me by Dr. Rogers, of Dorchester, showed: Red cells, 2,864,000; white cells, 2,000; hæmoglobin, 51 per cent. Differential count of 300 cells showed: Polymorphonuclear cells, 63.3 per cent; lymphocytes, 33.3 per cent; eosinophiles, 2.3 per cent; basophiles, .3 per cent.

I have never seen melanin in the leucocytes as Tschirkoff did in his two cases.

OSTEOMALACIA.

The blood has for a long time been supposed, on the authority of v. Jaksch (*Zeit. f. klin. Med.*, Vol. 13, page 360), to exhibit a diminished alkalinity, the bones being supposed to be eaten away by acids in the blood. Von Limbeck and many other observers have lately shown that the blood is normal in alkalescence.

21

Corpuscles and hæmoglobin are usually within normal limits quantitatively, but Neusser reports an increase of eosinophiles and the presence of myelocytes in the blood.

Ritchie[1] confirms Neusser and found also the young leucocytes more numerous than normal.

Fehling,[2] Sternberg,[2] Chrobak[2] found no increase of eosinophiles.

Rieder's case was normal in all respects: Red cells, 4,892,000; white cells, 5,600; eosinophiles, 3.6 per cent; polymorphonuclear cells, 61 per cent.

RICKETS.

1. Anæmia is always present in severe cases and often in moderate ones. This, together with the fact that many cases of rickets are associated with an enlargement of the spleen, has led to the use of the misleading term "splenic anæmia." There is no form of anæmia found in rickets that may not be found in other conditions (Morse).

Hock and Schlesinger found an average of 2,500,000 red cells in a considerable number of cases with and without enlarged spleen.

Von Jaksch describes a case in which the red cells sank from 1,600,000 to 750,000 within three months, and Luzet saw a similarly rapid process, the cells falling from 2,110,000 to 1,596,000 within three weeks. On the other hand, in Morse's admirable study of twenty well-marked cases the red cells averaged over 4,500,000 and not a case fell below 3,500,000.

2. The hæmoglobin is always relatively low; it averaged 63 per cent in Morse's cases, a color index of about .7. Felsenthal got similar results.

White Corpuscles.

It is often difficult to say whether or not the leucocytes are increased, owing to the occurrence of most cases in infants at an age when leucocytes are always higher than in adults—how much higher at any given age depends largely upon the degree of vigor and forwardness of development of the individual child.

In Morse's series, for example, the average age of the infants

---

[1] Edin. Med. Journal, June, 1896.

[2] Cited by Ritchie (loc. cit.).

is twelve months. And for this age none of the counts in his series seem to me necessarily abnormal. They are all under 16,000 except three, these three being 17,900, 18,800, and 22,000 respectively, the latter in a nine months' infant. Many of the counts seem to me subnormal for infancy (5,500, 7,200). Most observers find leucocytosis present in many cases, but not in all.

QUALITATIVE CHANGES.

Red Cells.

As in all anæmias of infants, the "degenerative" and " regenerative" changes are relatively common.

Polychromatophilic forms and nucleated corpuscles are frequently to be found, the latter often in great numbers but with a majority of the normoblast type.

White Cells.

Lymphocytosis is said to be marked, but, as with the question of leucocytosis, we are never quite sure whether the numbers are abnormal *for that age*, for lymphocytosis is the normal condition in infants' blood.

When, however, as in a case mentioned by Rieder, we find 75 lymphocytes in every 100 leucocytes, the child being four years old, we are surely dealing with a pathological condition. Another of his cases, a seven-months' child, rachitic, with 57 per cent of lymphocytes, seems to fall within normal limits. Not so with Morse's cases. The highest percentage of lymphocytes in his series was 69, in an infant of two months. I have similar counts in health at that age. The average of his twenty cases is 43 per cent, which is, if anything, rather low for that age. The same difficulty arises with regard to the reports of *eosinophilia* in rickets, since eosinophiles are always relatively numerous in infancy. Morse's highest figure was 7 per cent, his average 3 per cent. They were highest in cases with splenic tumor. In Rieder's four cases and in the three seen at the Massachusetts Hospital, no eosinophilia was present. Myelocytes in small number (.5–2. per cent) are not uncommon, and may be considerably more numerous.

CHAPTER IX.

BLOOD DESTRUCTION AND HEMORRHAGIC DIS-EASES.

1. PURPURA HÆMORRHAGICA.

THE blood is practically that of anæmia from hemorrhage (red cells and hæmoglobin reduced, white cells increased, occasional nucleated red corpuscles or polychromatophilic forms). Agello[1] has found methæmoglobin in the blood, and hence concludes that the disease is a poisoning of the corpuscles by ptomains absorbed from the intestine.

The blood plates are much diminished and may be entirely absent in the worst stages.

Bacteria of various kinds have been reported in the disease, but negative results are also common, and their presence is probably not significant.

The red cells may fall as low as 2,500,000, but are much oftener slightly or not at all diminished. In many mild cases there are *no* demonstrable blood changes. On the other hand, Osler mentions a case which sank to 1,800,000, and the loss of blood may give rise to a fatal anæmia of the microcyte type (see page 158).

Bensaude[2] has observed that in 16 cases characterized by *large hemorrhages* (2 = acute "infectious," 2 with tuberculosis, 2 chronic, 10 = Werlhof's disease) the clot shows no retraction and no transudation of the serum. Cases with *small hemorrhages* (toxic, rheumatic, cachectic, and nervous) do not show any such abnormal characteristics. Hence he concludes that at the outset of a case of purpura, observation of the clotting process may enable us to foretell whether or not the case is to be of a *severe* or of a *mild* type. He found the blood lesion above described to

[1] Riforma Med., Napoli, 1894, p. 103.
[2] La Semaine Med., 1897, p. 21.

be greatest during the hemorrhagic crises, slowly disappearing between them. Hayem has confirmed these observations. He finds the fibrin network almost invisible. Despite this and despite the absence of contraction in the clot, the actual rate of clotting is normal.

SCURVY.

There are no characteristic blood changes known. When hemorrhage is severe the red cells may sink very low, to 557,875 in a case of Bouchut's; Ouskow and Hayem saw counts of 3,500,000 and 4,700,000. The usual qualitative changes of secondary anæmia are present in severe cases; hæmoglobin suffers as usual more than the count of red cells.

Leucocytes are generally increased, whether from hemorrhage or from some complicating inflammatory process.

Barlow's disease may lower the red cells as far as 976,000—as in a case of Reinert's—the hæmoglobin being seventeen per cent and the white cells 12,000. This was the day before death. In any form of scurvy the blood plates may be much diminished.

HÆMOPHILIA.

The blood changes are practically those just described and show nothing characteristic of the disease. Coagulation is slower than normal and blood plates are sometimes very scanty. The white cells are sometimes persistently diminished as in the following cases:

I.

	Sept. 11th.	Sept. 14th.	Sept. 17th.	Sept. 20th.	Sept. 23d.	Sept. 24th.
Red cells	2,960,000	....	....	....	....	3,800,000
White cells	3,400	3,400	3,800	3,900	3,700	3,300
Hæmoglobin	42 per cent.	....	....	....	64 per cent.	49 per cent.

II.

February 8th.	February 28th.	
4,400,000	3,600,000	
5,000	5,000	} Daily nosebleed.
30 per cent.	28 per cent.	

BLOOD DESTRUCTION (HÆMOCYTOLYSIS).

I. Besides the slow destruction of corpuscles which takes place in any ordinary anæmia, we have a group of conditions under which a large number of red cells are suddenly destroyed in the circulation itself. This may take place by—

1. Separation of the hæmoglobin from the corpuscles so that it colors the serum.

2. Actual breaking to pieces of the red cells without separation of the hæmoglobin.

If normal blood is drawn and left to stand, the serum which separates from the corpuscles is not red-tinged or but very slightly so, *provided* all shaking and jarring are avoided. A very slight reddish tinge may appear in the serum even with most careful technique. In some conditions the hæmoglobin, while not actually separated from the corpuscles within the vessels, is so loosely connected to them that a considerable quantity separates post mortem and colors the serum in spite of the avoidance of any jar.

This condition is to be distinguished from true hæmoglobinæmia, in which the serum is actually colored before leaving the vessels, although the two conditions really represent only different degrees of vulnerability of the red cells.

We are surer of a diagnosis of hæmoglobinæmia when we find bits of broken-down cells in the fresh blood and the additional evidence of hæmoglobinuria or jaundice.

1. Severe forms of malaria, yellow fever, typhus fever, severe forms of septicæmia, and rarely scarlet fever may cause hæmoglobinæmia.

2. *Paroxysmal hæmoglobinæmia*, so-called, is a variety whose cause is unknown and which does not seem secondary to any other disease, unless a certain relationship to syphilis be established, and to malaria. The attacks are brought on by a great variety of causes (cold, muscular or mental strain, etc.). Some persons can always bring on an attack by putting the hand or foot into cold water.

Blood Examination.

Coagulation is very rapid, but the clot soon dissolves again (Hayem). The fresh blood occasionally shows deformities in the corpuscles or bits of broken cells, and lack of rouleaux if examined during a paroxysm. As a rule the corpuscles of the peripheral blood look normal. Frazer has recently reported a case in which he excited a paroxysm by a cold bath and studied the blood with great care.

Time.	Red cells.	White cells.	Per cent hæmoglobin.	Blood plates.
10 A.M. Before bath....	4,075,000	15,000	50	450,000
11.05 A.M. Twenty-five minutes after bath; urine pale.	3,633,300	21,800	50	696,000
11.45 (urine dark)	3,760,000	21,300	60	525,000
1.15 P.M................	4,200 000	21,500	50	4,250,000(!)
3.45 P.M	3,800,000	17,700	50	1,600,000
Next day, 1 P.M.........	4,100,000	18,700	50	500,000

The enormous increase of "blood plates" is striking. It is difficult to resist the conclusion that these blood plates were bits of broken red corpuscles. The serum was currant-jelly colored. The appearance of the corpuscles was quite normal.

All that is known of the disease is expressed by saying that for *some reason* the red cells are abnormally *sensitive*, so that any one of a variety of slight disturbances is sufficient to separate their hæmoglobin and set it loose in the plasma.

3. Extensive *burns* have been reported to cause hæmoglobinæmia with breaking up of the red cells, presumably through changes in the serum similar to those which make duodenal ulcer so common a sequel to bad burns.

4. Snake poison and scorpion poison may have similar effects.

II. Another group of corpuscle destroyers is that which works by changing the *hæmoglobin* to *methæmoglobin*. The most important of these is—

1. *Chlorate of Potash.*—This destroys the corpuscles and produces hæmoglobinæmia and the usual train of symptoms (jaundice, dark urine, etc.) due to this.

Brandenburg[1] examined the blood of a woman who had taken two and one-half ounces of chlorate of potash in water the night before. The blood showed *marked* leucocytosis, broken and

[1] Berliner klin. Woch., 1895, No. 27.

distorted red cells. In gross it was chocolate-colored and the serum after separation of the clot was brown. The red cells progressively decreased as follows:

	Red cells.	White cells.
First day	4,300,000	20,000
Second day	2,500,000	
Fourth day	2,300,000	
Fifth day	2,100,000	
Sixth day	1,900,000	
Seventh day	1,600,000	15,000 (death).

2. Ehrlich and Lindenthal[1] report the case of a patient who was poisoned with nitrobenzol. Ten hours after the blood was chocolate-colored and showed methæmoglobin bands. Under the microscope there were no changes till the third day, when poikylocytosis appeared.

	Red cells.	White cells.		Per cent hæmoglobin.	Nucleated red cells per cubic millimetre.
Fifth day	2,275,000	Much increased.		55	2,070
Seventh day	1,845,000	"	"	50	7,900
Eleventh day	1,600,000	"	"	44	24,700 (!)
Fifteenth day	905,000	"	"	40	12,000
Seventeenth day	1,102,000	"	"	..	1,300
Nineteenth day	900,200	"	"	..	540
" " death.					

The nucleated red cells were at first mostly normoblasts; later mostly megaloblasts.

3. *Antipyrin and antifebrin* in doses of thirty to forty-five grains may cause great cyanosis and dangerous prostration through transformation of the hæmoglobin and methæmoglobin. In certain persons much smaller doses produce the same effect.

4. *Phenacetin poisoning* (Kronig: *Berl. klin. Woch.*, 1895) may cause actual blood destruction with anæmia in case the patient survives the immediate effects of the deprivation of oxygen. A fatal case of *chloral* poisoning at the Massachusetts Hospital showed 14,400 leucocytes with 54 per cent of hæmoglobin.

5. *Phosphorus poisoning* (see Liver, page 290).

6. Workers in aniline dyes and nitroglycerine factories may

[1] Zeit. f. klin. Med., 1896, p. 427.

be severely poisoned by *nitrobenzol* compounds inhaled and producing methæmoglobinæmia.

7. *Pyrogallic acid and pyrogallol* as used in treatment of skin diseases may lead to death through destruction of the red cells. Chromic acid (for instance, as applied through the vagina) may have a similar effect.

Many other less common substances work the same ill-effects on the blood.

III. A third group of substances, of which *carbonic oxide gas* is the type, poison by combining chemically with the hæmoglobin and preventing its combination with the oxygen of the air.

1. *Illuminating gas* is for our purposes the most important of this group.

The appearance of individual blood cells is not altered nor do they break up, but the corpuscles are useless to breathe with, as they cannot take up oxygen.

The color of the blood is very *bright* red, much brighter than normal.

Red Cells.

Von Limbeck[1] found in two cases 6,630,000 and 5,700,000 respectively. The *volume* of these corpuscles (estimated by Bleibtreu's method) was greatly increased, amounting to 70.7 per cent (normal 41–48 per cent), so that apparently the size of the individual cells is increased.

Münzer and Palma[2] found 5,700,000 red cells in one case.

Leucocytes.

Eaton[3] reported four cases, in all of which the white cells were increased, the counts ranging between 15,000 and 22,000 per cubic millimetre.

Münzer and Palma (*loc. cit.*) found 13,300 in their case. Twelve such cases have been examined at the Massachusetts Hospital with the following results:

[1] *Loc. cit.*, p. 234.
[2] Zeit. f. Heilk., vol. xv., p. 1.
[3] Boston Medical and Surgical Journal, March 14th, 1895.

ILLUMINATING GAS POISONING.

Age.	Sex.	Red cells.	White cells.	Per cent hæmo-globin.	Remarks.
41	M.	....	31.200	..	Coma ; recovery.
49	M.	....	27,100	..	September 12th ; coma.
			19,900	..	September 13th, entirely well.
21	M.	....	26,000	70	Coma ; recovery.
19	M.	....	25,470	97	
40	M.	....	22,900	75	
			21,200	..	November 27th ; coma.
			15,500	..	November 29 ; convalescent.
60	M.	....	20,400	75	Coma ; recovery.
25	M.	....	20,360	110	Death.
45	M.	....	20,100	..	Coma ; death.
16	F.	....	18,500	84	Coma ; recovery.
19	M.	....	17,000	..	December 22d.
			17,500	..	December 23d.
		4,930,000	17,000		

Warthen[1] reports the same condition in a single case. Here the specific gravity was also very high (v. Limbeck finds that this is to be explained by the increase in the actual size of the corpuscles).

When there is any doubt as to diagnosis, the following test will settle it: Shake a small quantity of fresh-drawn blood into three times its volume of subacetate of lead. If the blood contains CO the mixture becomes of a fine red color; otherwise it turns chocolate-colored.[2]

2. Da Costa (*Med. News*, March 2, 1895) reported a considerable diminution in hæmoglobin of patients during *etherization*, especially anæmic patients, but the investigations of Lerber[3] do not confirm this.

Tansy Poisoning.—A single case examined at the Massachusetts General Hospital showed: Red cells, 4,600,000; white cells, 21,000; hæmoglobin, 70 per cent.

Corrosive Poisoning (Ammonia Fumes).—A patient whose throat was covered with a fibrinous pseudo-membrane in consequence of inhaling ammonia fumes showed a leucocytosis of 25,800. Red cells and hæmoglobin normal.

Opium Poisoning (Chronic).—The majority of cases of the

[1] Virchow's Archiv, vol. cxxxvi.
[2] Rubner : Zeit. f. anal. Chemie, xxx., p. 112.
[3] Inaug. Dissert., Basel, 1896 (see p. 10J).

morphine habit show normal blood, but in October, 1897, a man of twenty-six entered the Massachusetts Hospital for the morphine habit who showed at entrance 36,000 leucocytes per cubic millimetre. Five days later the count was 21,200. A differential count of 500 leucocytes made on this day showed: Polymorphonuclear neutrophiles, 71 per cent; small lymphocytes, 12; large lymphocytes, 10; eosinophiles, 6; myelocytes, 1. At the time of leaving the hospital he still showed a leucocytosis of 16,400. He had no fever and physical examination was entirely negative.

Ptomain Poisoning (Rotten Fish).—A mother and her four children were brought to the Massachusetts Hospital suffering from the effects of decayed fish eaten that day. The blood showed the following: (1), mother: leucoctyes, 21,600, of which 95.3 per cent were polymorphonuclear; (2), boy of seven years: leucocytes, 19,900; (3), boy of three years: leucocytes, 56,800, of which 92 per cent were polymorphonuclear; (4), girl of five years: leucocytes, 32,600; (5), girl of thirteen months: leucocytes, 55,400. The red cells and hæmoglobin were normal. All the patients made prompt recoveries.

ACUTE ALCOHOLISM.

It has been shown experimentally that in animals made drunk with alcohol, there is an invasion of the blood and tissues by micro-organisms from the intestine. It may be that some of the counts here recorded are thus to be explained.

ACUTE ALCOHOLISM.

Age.	Sex.	Red cells.	White cells.	Per cent hæmo-globin.	Remarks.
36	F.	....	15,900	..	Two weeks drinking hard. Temperature 102° ; died ; D.T.
38	M.	....	14,200	74	Temperature 101°.
42	M.	....	12,000	62	Temperature 101° ; D. T.
32	M.	3,946,000	10,200	30(?)	
44	M.	....	9,600	80	
29	F.	4,288,000	8,000	55	D. T.
37	M.	....	7,800	62	
60	F.	.. ....	7,450	65	
32	M.	....	5,700	68	Autopsy.
28	M.	....	5,600	..	D. T.

PART VI.

MALIGNANT DISEASE, BLOOD PARASITES, AND INTESTINAL PARASITES.

CHAPTER X.

MALIGNANT DISEASE.

THE BLOOD AS A WHOLE.

1. The specific gravity is reduced in most cases, running roughly parallel with the hæmoglobin.

2. Coagulation is normal or slower than normal in uncomplicated cases. When sloughing and inflammation are present it may be rapid.

3. Fibrin is usually normal; an increase means inflammation in or around the tumor or an inflammatory complication.

CANCER.

Red Corpuscles.

As in tuberculosis, we are frequently surprised to find but little diminution in the number of red cells. In all but very advanced cases this is the rule. It is a change of the individual red cells (pallor, loss of size, of weight, degenerative changes), rather than a reduction of numbers.

Nevertheless in the later cachectic stages of most cases of malignant disease, we do find a quantitative anæmia, the counts often running as low as 2,500,000 and occasionally sinking as low as in pernicious anæmia. Thus v. Limbeck records a case (complicated by repeated hemorrhages) with only 950,000 red cells per cubic millimetre. The lowest of my own cases was 1,457,000 per cubic millimetre.

There seems to be no considerable difference between cancer and sarcoma as regards their effect on the red cells. The following table summarizes our cases:

TABLE XXXIX., A.—GASTRIC CANCER.

Red Cells.

Between 1,000,000 and 2,000,000 .... 4 cases.
"   2,000,000 " 3,000,000.... ... 11 "
"   3,000,000 " 4,000,000.. ..... 23 "
"   4,000,000 " 5,000,000... .... 15 "
"   5,000,000 " 6,000,000 .... 16 "
Over 6,000,000 .... 3 "
                                   ──
Average, 4,090,000 +   72

Nucleated red cells present in eleven cases out of fourteen examined. Normoblasts always in majority. A few megaloblasts in three cases.

TABLE XXXIX., B.—GASTRIC CANCER.

Leucocytes per Cubic Millimetre.

Between 3,000 and 4,000 .... 1 case.
"   4,000 "   5,000 . . .. 4 cases.
"   5,000 "   6,000 .... 17 "
"   6,000 "   7,000 .... 9 "
"   ·7,000 "   8,000 .... 8 "
"   8,000 "   9,000 .... 8 "
"   9,000 " 10,000 .... 9 "
"   10,000 " 12,000 .... 6 "
"   12,000 " 15,000 .... 4 "
"   15,000 " 20,000 .... 12 "
"   20,000 " 30,000 .. .. 5 "
"   30,000 " 40,000 .... 3 "
                                      ──
                    Total. 167 counts in 86 cases.
Average, 10,600 +

As will be seen by consulting Table XXXIX., A, the count of red cells is sometimes above normal, doubtless due to concentration of the blood from some cause. Probably the same influence is at work in other cases, and many of those showing normal counts have really fewer red cells than they should. Such abnormally high counts are not rare, as the following examples show:

Author.	Case.	Affection.	Red cells.	Per cent hæmoglobin.
Osterspey [1]...	1	Cancer of the stomach.........	5,040,000	80
Osterspey....	2	Cancer of the liver and stomach	6,184,000	87
Osterspey....	3	Cancer of the gullet	8,280,000	48
Neubert [2]....	1	Cancer of the stomach.........	5,085,000	73
Neubert.....	2	Cancer of the liver	4,918,000	70
Reinert [3].....		Cancer of the stomach	6,200,000	77

I wish to lay some stress upon this point, because it has been stated by some recent writers (e.g., Grawitz: "Pathologie des Blutes," Berlin, 1896) that the red cells are almost always diminished in malignant disease.

The high counts in cancer of the gullet are obviously to be explained by the lack of liquid taken, the blood being greatly concentrated as in any other form of starvation.

That this increase is not invariably present (see Table XL., page 345) is doubtless because some œsophageal tumors permit the ingestion of liquid in normal amounts and of a certain amount of solids.

The highest counts in the Massachusetts Hospital series are in simple gastric cancer without any stenosis at either end of the organs (see Cases I., III., XVI., and XXI.), and the lowest count (1,632,000) was in a similar case just before death. Taking all the cases of cancer in this series together, *the average of the seventy-five cases at the time when treatment began was 4,140,-000 red cells per cubic millimetre.*

Hæmoglobin.

Bierfreund,[4] who has examined seventy-two cases with regard to their percentage of coloring matter, found that in relatively slow and long-standing cases it averaged 68.5 per cent, and in the worst cases 57.5 per cent. In cases of mammary cancer after operation the hæmoglobin is of course lower owing to hemorrhage, and Bierfreund noticed that as a rule the hæmoglobin began to rise toward normal much later than after opera-

[1] Dissert., Berlin, 1892.
[2] Inaug. Dissert., Dorpat, 1889.
[3] "Zählung d. Blutkörp.," Leipzig, 1891.
[4] Langenbeck's Archiv, vol. xli.

tions for non-malignant conditions—a week later on the average —and that it never reached the point at which it was before the operation.[1] The following table from Bierfreund is of interest as illustrating these points. Cases were examined before and after operation, and the examinations were continued daily after the operation until the hæmoglobin began to rise again. This occurred very late as compared with other operations.

Diagnosis.	Per cent hæmoglobin before operation.	Per cent hæmoglobin after operation.	Per cent loss.	Regeneration time.
Malignant tumor without complication.	68.5	53	15.5	23 days.
Very large or rapidly growing tumors.	56.6	38.4	18.2	27.8 days.
Tumors with "softening" or disturbances of function.	57.5	39.7	17.8	27 days.
Total, 72 cases.	Av., 60	Av., 42.8	17.2	Av., 25.9 days.

By "regeneration time" is meant the number of days elapsed after operation before the hæmoglobin begins to rise. After operations for other causes (non-malignant) the average regeneration time is fourteen to twenty days.

It is very important that these results of Bierfreund's should be tested. In Mikulicz's surgical clinic at Breslau all patients have their hæmoglobin tested regularly. In this country the surgical portion of the profession have not as yet taken hold of blood examination, and many questions about the blood in surgical affections remain unanswered.

Reinbach[2] examined 16 cases and found the hæmoglobin range between 18 to 70 per cent, with an average of 50 per cent.

Rieder's[3] cases average 53 per cent (sarcoma much lower— see below).

[1] This is all the more extraordinary because Bierfreund specially noted that even in patients who gained weight notably after the operation the hæmoglobin did not rise so high as it had been before operation; he watched them for months after it. Apparently the actual presence of the tumors is not the only cause of the lack of corpuscle substance.

[2] Langenbeck's Archiv, 1893, p. 486.

[3] "Beiträge z. Kenntniss d. Leucocytosis," Leipzig, 1892 (Vogel).

Laker [1] noticed the low hæmoglobin percentage in malignant tumors and thought it a help in excluding benign tumors or tuberculosis, in which the hæmoglobin is much less diminished.

In the 87 cases of malignant tumors in which I have notes of the hæmoglobin (see tables) the average is 58 per cent. Comparing this with the average count of red cells (4,140,000), we get a color index of .65, distinctly higher than the average of chlorotic cases, of which, however, the figures distinctly remind us. The highest cases of this series had 100 per cent and 90 per cent of hæmoglobin respectively, and the lowest 20 per cent and 22 per cent; in these last two cases the color indexes were .36 and .58 respectively, not excessively low. As pointed out by Taylor (loc. cit.) cases of malignant disease can be divided into three groups with reference to their blood:

1. Those with approximately normal blood.

2. Those with a low hæmoglobin but a nearly normal number of cells.

3. Those with great diminution both in cells and coloring matter.

Among our own cases at the Massachusetts Hospital about one-half fall under the second group, one-quarter under the first, and one-quarter under the third.

As the disease progresses, the red cells and hæmoglobin steadily go down (except in cancer of the gullet), and at the time of death 1,000,000 cells per cubic millimetre is not rare.

The color index usually remains below 1. Compared to most other varieties of secondary anæmia (e.g., those in tuberculosis or nephritis) a quantitative anæmia—that is, a loss of red cells as well as of hæmoglobin—is relatively more frequent. In general the degree of anæmia is parallel to the amount of cachexia, except when hemorrhage increases it (as in tumors of the stomach or uterus).

How far the anæmia may be due to actual destruction of cells by toxic (?) products of the tumors is doubtful. Grawitz found that the injection of extracts of cancerous tissues caused in rabbits a temporary dilution of the blood, so that the cells per cubic millimetre were diminished, and it may be that this plays some part in the causation of the low blood counts.

[1] Wien. med. Woch., 1886, Nos. 18 and 19.

Qualitative Changes.

(a) *The average diameter of the red cells* is often diminished either (as in chlorosis) by a diminution of the size of nearly every corpuscle, or by a less general shrinkage, many cells being of normal size. The very large forms seen in pernicious anæmia are rare in the anæmia of malignant disease, and never, I think, reach the size of the giant forms seen in the former condition. Very small cells, on the other hand, are as common in advanced cases as in any other form of anæmia, except chlorosis. Deformities and degenerative changes are very common in well-marked cases, often as great as in pernicious anæmia, though they may be slight or absent.

According to Strauer, the *deformities* found in malignant disease are greater than those found in any form of tuberculosis, and this fact he thinks of value in diagnosis. This observation has been confirmed by Taylor.

Degenerative changes are sometimes well marked, but seldom, if ever, reach so extreme a condition as occurs in many cases of pernicious anæmia.

(b) *Nucleated red corpuscles* are the rule in all advanced cases, and in some others. Taylor found them in one-half of the twenty-two cases examined by him. Malignant disease differs in this respect from tuberculosis and most other conditions involving secondary anæmia, in that the nucleated red cells are much more common in cancer and may appear even when there is no considerable loss of red cells (numerically) or even when the hæmoglobin is also normal (Schreiber). I have found them in four-fifths of all severe cases examined.

As a rule the nucleated corpuscles are of the normoblast types (including small forms with dividing nuclei), but in very cachectic cases we may find megaloblasts as well—always, so far as I know, fewer in number than in the normoblasts. This constitutes one of the points of distinction between pernicious anæmia and the severest types of secondary anæmia, such as occur in malignant disease. The megaloblasts, when present, are in the minority as compared with the normoblasts. For example:

22

Case I. { Five normoblasts. / Seen while counting 400 leucocytes.
          { Three megaloblasts. }

Case II. { Two normoblasts. } Seen while counting 500 cells.
         { No megaloblasts. }

Case III. { Five normoblasts. } Seen while counting 200 cells.
          { No megaloblasts. }

Cases could easily be multiplied.

The characteristics of the blood changes in malignant disease, then, so far as concerns the red cells, are those of secondary anæmia, which at times attains the severest type—but only when cachexia is marked, or when hemorrhage complicates the disease.

The specific gravity follows in a general way the hæmoglobin percentage.

On the *white corpuscles* in malignant disease a great deal of interest has centred, and very conflicting reports have been published. As the effects of cancer and sarcoma seem to be somewhat different we will consider them separately.

1. THE LEUCOCYTES IN CANCER.

(a) *Quantitative Changes.*

We should expect great differences in the blood of different cases if we consider what a wide range is included between the small, hard, slow-growing, curable cancer of the lip which may produce little or no impairment of the general health, and the "fulminating," rapidly growing cases with numerous metastases and profound prostration.

The former class of cases may show a blood normal in all respects, including a normal leucocyte count; while in the latter the blood may be so profoundly altered as to be confused with that of pernicious anæmia on the one hand, or with that of leukæmia on the other.

In a general way it may be said that the more "malignant" the cases the greater the changes in the blood.

The effect upon the leucocytes depends upon the following conditions:

1. The position of the tumor.

2. Its size, rapidity of growth, and the number, size, and position of its metastases.

3. The resisting power of the individual.

1. Position.—(*a*) Tumors of the gullet involving stricture but not extending to other tissues are often accompanied by a *diminution* of the leucocyte count, owing to the starvation which they produce. This is not true of all cases, as is shown in the accompanying tables, but when the leucocytes are *increased* there is usually an involvement of other organs as well.

(*b*) Cancers of the uterus and some of those of the stomach, by reason of the hemorrhage which they produce, are apt to be associated with a very high leucocyte count.

(*c*) Tumors of the thyroid and of the pancreas are said by some writers to cause a specially great leucocytosis. In my own experience, tumors of the kidney have shown very marked increase of white cells.

2. Size.—Other things being equal, the larger and more rapidly growing tumors show in most cases a greater leucocytosis than small, slow-growing ones.

Thus the cancers of the lip and of the pylorus, scirrhus of the breast or of the penis, show smaller counts than tumors of the liver, omentum, and kidney, which are apt to grow more rapidly. Metastases in the bone marrow are thought by some observers to give peculiar qualitative blood changes (see below).

In general, metastases, being a method of rapid growth, simply add to the leucocyte count.

These distinctions eliminate some of the apparent contradictions between the findings of different individuals who were simply describing cancers of different types. But even within a single type, there are very marked differences in different cases. For instance, Alexander[1] found the leucocyte count in cases of scirrhus of the breast to vary between 2,360 and 21,700. Similar differences have been reported in cancers of the stomach (*e.g.*, Schneider[2] finding leucocytosis in all of twelve cases, while Osterspey[3] in another series of twelve cases found leucocytosis in only two).

3. Resisting Power.—Possibly a part of these differences is to be explained by differences in the resisting power of the individual. But if this is so, we cannot measure the endurance of a given patient by his general health. As in the Civil War the

[1] Alexander : Thèse de Paris, 1887.
[2] Inaug. Dissert., Berlin, 1888.
[3] Inaug. Dissert., Berlin, 1892.

pale, city-bred men outlasted the healthy farmers, so here the tumor's rapidity of growth seems often to be greatest in the most vigorous young individuals, while dried-up old women will resist its advance for a longer period.

We come now to the conditions to be found in particular types of cancerous growth.

Surprisingly little work has been done on the blood in malignant disease, such cases usually being under the charge of surgeons who rarely value such investigations. Except for scattered counts here and there, all our knowledge of the corpuscles rests on the work of Hayem and Alexander in France, and Rieder, v. Limbeck, Pée, Sadler, Reinbach, Osterspey, Grawitz, Strauer, Schneyer, and Schneider in Germany.

CANCER OF THE BREAST.

Most of our data come from Hayem[1] and his pupil Alexander.[2]

1. *Scirrhus Growths.*—Number of cases, 14. Average leucocyte count, 11,400.   Highest count, 21,700; lowest, 2,360—the last is somewhat doubtful as to diagnosis; except for this case, which was in a very old, dried-up woman, the lowest count was 7,400.

In 10 out of the 14 cases, the count was over 10,000. In the 3 cases seen by the writer 2 showed no leucocytosis, 1 a considerable leucocytosis.

2. *Medullary (Encephaloid) Growths.*—Three cases, all over 10,000—average 11,300.

Effects of Operation.

The following figures from Hayem are also of interest:
CASE I.—Scirrhus of the Breast.

Before operation 21,700
Five weeks after operation (wound not
    quite healed) 10,000
Wound completely healed................ 6,200
Seven months after operation .... 8,990 (beginning to rise again)
    The growth recurred some months later and leucocytosis was again present.

[1] Hayem : "Du Sang," Paris, 1889, p. 947.
[2] G. Alexander : "De la Leucocytosis dans les Cancers," Paris Thesis, 1887.

CASE II.—Scirrhus of the Breast.

	First count.	Second count.
Before operation	11,500	11,450
After operation	8,500	6,200

CASE III.—Scirrhus of the Breast.

	First count.	Second count.
Before operation	11,000	12,400
After operation	8,400	

CASE IV.—Scirrhus of the Breast.

Before operation	7,400
After operation	1,800

CASE V.—Medullary Cancer of the Breast.

Before operation	10,000
After operation	9,000

Hayem considers that by watching the leucocyte count we can predict the coming of a recurrence before any physical signs are present. This he did in Case I. of the series just given.

I have seen no confirmation or refutation of this statement. It is one of the many points to which the attention of surgeons should be directed.

CANCER OF THE STOMACH.

Here we have a much larger body of data to judge from. Thus:

Hayem[1] in 12 cases found leucocytosis present in 5, absent in 7.

Schneider[2] in 12 cases found leucocytosis in 12 (all).

Schneyer[3] in 18 cases found leucocytosis in 4, and these 4 all under 11,000.

Osterspey[4] in 12 cases found leucocytosis in 5.

Rieder[4] in 6 cases found leucocytosis in 3.

Sadler[5] in 13 cases found leucocytosis in 2, and in both there were complications (abscess of liver, perforation of gullet with gangrene) to which the leucocytosis might be due.

[1] "Du Sang," Paris, 1889, p. 948.
[2] Inaug. Dissert., Berlin, 1888.
[3] Inaug. Dissert., Berlin, 1892.
[4] Loc. cit.
[5] Original-Mittheilungen aus der Klinik v. Jaksch, 1891.

Reinbach[1] in 4 cases found leucocytosis in 2.

Reinert[2] in 2 cases found leucocytosis in 2.

Laache[3] in 5 cases found leucocytosis in none.[4]

Despite these facts we have the record of a certain number of single cases in which the leucocytosis has been enormous. For instance, Welch in "Pepper's System of Medicine" mentioned a case in which the ratio of white to red cells was 1:25 (normally 1:750 ±). Eisenlohr's[5] case showed 1 white to 50 red, and Potain's[6] case showed 1 white to 48 red cells.

The Massachusetts Hospital series of 86 cases showed leucocytosis in 30 cases and none in 56 (see Table XXXIX., B). Out of those showing leucocytosis 10 were under 12,500, that is the leucocytes were but slightly increased, leaving only 20 out of 86 (or twenty-three per cent) in which the leucocytosis was very marked. Among these 20, the highest counts were 40,000 and 39,000, and the highest ratio 1:62.

In this series I have excluded all cases in which there was evidence of metastasis in other organs; this means excluding 7 cases, 6 of which showed leucocytosis, and helps to account for the low average leucocyte count in the other 86 cases.

In over three-fourths of these cases the diagnosis was made certain either by operation or by autopsy; all the others showed either a palpable tumor in old cachectic patients with pain and vomiting, or other equally clear evidence for the diagnosis. Doubtful cases have been excluded. As will be seen by the table, in some of the cases the counts were verified by repeated examinations, while in others only a single count—that made when the patient entered the hospital—was recorded.

As a rule, the high leucocyte counts were in the more cachectic cases; but this does not always hold. Cases 10, 11, and 28 in Table XXXIX., A, were very cachectic but showed no leucocytosis.

The position of the tumor in one or another part of the

[1] Langenbeck's Archiv, 1893, p. 486.
[2] *Loc. cit.*
[3] "Die Anämie," Christiania, 1883.
[4] Apparently, since he draws attention to the fact that there is leucocytosis in a case of cancer of the uterus.
[5] Deut. Arch. f. klin. Med., 1877, vol. xx.
[6] Gaz. des Hôp., 1888, No. 57.

stomach seemed to have no connection with the number of leucocytes.

On the whole, leucocytosis is relatively infrequent in cancer of the stomach, occurring in only about one-third of the early cases. As the disease progresses we may get a leucocytosis, particularly in case its growth is *rapid* and metastases are frequent and numerous; but some cases, particularly those in which the tumor is small and grows slowly, may run their entire course without any leucocytosis being present. In this respect they are like the majority of small, slow-growing cancers in other parts of the body (see below).

Hemorrhage or perforation is of course accompanied by an increase in the number of white cells—in fact the highest count in the present series (105,600) occurred in a case in which a cancer of the stomach with metastases in the liver perforated into the peritoneal cavity and started a virulent, quickly fatal peritonitis.

DIGESTION LEUCOCYTOSIS IN CANCER OF THE STOMACH.

A considerable body of statistics has accumulated to show that in the great majority of cases of gastric cancer the leucocytosis of digestion (see above, page 98) does not occur. R. Müller[1] noticed this fact in 5 cases of cancer of the stomach. Schneyer[2] in 18 cases found it invariably absent, while in 3 cases of benign stenosis of the pylorus a considerable digestion leucocytosis appeared, as was also the case in 7 out of 8 cases of ulcer of the stomach, the exception being a fatal case.

He found both incipient and advanced cases to be similarly affected. In 5 of his cases and in some of Müller's HCl was present in the gastric contents, so that the absence of digestion leucocytosis was not due to absence of HCl.

Hartung (*Wiener klin. Woch.*, p. 697, 1895) in a series of 10 cases (mostly advanced) found no digestion leucocytosis, whereas a marked increase occurred in cases of malignant disease of other organs.

Capps[3] in 17 cases examined at the Massachusetts General

[1] Prag. med. Woch., 1890, No. 17.
[2] Zeit. f. klin. Med., 1895, p. 475.
[3] Boston Med. and Surg. Journal, November 4th, 1897.

Hospital found a digestion leucocytosis in 2, the increase being respectively 3,270 and 3,850 cells over the count before the beginning of digestion. In the other 15 cases there was no increase after a large proteid meal. Since Dr. Capps' article 20 more cases have been investigated at the hospital, in 19 of which the digestion leucocytosis was absent. Thus in a *total of 37 cases only 3, or eight per cent, showed any digestion leucocytosis.* In 5 out of 10 cases of chronic gastric catarrh the digestion leucocytosis was present; it was also present in a case of benign stricture of the pylorus in a man of forty-nine on whom an operation was successfully performed later.

Three cases of ulcer of the stomach showed marked increase as did several cases of hyperacidity and other gastric disorders (see Diseases of the Stomach, page 280).

CANCER OF THE STOMACH WITH METASTASES.

Most writers have not separated the cases with metastasis from those without it. A glance at the seven cases of Table XXXIX., C, shows that with one exception leucocytosis was present throughout most of the disease.

TABLE XXXIX., C.—CANCER OF THE STOMACH WITH METASTASES.

No.	Age.	Sex.	Red cells.	White cells.	Per cent hæmoglobin.	Remarks.
1	48	M.	4,228,000	5,000	70	January 23d. Stomach and liver.
				6,200	....	January 28th, mealtime.
				7,300	....	January 28th, three hours later.
2	41	M.	4,272,000	10,000	57	Stomach, liver, and glands.
3	38	M.	5,432,000	10,190	52	January 6th. Stomach and liver.
				13,653	....	January 12th.
						January 22d, died.
4	66	M.	....	7,000	70	February 14th, no cachexia.
			5,168,030	14,400	62	March 6th, liver involved.
				19,600	....	March 12th.
				21,640	....	March 17th, cachectic.
5	Adult.	M.	3,352,000	16,000	....	Stomach, liver, and spleen.
6	54	M.	4,160,000	24,000	60	Stomach and liver.
				24,200		
				22,500		
7	47	M.	....	34,350	....	November 7th, cancer of stomach and liver.
				30,600	....	November 11th.
				105,600 I	....	November 14th, perforation peritonitis.

CANCER OF THE GULLET.

Most authors are agreed that *no increase*—in fact usually a decrease—of white cells is the rule in this disease. Thus Rieder found 6,900 in one case; Osterspey's two cases showed no leucocytosis, and Escherich and Pée found similar results.[1] This is probably due to the fact that the position of the tumor, by causing starvation, tends to lower the leucocytes, while it belongs to the class of small, slow-growing cancers which do not as a rule tend to produce leucocytosis.

Nevertheless, two of the five cases in the Massachusetts Hospital series (see Table XL.) *did* have leucocytosis, perhaps owing to some metastasis or complication. There was no autopsy in either.

TABLE XL.—CANCER OF THE GULLET.

No.	Age.	Sex.	Red cells.	White cells.	Per cent hæmo-globin.	Remarks.
1	58	M.	5,488,000	6,800	100	May 11th.
				6,800	..	May 18th.
2	46	F.	....	7,000	..	October 18th.
				10,600		
				5,400	..	October 19th, before food.
				6,600	..	October 19th, after food.
				9,860	..	October 20th.
3	51	M.	2,824,000	7,600	50	Before food.
				11,500	..	Four hours later.
4	56	M.	4,920,000	8,725	72	
5	36	M.	....	11,800	30	Hæmaturia also.
6	65	M.	....	11,100	68	
7	47	M.	....	15,400	80	
8	38	M	....	15,600	60	
9	67	M.	4,604,000	16,400	60	During digestion.
10	38	F.	4,560,000	20,600	50	

CANCER OF THE LIVER.

(See Table XLI.)

Out of fourteen cases, leucocytosis was present in eight—a larger proportion than in gastric cancer. The cases were not all primary in the liver or bile ducts, but none originated in the stomach, and in all the greater part of the growth was in the liver itself.

[1] Reinbach's two cases showed a diminution in the polymorphonuclear cells, which in all probability means a normal or diminished leucocyte count.

The comparatively great diminution in the red corpuscles will be noted in the Table XLI. The condition both of red and white cells is doubtless due to the rapid growth of tumors of the liver as compared, *e.g.*, with those of the stomach or lip (see below).

TABLE XLI.—CANCER OF THE LIVER.

No.	Age.	Sex	Red cells.	White cells.	Per cent hæmoglobin.	Remarks.
1	55	M.	4,170,000	5,000	..	Bile ducts = starting-point. Autopsy.
2	61	M.	3,824,000	5,200	52	
3	59	M.	4,570,000	8,000	..	Operated.
4	72	M.	4,100,000	9,000		
5	44	F.	4,953,000	7,800	69	January 4th, 1896. Autopsy.
			3,784,000	12,700	68	February 12th, 1896.
6	31	F.	4,572,000	8,000	62	
7	65	M.	....	10,300	58	
8	57	M.	....	11,150	50	
9	54	M.	4,072,000	9,300	..	Differential count of 1,000 cells: Poly., 82.4 per cent; small lymphocytes, 8.5; large lymphocytes, 8.1; old lymphocytes, 1.
10	50	M.	3,200,000	10,800	..	Primary in bile ducts. Autopsy.
11	?	M.	4,108,000	9,970	45	January 1st, 1896.
				11,200	..	January 3d, 1896. Autopsy
12	48	M.	4,160,000	14,100	?	July 17th.
						July 19th. Autopsy.
13	64	M.	2,768,000	15,800	45	May 6th.
			2,880,000	21,900	..	May 24th.
				1,530	45	May 28th.
			2,928,000	11,700	..	June 8th.
14	35	M.	3,800,000	9,800	..	November 3d.
				22,000	..	November 5th.
						November 6th. Differential count of 500 cells: Poly., 92 per cent; lymphocytes, 8. Autopsy.
15	48	F.	2,900,000	17,500	48	Differential count of 500 cells: Poly., 92 per cent; lymphocytes, 5.8; eosinophiles, .2; myelocytes, 2. Autopsy.
16	30	F.	3,660,000	17,200	82	Polynuclear cells, 83 per cent; Myelocytes, 1 per cent.
				16,800	..	
17	31	M.	3,120,000	18,700	52	December 20th.
				15,600	..	December 30th; before food.
				14,000	..	Four hours later.
18	Adult.	M.	4,408,000	25,500	70	
19	50	M.	4,544,000	35,600	..	November 29th, 1895.
				36,400	..	December 10th, 1896.
			3,136,000	23,000	..	January 15th, 1896.
			4,056,000	28,800	..	February 16th, 1896. Autopsy.

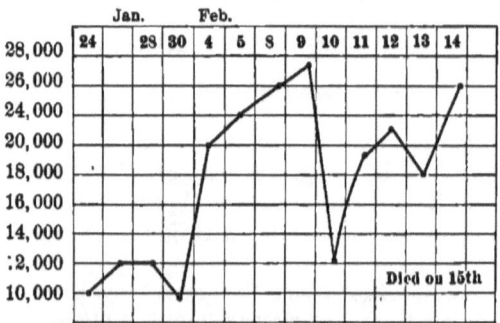

FIG. 86.—Chart of Leucocytes in a Case of Cancer of the Liver.

CANCER OF THE INTESTINE.

Here the counts range both high and low.
Hayem[1] found cancer of the rectum to show only 9,500 leucocytes. Reinbach[2] found in three cases of cancer of the rectum moderate leucocytosis.[3] Only four of the ten cases in our series (see Table XLII.) showed leucocytosis, and in one of these there was a complicating pylephlebitis which probably raised the count.
The red cells show little change.

TABLE XLII.—CANCER OF THE INTESTINE.

No.	Age.	Sex.	Red cells.	White cells.	Per cent hæmo-globin.	Remarks.
1	56	M.	4,408,000	12,700	60	Cancer of duodenal papilla with pylephlebitis. Autopsy.
2	41	F.	5,560,000	5,800	45	Cancer of cæcum. Operated successfully.
3	31	M.	4,921,000	8,800	..	Cancer of hepatic flexure. Opera.ed.
4	33	M.	4,368,000	5,800	83	Cancer of colon. Operated.
5	59	F.	4,800,000	5,500	33	Cancer of cæcum. Autopsy.
6	66	M.	4,268,000	7,150	78	Cancer of intestine (where ?).
7	50	F.	5,416,000	12,000	..	Cancer of rectum.
8	58	M.	4,160,000	15,200	50	Cancer of rectum (operation).
9	34	M.	....	15,500	40	Metastases, primary in sigmoid.
10	52	M.	....	7,400	55	Metastases, primary in sigmoid.
11	47	F.	....	9,300	63	Cancer of cæcum.
12	28	M.	.. ....	5,300	72	Cancer of cæcum. Operation.
13	52	M.	2,424,000	7,800	..	Cancer of cæcum.
			2,440,000	6,800	..	No digestion leucocytosis.

CANCER OF OMENTUM AND ABDOMINAL ORGANS GENERALLY.

The nine cases seen at the Massachusetts General Hospital in which cancerous tissue was pretty generally distributed through the abdominal organs, all showed leucocytosis with two exceptions (see Table XLIII., A).

[1] Loc. cit.
[2] Loc. cit.
[3] Apparently—that is, the percentage of adult cells was increased. He did not count the leucocytes as a whole.

TABLE XLIII., A.—CANCER OF OMENTUM AND ABDOMINAL ORGANS GENERALLY.

No.	Age.	Sex.	Red cells.	White cells.	Per cent hæmo-globin.	Remarks.
1	50	F.	....	Greatly increased.	Markedly diminished.	Primary in pancreas. Differential count of 400 cells: Poly., 84.5 per cent; small lymphocytes, 8; large lymphocytes, 5; eosinophiles, 2.5. Autopsy.
2	48	M.	....	7,250 6,500 7,300	....	May 13th.
					....	May 20th. No digestion leucocytosis.
3	42	M.	4,560,000	7,800	60	October 13th. Poly., 88 per cent; lymphocytes, 10; eosinophiles, 2.
				10,600	....	October 16th.
4	26	M.	....	9,000		
5	65	M.	....	11,700		
6	Adult.	M.	3,772,000	13.700	....	Autopsy.
7	Adult.	F.	5,500,000	26,200	....	Autopsy.
8	45	F.	....	27,400	....	Questions of aneurism. Autopsy.
9	Adult.	M.	....	Greatly increased.	Markedly diminished.	Differential count of 500 cells: Poly., 80 per cent; lymphocytes, 20.

CANCER OF THE KIDNEY.

Of five cases which I have examined (see Table XLIII., B) *all* showed very large leucocyte counts—viz., 25,000, 27,000, 28,500, 43,100, 82,000, and 91,000, an average of 54,000. In three of these cases, however, the tumors may have been sarcomata, as no microscopic examination was made. Most of the cases had fever, chills, and signs of inflammation, which may account for part of the leucocytosis.

TABLE XLIII., B.—CANCER (OR SARCOMA) OF KIDNEY.

No.	Age.	Sex.	Red cells.	White cells.	Per cent hæmo-globin.	Remarks.
1	53	M.	4,312.000	25,000	32	Differential count of 800 cells: Poly., 80.9 per cent; lymphocytes. 15.8; eosinophiles, 3.3. No nucleated red cells.
2	2	F.	3,756,000	27,000	..	Differential count of 500 cells: Poly., 66 per cent; lymphocytes, 29.5; eosinophiles, 2; myelocytes, 2.5; normoblasts, 24; megaloblasts, 2. Autopsy.
3	57	F.	5,200,000	28,500		Supposed leukæmia. Differential count of 500 cells: Poly., 81.8 per cent; small lymphocytes, 12; large lymphocytes, 4.2; eosinophiles, 2. Autopsy.
4	49	F.	3,360,000	43,100		Supposed leukæmia. Differential count of 1,000 cells: Poly., 92.9 per cent; lymphocytes, 6.2; myelocytes, .9; normoblasts, 2; megaloblasts, 1. Autopsy.
5	50	F.	4,111,000 2,780,000	82,000 91,000	.. ..	July 8th. Poly., 98 per cent; lymphocytes, 2.

Von Limbeck's [1] case mounted steadily from 18,514 to 80,541.

CANCER OF THE UTERUS.

In six cases Hayem [2] found no increase—the counts ranging from 4,575 to 9,500 with an average of 7,800.

Rieder, [3] on the other hand, in a single case found 30,800, and the three cases counted at the Massachusetts Hospital showed respectively 19,400, 22,250, and 34,900 (see Tables XLIV., A and B).

There is need of more data on this subject.

TABLE XLIV., A.—CANCER OF THE UTERUS.

No.	Age.	Sex	Red cells.	White cells.	Per cent hæmo-globin.	Remarks.
1	48	F.	2,696,080 3,232,000	19,400 30,700	20 27	October 26th. October 28th.
2	51	F.	....	34,900	....	Differential count of 1,000 cells: Poly., 88 per cent; small lymphocytes, 11.7; eosino-philes, .2; myelocytes, .1. Two normoblasts.
3	31	F.	2,889,680	22,250		
4	28	F.	....	20,170	75	Ureter blocked; anuria nine days. Autopsy

TABLE XLIV., B.—CANCER OF THE OVARY.

No.	Age.	Sex	Red cells.	White cells.	Per cent hæmo-globin.	Remarks.
1	30	F.	4,500,000	25,000	62	Operation.
2	....	F.	3,248,000	32,800	....	Operation.

CANCER OF THE PROSTATE.

| 1 | 45 | M. | .... | 10,200 | | |

CANCER OF THE LIP.

| 1 | 51 | M. | 7,000,000 | 6,300 | | |

CANCER OF THE BREAST.

1	31	F.	6,000,000	8,000		
2	?	F.	. ....	Not increased	....	Differential count of 600 cells: Poly., 72.4 per cent; lymphocytes, 25.4; eosinophiles, 2.2.
3	?	F.	....	Marked increase.	....	Differential count of 400 cells: Poly., 89 per cent; lymphocytes, 11.

CANCER OF THE NECK.

| 1 | 42 | M. | .... | Marked increase. | .... | Poly., 88.5 per cent. |

[1] *Loc. cit.*　　　　[2] *Loc. cit.*　　　　[3] *Loc. cit.*

TABLE XLIV., B (*Continued*).—CANCER OF THE PANCREAS.

No.	Age.	Sex.	Red cells.	White cells.	Per cent hæmo-globin.	Remarks.
1	54	M.	....	18,300	70 .	Metastases.
2	56	M.	....	17,600	....	Liver and spleen also.
3	64	M.	....	15,900	....	General peritonitis.

CANCER OF VERTEBRÆ.

| 1 | 62 | F. | .... | 13,200 | .... |

ADENOMA OF THE SUPRARENAL BODY.

| 1 | 59 | M. | .... | 24,200 | .... | Autopsy. |

Cancer of the lip has apparently been neglected so far as blood examination is concerned. Hayem, Rieder, and Reinbach give but one case each, the counts being respectively 7,000, 11,-600, and "not increased." In a single case at the Massachusetts Hospital I found 6,300.

The following scattered counts may be added: Cancer of tongue, 7,000 (Hayem); cancer of scrotum, 6,700 (Hayem); cancer of navel, 7,100 (Hayem); cancer of larynx, 7,200 (Hayem), 16,000 (Reinbach); cancer of ovary, 25,000 (Massachusetts Hospital) and "no increase" (Reinbach); cancer of neck, 20,000 (Massachusetts Hospital) and "no increase" (Reinbach); cancer of pancreas: Hayem, 2 cases—9,400 and 9,900; Schneider, 1 case—12,000; cancer of vagina, 9,800 (Rieder); cancer of penis, 7,000 (Hayem); cancer of thyroid, 70,000 (Hayem) (a very rapidly growing tumor); cancer of mediastinum, "marked increase" (Reinbach); cancer of prostate,[1] 10,200.

Qualitative Changes in the Leucocytes.

1. The percentage of polymorphonuclear neutrophiles is usually high in cases with leucocytosis and normal in those without it. This rule holds for perhaps three-fourths of the cases, but there are many exceptions to it. For instance, Taylor[2] reports 27,840 leucocytes with 65.6 per cent polymorphonuclear cells, 14,800 leucocytes with 66.2 per cent polymorphonuclear

[1] Braun (Wien. med. Woch., 1896, p. 582) mentions a cancer of the prostate in which the leucocytosis instead of being made up mostly by the adult leucocytes, was associated with a large increase of the small lymphocytes together with numerous eosinophilic myelocytes.

[2] Taylor: Internat. Med. Mag., July, 1897.

cells, 25,000 leucocytes with 58.2 per cent polymorphonuclear cells, 45,000 leucocytes with 43.7 per cent polymorphonuclear cells, the last a marked lymphocytosis. On the other
hand, he found 88.7 per cent of the polymorphonuclear cells in
a total leucocyte count of 3,000. My own experience is similar
—*i.e.*, 88 per cent of polymorphonuclear cells with a total count
of 7,800 leucocytes, though I have never seen so marked a
lymphocytosis as was present in 'Taylor's cases. He also
noted a relative increase in the large lymphocytes which my
counts have not shown.

Reinbach found in 8 cases with leucocytosis 89 per cent in
2 cases and 87, 86, 83, 81, 80, and 77 per cent in others. In
the Massachusetts General Hospital series the following percentages occurred: When no leucocytosis was present 88.7, 88,
86, 79, 66, 62.5, 62, 60, 57 per cent, etc. With leucocytosis,
96, 98, 92, 90, 90, 88, 87, 86, 84, 83, 74 per cent, etc. (See
Tables XXXIX., XLI., XLIII., XLIV.).

2. *Eosinophiles* are not always notably decreased (as they are
in many other leucocytoses) nor are they increased except when
bone metastasis occurs (see below). In Reinbach's 16 cases the
average percentage was 2 + per cent. In the Massachusetts Hospital cases the average was 1.2 per cent, but in 7 of the 38 cases
in which differential counts were made, no eosinophiles were
seen.

3. *Myelocytes.*—Perhaps more commonly than in other conditions except leukæmia and pernicious anæmia, we find in malignant disease small percentages of myelocytes, as the following
cases show:

CASE I.—Extensive abdominal cancer; great cachexia. Six
hundred cells showed:

Polynuclear neutrophiles.. .... 89.4 per cent
Lymphocytes................................... 10.   "
Eosinophiles 1   "
Myelocytes (3 in 600 cells) 5   "

CASE II.—Cancer of uterus; marked cachexia and leucocytosis. One thousand cells showed:

Polynuclear neutrophiles......................... 82.3 per cent.
Lymphocytes .... 17.3   "
Myelocytes (4 in 1,000 cells).................... .4   "

CASE III.—Cancer of uterus; died two days later. Red cor-

puscles, 7,000,000; white, 62,000.   Considerable stasis helps to
explain the count.   Differential count of 500 cells showed:

Polynuclear neutrophiles........................... 93   per cent.
Lymphocytes 6   "
Eosinophiles...................................... 0   "
Myelocytes (5 out of 500)......................... 1   "

Case IV.—Cancer of liver, jaundice and cachexia; died soon
after.   Differential count of 500 cells showed:

Polynuclear neutrophiles........................... 92. per cent.
Lymphocytes. .... 6.   "
Small myelocytes................................. 1.2 "
Large myelocytes (4 in 500) 8   "

Case V.—Cancer of abdomen; cachectic.   Differential count
of 1,000 cells showed:

Polynuclear neutrophiles........................... 82. per cent.
Lymphocytes .... 16.6 "
Eosinophiles.............................. .... 1.   "
Myelocytes (4 in 1,000) .... 4.   "

Case VI.—Cancer of stomach, liver, etc., with perforated
stomach; cachexia.   Leucocytes, 105,000.   Fifteen hundred
cells showed:

Polynuclear neutrophiles........................... 90.7 per cent.
Lymphocytes...................................... 4.8 "
Eosinophiles 2   "
Myelocytes (68 in 1,500)......................... 4.3 "

Case VII.—Cancer of uterus; cachexia.   In 1,000 cells there
were:

Polynuclear neutrophiles........................... 88. per cent.
Lymphocytes .... 11.7 "
Eosinophiles............................ 2   "
Myelocytes 1   "

Case VIII.—Cancer of kidney; great cachexia.   In 1,000
cells there were:

Polynuclear neutrophiles........................... 92.9 per cent.
Lymphocytes...................................... 6.2 "
Myelocytes....................................... 9   "

CASE IX.—Cancer of kidney; great cachexia. Leucocytes, 27,000. Five hundred cells showed:

Polynuclear neutrophiles.......................... 66. per cent.
Lymphocytes....................................... 29.5 "
Eosinophiles...................................... 2. "
Myelocytes.. 2.5 "

CASE X.—Cancer of liver. Five hundred cells showed:

Polynuclear neutrophiles.......................... 92. per cent.
Lymphocytes....................................... 5.8 "
Eosinophiles...................................... .2 "
Myelocytes.. 2. "

About one-half of all the cases of cancer examined by me have shown myelocytes.

Epstein (*Wiener med. Presse*, December, 1894) in a case of cancer with metastatic bone nodules noticed large numbers of nucleated corpuscles (normoblasts and megaloblasts) and myelocytes, but I think the association was a mere coincidence, since I find that myelocytes and erythroblasts are very commonly present in cachexia from any cause.

SARCOMA.

In general the effects of sarcoma are like those of cancer, but *worse*. Great anæmia and higher leucocyte counts are the rule. The literature of the subject is rather scanty.

Red Cells.—Hayem in a case of osteosarcoma counted the red cells at 663,400 per cubic millimetre.

Laker[1] describes an "abdominal cystosarcoma" in which two counts of red cells showed 2,800,000 and 2,500,000.

Von Limbeck[2] in 1 case found 1,118,000, and in another 2,-240,000. Both were osteosarcomata.

Sadler[3] in 3 cases found 2,710,000, 3,637,000, 4,500,000.

Rieder[4] in 3 cases (all osteosarcomata) found 1,846,160, 3,-770,000, and 3,995,000.

The Massachusetts Hospital blood counts include 15 cases in which the red cells were counted (see Table XLV., A and B), the average being 4,400,000, not nearly so low as that recorded

[1] Wien. med. Woch., 1886, p. 926.
[2] *Loc. cit.*, p. 343.
[3] *Loc. cit.*, pp. 88, 89.
[4] *Loc. cit.*, pp. 98, 100.

23

by other observers; still low counts occurred (2,706,000, 2,637,-000, 3,842,000).

The qualitative changes in the red cells consist (as in cancer) of the "degenerative" changes (deformities in size and shape, englobular changes) present in marked cases, and the presence of nucleated corpuscles, when cachexia is marked.

TABLE XLV., A.—SARCOMA WITH LEUCOCYTOSIS.

No.	Age.	Sex.	Red cells.	White cells.	Per cent hæmo-globin.	Remarks.
1	......	....	4,188,000	98,000	....	Polynuclear cells, 90.2 per cent.
2	......	....	4,312,000	25,000	32	Polynuclear cells, 80.9 per cent.
3	......	....	4,000,000	44,600	42	Polynuclear cells, 70 per cent (infant of twenty months).
4	21	F.	2,706,000	56,000	....	Sarcoma of kidney. Autopsy.
5	35	F.	4,560,000	17,000	65	Melanotic sarcoma all abdominal organs (bone metastasis ?). November 30th, 1895. Differential count of 600 cells: Poly., 71 per cent; small lymphocytes, 11; large lymphocytes, 5.2; eosinophiles, 12.4 (!); myelocytes, 4.
				23,900	....	December 7th.
				33,400	....	December 13th.
				37,900	....	December 19th.
				41,200		
				33,000	....	December 22d.
				36,000	....	December 26th.
				40,200	....	January 14th.
				55,400	....	January 28th.
6	46	M.	4,700,000	16,000	....	Sarcoma of abdominal organs.
				19,000	....	Three days later. Autopsy.
7	32	M.	2,630,000	24,000	50	General sarcomatosis.
			2,900,000	21,000	....	One week later. Autopsy.
8	24	M.	4,352,000	13,600	....	Sarcoma of kidney.
9	41	M.	3,842,000	61,100	55	Sarcoma of lung, etc. Autopsy.
10	68	F.	6,200,000	16,000	....	Sarcomatosis.
11	48	M.	....	Marked increase.	....	Differential count of 700 cells: Poly., 70 per cent; lymphocytes, 22; eosinophiles, 1; myelocytes, 7. Sarcomatosis.
12	57	M.	4,180,000	13,000	47	Melanotic sarcoma of abdominal organs.
				16,250	....	One week later.
				15,180		
13	Adult.	M.	....	18,000	....	Sarcoma of abdominal organs.
14	......	....	....	Great increase.	....	Osteosarcoma (thigh). Differential count of 500 cells: Poly., 74 per cent; small lymphocytes, 19; large lymphocytes, 6; eosinophiles, 1.
15	......	....	....	Great increase.	....	Sarcoma of abdominal organs. Differential count of 800 cells: Poly., 84 per cent; lymphocytes, 15.5; eosinophiles, 5.
16	......	....	....	13,200	....	Sarcoma of abdominal wall.
17	36	M.	....	6,700		

TABLE XLV., B.—SARCOMA WITHOUT LEUCOCYTOSIS.

No.	Age.	Sex.	Red cells.	White cells.	Per cent hæmo-globin.	Remarks.
1	29	M.	5,280,000	8,200	....	Sarcoma of testicle.
2	37	F.	4,980,000	9,000	78	Sarcoma of ovary.
3	?	M.	4,946,000	9,000	....	Osteosarcoma of shoulder.
4	24	M.	4,952,000	6,000	....	Small recurrent sarcoma of groin.

Small tumors are often without any effect on the blood (see

Table XLV., B). According to v. Limbeck' this is oftener true than in cancer.

Hæmoglobin.—Reinbach's[2] 20 cases ranged between 23 and 75 per cent, averaging 52 per cent.

Bierfreund[2] in 29 cases found variations between 40 and 75 per cent.

Von Limbeck's 2 cases had 28 and 48 per cent respectively.

Rieder's[4] 4 cases showed at the beginning of treatment 29, 56, 57, and 65 per cent respectively, but in 1 case the hæmoglobin went down gradually while under observation until it reached 6 per cent (!), the lowest point, Rieder says, that he has ever seen in any disease.

Sadler's[2] cases showed 33, 45, and 78 per cent.

In the 5 cases of Table XLV. in which this point was noted, the average is 58 per cent.

On the whole, the coloring matter seems to be more diminished than in most cases of cancer.

Leucocytes.—The following tables, slightly modified from v. Limbeck, show the important points.

No.	Observer.	Diagnosis.	Count.
1	Hayem.	Osteosarcoma.	11,250
2	Alexander.	"	52,700
3	"	"	16,430
4	"	"	16,275
	"	"	17,050
5	"	"	15,900
	"	"	15,570
6	"	"	13,020
7	"	"	10,950
	"	"	12,090
8	"	"	11,248
9	Rieder.	"	12,700
	"	"	10,900
10	"	"	9,100
11	"	"	8,000
12	v. Limbeck.	"	32,000
	"	"	26,800
13	Reinbach.	"	20,000
14	"	"	13,000
15	Massachusetts Hospital.	"	21,000
16	" "	"	9,000
		Average,	17,000 ±

[1] *Loc. cit.* [2] *Loc. cit.* [3] *Loc. cit.*
[4] *Loc. cit.* [5] *Loc. cit.*

No.	Observer.	Diagnosis.	Count.
1	Hayem.	Lymphosarcoma.	11,700
2	Alexander.	"	19,910
3	"	"	19,530
4	"	"	11,696
5	"	"	11,470
6	"	"	10,540
7	v. Limbeck.	"	55,100
8	"	"	38,000
9	"	"	10,800
10	Sadler.	"	33,248
11	"	"	19,299
12	"	"	9,044
		Average,	20,000 +

No.	Observer.	Diagnosis.	Count.
1	Rieder.	Melanosarcoma.	41,600
2	"	"	28,500
3	"	"	22,300
4	Reinbach.	"	25,000
5	"	"	8,000
6	Massachusetts Hospital.	"	37,900
7	" "	"	13,000
		Average,	25,100 +

For other sarcomata, see Table XLV., A and B.

On the whole, leucocytosis appears to be more constant and of greater extent in sarcoma than in cancer.

Qualitative Changes.

1. The increase of polymorphonuclear leucocytes which we find in most forms of leucocytosis is not always present in sarcoma[1] and seems to be less frequent than in cancer (see Cases 5, 11, 14, Table XLV.)

As in cancer, it may be present when no increase in the total leucocyte is to be found, and may be the only indication of any disease in the organism.

2. A few cases are on record in which a large percentage of *eosinophiles* has been present.

Reinbach found 48 per cent of eosinophiles in a case of sarcoma of the neck with sloughing and ulcerative endocarditis, the

[1] Palma (Deut. Med. Woch., 1892) reports lymphocytosis in sarcoma.

percentage continuing over 40 for several weeks.[1] Autopsy showed sarcomatous nodules in the bone marrow. In another case, a tumor of the abdomen, the eosinophiles were 10.5 per cent, and in two others 8 per cent.

A case of apparent sarcoma of the abdominal organs (no autopsy) at the Massachusetts General Hospital in January, 1896, had 12.4 per cent of eosinophiles.

Such cases should certainly make us think of bone metastases, and Neusser speaks of osteosarcomata as being accompanied by eosinophilia, but the evidence is as yet fragmentary.

3. *Myelocytes.*—Reinbach's case just described had a low percentage of myelocytes.

The following cases illustrate the same point:

CASE I. is a case of sarcomatosis in a man in whom sarcomatous nodules were distributed all over the internal organs and in the skin. A differential count of 700 white cells showed in his case:

Typical myelocytes (over 15μ) .... 2 per cent.
Small myelocytes (under 15μ) .... 5 "
Lymphocytes .... 22 "
"Polynuclear neutrophiles" .... 70 "
Eosinophiles .... 1 "

The autopsy showed no special lesions in the spleen, glands, or bone marrow, except those due to the sarcomatous nodules.

[1] The full counts are as follows:

April 4th, 1892.	May 20th, 1892.
Red cells.......... 5,396,000	Red cells.......... 4,512,000
White cells........ 120,000 (!)	White cells........ 52,000
Hæmoglobin........ 60 per cent.	Hæmoglobin....... 55 per cent.

DIFFERENTIAL COUNTS.

	April 4th.	May 1st.	May 20th.	May 26th.
	Per cent.	Per cent.	Per cent.	Per cent.
Poly. neut............	48	51	55 +	51 +
Eosinophiles	48	46	42	44 +
Lymphocytes	2.7	2.32	1.5	3.2
Myelocytes	1	.68	.64	.8

CASE II.—Sarcoma of abdominal wall. Differential count of 800 cells showed:

Polynuclear neutrophiles... .... 84. per cent.
Lymphocytes........................ 10.5   "
Large lymphocytes .... 5.   "
Eosinophiles 2   "
Myelocytes 3   "

CASE III. (No. 2, Table XLV., A).—Six hundred cells contained:

Polynuclear neutrophiles......................... 71. per cent.
Lymphocytes..................................... 16.2   "
Eosinophiles .... 12.4   "
Myelocytes...................................... .4   "

Summary of Blood Changes in Malignant Disease.

1. Small, slow-growing tumors and the early stages of all tumors may have no effect on the blood appreciable by our present methods of examination.

2. In advanced cases the red corpuscles often become thin, light, and pale, and finally their number may be greatly decreased, the counts running sometimes as low as in pernicious anæmia. In this respect, as in others, sarcomata seem to injure the blood more than cancers.

3. The color index is always below 1, but is rarely as low as we find it in severe chlorosis.

4. Normoblasts and megaloblasts (the latter being in the minority) may occur, the former even in the absence of severe anæmia. Deformities in size and shape are common.

5. Leucocytosis is present in the cachectic end-stages of many cases, but is frequently absent in small tumors of slow growth and without metastases. The polymorphonuclear cells are often relatively increased.

6. Fibrin is not increased.

Diagnostic Value.

1. When we are dealing with an obscure, deep-seated disease, if hemorrhage is excluded, the presence of persistent leucocytosis suggests suppuration or malignant disease (rather than tuberculosis or syphilis, for example), and excludes any simply

functional or hysterical affection. The *absence* of leucocytosis, however, does not exclude malignant disease, though it makes suppuration very unlikely.

2. Between malignant disease and suppuration—if the other signs and symptoms do not decide—there may be nothing in the blood to decide. In decided pyæmia we may get pyogenic cocci from the blood by culture, but a negative result would not exclude the suppurating focus.

The *absence* of any increase of fibrin in the blood speaks against suppuration, and therefore in favor of malignant disease; but the presence of increased fibrin network is not decisive either way, as it may be met with in connection with neoplasms, though more common in suppuration.

3. Between malignant disease and hemorrhage—a marked anæmia favors the latter, provided the case is a recent one; for the anæmia of malignant disease is comparatively slow to develop. The leucocytes give no help.

4. Between cancer and ulcer of the stomach, if there has been no recent hemorrhage, leucocytosis favors cancer; but its *absence* is of no weight either way.

The hæmoglobin is said to decrease steadily in cancer, while in ulcer it tends to return toward normal after the cessation of hemorrhage.

The presence and persistence of digestion leucocytosis speak against cancer, and its absence in favor of cancer. It must be remembered, however, that any variety of *catarrh* or *dilatation* (should such be present) can also prevent digestion leucocytosis, and that the latter is not invariably present even in health.

5. Between cancer of the liver or bile ducts on the one hand and *simple* gall-stone colic or gall-stone obstruction, the presence of leucocytosis favors cancer. As usual, however, its absence does not exclude cancer, and we must bear in mind that gall stones *with cholangitis* may raise the leucocyte count as much as cancer. Simple cysts or echinococcus cysts cause no leucocytosis, nor does syphilis of the liver.

6. The appearance in the blood of large numbers of eosinophiles, myelocytes, and nucleated corpuscles during the course of a malignant disease points to a bone metastasis.

7. When a leucocytosis which has disappeared after removal

of a neoplasm reappears, we may expect recurrence of the growth shortly.

8. A steadily increasing leucocytosis in a case of malignant disease points to a rapidly growing tumor or to the occurrence of metastasis.

9. Between malignant disease and pernicious anæmia the diagnosis rests on the following points:

I. Color index low in malignant, apt to be high in pernicious anæmia.

II. Leucocytes often increased in malignant, diminished in pernicious anæmia.

III. Lymphocytes often decreased in malignant, increased in pernicious anæmia.

IV. Average size of red cells often decreased in malignant, and often increased in pernicious anæmia.

V. If nucleated red corpuscles are present the normoblasts are in a majority in malignant disease, and in a minority in pernicious anæmia.

10. The presence of leucocytosis is against the benignness of any tumor.

11. When no actual increase of leucocytes is present, an increased percentage of the polymorphonuclear variety among those present may have the same significance as a leucocytosis.

CHAPTER XI.

EXAMINATION FOR THE PLASMODIUM MALARIÆ AND ITS PRODUCTS.

I. *Time for Examination.*—It is often stated that the organism is most easily found during the chill. But this is not the writer's experience. During a chill it is often difficult and sometimes impossible to find the organisms. Eight hours before or after a chill is the most favorable time (Thayer), although parasites have been found as late as forty-eight hours after the last chill. During the chill many organisms retire to the internal organs.

The number of organisms varies a great deal. In some cases they are present in every field of a one-twelfth immersion lens, while in others we may find only one after an hour or more of patient search. In the majority of the cases occurring near Boston, it needs but a few minutes' search to find them if the blood be taken within twelve hours before or after a chill, and provided no quinine has been lately given. Occasionally in mild cases the organisms are very scanty; and it may be almost impossible to find any. The quartan and æstivo-autumnal forms of malaria are so rare in New England that I shall not attempt to describe in detail the parasites found in them, but shall confine myself mostly to the parasites of common tertian and double tertian fevers with which I am personally familiar.

II. *Method of Examination.*—A slide of fresh blood is prepared as above described (pages 6–8) and examined with a one-twelfth immersion lens.[1] Lower powers should not be used, although in skilful hands they are often sufficient. Portions of the slide in which the corpuscles do not overlie each other should be chosen for examination. As we pass the slide along beneath the lens it is well to be on the lookout for any *specially large* or *specially pale* corpuscle. Such a one will catch the eye if we

---

[1] In cold weather both slide and cover should be warmed before using. Indeed this is always well, as it makes the corpuscles spread better.

are on the watch for it, even though the slide is being passed along very rapidly, and all such should be carefully examined.

Another thing to watch for is anything *black or dark brown*. If the slide is not perfectly clean, or if the cover-glass has touched the skin in collecting the blood, there will often be black spots which make us pull up short and examine, only to find that they are bits of dirt. This loses time, and hence, as above noted, the importance of care and cleanliness in the earlier stages of the process.

Besides any strikingly pale or swollen corpuscle or any black dots, we should be on the lookout for any *movements* in the field. The movements of Müller's "blood-dust" (see page 59) are often mistaken by beginners for those of the malarial organism. Their greatly smaller size and extracorpuscular position serve to distinguish them in most cases. I have sometimes thought I saw pigment in these bodies. If, as Stokes believes, the "blood-dust" is derived from the leucocytes, it is possible that they might carry out with them some pigment ingested by the leucocyte.

III. *The Malarial Organism.*—(*a*) "Hyaline Forms." In the earlier stages of its growth, *i.e.*, during and soon after the chill, the organism is not pigmented, but appears only as a light spot in the pale greenish-yellow of the corpuscle. It practically is never to be seen outside the corpuscle. Most malarial organisms are to be found within the corpuscle, and *only there.*[1]

For those who have not examined many specimens of malarial blood it is a very difficult thing to find the organism at this stage of its growth, and the number of mistakes in diagnosis is very large. I always look with great suspicion on any report of malarial blood as containing *only* "hyaline forms."

In the later stages, when the organism has become well pigmented, there is nothing that at all resembles it, and those who have seen and watched it a few times can hardly mistake anything else for it. Not so with the so-called "hyaline" or youngest form of the organism. Personally I think the *name* "hyaline bodies" is responsible for a part of the mistakes. We are led to expect something more shiny and refractile than the organism

[1] Except degenerate forms, free flagellæ, and spores at the moment of segmentation (*rarely* to be seen). Crescents and ovoid bodies are intercellular.

really is, and so are misled by the brilliant white circles to be found at the centre of many normal corpuscles under certain conditions of light and partial drying up. Time and again I have been asked to look at malarial organisms (always the "hyaline" forms), and found nothing more than one of these effects of light which can be found in any normal blood, if the conditions are right. There are certain marks by which we can exclude these artifacts from consideration:

I. They are generally far too numerous to be malarial organisms. One usually finds a dozen or more in a field which would be almost unheard of with the plasmodium malariæ.

II. They are generally in the centre of the corpuscle, while the young malarial organism is almost never at the centre.

III. They are almost invariably round, the malarial organism being generally more irregular and branching.

IV. They seem to increase and diminish in size as we focus up and down upon them, while the malarial organism only grows dimmer or clearer.

V. They are, as before mentioned, more brilliantly white and shiny than the malarial organism, which has often a faint tinge of yellow, although much paler than the surrounding corpuscle substance.

VI. Their edges are sharper, the malarial organism often fading off very gradually into the corpuscle color.

VII. Their movement is different. The malarial organism is not at all the only thing to be seen moving in the blood, as has sometimes been stated. The red corpuscles have the Brownian motion, and as they begin to crenate often move very actively. But their motion is very different from that of the hyaline malarial organism, for the latter changes both its shape and its position in the corpuscle quite rapidly, while the motion of the light space in an ordinary red cell is a wavy undulation of the outlines back and forth without any considerable change of shape.

(b) As soon as the organism gets any pigment (and there are very few times in the cycle of a malarial case when there are not some pigmented organisms present), the active rapid motion of the black pigment dots is unlike anything else seen in the blood, and when once recognized can never be forgotten or mistaken. It is only when the pigment has ceased moving (owing to the death of the organism) that the differentiation between dirt and malarial pigment becomes difficult.

Sometimes it is really difficult to distinguish motionless pigment in a malarial organism from dirt even on careful scrutiny. The best way is to get a fresh slide when the pigment is in motion.

To any one fairly familiar with the appearance of pigmented forms of malarial organisms, failure to find them in a case of malaria is due generally (1) to too thickly spread a layer of

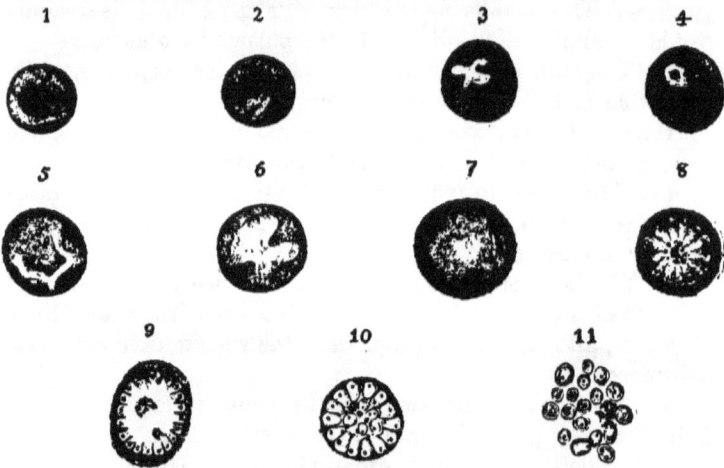

Fig. 37.—The Parasite of Tertian Malaria (after Thayer). 1, Normal red cell; 2 and 3, hyaline parasites; 4, 5, 6, 7, pigmented forms; 8, 9, 10, 11, segmentation.

blood, the corpuscles overlying each other; (2) to not looking long enough (Figs. 37 and 38) ; (3) to lack of proper light.

I have not attempted to go into the marks by which we can differentiate the tertian, quartan, and æstivo-autumnal forms of the organism—for clinical evidence usually suffices to determine this point.   For information on this and all the finer points in regard to the life history and habits of the organism W. S. Thayer's admirable monograph should be consulted.   Here it is sufficient to say that as the paroxysm draws near, the pigment granules begin to work in toward the centre in radiating lines until they are all collected in a solid black mass.   While this is going on, the pigment granules not infrequently gather into short rod-like masses not at all unlike bacilli.

Round the central mass of pigment, indistinct radiating divisions may sometimes be seen just before the organism breaks up. These divisions have been compared to the petals of a flower, but it is very difficult to see more than the faintest indi-

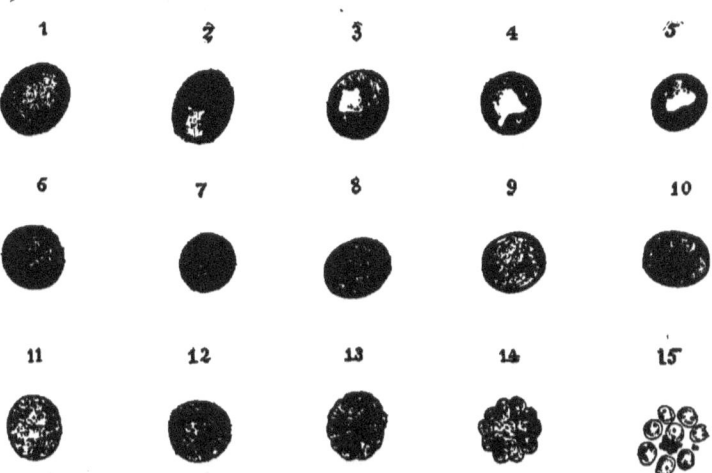

Fig. 38.—Parasite of Quartan Malaria (after Thayer).   1, Normal red cell; 2, hyaline parasite; 3 to 11, pigmented forms; 12 to 15, segmenting forms.

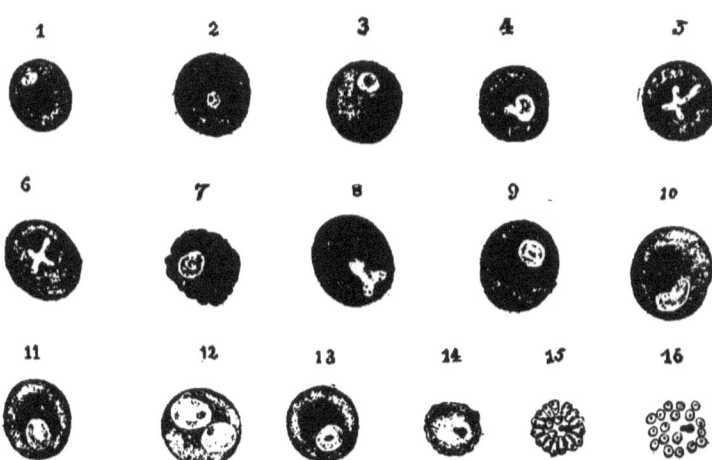

Fig. 39.—Parasite of Æstivo-Autumnal Malaria (after Thayer).   1 to 6, Young forms; 7 to 13, mature forms; 14 to 16, segmenting forms.

cations of such an arrangement in most specimens. The corpuscle itself is by this time wholly lost to sight.

(c) The next stage, that of segmentation, is less commonly seen than those just mentioned, and is only to be satisfactorily observed by using a warm stage (*vide supra*, page 8) and spending considerable time on the watch for it. Around the central pigment mass we may sometimes see in ordinary specimens (without warm stage) the faint outlines of a group of small spherical, colorless bodies (*vide* Fig. 2, 9, Plate I.) which are the new generation of young organisms.

Now we should expect that with the next step in the process we should find these young plasmodia free in the plasma or entering a fresh set of red corpuscles. But in the peripheral circulation this is rarely if ever observed. Thayer in his immense experience has never seen them. The next evidence we have of the organism is as a "hyaline" body inside the corpuscle again.

Almost all stages of the growth of the plasmodium which we can watch in the blood drawn from the peripheral circulation take place within the corpuscle. It is true that as the pigmented organism gets towards its full growth, and before the granules have begun to gather at the centre, we may find it very difficult to find any trace of corpuscle substance around the margin of the plasmodium. Sometimes we see a ring of non-pigmented glistening white substance outside the moving black dots (see

Fɪɢ. 40.—Flagellate Malarial Organisms (after Thayer).

Fig. 2, 7, Plate I.) standing out *light against the darker plasma*. This I suppose to be the remains of the corpuscle. It is not described or pictured in the standard works on the subject.

Occasionally we do find pigmented bodies wholly outside the corpuscle, either partly or fully grown. In the intracorpuscular forms the distinction between plasmodium and corpuscle substance is not, I think, so sharp and clear as one would be led to expect from the plates in standard works. With average eyes and lenses the outline of the organism, as distinguished both from its pigment granules and the surrounding corpuscles, is not easy to see. It is the moving pigment granules that attract our notice.

(d) It remains to speak of three comparatively small points:

1. The presence of flagella.

2. Pigmented leucocytes.

3. Crescents and ovoids.

1. Toward the end of the life history of a malarial parasite, it sometimes makes its presence very obvious in the microscopic field by knocking about the surrounding corpuscles with its arms or "flagella." Exactly why and under what conditions it shows or fails to show these appendages is not known.' They are about two or three times as long as a red corpuscle and one-sixth or one-eighth as wide. They are usually to be inferred rather than directly seen, as they are nearly transparent. Our

¹ McCallum has recently offered interesting evidence that they are sexual organs.

FIG. 41.—Flagellate Malarial Organisms.
(After Manson's photographs.)

attention is attracted by an active motion among a group of red
cells apparently of spontaneous origin.   Gradually we make out
a filmy whip-like tail attached to an adjacent malarial parasite.
Sometimes there is pigment dotted along the flagellum itself,
and then we can make it out more easily.   Its distal end is
especially apt to be pigmented, and by the help of this pigment we make out that it is bulbous, while similar swellings can sometimes be seen at other points along the flagellum (see Fig. 41).   Such a flagellum may break off and dart
about free among the corpuscles.   As the pigmented end is
sometimes all that we can see of it, this gives rise to the appearance of a very small, *actively locomotive* pigmented body free
among the corpuscles, and its course may be followed through
several fields.

When the flagella have ceased moving, their presence is generally detected, if at all, by an irregular line of pigment dots
about 20 μ long, which will be shown by careful focussing to be
contained within a nearly transparent membrane.

Very often we find a leucocyte in process of closing round
the flagellated parasite.   Manson has lately succeeded in staining the flagellæ, and the accompanying photographs are from
his stained specimens.

2.   Pigmented leucocytes, containing the whole or part of
malarial organisms or simply blocks or granules of black pigment, are usually to be found in the blood near the time of the
chill.   The pigment is to be carefully distinguished from the
granules present in most leucocytes, which in certain lights look
quite dark even if unstained, dark enough to be mistaken for pigment by the untrained eye.   Careful focussing and changing the
light will easily determine which we are dealing with, provided
we are familiar with the appearances of leucocytes in the fresh
unstained blood.   In certain forms of the disease in which the organisms themselves retire to the internal organs, the presence of
pigmented leucocytes may be the only evidence of the disease to
be found in the peripheral blood and is therefore of the greatest
importance.

3.   Crescentic forms are not often seen in New England.
They are found only in the æstivo-autumnal forms of malaria
which occur chiefly in the South and West and have been seldom
reported in any Northeastern State except in patients who have

brought them from the South and West.   I have never seen these crescentic forms except in the stained specimens of other observers, and my ideas of them are mostly second-hand (Fig. 42). Full account of them will be found in the monograph of Thayer's above referred to.

Hitherto I have spoken wholly of the appearance of the par-

1   **2**   **3**

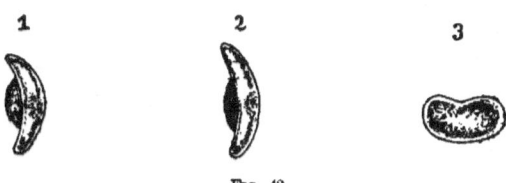

Fig. 42.

asites in the fresh unstained blood, this being by far the simplest, easiest, and surest way of finding them and the only way of studying their development.   In cases in which we cannot make a microscopic examination at the bedside, we can sometimes preserve the organism alive between slide and cover-glass, until we can get it to the nearest microscope, even if this takes several hours.   I have carried specimens in my handbag a whole morning and yet found the pigment of the malarial parasite in motion at the end of that time.   Warm weather favors this. When it is necessary to keep the specimen some time before examination, it is best to paint on the slide a ring of vaseline or any gummy substance, and allow the drop of blood to spread out inside this ring so that the margins of cover glass are glued to the slide by the oily substance and the entrance of air is prevented.   The cedar oil ordinarily used for immersion lenses answers the purpose very well.   Both slide and cover should be gently warmed before spreading the drop of blood.

Many physicians who cannot possibly carry a microscope about with them can easily find room for a few slides and cover-glasses and they may be of great service.

When specimens have to be sent by mail, or for long distances, or in cold weather we have to fall back on dried specimens prepared as described on page 43, provided always that a

24

bedside examination is impossible. These can be stained by one of the following methods:

Leave the specimen for half an hour or more in equal parts of ether and absolute alcohol; dry them in the air, stain for from one-half to five minutes in a one-half-per-cent solution of eosin in sixty-per-cent alcohol, wash in water, dry and stain one - half to one minute in concentrated watery solution of methylene blue; wash again in water, dry in filter paper, and mount in Canada balsam.

Personally I have found this method rather unsatisfactory on account of the different intensity of different eosin stains and the consequent need of finding out by experiment how long (within the limits of one-half to five minutes) the specimen is to be stained before a distinct yet not violent red color is attained in the protoplasm of the corpuscles. The blue stains the plasmodium itself in contrast with the pink corpuscle substance around it; the pigment granules remain, as in the fresh specimen, black or brownish black. (See Fig. 3, Plate I.)

Some find the stain of Plehn simpler and more satisfactory as well as quicker. By this method we leave the specimens only three or four minutes in *absolute alcohol* and then stain five or six minutes in the following mixture:

Concentrated watery solution methylene blue............. 60
One-half-per-cent solution of eosin in seventy-five-per-cent
    alcohol... 20
Distilled water... 40
Twenty per cent NaOH................... .... 12 gtt.
Wash in water and mount in Canada balsam.

The trouble of double staining and the uncertainty as to the length of time are avoided by this solution, and the parasites are sometimes beautifully stained. Yet on the whole I have had better success with the eosin and methylene blue despite its difficulties. The ordinary Ehrlich-Biondi mixture may also be used to demonstrate pigmented forms. The organism itself does not stain at all with this mixture but stands out light against the yellow of the corpuscle, the pigment looking as it does in the live parasite. The hyaline forms need some other stain for satisfactory recognition, but it is sometimes convenient to use the same stain for the differential count and the malarial organism, as for instance when we have only one cover-glass preparation in a case of doubtful diagnosis. Fixing the specimen in alcohol and ether is here far better than heat; otherwise the technique is as above described under Triple Staining (page 44). The general appearance of the organism so stained is shown in Fig. 43.

FIG. 43.

If the organisms are fairly numerous and the technique is good we can find them by this method even in preparations months old. In general, however, it is very inferior to the examination of the live organism in the fresh blood, and gives many more chances for error.

So much for technique.

We often hear reports of fruitless search for the parasite in the blood of malarial patients, but the regularity with which they are found at all the larger hospitals and by all practised observers in this and other countries leaves no doubt that they are to be found in every case during some portion of the cycle. The practice of taking blood during a chill contributes, I believe, to the number of unsuccessful endeavors to find the organism; as mentioned above, this is the worst, not the best time to look for them. Too thick a layer of blood between slide and cover accounts for some failures, as I have found in personal experience.

No doubt, in many cases in which we fail to find the organism in supposed malaria a faulty diagnosis is the reason. Many of the cases in which latent malaria is supposed to have "come out" after a surgical operation are exploded by the negative examination for parasites and the positive indications of pus-pocketing which are afforded by a marked leucocytosis (never present in simple malaria), and the fact of insufficient wound drainage is often disclosed in this way. Whenever we see the leucocytes increased we begin to doubt the existence of an uncomplicated malaria; if, furthermore, we see no signs of any pallor of the corpuscles we doubt the presence of malaria still more, as there is no more rapid deglobularizer than the malarial organism.

How long after a chill the organisms may still be found in the peripheral blood is difficult to decide, but certainly they can be found any time within twenty-four hours after the last chill, unless quinine has been given, and sometimes even if it has been given.

OTHER CHANGES IN THE BLOOD.

Red Corpuscles.—The following is from Thayer's remarkable monograph:

" A reduction in red corpuscles follows each paroxysm; these reductions are more marked after the early paroxysms than after those occurring later. When a certain degree of anæmia has been reached the losses per paroxysm are much less. When the number of corpuscles is reduced to 2,000,000 or 1,000,000 there is little tendency toward a further fall; sometimes there may be slight rises in the curve between the paroxysms; often, however, the number of corpuscles remains stationary for weeks.

" In pernicious cases the number of corpuscles may fall between paroxysms." Kelsch has seen the count decrease to as small a number as 500,000 per cubic millimetre. The diminution is greater the longer the disease lasts and the more intense its manifestations.

During the paroxysms, particularly the earlier ones, the red cells tend to *increase* in number.

In tertian and quartan fevers there is a rapid and almost complete restitution of the corpuscles during the afebrile period.

In æstivo-autumnal fevers the number of red cells bears a direct relation to the number of organisms. Crescentic bodies seem to have no influence on the number of red cells.

When after a paroxysm the number of corpuscles has been greatly diminished the succeeding paroxysm may be followed by a slight reduction only or even by an increase.

Bignami and Dionisi distinguish three types of post-malarial anæmia:

1. Ordinary secondary anæmia, but with leucopenia instead of leucocytosis; such cases usually recover.

2. Anæmia practically identical with pernicious anæmia, megaloblasts being present, and ending fatally.

3. Anæmias which are progressive, because the bone marrow cannot compensate for the losses of corpuscles.

The rapidity of the diminution in red cells may be very great. Kelsch's count of 500,000 cells per cubic millimetre, mentioned above, was after thirty days' illness. Grawitz has seen a loss of 4,000,000 cells in six days.

Qualitative changes are those of severe secondary anæmia, deformities in size and shape, normoblasts, occasional megaloblasts in the worst cases, motility in the "pale, ghostly" cells.

Hæmoglobin.—The loss of hæmoglobin bears usually a direct relation to the number of parasites in the blood. As a rule, the corpuscles and hæmoglobin are diminished proportionally (color index =1) but sometimes the hæmoglobin is reduced disproportionately.

In convalescence the restitution of hæmoglobin is often incomplete; persons living in malarial districts have often a slightly smaller percentage of hæmoglobin than those living elsewhere.

The rapid diminution in hæmoglobin is a valuable point in differential diagnosis between malaria and typhoid or pneumonia.

White Cells.—The number of leucocytes is usually subnormal, but show a slight increase at the beginning of the paroxysm. Following this increase there is a rapid decrease continuing throughout the paroxysm. The small number of leucocytes is to be seen at the end of the paroxysm when the temperature is subnormal. From this time it shows a gradual increase until the beginning of the next attack (Billings).

In a general way the white cells follow the same course as do the red.

The differential count shows a lymphocytosis whenever the white cells are subnormal, the larger forms of lymphocytes being especially numerous, while the polymorphonuclear cells and eosinophiles are scanty.

In four cases of post-malarial anæmia Billings found quite marked leucocytosis.

The occurrence of pigmented leucocytes has already been mentioned.

Grawitz and others have noticed an increase of eosinophiles in post-malarial anæmia. I have frequently found small percentages of myelocytes, three per cent being the highest in my experience.

MALARIAL HÆMOGLOBINÆMIA.

During the paroxysms of this form of the disease, the number of the red cells is much diminished, rouleaux not formed, marked poikilocytosis with nucleated forms. The leucocytes are increased. The regeneration is very swift, twenty-four to forty-eight hours being usually sufficient to re-establish normal conditions.

FILARIA SANGUINIS HOMINIS.

Although most commonly found in tropical countries, one species of this worm is not very uncommonly found in various parts of the United States. Any case of chylous urine or elephantiasis should lead us to make a careful examination of the blood for the filaria. There are at least four species of filaria, one of which is present in the blood chiefly at night, another chiefly during the daytime, and another continuously. Only the *filaria nocturna* has thus far been seen in America (Fig. 44).

In examining for the filaria a slide of the fresh blood is pre-

Fig. 44.—The Filaria Sanguinis Hominis. The head, curled up, is seen at the right of the cut, the tail at the left. Instantaneous photomicrograph. Four hundred diameters magnification.

pared in the usual way, *but after 8:30 o'clock in the evening,*[1] and examined at once. The embryo of this parasite (which is what

[1] In persons who sleep in the daytime and work at night the habits of the filaria are said to become reversed, so that it appears in the peripheral circulation chiefly in the daytime, and is to be looked for then.

we find in the human blood) is from one-ninetieth to one seven-tieth of an inch in length, *i.e.*, about fifty times the diameter of a red cell, and about the width of a red corpuscle. Seen in the blood it retains its vitality and motile power for a considerable time, so that its motions may continue a week or more between slide and cover-glass. Cold has little effect upon it, even freezing temperature failing to do more than make the movements slower.

A distinction can generally be made out between the embryo proper and its sheath (see Fig. 45). From this sheath the embryo escapes when in the blood of the mosquito, which insect

Fig. 45.—Tail of Filaria, showing prolongation of the sheath beyond the end of the embryo itself. Magnified 800 diameters.

acts not infrequently as intermediary host and conveys the parasite indirectly from man to man through the medium of water. After sucking in the organism with the blood the mosquito lays its eggs and dies in some neighboring pond or stream whence the filaria again gains access to men.

It is a long, slender, snake-like, gracefully shaped worm, and when alive its activity is so great that measurements and observations of its structure cannot be made till it is paralyzed by approaching death (Fig. 46).

Posteriorly it tapers for one-fifth its length down to a very sharp point. The extreme end of the tail often looks as if ar-

FIG. 46.—The Movement of a Single Filaria during Four Successive Exposures of one-fifth of a second each, the entire series occupying less than five seconds. Magnified 800 diameters.

ticulated, for it does not harmonize with the general curve of the body, but lies bent at an angle. Toward the head it tapers very slightly and when alive a "pouting" movement as if of breathing can be seen at its very extremity. About the middle of the body a granular aggregation can be made out along the central axis of the animal. Except for this granular portion the parasite is so translucent that it is not easy to make it out at first. The distinction of body and sheath mentioned above, appears as a "clear space" at each end of the body (vide Fig. 45). After the motions have ceased it becomes darker and traces of transverse striation may be seen (Fig. 47).

It has no locomotive power and confines itself to wriggling in the same spot. Saussure[1] says he has watched them "fighting with each other for hours."

The head of the filaria is said by some authorities to be sup-

[1] Philadelphia Medical News, June 28th, 1890, where he reports twenty cases seen in Charleston, S. C.

FIG. 47,—Head of Filaria. Shows structure and beginning granular degeneration. Magnified 1,500 diameters.

FIG. 48.—Head of Filaria Magnified 1,500 Diameters. The blur in front of the head may be
due to the motion of flagella.

plied with feelers or flagella, and Manson describes what he calls a "cephalic armature" or fang (Fig. 48).

The same organism can sometimes be found in the chylous urine, but not every case of chyluria is due to the filaria sanguinis hominis. In a considerable proportion of cases no such organism is to be found.

Henry (*Med. News*, May 2d, 1896) succeeded in staining the parasites *intra vitam* by giving the patient considerable doses of methylene blue internally for some weeks. Only a faint

Fig. 49.—Head of Filaria Overlapping a Red Corpuscle. The appearance might be mistaken for the cephalic end of a sheath.

bluish tinge was imparted, however, to the organism by this method.

For finding the parasite it is best to use a low power, not an immersion lens, and the whole of several slides should be looked over.

Specimens can be dried and preserved for staining provided we do not heat them over a lamp or pass them through a flame. Manson[1] stains with eosin and mounts in "glycerin jelly" (Fig. 49).

Several other species have been observed in England in negroes from the Congo River, but not hitherto in America. But as it frequently is to be found in persons who have no symptoms whatever, it may well be that some of these other species would be found here if one took the trouble to seek out natives of Southern China (one out of every ten of whom carries

[1] The "Filaria Sanguinis Hominis," by Patrick Manson, M.D., Amoy, China, 1883.

about the filaria in his blood), or of Central Africa, or other
tropical regions.

SPIROCHÆTE OF RELAPSING FEVER.

During the febrile paroxysms of relapsing fever, and for
one or two days before them, Obermeyer and others have found

Fig. 50.—Spirochætes of Relapsing Fever in Human Blood.

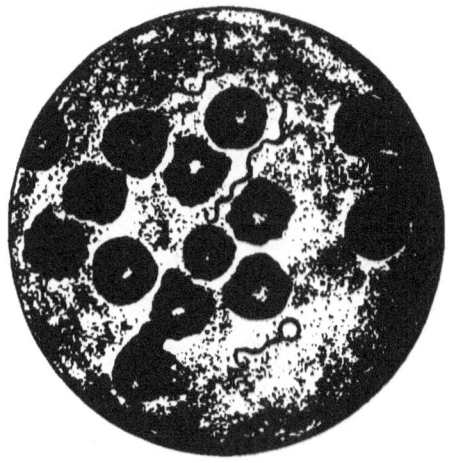

Fig. 51.—Spirochætes of Relapsing Fever in Human Blood.

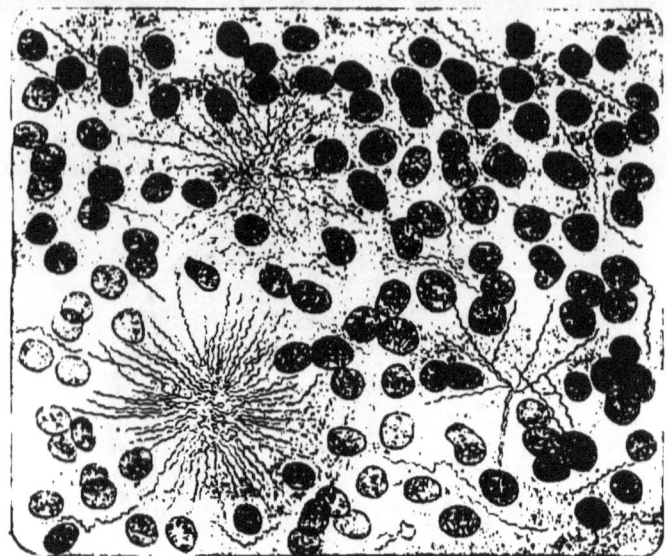

FIG. 52.

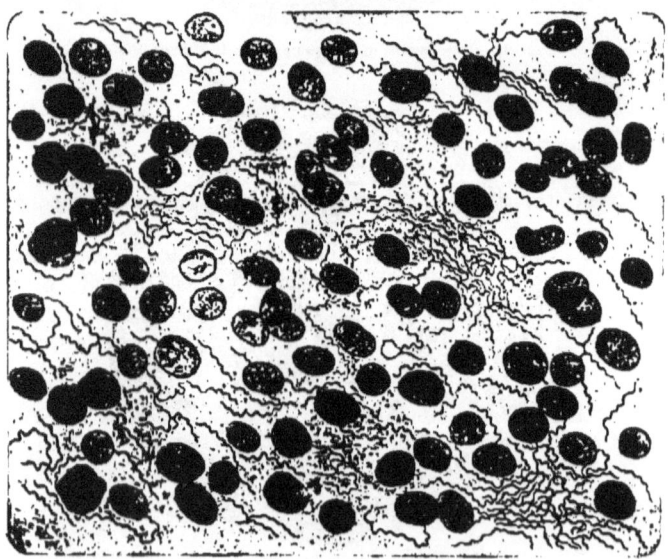

FIG. 53.

Spirochætes of Relapsing Fever.

constantly present in the peripheral circulation a parasite whose length averages about six times the diameter of a red corpuscle. Even under high-power lenses it is a mere thread in width, curled upon itself like a corkscrew and actively motile, so that in examining the blood with a low power we get "a peculiar impression of disturbance" among the red cells.

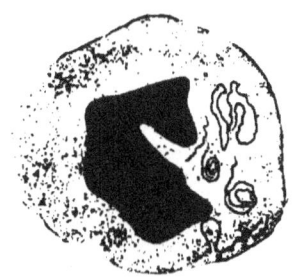

The number of twists in this spiral-shaped organism varies a good deal, and one of its motions consists in contracting and extending itself like a spiral spring. It can thus multiply its own length three or four times. It has also a delicate, wavy, but rapid motion along its long axis. The whole thread, or a part of it only, may have these motions. Further, the whole parasite has power of locomotion apparently independent of the currents in the blood plasma of a slide and cover-glass specimen. Its locomotion is slow compared to the movements above described. Particularly in the blood post mortem they are apt to wind themselves into each other so as to seem much larger than they actually are, and sometimes a large "nest" of them may look like a leucocyte, except for the fine wavy threads which can be seen in motion at the periphery of the mass.

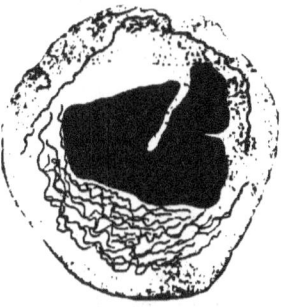

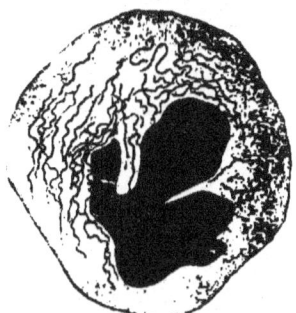

Fig. 54.—Leucocytes Containing Spirochætes.

The number present in the blood is very much smaller at the beginning of a paroxysm than after the second day. During the first few hours of a febrile period Mocyntkowsky could find only one spirochæte in ten or twenty microscopic fields, while later on he saw twenty or thirty of them in a single field. There are usually more parasites with each successive paroxysm.

Blood taken from different parts of the body often shows a great difference in the number of organisms to be found. The life history of a single parasite seems to be very short, but they multiply with the greatest rapidity. Albrecht has seen them so increase within six hours that whereas at first he saw only a few in the whole slide he later found many in each field. As the spirochæte dies, its movements get languid and finally it breaks up into small granular bits (spores?).

Between paroxysms the spirochætes are not found, but there are to be seen peculiar highly refractile globules compared by v. Jaksch to a diplococcus. The latter author believes that he has seen these develop into the spirochæte at the beginning of a paroxysm and hence believes them to be spores.

This spirochæte is found in all cases of relapsing fever and in no other known disease, so that like the plasmodium malariæ it is pathognomonic and of the highest importance.

Anæmia and leucocytosis (during the paroxysm) are among the secondary results of the presence of this parasite in the blood.

A certain resemblance has been noted between the spirochæte and a free flagellum broken off from a malarial parasite, but the clinical history and the presence or absence of other evidence of malaria in the blood would easily decide the question of diagnosis.

Technique of Examination.—As in looking for the malarial organism it is best to examine the blood fresh between a slide and cover-glass (*vide supra*, page 7) and to use an oil immersion lens. In dried specimens the organism can be stained with fuchsin, but it is much more difficult to recognize than in the fresh blood. Phagocytosis (see Fig. 54) can easily be watched in the peripheral blood.

DISTOMUM HÆMATOBIUM.

Bilharz found this parasite post mortem in the large internal veins (portal, splenic, mesenteric, etc.), but as it has never been seen in the peripheral circulation its clinical importance is thus far *nil.*

BACTERIA IN THE BLOOD.

(a) *Cover-Glass Specimens.*—Bacilli of anthrax, tuberculosis, glanders, grippe, typhoid fever, and tetanus have been demonstrated in the blood of human beings as well as have the pyogenic streptococci and staphylococci, the diplococcus lanceolatus, the gonococcus, and the bacillus coli communis. Nevertheless it is exceedingly difficult and frequently impossible to find them, and no considerable practical use has as yet been made of the cover-slip examination of blood for micro-organisms.

Gunther's method is an excellent one. Cover-glass specimens of the blood are prepared as above described (page 43), and left a few seconds in five-per-cent acetic acid to render the red cells invisible; the acetic acid is then shaken (*not washed*) off and the cover-glass held over the mouth of a bottle of strong ammonia water to neutralize the remaining acid. The covers are then stained with the Ehrlich-Weigert solution,[1] mounted in balsam, and examined with a one-twelfth immersion lens.

(b) *Cultures* (see above, page 47).

. ANÆMIA DUE TO INTESTINAL PARASITES.

The bothriocephalus latus, ankylostoma duodenale, and a few other parasites are capable of producing by their presence in the intestine a very severe anæmia, which may be indistinguishable from pernicious anæmia. As yet no such case has been reported in this country, but Askanazy'[2] and Schaumann'[3] have carefully studied the disease in Germany and found that the blood may correspond exactly with that of pernicious anæmia, including the presence of high color index and of a majority of megaloblasts among the nucleated red cells present. Yet such cases may be rapidly and permanently cured by expelling the parasites from the intestine. No special description of the blood states need be given, as they present nothing which has

[1] To 6 c.c. of distilled water add ten drops of aniline oil and filter. To the filtrate add a saturated alcoholic solution of gentian violet till slight (transient) turbidity appears. On the surface of this solution in a watch glass float the cover-glass face downward for twenty-four hours.

[2] Vereins-Beilage der Deut. med. Woch., 1895, Bd. 148.

[3] "Bothriocephalus-Anæmia," Berlin, 1894 (Hirschwald).

not been already described under pernicious anæmia or severe symptomatic anæmia.

ASCARIS LUMBRICOIDES.

The reports of Jenner's Hospital at Berne for 1890 include a case in which the blood showed only 2,450,000 red cells before driving out the parasite with santonin, and 4,200,000 two weeks later.

CHAPTER XII.

THE BLOOD IN INFANCY.

I. *All the signs by which sickness is shown in the blood of adults are exaggerated in children.* Their blood is apparently more sensitive to the action of any morbid influence. Causes leading to but slight anæmia or leucocytosis in the adult, produce grave anæmia and very marked leucocytosis in children. Into the reasons for this I shall not attempt to enter. The increased toxicity of their serum compared to that of adults, and the relatively recent establishment of the functions for producing and destroying blood have been suggested as explanation.

Comparatively slight hemorrhages, gastro-intestinal or respiratory disorders, which would not impoverish an adult's blood may produce considerable anæmia in a young child.

II. All forms of anæmia in infancy are apt to be associated with enlarged spleen.

III. I have already alluded to the polycythæmia and leucocytosis of the new-born, and the gradual fading out of these relative abnormalities as the child grows up. In judgments as to the presence or absence of leucocytosis in infancy, these physiological variations are too often lost sight of, especially as the proper leucocyte count for any given infant depends not simply on its age but on the backwardness or forwardness of its development. As with the fontanelles, the growth of the blood toward adult conditions may be retarded by congenital weakness (infantile atrophy, marasmus) or inherited disease (tuberculosis, syphilis) as well as by acquired sickness (rickets, cholera infantum).

Under the influence of any of these drawbacks a sick child's blood may be no further developed at three years than that of a healthy child of eighteen months.

IV. When we remember that in early infancy the leucocytes differ from those of adults not only in number but in that the lymphocytes are relatively more numerous ("lymphocytosis of infancy"), we shall understand that any influence like rickets

25

or syphilis which retards development, will show lymphocytosis together with the increased leucocyte count. Qualitatively as well as quantitatively the blood reverts to a more infantile condition.

V. This shows itself not merely in the leucocytes but in the red corpuscles. During the first days after birth the infant's blood shows greater *variations in size and shape* than that of adults, as if the type were not yet quite fixed. The majority of authors also find a few normoblasts in the first few days of life. These are not invariably present, doubtless because in some children the blood at the time of birth is more developed than in others.

Under pathological conditions the red cells revert to this earlier type and deformed or nucleated corpuscles are plentiful. This is more marked than in anæmia of the same grade occurring in adults. An anæmia that shows but thirty nucleated erythrocytes per cubic millimetre in an adult might show ten times that number in a child.

VI. As we said before, all blood changes are exaggerated in infancy. This includes such physiological changes as the digestion leucocytosis or that following cold bathing as well as pathological leucocytosis and anæmia, and changes in the degree of dilution or concentration of the blood seem to be similarly exaggerated, as is seen, *e.g.*, in the physiological variations in the specific gravity of the serum (Hock and Schlesinger[1]).

VII. The *hæmoglobin*, though relatively high at birth and for the first few weeks, is lower than that of adults during the rest of childhood. The high percentages of the earliest weeks are not due to a polycythæmia, but to a genuine increase of hæmoglobin in the individual cells (Schiff[2]), color indexes being often over 1.

It is indispensable, therefore, that we should know the age and degree of development of a child before we can draw accurate inferences from its blood. In many of the cases reported in literature we are unable to judge whether the blood condition is pathological or not, because the age of the child is not given. For example, v. Limbeck[3] quotes a case of acute gastritis re-

[1] Hock and Schlesinger Centralb. f. klin. Med., 1891.
[2] Schiff: Zeit. f. Heilk., vol. xi., 1890.
[3] v. Limbeck: *loc. cit.*, p. 373.

ported by Fischl[1] as having an unusually high percentage of lymphocytes (59.4 per cent). But this is physiological in the first days of life, and may have been so in this case, the age not being given.

Observations of this sort should always represent a comparison between the conditions present *before* and *during* the sickness in question.

Bearing these general considerations in mind, we shall be better able to find our way among the complications and perplexities of the blood conditions in infancy.

THE ANÆMIAS OF INFANCY.

As above mentioned, anæmic infants are apt to have enlarged spleens. This may be due either to the anæmia or to some disease accompanying or underlying the anæmia (*e.g.*, rickets, syphilis). It seems more probable that the hypertrophy is not directly or exclusively dependent on the anæmia, inasmuch as similar blood changes are found without splenic enlargement. By far the greater number of reported cases of severe infantile anæmia are accompanied or caused by such diseases as rickets and hereditary syphilis, both of which may cause splenic hyperplasia even when no anæmia is present. It seems probable that the anæmia and the enlargement of the spleen are alike symptomatic of an underlying disorder.

1. Some writers (*e.g.*, Luzet[2]) divide the anæmias of infancy into two classes : those with splenic enlargement and those without it. Luzet considers that the former class is severer than the latter and more apt to show large numbers of nucleated red corpuscles than those with normal-sized spleens. This classification, however, does not always hold. We may have very severe anæmia without splenic enlargement and splenic enlargement with slight anæmia, and the presence or absence of numerous nucleated red corpuscles is governed by conditions other than the size of the spleen.

2. Another classification of children's anæmias was proposed in 1892 by Monti and Berggrün ("Die chronische Anämie im Kindesalter," Leipzig, 1892). They divided the cases into

---

[1] Fischl: Zeit. f. Heilk., 1892.   [2] Luzet: Diss., Paris, 1891.

the *mild* and the *grave*, each group being subdivided into those with leucocytosis and those without it.

Secondary anæmia of infancy =
$$\begin{cases} \text{Mild} = \begin{cases} \text{With leucocytosis.} \\ \text{Without leucocytosis.} \end{cases} \\ \text{Grave} = \begin{cases} \text{With leucocytosis.} \\ \text{Without leucocytosis.} \end{cases} \end{cases}$$

They rightly discard the term "splenic anæmia," corresponding as it does to no single set of blood changes. The above classification puts pernicious anæmia, leukæmia, and anæmia infantum pseudoleukæmica (v. Jaksch) in a different category.

(*a*) Mild cases of secondary anæmia show no deformities in the shape or size of the red cells. The color index may or may not be low. The cases with leucocytosis are much more numerous than those without it and more apt to have a low color index; in other words, the loss of corpuscle substance is greater and the cases are approaching the imaginary boundary between "mild" and "grave."

(*b*) The grave cases have poikilocytosis, and of course a greater reduction of corpuscle substance.

"Chlorotic" conditions, and most but not all those with enlarged spleen, come under this heading; also most of those due to hereditary syphilis, prolonged diarrhœa, and rickets.

In 1894 Monti [1] gave the following classified lists of the commonest antecedents of secondary anæmia in infancy:

1. Congenital, due to....
$$\left\{ \begin{array}{l} \text{Syphilis,} \\ \text{Tuberculosis,} \\ \text{Malaria, etc.} \end{array} \right\} \text{In the mother during pregnancy.}$$

2. Acquired..

1. Hemorrhage.
$$\left\{ \begin{array}{l} \text{From navel.} \\ \text{After circumcision.} \\ \text{Scurvy, purpura, hæmophilia, Werlhof's disease, melæna.} \end{array} \right.$$

2. Other causes.
$$\left\{ \begin{array}{l} \text{Inanition.} \\ \text{Bad hygiene (lack of light, air, etc.).} \\ \text{Post-febrile.} \\ \text{Nephritis, diarrhœa, serous effusions.} \\ \text{Syphilis.} \\ \text{Rickets.} \\ \text{Suppuration.} \\ \text{Diseases of liver, spleen, bone, or lymph glands.} \end{array} \right.$$

He points out that cases with leucocytosis are usually graver than those without it and may develop into pernicious anæmia;

[1] Wiener med. Woch., 1894.

also that the presence of leucocytosis does not point to malignant disease, suppuration, or any of the causes which usually
account for it in adults.

Grave cases with leucocytosis in infants under twelve months
are apt to develop into the anæmia infantum pseudoleukæmica,
or into true leukæmia or pernicious anæmia.

On the whole, the division of Monti and Berggrün seems
much better than that according to the particular causes, e.g.,
"rachitic anæmia," "syphilitic anæmia," etc., for there is no
particular set of blood changes that follows rickets, syphilis, or
any other disease. In connection with various diseases of infancy, and particularly with those last named, we may have
anæmia of any grade of severity from that reducing the red
cells to 4,000,000 down to cases with only 500,000 red cells per
cubic millimetre or even less. The worse the case is the more
likely is it to be accompanied by leucocytosis and the more numerous will be the nucleated red corpuscles, always more numerous here than in anæmia of adults.

In *syphilis*, hereditary or acquired, the red cells may fall below 1,000,000 and the leucocytes may rise as high as 58,000
(Loos). The hæmoglobin may be proportionally diminished,
or may be even lower than the percentage of red cells, so that a
"chlorotic" condition obtains.

Such cases have been called *chlorosis*, but it seems better to
confine this term to anæmia of unknown origin and favorable
course occurring in women soon after puberty, since obviously
secondary cases may have similar blood.

Rickets in a case observed by v. Jaksch caused a fall of the
red cells to 750,000 and Luzet counted 1,590,000 in a similar
case. The hæmoglobin is usually low, but Hock and Schlesinger found 60 per cent with 2,300,000 red cell, a color index of
1.2 +.

Leucocytosis may occur even when no anæmia is present.
Hock and Schlesinger found 45,000 leucocytes in a rachitic child
of sixteen months, sound in other respects and not anæmic.
Acute gastritis causes at first only leucocytosis (with increased
percentage of lymphocytes). If it becomes chronic the reduction
of red cells is severe. Hayem found only 685,000 red cells per
cubic millimetre in an infant of two months, though recovery
eventually took place.

In *tuberculosis* of lungs and peritoneum in a child of seven, Monti and Berggrün counted 3,230,000 red and 17,200 white cells with 52 per cent of hæmoglobin.

Qualitative Changes.

The exaggeration characteristic of all blood changes in infancy extends to the presence of nucleated red corpuscles, which in all forms of severe anæmia are very numerous. What has been described above (page 91) as the typical megaloblast, a large pale-stained nucleus in a very large cell (see Plate IV.), is relatively rare in infancy. The nuclei are almost always deeply stained whatever their size, and apt to be small. Dividing nuclei are very common, both by karyolysis and karyokinesis. These changes are most often found in the anæmias of the severest type and those which resemble leukæmia (see below, page 397), but may occur in any marked secondary anæmia. Polychromatophilic and "degenerative" changes are very common in severe cases.

The increased leucocyte count, so frequently found, is often made up of a majority of lymphocytes. This change, as above said, is not characteristic of rickets, syphilis, or any other cause of anæmia, but it is to be regarded as a mark of the arrest of development or reversion to an earlier type of tissues brought about by various diseases in early infancy. Sometimes the large lymphocytes and sometimes the small are in excess.

A further qualitative change already alluded to (see above, page 121) is the occurrence of *myelocytes*. We have seen that small percentages of these cells are not uncommonly seen in the anæmias of adults. Now this, like all other blood changes, is exaggerated in infancy. Myelocytes are more apt to appear and in greater numbers. Their presence is not characteristic of any one disease, but they are commonest in the severer types of secondary anæmia, such as those following syphilis and rickets. Their significance is about the same as that of normoblasts. At times, however, they are so numerous as to make us hesitate somewhat before we exclude splenic-myelogenous leukæmia.

This brings us naturally to the discussion of *the difficulty of distinguishing the different blood diseases in infancy*, which naturally centres in the question of the existence and nature of the so called

"ANÆMIA INFANTUM PSEUDOLEUKÆMICA."

Von Jaksch's[1] decription of this disease (which he was the first to recognize) includes the following elements:

1. Grave anæmia—*e.g.*, 820,000 red cells per cubic millimetre in one case.

2. Extensive leucocytosis—*e.g.*, 54,660 white cells per cubic millmetre, in the same case.

3. Great variations in the form, size, and staining of the white cells.

4. Deformed, degenerated, and nucleated red cells.

Von Jaksch admits that none of these blood changes are characteristic of the disease, but thinks that its title to the position of a distinct and separate disease rests upon *clinical* data, the more important of which are: (1) A great enlargement of the spleen without any such accompanying enlargement of the *liver* as is usually found in leukæmia (the lymph glands are sometimes enlarged). (2) A relatively good prognosis. (3) Post mortem we find no positive evidence of leukæmia.

This description was given by v. Jaskch[1] in 1889. He stated the relation of white to red corpuscles as 1:12, 1:17, and 1:20 in the cases seen by him. Later he reported three cases in one of which the white cells numbered 114,150, and the red 1,380,-000. The differential counts are not carefully given.

Almost at the same time Hayem[2] reported a similar case, and noted the abundance of nucleated red corpuscles many of which were undergoing mitosis. This was verified by Luzet[3] in May, 1891 (*Arch. gén. de Méd.*), who reported two cases. His description of the disease differs considerably from that of v. Jaksch. He finds no greater difference between liver and spleen than often exists in true leukæmia. The course of the disease, though sometimes chronic, usually ends in death. The leucocytosis in Luzet's cases was less marked than in those of v. Jaksch and not greater than that occurring in many anæmias of children. He dwells particularly on the large number of nu-

[1] Von Jaksch : Wien. klin. Woch., 1889, Nos. 22, 23.
[2] Hayem . Gaz. des Hôpitaux, 1889, No. 30.
[3] Luzet : Diss., Paris, 1891.

cleated red cells, and the *frequency of mitosis* and considers *this* the most important diagnostic point.

Although Luzet's continues to use the name suggested by v. Jaksch, he describes the disease so differently that it is difficult to see why the same title should be given to it. He agrees with v. Jaksch in thinking that it is not simply a severe secondary anæmia due to syphilis, rickets, tuberculosis, or infectious disease.

Somewhat similar cases had already been described by various Italian writers (*e.g.*, Fede) under the title of "*Infective Splenic Anæmia of Infants.*"

Among others who have written on the subject are Baginsky,[1] Senator,[2] Fischl,[3] Andeoud,[4] Monti and Berggrün,[5] Felsenthal,[6] Raudnitz,[7] Epstein,[8] Alt and Weiss,[9] Hock and Schlesinger,[10] Crocq,[11] and Rotch.[12]

The majority of these writers report very little as to the differential counts of white corpuscles. An increased percentage of the polymorphonuclear forms is mentioned by many, but Rotch in a case with 1,311,250 red cells and 116,500 white cells found only 16 per cent of the polymorphonuclear variety with 46 per cent of small lymphocytes, 34 per cent of large lymphocytes, and 4 per cent eosinophiles. A second case had only 14 per cent of polymorphonuclear cells and 84 per cent of lymphocytes (large and small).

Von Jaksch noted the lack of any relative increase of eosinophiles, supposing this to be a means of distinguishing his cases from true leukæmia. Luzet, on the other hand, found eosinophiles numerous. (This of course has no weight for or against leukæmia.)

Klein (*loc. cit.*) noted the occurrence of myelocytes in small number.

[1] Baginsky : Arch. f. Kinderheilk., 1892, vol. 13.
[2] Senator : Berlin. klin. Woch., 1892.
[3] Fischl : *loc. cit.*
[4] Andeoud : Rev. de méd. de la Suisse rom., 1894, p. 507.
[5] Monti and Berggrün : *loc. cit.*
[6] Felsenthal : *loc. cit.*
[7] Raudnitz : Prag. med. Woch., 1894, p. 6.
[8] Epstein : Prag. med. Woch., 1894, p. 6.
[9] Alt and Weiss : Centralb. f. med. Wissenschaft, 1892.
[10] Hock and Schlesinger : *loc. cit.*
[11] Crocq : "Étude sur l'Adénie," etc., Brussels, 1891 (Lamartin).
[12] Rotch : Pædiatrics, 1895, p. 361.

The discrepancy of these different reports is suggestive. The chief importance of the heterogeneous group of cases which have received the name of *anæmia infantum pseudoleukæmica* seems to me to be as a proof of the difficulty of distinguishing the various blood diseases in infancy.

Among the cases reported under this name are some which might be any one of the following list: Pernicious anæmia, secondary anæmia with leucocytosis, Hodgkin's disease, lymphatic leukæmia, and probably splenic-myelogenous leukæmia.

(a) Most of the few reported cases of pernicious anæmia in infancy have shown moderate leucocytosis (as compared with adult blood), a fact which deprives us of one of the means of distinguishing the disease from secondary anæmia. The reports as to nucleated corpuscles very rarely separate normoblasts from megaloblasts, and we have no way, therefore, of being sure on this important point. The high color index and large diameter of the red cells are occasionally seen in other anæmias of infancy and are not always present in pernicious cases. The great fatality of all kinds of anæmia in infancy prevents our calling a case *pernicious* because of a fatal termination. Enlargements of liver and spleen occur in many cases of each type of infantile anæmia, and occasionally in pernicious anæmia of adults. They do not, therefore, exclude pernicious anæmia in infancy.

Bearing these facts in mind, it is evident that some of Luzet's cases of "anæmia infantum pseudoleukæmica" may have been pernicious anæmia. Von Jaksch's own cases may have been either (a) Hodgkin's disease with leucocytosis, (b) grave secondary anæmia with leucocytosis (Monti and Berggrün), or (c) leukæmia.

(a) Hodgkin's disease, which v. Limbeck finds to be very common in infancy, may affect the liver and spleen and not the external lymph glands, and may be accompanied by anæmia and leucocytosis such as v. Jaksch describes. Epstein considers that this is the case, and denies the existence of any such disease as the anæmia infantum pseudoleukæmica.

(b) As any anæmia secondary to rickets or syphilis may have enlarged spleen and liver and marked leucocytosis, we cannot tell from v. Jaksch's description that we are not dealing in his cases with secondary anæmia.

(c) Since v. Jaksch does not give any accurate differential

count of the leucocytes, there may have been large numbers of myelocytes in his cases for all we know, or an overwhelming percentage of lymphocytes, *i.e.*, either type of leukæmia.

One of the cases reported by Rotch as "anæmia infantum pseudoleukæmica" had 80 per cent of lymphocytes in a leucocyte count of 116,500, the ratio of white to red cells being 1:11, and the nucleated corpuscles abundant. The external lymph glands as well as the liver and spleen were enlarged. How such a case is to be distinguished from lymphatic leukæmia without autopsy I cannot see. Large numbers of nucleated corpuscles with mitoses (present in this case) are to be found in any anæmia of infancy where the red cells, as in this case, have sunk as low as 1,311,500, and therefore do not exclude leukæmia.

Von Jaksch protests that his cases are not secondary to rickets or any other disease, but Fischl[1] in a careful study of all the published cases finds that out of a total of eighteen cases, sixteen had severe rickets and two hereditary syphilis.

The writings of Raudnitz, Ebstein, Felsenthal, Fischl, and v. Limbeck, which deny the separate existence of the anæmia infantum pseudoleukæmica, are convincing to me, and are reinforced by the few cases of bad anæmia in children which I have seen. We must distribute the cases of anæmia with leucocytosis and large spleen under pernicious anæmia, secondary anæmia, and leukæmia.

But our problem is not yet nearly solved. All we have gained is the belief that v. Jaksch's new disease does *not* help us to classify these doubtful cases. The difficulty is still very great. The following cases reported by Dr. Vickery in the *Medical News* for December, 1897, illustrate this:

CASE I.—A male child of sixteen months with symptoms of grave anæmia, greatly enlarged spleen and slightly enlarged liver, showed the following figures: Red cells, 2,500,000; white cells, 22,000. Differential count of 500 cells showed: Lymphocytes, 53.8 per cent (46.2 of the smaller type); polymorphonuclear cells, 29.4 per cent; eosinophiles, 6.2 per cent; myelocytes, 10 per cent.

While counting these, 147 nucleated red corpuscles were seen, of which 21 were normoblasts, 50 megaloblasts, and 47 microblasts; 6 showed mitosis in their nuclei.

The child died shortly after without any complication or

[1] Fischl Zeit. f. Heilkunde, 1892.

intercurrent disease. No autopsy. No evidence of rickets or syphilis or other previous disease.

CASE II.—Young infant with enlarged external lymph glands and very large spleen.   July 14th, 1897—Red cells, 4,300,000; white cells, 31,000; hæmoglobin, 60 per cent; polymorphonuclear neutrophiles, 57.5 per cent; small lymphocytes, 26 per cent; large lymphocytes, 15 per cent; eosinophiles, 0.5 per cent; myelocytes, 1 per cent.

One or two nucleated red corpuscles in every field.   Out of 100 of them 89 were large and 11 small.   Many showed mitosis. Polychromatophilic forms numerous.   July 19th—Seventeen megaloblasts seen while counting 1,000 white cells.   Blood is otherwise about the same.   The case was lost sight of and not traced.

Now I see no reason for supposing these cases to represent a new type of disease, and yet I cannot feel perfectly safe in classifying them as primary anæmia, secondary anæmia, or leukæmia.

(a) Primary or pernicious anæmia should have a lower count of red cells.   The percentage of myelocytes in the first case (ten per cent) is higher than in any other case of pernicious anæmia on record, though in one adult case with autopsy I found 9.2 per cent with a leucocytosis of 12,500, or 1,150 myelocytes per cubic millimetre, against 2,200 per cubic millimetre in this case.

(b) It is hard to call an anæmia secondary which kills with no complications and when there is no evidence of any disease to which it can be secondary.

(c) For splenic-myelogenous leukæmia the total leucocyte count and the percentage of myelocytes are very small in either case.   Still the leucocyte count may drop very low in leukæmia even without any inflammatory complication.   Such a case is reported by Osler, in which the leucocytes fell to 7,500, of which only 300, or four per cent, were myelocytes.

Hayem (loc. cit., page 864) in a ten months' child counted 2,712,500 red and 33,000 white cells, almost the same figures as in the case just quoted.   [Hayem unfortunately gives no differential count, but apparently considers the case leukæmic because of the enormous number of nucleated red cells, many with mitoses.]

Morse's case of leukæmia in infancy had 2,900,000 red and 48,000 white cells.   Twenty-one and four-tenths per cent of the leucocytes, or about 10,000, were myelocytes. The same abundance of nucleated red cells (some with mitoses) were here present as in Hayem's case, so that there is evidently nothing peculiar in their presence in the disease described by v. Jaksch, as Luzet supposed.

These cases show that leukæmia may at certain periods present just such a blood picture as was present in the above-quoted case and that the number of leucocytes in the leukæmia of infants may be no greater than that in any anæmia with the leucocytosis so common in children.

It seems to me the most natural conclusion to be deduced from these facts is that we meet with cases in infancy *which are apparently intermediate between leukæmia and pernicious anæmia.* I have pointed out elsewhere that there are many points of resemblance between the two diseases. The case of leukæmia reported by Osler showed at one period—the period of remission—a fall in the number of leucocytes and in the percentage of myelocytes till the blood was practically that of pernicious anæmia.

Dr. Rotch's case (above quoted) is another in which the diagnosis seems to lie somewhere intermediate between the two diseases, anæmia and leukæmia.

The case which I have quoted above seems to me on the whole nearer to the type of pernicious anæmia than of leukæmia, and Dr. Rotch's nearer to the latter than to the former; but each is really intermediate, *so far as the blood goes,* between the two diseases. I have no intention of suggesting that the organic lesions in these cases are intermediate between leukæmia and pernicious anæmia. It is simply the blood that is so.

Engel's case, reported in Virchow's *Archiv,* Vol. 135, suggests the same thing. He calls the case one of "*pseudo-pernicious anæmia.*" Meylocytes were abundant.

Polymorphous Condition.

This illustrates that "polymorphous" condition of the blood which v. Jaksch supposed to be characteristic of the anæmia infantum pseudoleukæmica. The same thing was very marked in all the bad cases of anæmia which I have seen, including the case above mentioned, and a case of true leukæmia in a girl of eight. The impression one gets from the field of a stained specimen is that *no two white corpuscles are alike.* Every species is subdivided into several sub-varieties and all stages of degeneration are to be seen in each variety. But this is characteristic of any very severe infantile anæmia and not of any single type.

LEUKÆMIA.

In Morse's careful article of August, 1894 (*Boston Med. and Surg. Journal*), twenty cases of leukæmia in infancy are collected. As he rightly says, probably most of these cases were not genuine. Only one of them includes a differential count, and this is in a lymphatic case. Morse's is the only one of the splenic-myelogenous type on record in which the diagnosis is made reasonably certain by a color analysis. Fischl in 1892 said that there was *no* case on record with a differential count.

A case was seen in 1890 by Dr. F. C. Shattuck, which was apparently acute, the symptoms appearing only six weeks before death. Cover-glass preparations examined by W. S. Thayer showed a ratio of about 1 white to 20 red cells. The differential count[1] showed: Small lymphocytes, 97.9 per cent; large lymphocytes, .7 per cent; polynuclear cells, 1.4 per cent; eosinophiles, .08 per cent.

The other case reported by Morse has been mentioned above.

Charon and Giratea[2] have recently reported a case in a child of eight with 880,000 red cells, 305,000 white cells, and 39 per cent of hæmoglobin. It was apparently of the myelocyte type. E. Müller thinks that there are about five other (German) cases on record, all of acute leukæmia and all with a similar blood count, though in some the large lymphocytes (without neutrophilic granules) have been described as "myelocytes."

Müller[3] has lately reported with great care three cases of leukæmia, all of them in boys four years old—all apparently acute, all of the gastro-intestinal type—*i.e.*, the glands and follicles throughout the whole length of the alimentary tract being

[1] Reported by Thayer in the Boston Medical and Surgical Journal, 189?, vol. 128, p. 183.
[2] Bull. d. Soc. Roy. d. Sciences Méd., etc., Bruxelles, 1897, No. 7.
[3] Jahrbuch für Kinderheilk., 1896, vol. 43.

the chief seats of infiltration, though the liver and spleen were also enlarged. The counts were as follows:

	CASE I.				CASE II.	CASE III.
	April 30th.	May 1st.	May 2d.	May 3d.		
Red cells............	1,508,000	1,684,000	1,362,000	1,232,000	2,290,000	1,308,000
White cells..........	109,500	93,800	46,000	6,800	206,000	420,000
Hæmoglobin........	40%	....	....	Death.	25%	
Polymorphonuclear neutrophiles		2%		Many.	1%	.7
Small lymphocytes[1]..	85% (8-10 μ diameter).			Few.	15%	2.
Large lymphocytes ..		13%		Few.	84%	97.3
Eosinophiles	....			Many.	....	.01
Normoblasts.........	Few.				Two normoblasts seen in counting 1,135 leucocytes.	Seven seen in counting 1,118 leucocytes.
Megaloblasts........	Few.					

[1] All with large pale nuclei.

APPENDIX.

NEUSSER'S PERINUCLEAR BASOPHILIC GRANULES.

Using the following modification of Ehrlich's tricolor mixture, Neusser' believes that he can bring out certain characteristics in the leucocytes of value in diagnosis and prognosis.

	Acid fuchsin	50 c. c.
Saturated aqueous solution of	Orange G	70 "
	Methyl green..........	80 "
Distilled water		150 "
Absolute alcohol.....................................		80 "
Glycerin...		20 "

Cover slips stained with this mixture show in certain diseases (*e.g.*, gout, leukæmia) a grouping of dark blue-stained granules around the nuclei of the mononuclear leucocytes and over and around the nuclei of polymorphonuclear leucocytes. These granules appear to take up only the basic part of the tri-color mixture.

For Neusser's conclusions regarding the meaning of these granules, the reader is referred to pages 258 and 318. The researches of Futcher have in my opinion utterly disproved Neusser's claims. The granules are of no known clinical significance and certainly have no direct relation to gout or any other alloxuric diathesis. I have a triple stain (*not* made up for the purpose) which brings out Neusser's granules in *every* blood, normal or abnormal.

[1] Wien. klin. Woch., 1894, No. 39.

PART VII.

EXAMINATION OF THE SERUM.

CHAPTER XIII.

THE CLUMP REACTION.

GENERAL DESCRIPTION.

ALTHOUGH this phenomenon is to be obtained in various infections, natural as well as experimental, and with various body fluids, I shall describe as a typical case of it the reaction which takes place when the blood serum of a patient ill with typhoid fever is added in certain proportions (*vide infra*) to a young bullion culture of well-certified and virulent typhoid bacilli. In a drop of such a mixture, examined between slide and cover-glass[1] with a magnification of 300 diameters or more (an immersion lens is not necessary), we notice, as soon as the serum and culture are mixed, *either* a marked slowing of the progressive movements of the bacilli *or* an unequal distribution of them in the different parts of the preparation, some parts showing the bacilli closely crowded, while in others they are more scattered. Whichever of these changes occurs first, the slowing of locomotion or the tendency to grouping, the other soon follows, and then both processes go on together, as admirably described by Biggs and Park:[2]

"Some of the bacilli soon cease all progressive movement, and it will be seen that they are gathering together in small groups of two or more, the individual bacilli being still somewhat separated from each other. Gradually they close up the spaces between them, and clumps are formed. According to the

[1] Hanging-drop preparations are often recommended, but a simple slide and cover-glass are as good for the purposes of this reaction.

[2] American Journal of the Medical Sciences, March, 1897.

completeness of the reaction, either all the bacilli may finally become clumped and immobilized or only a small portion of them, the rest remaining freely motile, and even those clumped may appear to be struggling for freedom. With blood containing a large amount of the agglutinating substances all gradations

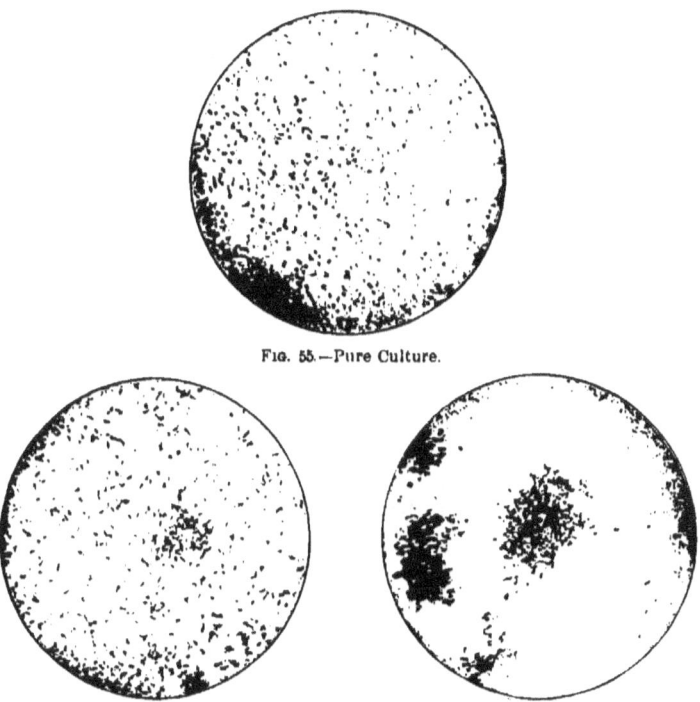

FIG. 55.—Pure Culture.

FIG. 56.—Partial Reaction. FIG. 57.—Typical Clumping.

in the intensity of the reaction may be observed, from those shown in a marked and immediate reaction to those appearing in a late and indefinite one, by simply varying the proportion of blood added to the culture fluid" (see Figs. 55, 56, and 57).

The process may go on gradually and be much more distinct at the end of half an hour.

The groups or clumps above described constitute the important part of the reaction for diagnostic purposes. Of the loss of motility more will be said later.

26

The clumps may hang together for a long time. They have been observed unchanged for one hundred and forty-four hours. On the other hand, they may be dissolved in a few hours and the bacilli regain their motility.

In watching the formation of the clumps it is easy to see that the bacilli are positively attracted to each other and do not drift passively into a heap. The loss of motility is not the cause of the clumping, as they often begin to approach each other while in vigorous motion. The power of locomotion is lost much sooner than are the squirming and spinning motions, which often persist among the bacilli in the peripheral parts of the clumps as well as outside them.

The clumps tend to adhere to the under side of the cover-glass.

Specimens can be fixed and stained with the bacilli in clumps —contrasting strongly with the even distribution of the bacilli in ordinary stained preparations.

TECHNIQUE OF THE CLUMP REACTION IN TYPHOID FEVER.

Our account of the methods of obtaining the clump reaction may be divided into the following parts:

1. The body fluids to be used and the methods of obtaining them.
2. The cultures.
3. Dilution and the time limit.

1. THE BODY FLUIDS TO BE USED.

Experiments have proved that the reaction can be obtained with the following fluids:

(a) The whole blood, fluid or dried.

(b) The plasma and serum, fluid or dried.

(c) The fluid obtained by blistering.

(d) The fluid *normally* present in the pericardium, pleura, peritoneum, and joints; *not* in rapidly accumulated effusions.

(e) The *milk* and colostrum of women suffering from typhoid during lactation.

(f) *Pus* from persons suffering with typhoid—whether the bacilli of Eberth are present in the pus or not.

(*g*) *Tears*—naturally (*i.e.*, gradually) secreted. If secreted in response to the irritation of ammonia fumes, the tears do not produce clumping.

(*h*) Some observers also find it in the fluid of œdema and in the bile. Others do not.

(*i*) The clumping persists in the above-named fluids after death and even in putrefaction. The "juice" of the spleen, kidneys, and rarely of the liver, will give the reaction feebly.

(*j*) Though present in the placental blood of pregnant typhoid patients, it does not usually exist in the fœtus.

The saliva, gastric juice, and sweat do not produce the reaction, so far as known. The aqueous humor sometimes does.

The urine and fæces sometimes do and sometimes do not give it, but these excretions in normal persons may also produce the reaction, so that they cannot be made clinically available.

Of all these fluids, the blood, the serum, and the fluid of blisters are the only ones used in clinical work, both because of their greater convenience, and because the clumping power is much more marked in the blood and blister fluid than in any of the others.

1. Use of the Whole Blood—Fluid.

The advantages of this method are (*a*) its quickness, and (*b*) the small amount of blood (*one drop*) sufficient for the test.

Its *disadvantages* are (*a*) that the corpuscles interfere slightly with the fields in which the reaction is to be watched, and (*b*) that they sometimes lead to the formation of false clumps ("pseudo-amas"), which simulate those present in the real clump reaction, and lead to false inferences. Both these objections are trifling, however, as the corpuscles can be excluded by waiting a minute or two until they settle, leaving a clear liquid above in which the reaction can be observed. The false clumps are rarely seen, and can be differentiated from the true by careful technique (see below).

I have used this method in many cases and always found it satisfactory and convenient. Widal, McWeeney, Delépine, Coleman, and others have employed it with success. It is most suitable for the "quick method" (see page 406), and is chiefly employed in this way.

Procedure.—Suck up some water with a medicine-dropper and

expel ten drops of it into a watch-glass. Then empty and dry
the dropper, draw up from the watch-glass the ten drops just
expelled, and mark with a file on the side of the dropper the
point up to which the ten-drop column extends. Mark also the
point to which one drop (expelled and then sucked up again as
before) will rise.

Ten drops of the bouillon culture of the bacilli to be used
are then expelled into each of several small test-tubes, and one
of these tubes is carried to the bedside. After pricking the
ear as if for blood examination[1] (see page 6), put the end of the
medicine-dropper into the blood drop, and carefully draw back
the rubber bulb (which has been previously pushed down over
the glass part of the dropper) until the blood rises to the mark
for one drop. Wipe from the outside of the dropper any blood
that may adhere there and then expel the drop into one of the
little test-tubes containing the ten drops of bouillon culture. In
this way blood can be taken for examination from a dozen
patients in as many minutes.

2. *Whole Blood—Dried.*

This method, though previously described and tested by
Widal, was first put into effect in large numbers of cases by
Wyatt Johnson, of Montreal, for the use of the Board of Health
of Quebec, by whom specimens of dried blood sent by mail were
examined and diagnoses returned as with diphtheria cultures.
It was subsequently employed on a large scale by the Boards of
Health of New York and Chicago.

The advantages of the method are (*a*) the ease and quickness
with which the blood can be obtained, (*b*) the convenience for
transportation by mail, and (*c*) that it does not deteriorate or
become contaminated by bacterial growth, as specimens of fluid
blood or serum are so apt to do. Its clumping power is fully
equal to that of the serum *in most cases.*[2]

These advantages are very great and would surely lead to the

---

[1] Squeezing and milking the ear are of no harm in this procedure and
enable us to get on with a trifling and painless puncture.

[2] Widal and Delépine think the fluid serum is slightly more powerful than
the dried blood. Johnson admits that in one-tenth of the cases the serum is
the more powerful. I have obtained reactions with the dried blood in only
seven-eighths of the cases in which I got them with the fluid serum.

immediate and universal adoption of this method were it not for the following serious drawbacks:

(a) It is *difficult to measure the amount of blood* to be used in the test. This is important, because, as we shall see later, a positive reaction means not simply a clumping, but *a clumping in a 1 : 10 dilution of the blood*, to get which we need to know just how much blood we are dealing with. When we take the blood from a patient ourselves we can use the marked medicine dropper, as above described, but when blood is received through the mails for examination or taken by any one who does not measure it in some way, we cannot accurately gauge the dilution.

(b) It is agreed by all who have used the method extensively that the clumping may occur with the blood of healthy people and hence confuse our inferences. Whether these " false clumps" are due, as Widal supposes, to masses of fibrin and débris in which the bacilli become entangled, or whether they are formed in the ordinary way, there can be no doubt that they occur occasionally when dried blood is used. Johnson has succeeded in avoiding such errors in his own work by the use of attenuated culture (*vide infra*).

These objections have led most observers to prefer the fluid serum, but when we have not the apparatus necessary for collecting and preserving fluid serum, or when such apparatus could not be transported, the method is of great value.

Procedure.—The blood should be dried either upon a glass slide or on a piece of glazed paper or card. Any absorbent substance is less available. Glass is easier to sterilize than paper. Several large drops should be placed in different parts of the glass or paper and *thoroughly* dried.

If paper has been used, we cut out the dried blood drop with a pair of scissors, keeping close to the blood all round, and drop it into a test-tube containing one or two drops of water, in which with some sharp-pointed instrument we mix the dried blood, freeing it as well as possible from the paper.

To the liquid so obtained add eight or nine drops of the bouillon culture of bacilli and proceed in the ordinary way. Or we may drop the fragment of paper holding the blood directly into ten drops of bouillon culture—using the bouillon itself to soak off the blood from the paper.

When the blood is collected on glass, it may be dissolved by putting water on the glass and rubbing the dried blood in it until a decided red tinge is obtained. A drop of this mixture is then diluted and mixed with the bouillon culture. Johnson does not pay much attention to the dilution of the mixture of dried blood and water, before examination, as he does not find it necessary with his attenuated cultures. If necessary blood can be collected in wire loops of a given size, fairly accurate dilutions can be made.

A. The Fluid Serum—Quick Method.

The ear is pricked in the ordinary way and about twenty drops are forced out by strong squeezing. The blood is received in a small (preferably two-inch) test-tube, with the edge of which each drop is scraped off the ear; or we may suck the blood into a capillary pipette and expel it again into a test-tube or other receptacle. There is no need of cleansing the skin or sterilizing the test tubes in this method of procedure, as the whole process is finished up so rapidly that there is no time for contaminating organisms to grow.

The blood when collected may be at once centrifugalized, and the plasma used for the test, or we may wait till clotting occurs and use the serum. When blood is collected in test-tubes, it is convenient to free the edges of the clot from the tube all round with some sharp instrument, so that the serum may not be pinned down underneath the clot, as it often is. If this is done, a drop of serum can be had within two or three minutes, and is then mixed with ten drops of bouillon culture, as above described, and examined at once between slide and cover-glass.

(Dried serum can be used in the same way as dried blood, but has no special advantages and has not been frequently employed by any observer.)

B. The Fluid Serum—Slow Method.

This was the way originally described by Widal, or rather applied by him to the diagnosis of disease.

The serum must be collected *aseptically*, and many have therefore preferred to take it from a vein of the elbow, which is punctured with a sterile syringe, as described on page 47.

Durham cleans the skin of the ear with a two-per-cent solution of lysol, sucks blood into a sterile pipette, and blows it out again into a sterile test-tube to wait for clotting.

Or, if we desire to keep and transport the fluid serum, it is sucked into the bulb of a modified Pasteur's pipette (sterile), such as is shown in Fig. 58, which is then sealed by heat at the points A and B. In this way the serum will keep for an indefinite period and can be sent across the ocean, as was recently done at the request of the New York Health Department.

When we are ready to use the serum, one of the pointed ends of the sealed bulb is broken off and the serum expelled by gently warming the other end.

The serum aseptically collected by one of the above-described methods is then added:

1. To ten times its volume of bouillon culture of bacilli, i.e., eight drops to five cubic centimetres of culture, in a test-tube, which is then left from eight to twelve hours in the thermostat at 37° C.; or

2. The serum may be added to ten times its volume of pure *sterile* bouillon, and then a trace of the dry agar culture of bacilli added with a platinum loop and *thoroughly* mixed with the bouillon by rubbing the loop against the inside of the test-tube, which is then kept twenty-four hours at 37° C. If the first of these ways is used, we get the effect of the serum on the fully grown bacilli; in the second way—which usually needs fully twenty-four hours—it works on the nascent and immature organisms.

FIG. 58.

Whichever method is used, we find that within from eight to twenty-four hours a remarkable change takes place in the appearance of the culture when serum from a case, e.g., of typhoid fever, is added to typhoid bacilli, nascent or full-grown. The uniform turbidity of the bouillon is gone and the liquid is either clear with an abundant flocculent sediment at the bottom of the tube, or is filled with coarse whitish particles separated from each other by clear bouillon. The latter change may take place the instant the serum is added to the culture, but usually needs from six to eight hours, and the full end reaction is often not completed till twenty-four hours elapse. Fraenkel finds the reaction most marked in twelve to fourteen hours—less so in twenty-four.

A control tube containing the same proportions of the same culture and of a healthy person's serum should always be put into the thermostat along with the serum to be tested. Occasionally in such a control tube fine but visible whitish dust forms, *but such dust usually disappears later of itself, or can be dissolved* and the original diffuse turbidity produced *by shaking the tube*, while shaking a tube in which the true clump reaction has taken place will not break up the clumps nor restore the original turbidity.

As above suggested, the microscopical examination of the "dust" seen in such a test, or of the precipitate formed at the bottom of the tube, shows it to be made up of clumps of bacilli similar to those seen in the quick method, but generally larger.

The reaction is considerably less typical when the serum used is dark-colored, but the effects of shaking the tube and the comparison with the control usually enable us to decide.

Some precipitate and clumping may occur in cases not typhoid: (*a*) when the bouillon has not been filtered and contains sediment, in which the bacilli may become entangled; (*b*) when a large amount of the dry culture is added (in trying the slow method on nascent bacilli) and not thoroughly mixed with the bouillon; (*c*) in case the platinum loop is not quite cooled before the agar culture is taken upon it; (*d*) in case the culture is impure or the serum not aseptic.

3. *Blister Fluid.*

Biggs and Park find the fluid obtained by blistering the most satisfactory. A fly-blister the size of a five-cent piece is applied, and in from six to eighteen hours a blister has formed. The serum from the blister is collected with a capillary tube, the ends of which are then sealed. This serum is admirably clear and free from blood corpuscles and answers the purpose well.

This method has never been extensively used by other observers, except Puglieri.

Advantages and Disadvantages of the " Quick Method" and of the " Slow Method."—In favor of the quick method are: (1) *its quickness*, (2) the small amount of blood needed, and (3) absence of any need for asepsis and of any danger of contamination.

Against it are: (a) the occasional occurrence of pseudo-reactions or false clumps, which will be discussed on page 418; (b) that it needs a microscopic examination instead of being evident to the naked eye, as in the slow method;[1] (c) that it needs watching and cannot be left to "go on of itself."

In favor of the slow method are:

(1) That to some observers it appears more reliable and less apt to give pseudo-reactions.

(2) That it can be seen with the naked eye.

(3) That we do not need to watch it but simply to note the results at the end of from eight to twenty-four hours.

Against it are its slowness, the danger of contamination, the need of a large quantity of blood and of a thermostat.[2]

On the whole the great majority of observers prefer the quick method, and it has been used in three-fourths of the reported experiments. My own experience has been exclusively with the quick method.

Breuer, Catrin, and Vanlair and Beco are the only ones who distinctly prefer the twenty-four-hour method in all cases.

2. The Cultures of Typhoid Bacilli to be Used.

1. The stock cultures grow best on agar.

2. Ordinary peptone bouillon, free from sediment, is the best medium for the test culture. It should be just on the verge of litmus acidity, giving no blue to the red paper and requiring 3.5 per cent of normal alkali to render it neutral to phenol-phthalein.

3. All observers agree that the cultures should be *young*—that is, that the transplantation to bouillon should have taken place not more than from twelve to twenty-four hours before the culture is used. Many observers find even the twenty-four-hour culture too old and prefer a twelve- to twenty-hours-old culture in all cases.

4. The virulence and motility of the culture are very important. Most observers agree that the more virulent the culture the more readily and characteristically it is clumped by typhoid serum. Biggs and Park noticed that one culture of peculiarly

---

[1] Greene states that with the quick method a mottling of the specimen can be seen with the naked eye.

[2] Pick states that no thermostat is needed, and that sedimentation takes place readily at room temperature.

great virulence recently received from Pfeiffer of Berlin worked much better in their cases than any other of the cultures used. I have repeatedly noticed that cultures recently taken from autopsies on patients who had died during the acme of the fever were much more easily clumped than those taken in autopsies on patients who had succumbed late, after the temperature had been normal for some time. I have also noticed that virulent cultures grown for a long time in the thermostat with weekly transplantations gradually lost a good deal of their susceptibility to the clumping power of typhoid sera.

Presumably these changes mean a loss of virulence in the culture, especially as they have always been accompanied by a diminution in the rapidity of motion in the bacilli. Cultures fresh from an autopsy usually show *furious* motility, the bacilli darting about like a swarm of insects, but after repeated transplantations and long sojourn in the thermostat a good deal of this motility is gradually lost. *Cultures kept at room temperature preserve their motility for much longer periods.*

For those who have no opportunity to test the virulence of organisms on animals, the motility is the best guide to virulence, and the rule should be: *Among the available cultures select that having the most rapid motility.*

4. Certain cultures contain small clumps of bacilli *before any serum has been added to them.* This is a very important point and has doubtless misled many. In consequence of this possibility every culture must be examined *each time* that a test is made. It is not sufficient to examine each culture once for all, as cultures vary slightly from day to day and also vary in different portions of the culture tube. For instance, ten drops taken from the middle of the bouillon may be found free from clumps, while if the next ten drops be taken from the surface or from the bottom of the liquid, they may contain clumps.

This point has been strongly insisted on by Widal, Rénon, and others.

5. It is hardly necessary to say that the cultures used must have been submitted to all the regular tests for the recognition of the typhoid bacillus, and that the greatest care must be used to avoid their contamination.

The Use of Suspensions or Emulsions of the Bacilli instead of Cultures.

A few observers—particularly Durham and Grüber—have preferred to use a mixture of small bits of solid agar culture and bouillon instead of bouillon cultures. The majority of writers prefer cultures.

The Use of Attenuated Cultures.

Johnson finds that with his methods of technique (dried blood and no definite dilution) pseudo-reactions were not uncommon with the blood of healthy people.

He avoids this by using attenuated cultures—*i.e.*, old stock agar cultures kept at room temperature and not transplanted more than once a month, from which he planted his bouillon cultures. This gives a bacillus of reduced virulence and slow, gliding motion, which is clumped far less readily than the virulent varieties. Bouillon cultures of this kind from twelve to twenty-four hours old he found to react in fifteen minutes with all typhoid sera and not with other sera even after forty-eight hours' waiting.

Durham, Biggs and Park, and Delépine, on the contrary, found such cultures unsatisfactory, in that it was not possible to avoid pseudo-reactions with sera of diseases not typhoid. I have been equally unsuccessful with this method, and believe with Biggs and Park that the most virulent cultures are the most reliable, if fluid blood or serum is used. When dried blood *must* be used, the attenuation of cultures as advised by Johnson is probably the best plan.

The Clump Reaction with Dead Bacilli.

One of the most remarkable and interesting features of the clump reaction is the possibility of obtaining it with bacilli that have been killed by heat or by formol.

Widal observed that bouillon cultures of typhoid bacilli exposed to a temperature of 57°–60° C. for one-half to three-quarters of an hour lost scarcely any of their susceptibility to the clumping action of typhoid serum, though they are quite dead. Higher temperatures (70°–120° C.) take away more and more of the susceptibility to clumping and *also cause the formation of false clumps without the addition of any serum whatever.*

Similarly one drop of ordinary formol mixed with one hundred and fifty drops of bouillon culture of Eberth's bacilli kills them, but apparently "embalms" them, so that their susceptibility to clumping is scarcely if at all lessened, even after the lapse of five months.

The bacilli gradually sink to the bottom of the tube, but when shaken up distribute themselves evenly throughout the medium and can be used like fresh cultures for diagnostic purposes. Bordet has noted the same thing with cultures of the cholera-vibrio killed with chloroform.

These facts seem at first sight to conflict with the statement made above, that fresh, motile, and virulent cultures are best, and that old ones are not reliable. But it may be, as Widal supposes, that the rapid action of heat or formol on virulent cultures preserves unchanged the power which prolonged growth in old media destroys. If this be true, it will enable us to dispense with our thermostat and careful nursing of cultures, since a single first-rate culture can be thus "embalmed" and preserved for use at all times and under all circumstances.

Widal's results with this method have not yet been confirmed by others.

3. DILUTION AND THE TIME LIMIT.

I. Dilution.

We have mentioned without explanation in various parts of this chapter that the blood serum or other fluids used must be diluted with at least ten times their volume of bouillon culture before any observation is made as to their action on the bacilli of typhoid fever.

The reasons for this dilution and for the proportions 1:10 are the following:

It has been found, as mentioned above, that the mere formation of clumps in bouillon cultures of Eberth's bacilli is not a power exclusively possessed by typhoid serum. The serum of persons suffering from other diseases and even of healthy persons will form clumps exactly like those formed by typhoid bacilli, *provided it is not diluted.* The only known peculiarity of the typhoid serum is that its clumping power is *greater* than that of other diseases, and persists in spite of dilution, while the sera of diseases other than typhoid lose their power to clump typhoid bacilli when diluted ten times or more.

II. Time Limit.

But even this statement must be further limited. The sera of various other diseases, and of healthy persons, will sometimes clump typhoid bacilli *even in a 1:10 dilution, provided we give them time enough.* We must therefore limit the period within which a serum must "come up to the scratch" and do its work, if it is to be considered a typhoid serum.

Following Grüber and Durham, a time limit of *one-half hour* has been adopted by Grünbaum, Block, Haedke, Park, and others.

All that these more or less arbitrary figures stand for is this: that *hitherto no one has reported any considerable number of cases in which the serum of any disease or of healthy persons has clumped typhoid bacilli within one-half hour, when diluted 1:10 and used with unimpeachable technique.*

Johnson finds dilution unnecessary with his methods of preparing the cultures, and Widal only lately has admitted the necessity of a time limit, but the majority of careful and non-partisan observers are agreed that these precautions are necessary unless attenuated cultures are used. If at any time cases are reported in which, despite these precautions, a clumping of typhoid bacilli has occurred with non-typhoidal sera, it will be necessary to raise the dilution to 1 : 15 or 1 : 20. Indeed there are many who think it should now be placed at one of these two figures or even higher. Many German observers prefer to use a dilution of 1 : 40 or 1 : 50 and a time limit of one or two hours. This amounts to about the same thing as 1 : 10 dilution with a limit of fifteen minutes.

The clump reaction in typhoid fever is to be considered specific and pathognomonic only in the sense that it occurs more readily and in presence of greater dilution in typhoid than in any condition yet reported. (For details and exceptions on these points see page 370.)

The serum of most cases of typhoid fever during the second

week will clump typhoid bacilli when diluted 1:40, and many
sera preserve the power even at 1:100 or higher. Widal has
seen it as high as 1:12,000. The following table .from Biggs
and Park illustrates these points well:

Case.	History, symptoms, and diagnosis at time of taking blood specimens.	Corrected diagnosis on completion of illness.	Reaction of bacilli in broth cultures to serum in different dilutions.		Reaction.
			Amount of serum.	Amount broth culture.	
1	Adult; sick four weeks, continuous high fever; pleurisy; "tuberculosis" with possibility of typhoid.	Tuberculosis.	1	1	Not appreciable.
2	Boy; sick two weeks; continued moderate fever, abating when test was made; prostration, constipation; no typhoid symptoms except fever and prostration; "atypical typhoid fever."	Uncertain.	1	1	Not appreciable.
3	Adult; symptoms of acute articular rheumatism only; "acute articular rheumatism."	Acute rheumatism.	1 1 1	1 4 9	Delayed moderate. Delayed very slight. Not appreciable.
4	Adult; just convalescent after sickness giving characteristic symptoms and physical signs of pneumonia; "pneumonia."	Pneumonia.	1 1 1 1	1 4 9 19	Immediate marked. Delayed moderate. Delayed slight. Not appreciable.
5	Adult; continued high fever; enlarged spleen; typhoid bacilli obtained from spleen; "typhoid fever."	Typhoid fever.	1 1 1	1 4 9	Immediate. Delayed incomplete. Delayed very slight.
6	Adult; relapse after four weeks of continuous fever with typhoid symptoms; "relapse after typhoid fever"	Typhoid fever.	1 1 1 1 1	1 10 50 100 200	Marked immediate. Marked immediate. Marked immediate. Delayed moderate. Delayed slight.
7	Adult; seven days continued high fever; typhoid symptoms; two days later an atypical rash; "typhoid fever."	Typhoid fever.	1 1 1 1 1	1 9 49 99 199	Marked immediate. Marked immediate. Marked immediate. Delayed but marked. Delayed moderate.

The Microscopic Examination.

An artificial light is preferable. The use of hanging-drop
preparations is unnecessary, as a simple slide and cover-glass is
satisfactory. A hanging-drop cell may be extemporized by
cementing with marine glue a small brass curtain ring to a slide,
and inverting the cover-glass within it, as advised by Stokes.

SERO-DIAGNOSIS OF TYPHOID.

I have collected over 3,000 cases of supposed typhoid fever in which the clump reaction was tested as above described either with the fluid or dried blood.   Of these, 95 per cent showed a serum reaction at some time in their course; 2,500 odd controls showed about 2 per cent of positive results in cases other than typhoid.   Altogether then about 5,500 cases have been tested.   If we leave out the reports of those whose experience covers less than 100 cases, we have left 4,339 cases observed by 18 physicians in which the percentage of error is 2 per cent only.

There seems to me no doubt of the fact that the serum reaction is present *in some part of the course* of 95 or more per cent of all cases of typhoid fever, and absent in 95 or more per cent of all other conditions.   But it is also true that it is absent in some part of the course of many cases of typhoid —usually in the earliest or latest days of the fever—and this fact makes it necessary to retest every case in which a negative result has been found, and even in some cases to make a considerable number of tests before a positive result is obtained.   My own experience covers 202 cases of typhoid, all but 7 of which were positive, and in 4 of these there was no opportunity of retesting.   In the last 108 cases, all of which were carefully retested, there has not been a single failure, though in some the reaction was very late.   Out of 376 controls one reacted like typhoid, a case of pernicious anæmia in a negro.

How early does the reaction appear?

Few of the many observers who have written on this point have discussed how the beginning of the disease is settled and what they mean, *e.g.*, by the "fifth day of the disease."   It might be dated from the first day of malaise and indisposition, from the nose-bleed or the beginning of headache, or from the time of going to bed.

Allowing for such serious uncertainties as this, we find that while the majority of observers record the sixth to eighth day as the earliest on which the reaction appears, there are quite a number of cases mentioned in which it was seen on the fourth or fifth day; a few record reactions present on the third day, and two or three on the second day.

As above mentioned, we have no way of knowing what the "second day" means in these cases.

In my own observations I have called *the first day in bed the first day of the disease* (though I am aware that many patients are sick some time before taking to bed), because it was the only date that could be definitely fixed in all cases. With this nomenclature I have found the reaction present on the first day in two cases and on the second in three cases.

Counting from the first day on which the patient felt sick *in any way*, the *fifth day* is the earliest reaction day in my series. In these figures we have always to remember that in no case was the blood tested at all previous to the day on which the positive test occurred, so that their meaning is: *In some cases* (what proportion of all is unknown) *the serum reaction occurs at least as soon as the fifth day of malaise or the first day in bed, and perhaps sooner.* Not infrequently the reaction antedates the appearance of rose spots, splenic enlargement, or the diazo reaction by several days. On the other hand, I have known the bacilli to be isolated from the stools before the serum reaction appeared; but this is rare.

Experiments on animals show that the clump reaction appears in the blood on the third to eighth day after inoculation with dead typhoid bacilli.

How late in the disease does the reaction last? The majority of observations agree that in mild cases the reaction may die out even before the end of the fever. On the other hand, the reaction usually lasts several months, and Widal found it still present after one year in 3 out of 22 cases in which he tried it. These 3 subjects had had very severe cases of typhoid three, seven, and nine years previously. It has been reported present twenty and even thirty years after the fever. Biggs and Park found the reaction more constant in the fourth week than at any other time—76 per cent of their cases tested between the thirtieth and sixtieth days still showed the reaction, and 5 of 8 cases still reacted after three to four months.

The reaction almost always persists in relapses, even to a second or third relapse, and occasionally it is present *only in relapse and not in the original attack at all.* Biggs and Park record a case in which the diagnosis was proved during the original attack by puncture of the spleen, which showed a pure culture of Eberth's bacilli, yet no serum reaction was present until the second day of the relapse. I have observed several similar cases, and quite frequently not found the reaction until convalescence. The failure to follow up such cases as these accounts for many negative reports. In one of Elsberg's cases the total duration of the clumping power in the blood was only eight days; in another only twelve days.

The continuance of the reaction after the fall of the temperature is no indication (as some have supposed) that relapse is coming, for in many such cases no relapse follows. Very frequently the reaction is absent on a given day though present the day before and after.

The Intensity of the Reaction.

Widal and others have studied the intensity of the reaction at different periods of the disease, judging by the amount of dilution which could be practised without destroying the power of a given serum.

Examples of this have already been given in the table on page 363. The majority of typhoids in the second and third week yield serum which will clump Eberth's bacilli when diluted 1 : 40 and many cases will do so even at 1 : 100. Strangely enough, some typhoid sera clump better when diluted 1 : 16 or more than when undiluted. This has been repeatedly noted by Grünbaum.

Widal and Sicard record clumping with a dilution of 1 : 12,000 and 1 : 1,800 and consider that in the active stages of the disease a dilution of 1 : 60 or 1 : 80 does not usually present the reaction, while in convalescence the power of the serum falls off gradually and is not always present even at 1 : 10.

Biggs and Park find one-half their typhoid cases furnish serum with the power to clump in 1 : 40 dilution by the end of the first week, and have occasionally noted the reaction even with a dilution of 1 : 200.

Jemma found the reaction most intense at the acme of the fever and greater during the evening exacerbation of fever than in the morning.

27

EFFECTS OF THE SERA OF OTHER DISEASES.

Negative results are reported in the following list of diseases experimented on as controls: Pneumonia, typhus, Malta fever, tuberculosis in its various forms, including miliary tuberculosis, tubercular meningitis, pneumococcus meningitis (purulent) and epidemic cerebro-spinal meningitis, diphtheria, influenza, ulcerative endocarditis, erysipelas, puerperal septicæmia, gonorrhœal septicæmia, measles and scarlet fever, tonsilitis, acute articular rheumatism, malaria, leprosy, syphilis, bronchitis, pleurisy with effusion, acute and chronic nephritis, mumps, otitis media, catarrhal jaundice, sciatica, acromegalia, hysterical vomiting, Graves' disease, gangrene of the lung, appendicitis, abscess and cirrhosis of the liver, acute febrile gastro-enteritis ("embarras gastrique"), cancer of the various organs, alveolar abscess with fever, osteomyelitis, bubo with fever, arthritis deformans, chronic laryngitis, intestinal obstruction, general peritonitis, leukæmia, Hodgkin's disease, pernicious anæmia, diarrhœa, chronic gastritis, gallstone colic with fever, dysentery, acute mania, stuporous melancholia, synovitis, neurasthenia, varicose veins, orchitis, suppurative thyroiditis, perinephritis, cystitis, pericarditis, empyema, brain abscess, valvular heart disease, diabetes, gas poisoning, alcoholism, and eclampsia.

The important diseases of this list, such as pneumonia, tuberculosis, meningitis, and typhus, have been tried many times. Biggs and Park got a positive result in one case said to be typhus. There is a chance of mistaken diagnosis here.

Positive Results of the Sera of Other Diseases with Typhoid Bacilli.

Many of the supposed contradictions of the law, that the *typhoid bacilli are clumped within one-half hour only by typhoid serum when a dilution of one part of serum to ten or more of culture is used,* are due to faulty technique. Such are probably the cases reported by Ferrand and Theoari (septicæmia), Villies and Battle (malaria), Gehrmann and Wynkoop (pneumonia, bronchitis, pleurisy), and Stern (otitis media).

On the other hand there are a few cases reported by careful observers in which a genuine clumping of typhoid bacilli has been caused by the sera of other diseases, viz.: Pernicious malaria, comatose, one case (Block); diabetic coma, one case (Block); jaundice, one case (Catrin); tubercular meningitis, one case (Jez), and a few more.

A case of malaria, reported by Catrin, with positive reaction of the serum on typhoid bacilli, was in a subject who had had typhoid five years before. In view of Widal's and Fraenkel's results, this cannot be counted an exception to the general law. The same is true of Grünbaum's much-quoted cases, which he reported *not* as exceptions but to emphasize the necessity of proper dilution. Using a proportion of 1:1 instead of 1:10, he got clumping of typhoid bacilli with the sera of jaundice (two cases), meningitis and bronchitis (one case each).

The cases reported by Johnson, Brannan, Thomas, Reed, and other observers, in which the dried blood of healthy persons and persons with various diseases other than typhoid has clumped typhoid bacilli, are probably owing to the uncertainties connected with that method of procedure.

In most cases in which the fluid serum was also tried it gave no reaction.

The discovery that the bacillus of psittacosis and the "bacillus enteritidis" of Gärtner are somewhat sensitive to the action of typhoid serum (see page 421) has led to the fear that infections due to those bacilli might be mistaken for typhoid, but this is wholly an assumption, as in the few cases of these infections which have been studied the serum has not affected typhoid bacilli.

Further, it is only by a concentrated artificial typhoid serum that the bacillus of Gärtner is clumped, and the clumping of the psittacosis bacillus is quite different from that of the typhoid bacillus, the clumps of the former being very small and few; with the twenty-four-hour method no precipitate forms.

Summary of Negative Results.

Out of over three thousand cases of various diseases not typhoid, not over a dozen have been proved to clump typhoid bacilli with proper technique. It is quite possible that further improvements in technique may enable us to prevent even this very small error.

EFFECTS OF TYPHOID SERUM ON OTHER BACILLI.

(a) On the Bacillus Coli Communis.

Any blood serum mixed 1 : 10 with a bouillon culture of colon bacilli may cause the formation of *small* clumps without considerable loss of motility. The effect of typhoid serum does not differ from that of other sera, and the clumps which it forms are much smaller and looser than those seen in the typical typhoid clump reaction. Different cultures of colon bacilli differ a good deal in their susceptibility to typhoid serum, and Vanlair and Beco consider that no difference can be made out in certain cases between its effects on typhoid bacilli or on colon bacilli. The majority of observers, however, find a decided difference, especially with the twenty-four-hour method. *Undiluted* typhoid serum acts more strongly on colon than on typhoid bacilli, according to Grünbaum.

Biggs and Park found that "a number of varieties of motile bacilli other than typhoid bacilli are clumped by the serum of persons suffering from typhoid fever, even when the serum is used in quite high dilutions."

Rodet noted that only a very slight effect is produced by typhoid serum on colon bacilli until a dilution of one part of serum to two of culture is reached.

Fraenkel tested a large number of colon cultures without getting any decided effect from the addition of typhoid serum.

Courmont found that some cultures of the colon bacillus are clumped by typhoid serum.

Widal saw no difference between the effect of typhoid serum and that of other sera on colon bacilli, but Vedel thinks that young cultures are better clumped by typhoid serum than by other sera.

Johnson, who studied a large number of cases, says: "A complete colon reaction we have found to be exceptional in ordinary typhoid, and its presence would indicate a condition of coli intoxication," which may be held to sum up the discussion up to the present time.

(b) On the Bacillus Enteritidis (Gärtner).

Grüber and Durham, using powerful artificial sera from animals immunized against Eberth's bacillus, were able to obtain a clumping of Gärtner's organisms. No experiments with human serum are recorded.

(c) On the Bacillus of Psittacosis.

Psittacosis is a disease affecting parrots and occasionally transferred by them to human beings. A bacillus has been found by Nocard in the marrow of the parrot's wing-bones which is considered the cause. Typhoid serum has an effect on bouillon cultures of this bacillus, which is to be distinguished quantitatively from the clumping of typhoid bacilli by typhoid serum; the heaps of psittacosis bacilli are much fewer and smaller, and in the twenty-four-hour method the turbidity of the cultures does not disappear.

(d) The Klebs-Loeffler Bacillus and Pus Cocci.

Courmont finds that typhoid serum clumps Klebs-Loeffler bacilli and staphylococci, but is without effect on the streptococcus and the bacillus pyocyaneus.

Summary of Clinical Evidence on the Sero-Diagnosis of Typhoid Fever.

The blood of over ninety-five per cent of all cases of typhoid shows a clumping power in some part of their course, but in at least half the cases this does not appear until the second week of the disease, while in a small number of cases it first appears in relapse or convalescence. The clumping power may disappear before the defervescence and may be present only eight days in all; as a rule it persists from the sixth or eighth day until convalescence is established.

In diseases other than typhoid a clump reaction is very rarely to be obtained, provided a dilution of at least 1:10 is used with a time limit of one-half hour. There is no one disease in which clumping is especially apt to occur.

Clinically the reaction is of considerable value, especially when the diagnosis is in doubt after the first week of the disease.

Sero-Diagnosis of Diseases Other than Typhoid.

1. *Cholera.*

Grüber and Durham first showed that human cholera serum would clump cholera vibrios, following the researches of Pfeiffer *in vivo* by demonstrating a similar reaction *in vitro*.

Achard and Bensaude have applied this to the actual diagnosis of cholera in man with considerable success. In fourteen cases, thirteen clumped readily; two of these were on the first day of the disease. Thirty control cases were negative. The presence of the pellicle renders it unsafe to use bouillon cultures except such as have no pellicle, for bits of it are much like true clumps. Suspensions of twenty-hour gelatin cultures are more convenient. The dilution and time limit are the same as in typhoid. Some cases will react even in 1:120 dilution. The reaction can be performed with dried blood and persists into convalescence (seven months or more).

2. *Pyocyaneus Infections.*

The bacillus pyocyaneus has been shown to be in all probability the cause of certain cases of dysentery, broncho-pneumonia, otitis media, nephritis, pericarditis, cystitis, and of a hemorrhagic septicæmia with enteritis in the new-born.

Roger and Charin found in 1889 that the bacillus pyocyaneus is serum of animals immunized against this bacillus. Durham repeated these observations in 1895 and confirmed them.

Here we have the clinical infection and laboratory clump-reaction experiments, but so far as I am aware no one has yet brought the two together or tried the serum of patients with pyocyaneus infections on cultures of the bacillus.

3. *Diphtheria.*

Widal reports no success in attempts at the sero-diagnosis of diphtheria, and Fraenkel has not been more successful. Nicolas and Charrin found that, although no true serum reaction could be obtained in diphtheria previous to antitoxin treatment, the injection of antitoxin produces in the patient's serum a decided clumping power over the Klebs-Loeffler bacilli within twenty-four hours of the time of injection. This is especially marked in the twenty-four-hour method, using the *nascent* bacilli, as described on page 407. The serum retains its clumping power for about two weeks after the injection of antitoxin, and then gradually loses it. Outside the body the diphtheria antitoxin easily clumps Klebs-Loeffler bacilli.

4. *Pneumococcus Infections.*

Washburn in 1895 noticed that pneumococci, when mixed with artificial antipneumococcus serum and left twenty-four hours at 37°C, were clumped in masses at the bottom of the tube, leaving the upper portions of the liquid clear. In other words he got a typical twenty-four-hour clump reaction, using a powerful artificial serum. The same fact had previously been observed by Metchnikoff in 1891 and by Issaef in 1892, and has been recently confirmed by Mosny.

Widal has been entirely unsuccessful in finding any clumping with the serum of pneumonia patients, and Block finds the lumping of pneumococci very slow and unsatisfactory. Bezancon and Griffon get similar results.

5. *Colon-Bacillus Infections.*

In view of the frequent association of this bacillus with disease, especially with the cystitis of young girls, it is important that the possibility of a sero-diagnosis of colon-bacillus infections should be studied, but as yet very little has been done in this direction.

Grüber and Durham showed that serum from animals artificially immunized against the colon bacillus would clump that bacillus strongly, but Widal's early experiments with supposed cases of colon-bacillus infection did not show any decided reaction, nor did the serum of typhoids which showed post-mortem a secondary colon-bacillus infection react during life on cultures of this bacillus.

Widal has lately claimed that in any case of colon infection only the *particular* race of bacilli which are actually causing the case in question can be specifically clumped by the serum of that case. In a case in which he first isolated the bacillus and then used it with the patient's serum he got a clumping as high as 1 : 1,000 dilution. Lesage in an epidemic of infants' diarrhœa found that the serum of 40 out of 50 cases clumped the colon bacillus isolated from the stools. Each of the 40 sera clumped each of the 40 cultures isolated from the 40 cases. The colon bacillus of the normal intestine of infants of the same age was not at all affected by the serum of the sick children, nor did the serum of normal infants clump the organisms from the infected children. This tends to confirm Widal's assertion. Apparently this epidemic was due to a single bacillus which could be easily isolated and used for experiment. The difficulty of isolating the bacillus of every case that is to be tested renders the method of very limited clinical value.

6. Malta Fever.

Wright and Smith tested the serum of 15 cases of Malta fever with the microccocus melitensis of Bruce, and found a strong clump reaction to occur (1:50 in most cases). On the typhoid bacillus the serum of these cases had no action. Sixteen cases of typhoid showed no reaction with Bruce's organism. The evidence in favor of this organism as the cause of Malta fever is strengthened by these facts.

7. Peripneumonia of Cattle and Hog Cholera.

Arloing finds that the serum and other body fluids of cattle suffering from peripneumonia have a marked clumping power on the pneumobacillus bovis.

Dawson has had similar positive results working with the bacillus of hog cholera. Hog-cholera serum had no effect on the typhoid or colon bacillus.

8. Proteus Infections.

Infections with the proteus vulgaris or proteus mirabilis have been considered causative in cases of mastoid abscess, meningitis, and Potts' disease. When found by culture at autopsies the question often arises whether they have wandered in after or at the time of death, or whether they were really concerned in the etiology of the case. The investigations of Achard and Lannelongue appear to give us the means of answering this question. They found that cultures of the two species of proteus above mentioned were markedly clumped by the serum of animals rendered immune to them by inoculations. This power

persists after death and even in putrefaction, and if present at
any given autopsy proves that the infection did not take place
during the last two days of life, since it takes *at least three days*
to bring the clumping power into the serum by artificial inoculation.

9. Oidium Albicans.

Roger showed that the oidium was well clumped by the
serum of animals immunized against it, and these observations
have been confirmed by Charrin and Ostrowsky. No experiments with human thrush have as yet been reported.

10. The Bubonic Plague.

Zabolotny [1] studied forty cases at Bombay in April, 1897, and
found the reaction absent in the first week, present in 1 : 10 dilution in the second week, and in 1 : 50 dilution in the third or
fourth week. He noted that the action of the infected serum
seemed to deprive the bacilli of their capsules. In an editorial
in the *Arch. Russes de Pathologie*, May 31st, 1897, it is stated that
the reaction increases in intensity until the fourth week of the
disease and then declines; also that it is most marked in the
severest cases. Feindel (*loc. cit.*) states that in the acute pneumonic cases the reaction is absent.

11. Yellow Fever.

Sanarelli [2] states that the organism which bears his name is
clumped very strongly and speedily by the serum of dogs immunized against his bacillus. By normal human serum it is not
clumped at all. By patients with yellow fever it clumped very
slowly. Post mortem the serum clumps more readily but very
variably. Pothier's [3] experience in the recent New Orleans epidemic has been similar.

12. Relapsing Fever.

(a) *Diagnosis.*—In countries where this disease is common
the difficulty of diagnosing cases between attacks (when the

[1] Deut. med. Woch., 1897, p. 392.
[2] Annales de l'Institute Pasteur, October 27th, 1897.
[3] Personal letter.

spirochætes are absent from the blood) is frequently met with. Löwenthal has perfected a method by which in most cases the diagnosis can be made by means of the effect of the serum of suspected cases on the spirochætes of other active cases. The organism cannot be cultivated as yet, so that a diagnosis of this kind is possible only during epidemics when fresh blood containing the organism can be obtained. A drop of blood from the suspected case is mixed with a drop from a patient then undergoing a paroxysm, and the two are sealed with wax between slide and cover-glass and left in the thermostat for half au hour together with a mixture of normal blood and blood containing spirochætes as a control. At the end of that time, if the case be one of relapsing fever, the organisms in contact with the blood from that case *cease their motion*, while those in the control are lively. It is not a clump reaction but a direct bactericidal effect which persists in the serum nearly up to the time of the next attack. The diagnosis so made by Löwenthal in forty cases was verified in every case by the course of the disease. In this way mild or abortive cases with few organisms in the blood can also be identified.

(b) *Prognosis.*—If the above bactericidal power lasts as late as the seventh day from the last attack, and in sufficient intensity to immobilize the spirochætes in *one hour* or less, there will be no relapse. If these conditions are not fulfilled relapse is sure to follow unless prevented by treatment. Löwenthal has verified this prognostic use of the serum in over one hundred cases.

13. Miscellaneous Reports on Other Infections.

(a) Grünbaum (*Lancet*, February 13th, 1897) states that a "non-motile diplococcus" from a case of *scarlet fever* was clumped by the serum of another case of scarlet fever.

(b) Delépine (*Medical Chronicle*, October, 1896) refers to successful experiments with the *tetanus bacilli*—its antitoxin having a decided clumping action upon it. The serum of normal horses clumps the tetanus bacillus to some extent and that of tetanized horses clumps it intensely. In eight cases referred to by Feindel[1] the bacillus was clumped by the serum of human tetanus.

[1] Arch. Gén. d. Médecine, October, 1897.

(c) Durham (*Lancet, loc. cit.*) speaks of the present antistrep-tococcus serum (Marmorek's) as having strong clumping power on *streptococci*, but Masino [1] finds very few cultures react to it.

(d) Gilbert and Fournier (*Compt. rend. de la soc. de biol.*, December 25th, 1896) mention two cases of human psittacosis whose serum clumped well the bacilli obtained from another human case as well as those taken from parrots. Clumping was present on the fourth and fifteenth days respectively.

SERO-PROGNOSIS.

It is agreed by all observers that in a very general way severe cases have more marked reactions than mild ones, but beyond this, in the opinion of the best judges, we cannot yet go.

Widal, Fraenkel, Biggs and Park, and Johnson have attempted no sero-prognosis, and my own observations are entirely in accord with this. The reaction may be strong in mild cases and feeble or absent in fatal ones.

Certain writers, however, especially Breuer, Courmont, Catrin, and Ullmann and Wöhnert, have thought the reaction of prognostic value, an intense and early reaction seeming to them of evil omen. Further evidence on this point is much needed.

[For bibliography, see page 429].

[1] La Semaine Médicale, 1897, p. 114.

BIBLIOGRAPHY.

I⊤ has seemed to me best to give a list only of the books and articles which I have found most useful, since the general bibliography of the subject is now large enough to form a volume by itself. Most of the larger works here described contain extensive bibliographies—especially that by Grawitz.

Text-Books.

1. Hayem: "Du Sang," Paris, 1889, 8vo, 1035 pages (French). This valuable book is the largest that I know of on the subject, and contains a mine of information on the morphology of the blood in health and disease, mostly from the author's own experience, literature being but little referred to. It contains a comparative anatomy of the blood and a long account of blood development. Unfortunately, it is dominated throughout by a theory of blood formation which has never gained acceptance by any other authority. It is very full on the subject of fibrin formation and of chlorosis. The illustrations are excellent.

2. v. Limbeck: "Grundriss ein. klin. Pathologie des Blutes," Jena, 1896, 8vo, 383 pages (Fischer). The second edition of this book, which appeared in February, 1896, is more than twice the size of the first edition (1892)—a fact illustrating the rapidity of the subject's growth. It is on the whole the best general text-book known to me, being equally full on all parts of the subject, including, for example, technique (which Grawitz omits) and of the chemistry of the blood, which is at present the author's special interest and on which Hayem is meagre. The illustrations are poor and the type is trying to the eyes. The writer shows little personal experience with the morphology and micro-chemistry of the blood, and this is the weakest side of the book. A large part of the book is concerned with the physiology of the blood.

3. Grawitz: "Klinische Pathologie des Blutes," Berlin, 1895, 8vo, 333 pages (Enslin). Issued in April, 1896. This book is largely devoted to the matter indicated by the title and contains no account of blood technique, and only thirty pages on the normal anatomy and physiology of the blood, while two hundred and seventy concern the blood in disease. The arrangement of the book is very clear and helpful. The author's main interests are in the estimation of the dried residue of the blood in various diseased conditions and in the bacteriology of the blood, so that the book is specially full on these topics. The illustrations are poor. Type and paper are excellent.

4. Ehrlich and Lazarus: "Die Anaemie," Wien, 1898, 8vo, 142 pages

(Hölder). An account of the normal and pathological histology of the blood not only in anæmia, but in all diseases of the blood, containing the latest researches and admirably clear as regards the microscopic appearances. This is Ehrlich's latest utterance—his last book previous to this being issued in 1891 (*vide infra*). It contains also a good deal of interesting theoretical discussion on the sources and formation of the elements of the blood. There are but three rather indifferent illustrations (uncolored). The book forms part of vol. iii. in Nothnagel's new "Special Pathology and Therapeutics," but is issued separately.

5. Coles: "The Blood: How to Examine it," etc., London, 1898 (J. and A. Churchill), 8vo. A very clear account of our present knowledge on the subject. Especially full on technique.

6. Schmaltz: "Pathologie des Blutes und die Blutkrankheiten," Leipzig, 1896, 16mo, 268 pages (Naumann). A much smaller book than any of the others and including the symptoms, pathology, and treatment of blood diseases, as well as a pathology of the blood itself. Specific gravity of the blood is a point of special interest with the author. There are no illustrations. The book is excellent as far as it goes, well arranged, and clear.

These are the best text-books known to me on the whole subject. None of them have been translated.

Text-Book Articles on Blood Diseases.

1. Stengel's article in vol. vii. of the "Twentieth Century Practice of Medicine" is by far the best text-book article in English that I know of.

2. Osler, in the "American Text-book of the Theory and Practice of Medicine," vol. ii. (Philadelphia, 1894, Saunders), writes an excellent fifty-page article on "Diseases of the Blood." It covers, of course, only the blood diseases proper without much account of the blood in other conditions.

3. The article "The Blood in Infancy," in Rotch's Pædiatrics, covers this branch of the subject very thoroughly.

These are the best articles in English that I know of.

4. The article on "La Pathologie du Sang," by Gilbert, in the five-volume "Traité de Médecine" edited by Charcot, Bouchard, and Brissaud, Paris, 1892 (Masson), is inferior to those last mentioned and is mostly an echo of Hayem's work above referred to. Theories long exploded (*e. g.*, that eosinophiles are pathognomonic of leukæmia) receive the author's sanction. The article is one hundred large octavo pages long and is intended to cover the whole subject.

5. Griffith's eighty-page article in Keating's "Cyclopædia of the Diseases of Children," vol. iii., p. 755 (Philadelphia, 1890, Lippincott), is now a good deal out of date.

6. The articles on blood diseases in the latest editions of the text-books of Osler, Strümpell, Da Costa, Flint, and Fagg, contain relatively little about the blood itself.

Treatises on Special Portions of the Subject.

1. Reinert's "Die Zählung der Blutkörperchen," Leipzig, 1891 (Vogel), 246 pages, is an admirable account of the avoidable and unavoidable errors in blood examination, and the best methods of reducing error to a minimum. A number of careful examinations of the blood in health and in various diseases are also given ; and an outline of the scope of blood diagnosis closes the book.

2. v. Noorden's "Chlorosis" (Wien, 1897, 8vo, 209 pages) is by far the best piece of work so far published on this subject. The clinical and therapeutic sides of the subject are fully treated, as well as the hæmatological pathology.

3. Türk's monograph on the "Condition of the Blood in Acute Infectious Disease" is an admirable résumé of German and French literature on the subject, together with a detailed study of fifty-two cases. Published at Wien and Leipzig, 1898 (Braumüller), 347 pages, 8vo.

4. Rieder's "Beiträge zur Kenntniss der Leukocytosis," Leipzig, 1892 (Vogel), 220 pages, is an admirable work in all respects, although now considerably out of date. It shows, as very few of the foregoing treatises do, a practical acquaintance, on the author's part, with the details of blood morphology and microchemistry. A very large number of blood counts in many diseases are recorded.

5. Löwitt's "Studien zur Physiol. und Pathol. des Blutes u. der Lymphe" (Jena, 1892 [Fisher], 8vo, 138 pages) is mostly concerned with experiments on animals and intended to throw light on the theory of leucocytosis. The conclusions of the book have not been generally adopted, though its facts have been mostly verified.

6. Thayer and Hewetson's book, on the "Malarial Fevers of Baltimore," leaves nothing more to be desired in that direction. It is two hundred and fifteen pages long, published by the Johns Hopkins press of Baltimore in 1895. It contains a summary of the literature of the subject, an analysis of six hundred and sixteen new cases, and some admirable colored plates. It is a model of its kind in every respect, and an ideal for others to aim for.

7. Ehrlich's "Farbenanalytische Untersuchungen" (Berlin, 1891 [Hirschwald], 137 pages) contains nine short essays by Ehrlich and three by his pupils. Considering the reputation of the writer they are at the present day rather disappointing reading, and contain little that is not better expressed elsewhere.

8. Weiss's "Haematologische Untersuchungen" (Wien, 1896 [Prockaska] 112 pages, 8vo) contains many valuable studies on various points.

9. Under a somewhat different heading come the sections on the examination of the blood in v. Jaksch's "Clinical Diagnosis" (English translation, London, 1893, Griffen & Co.), a seventy-five-page article containing many inaccuracies ; and Lenharz: "Microscopie und Chemie am Krankenbett" (Berlin, 1896, Springer), a fifty-page article.

Magazine Articles of Special Value.

1. On Concentration and Dilution of the Blood—Oliver: Lancet, June 27, 1896.

2. On Leucocytosis—Goldschneider and Jacob: Zeit. für klin. Med., 1894, vol. 25. Krebs: Inaug. Dissert., Berlin, 1893. Sadler: Forschr. d. Med., Supplement-Heft, 1892. Also Klein, in Volkmann's Sammlung klinischer Vorträge, December, 1893, and of course Rieder and Türk above referred to.

3. On Anæmia—Dunin: Volkmann's Sammlung. klin. Vorträge, 1896, No. 135. Romberg: Berlin. klin. Woch., June 28, 1897.

4. Parasitic Anæmia—Schaumann: Zur Kenntniss der sog. Bothriocephalus Anämie, Berlin, 1892, 214 pages; and Askanazy: Zeitschr. f. klin. Med., 1895, p. 492. Brown: Journal of Experimental Medicine, May, 1898 (Trichinosis).

5. Leukæmia—Fraenkel: Deutsche med. Wochenschrift, 1895, p. 639. Fraenkel: 15th Congress für inn. Medicin. Wiesbaden, 1897. Benda: *Ibidem.* Dock: Moscow Internat. Congress, 1897.

6. Pernicious Anæmia—Discussion by Birch-Hirschfeld, Ehrlich, Troje, and others, at the XI. Congress f. inner. Med. (Leipzig, 1892).

7. Pneumonia—Billings: Bulletin of the Johns Hopkins Hospital, November, 1894. Diphtheria—Billings: New York Medical Record, April 25, 1896. Typhoid—Thayer: Johns Hopkins Hospital Reports, vol. iv., No. 1. Engel: 15th Congress für inn. Med., Wiesbaden, 1897. Exanthemata—Felsenthal: Arch. f. Kinderheilk., 1892, p. 78. Zappert: Zeitschr. f. klin. Med., 1893, No. 23. Small-pox—Pick: Arch. f. Dermatol. und Syph., 1893, p. 63. Sepsis—Roscher: Inaug. Dissert., Berlin, 1894. Cholera—Biernacki: Deutsche med. Wochenschr., 1895, No. 48. Diabetes —Bremer: Moscow Internat. Congress, 1897.

8. Syphilis—(a) Reiss: Arch. f. Dermat. und Syph., 1895, Hf. 1 and 2. (b) Justus: Virchow's Arch., 1895.

9. Tuberculosis—(a) Dane: Boston Medical and Surgical Journal, May 28, 1896. (b) Stein und Erbmann: Deutsche med. Wochenschrift, 1896, No. 56, p. 323. (c) Grawitz: Deutsche med. Wochenschr., 1893, No. 51.

10. Malignant Disease—Taylor (International Medical Magazine, July, 1897). (a) Sadler: *Loc. cit.* (b) Reinbach: Langenbeck's Archiv, 1893, No. 46. (c) Strauer: Dissert., Greifswald, 1893.

11. Bacteriology—Sittmann: Deutsches Arch. f. klin. Med., vol. 53.

12. Diseases of the Stomach (especially Cancer)—Schneyer: Zeitschrift f. klin. Med., 1895, p. 475. Osterspey: Inaug. Diss., Berlin, 1892.

13. Eosinophiles—Zappert: Zeitschr. f. klin. Med., 1893, vol. 23.

14. Hæmoconien—Müller: Wien. med. Presse, 1896, No. 36.

INDEX.